THE
LIVING KING
AND THE TWELVE KINGS

THE LIVING KING

AND THE TWELVE KINGS

BY DAVID JIMENEZ

◆ BOOK ONE ◆

TATE PUBLISHING

AND ENTERPRISES, LLC

Published by Tate Publishing & Enterprises, LLC
127 E. Trade Center Terrace | Mustang, Oklahoma 73064 USA
1.888.361.9473 | www.tatepublishing.com

Tate Publishing is committed to excellence in the publishing industry. The company reflects the philosophy established by the founders, based on Psalm 68:11,

"The Lord gave the word and great was the company of those who published it."

Book design copyright © 2016 by Tate Publishing, LLC. All rights reserved.
Cover design by Kyle Cotton and Nino Carlo Suico
Interior design by Manolito Bastasa
Illustrations by Kyle Cotton with Copyright 2014 by David Jimenez and Kyle Cotton

Published in the United States of America

ISBN: 978-1-68237-403-0
1. Juvenile Fiction / General
2. Juvenile Fiction / Fantasy & Magic
15.10.20

ACKNOWLEDGMENTS

The Living King and the Twelve Kings is specifically dedicated to my beautiful and kind wife, Erika. Erika, my lovely wife, you truly are everything to me. You are my inspiration. You are my light, my motivation, and you are the love of my life. I have to thank you for everything you have done for me and our girls. You are truly a special wife and a very special mother. Every day, you impress me with your goals, your ambition to serve your family, and your drive to work with us.

Your smile lights up the room and really lights up my life. Your words of wisdom and encouragement to me every day are priceless. I wrote this book with a passion to show the real you, a passionate wife and dedicated mother who protects her young and your husband.

Thank you for everything, mi amor. I wake up every morning not to look forward to the day, not to work, to deal with every-thing, not even for the good this life has to offer us. I wake up every morning to see my best friend sleeping next to me and for me to have another opportunity to say I love you.

Happy nineteenth wedding anniversary, Erika. You are the same as I remember you the day we wed, beautiful and sweet as always.

As the book shows, you are truly my queen Erika, and I will always honor and protect you.

Love,
David

Contents

1

THE KINGS

AND SO THERE were twelve kings, twelve wise men who followed the High Living King, and He was Yesu. Yesu was the Almighty King, and He alone ruled the kingdom of Heirthia. He had grace, He gave love, He was powerful, but all He wanted was for His people to rule the land. The kingdom of Heirthia was created by Yesu's father, Jeinua.

Jeinua was the God of all, and He was good. Yesu ruled the world of Heirthia with His father's blessing, and so, with Yesu's wisdom and almighty power, He conquered all evil and ruled and blessed all the land. His ways and kindness brought peace and tranquility among the twelve kings, the twelve lands, and all the people and creatures. Anyone who would try to break this would face the twelve kings, who were unbreakable through their bond with Yesu.

Because of this, Yesu dwelled in different lands, oceans, deserts, mountains, just watching and living among all creatures. He left the world of Heirthia to the twelve kings to rule for eternity and, ultimately, to His people. Although all knew who Yesu was, only few ever saw Him or ever saw His great power.

Although each of the twelve kings owned and ruled their own lands, they would serve and fight to their deaths to serve the wise and great Yesu, who brought peace. Each of these twelve kings had a unique talent which proved to be great and powerful. Each of the twelve kings was granted this power by Yesu, and it proved to be powerful if used wisely.

Yesu granted these powers so that each king would rule his land in an honorable way, spreading peace throughout the lands. These kings came from the School of Youngs. The land of Heirthia is a land of kings, queens, princesses, great warriors, castles, chariots, fairies, wizards, and creatures of all kinds.

The School of Youngs brought together young lads and ladies to learn and train to be true kings and queens of all the lands of Heirthia. These students were known as the Youngs. Young kings and queens they were, but before they could be honored as true kings and queens, they had to master all their courses to prove their worth, loyalty, and honor. It was indeed a very special school. Chosen children of age 10 were summoned, and indeed it was a great honor as not every child was summoned.

These Youngs would pack their belongings and spend their school year at the School of Youngs, which was at the heart and center of Heirthia.

At the School of Youngs, the students trained how to be kings and queens. They learned to battle by sword fight. Some Youngs learned the talent of wizardry. Some learned the talent of transformation while others learned many other talents. However, one of the most important aspects of the School of Youngs was for the older Youngs to find their true love.

After all, each of the Youngs was either a young prince or princess, and thus, it was the duty of each from the very young age of ten to grow up together as friends, to be true friends and companions, to honor and respect each other, and to ultimately join in matrimony once they chose their love. Indeed, true love came out of the School of Youngs, and so the purpose was for these princes and princesses to learn to be courageous, to be loyal and faithful to their king or queen, and to learn to be true warriors when necessary. A fine school it was.

The land of Heirthia was so beautiful. It was a land so rich in forests, grasslands, trees, flowers, and creatures of all kinds and sizes. Rivers ran freely and were pure. Yesu's castle (which was surrounded by beautiful gardens, acres of wood, and scents from all the wonderful plants and flowers) was at the center of Heirthia. Yesu's castle was beautiful and enormous. It was made of pearls as white as snow. Jewels surrounded the doorframes, the gates were of fine wood carvings of honorary warriors, and the doors were so large even a twenty-foot giant could walk right in.

All the people in Heirthia knew that the castle was special and that within its center, deep in its dungeons, right at the heart of its foundation, there was a great power like no other. A power that if put into the wrong hands could destroy all and would grant all the powers and privileges of the entire universe.

However, to gain such power, to earn such honor, one would have to pass the Seven Wishes of Greatness, seven tests that would truly measure the heart of a brave soul. These tests were (1) the test of faith, (2) the test of love, (3) the test of wisdom, (4) the test of sacrifice, (5) the test of hope, (6) the test of humbleness, and, the most difficult of all, (7) the test of forgiveness.

Although many tried, no one had ever conquered the Seven Wishes of Greatness, and all who had tried ended in death. This was the trade-off. If one dared to begin the Wishes, he or she either conquered the test or died instantly, or so the legend goes. Because of this, Yesu's castle remained sacred to all the people, and no one ever entered or dared to face the Wishes.

The world of Heirthia was a great world full of wonder. Directly to the north of Yesu's castle was the kingdom of Exsul, the largest land of Heirthia, where mountains of stone stood tall and grand. To the east of Exsul was the kingdom of Juliet, which was the land of the great ocean, and to the far east of Juliet stood the kingdom of Flora, a land filled with flowers. To the west of Exsul was the kingdom of Demble, the land of the beautiful forest, tall pines, great oak trees, and dynamic evergreens. To the far west was the kingdom of Castillo, the land of spring waters, waterfalls, and crystal clear rivers.

In order to rule these lands, however, it would take more than just a ruler. It would take anointed kings. Because of this, out of all the talents and powers granted to the twelve kings, five were much greater than the others—five chosen kings, kings with honor and faith. Their powers combined could single-handedly take over Heirthia. These powers were known as the Quint Fey.

The first and most trusted of the five was King Simon Peuro, "the Magnificent." He was the most trusted of the twelve to receive one of the Quint Fey. His talent was that of great speed and an inner power like no other. King Simon was about forty-three years old, in his prime. He had short brown hair, medium-color skin, hazel eyes, and broad shoulders. He was handsome and well built, and his hands were so rough from all the battles of his life.

King Simon's power, granted by Yesu, was that of the beautiful silver-and-gold Sword of Yesu. It was the most powerful sword in all the land. Only Yesu was greater. On one side of the sword was the powerful lion representing authority, strength, rule, and pride. The other side of the sword showed the valiant eagle. This represented honor, valiance, and peace. Although beautiful, the Sword of Yesu had immense powers, and one swing of the mighty blade could cut through the strongest metal or the thickest stone.

The Sword of Yesu was created by Yesu himself. Yesu prayed one day to His Father that a strong and mighty sword be created for the people of Heirthia, and so Yesu went on a journey into all the lands of Heirthia, gathering all precious metals from each corner of the land. Once he did this, he returned to his castle and went into the dungeon to face the Seven Wishes of Greatness, a feat that no one had ever accomplished.

Through His powers, wonders, and greatness, Yesu went through each test without trouble and defeated each endeavor. It was at this point, with the power vested within him, that Yesu created the Sword of Yesu with the metals He had obtained and blessed the sword with such power through the blessing of His Father. As He blessed the sword, there was a bright light that radiated out of the castle and lit up the sky throughout Heirthia. The people were indeed amazed.

The Sword of Yesu was created to protect the people of Heirthia. Yesu granted King Simon this sword because King Simon was loyal, honest, and the most noble of them all. Only King Simon was worthy enough to carry such honor. King Simon did indeed have a peaceful heart. King Simon ruled the land of Exsul, the great land of the North. Exsul was a land of the brave. The people here believed in loyalty and honor and had the talents of inner strength.

Out of all the twelve, King Simon would counsel the rest and would lead them through all their battles. Thus, King Simon was their leader through the blessing of Yesu.

Second of the Quint Fey was King Aniser, "the Brave." He had the talent to cure and heal with his hands, and because of his bravery, Yesu granted King Aniser the power of the Lion Heart Medallion.

A remarkable piece it was. The medallion was made of beautiful diamond, with the emblem of a lion to symbolize the great

Lion King. The medallion came from the true heart of Yesu. Yesu battled the all-powerful Brinstow, the great lion cat. Upon the hills of Demble, Yesu summoned the great cat out of his lair. All people feared the power and strength of the lion cat, which feared nothing. With a great roar, Brinstow challenged Yesu, but Yesu was not moved. Brinstow stood in a stance to charge Yesu. It growled, which would make any person tremble. From within the lair, out came Brinstow's pride of lionesses and other lions. There were about ten of them, and they all surrounded Yesu and growled. It was a chilling sound. Brinstow stood as tall as seven feet, and he was ten feet long. Yesu stood there with no fear in His heart. Yesu locked eyes with the great cat.

"I am your master," called Yesu. The other cats stood in amazement at what Yesu was saying.

Brinstow then became even more angry. He let out an awesome roar and charged with such great speed. Yesu did not move, and as the great cat drew closer, Yesu raised his right hand and whispered, "I command you, stop."

Brinstow, amazed at what he had seen, stopped his charge and slowly stepped back. For the first time, Brinstow was afraid. Once he realized that Yesu was the Almighty King, he bowed down and humbled himself. At this point, the pride, being compelled, bowed down to the great Yesu too. Yesu went forth to the great cat and placed His hand upon the cat's head. Yesu then reached down into His pocket. There, in his hand, was a great diamond.

Yesu ordered, "Let out your greatest roar, my friend. Pour all your heart into this diamond so that the people of Heirthia may be protected by your authority."

Then and there, the great cat raised his mane, stood with such pride, and opened his mouth. *Roar!* The entire world of Heirthia was shaken, and the roar was blessed into the Lion Heart Medallion with a bright light emanating out of it, and the magic and power drafted through the wind from the great cat into the diamond, and so it was then captured forever.

Before Yesu left the great cat, He said, "Brinstow, the great cat, do not disturb the people, but the creatures and animals of this world, I grant to you. You are never to interfere with the people. My power shall summon you in times of great need."

Brinstow bowed down and then ran into the distance, where his pride followed him.

With the medallion around the neck of King Aniser, King Aniser could transform into a fierce and powerful lion with a roar that would shake the inner core of Heirthia and beyond. King Aniser had long bright yellow hair and striking honey-colored eyes. His skin was light and thin, and his body too was certainly built for battle. King Aniser was forty-one years old.

King Aniser was King Simon's best mate, and the two together would lead all the other kings. Although King Aniser could transform, he also had the difficult but possible ability to transform his most noble companions so they could join him in battle. The enemies knew that King Aniser could transform, and they were afraid. King Aniser ruled the land of Demble. Demble was the great land of the northwest. The people here were known for their kind hearts and peaceful ways, but they also had the talent to cure and heal.

The third of the Quint Fey was King Jemis, "the Brilliant." King Jemis found favor with Yesu because of his talent was in his ability to think and move quickly, but more so because King Jemis had the remarkable talent of discernment of people and creatures.

King Jemis had black hair, long and straight. He had dark-colored facial hair around his lips. His eyes were light brown, and he was not very tall, but he was well built. His arms were remarkably built. King Jemis was forty years old. Yesu granted King Jemis the power of the Falcon Bow. The Falcon Bow came from the bond of Yesu with Kadis, the great falcon.

Kadis was an enormous falcon from the mountains of Exsul, and he was unstoppable. He stood twelve feet tall, with a wingspan of over thirty-three feet. His colors were that of dark brown and black stripes. He was very respected. The falcon warrior was the king of the birds, and would strike faster than anything in all of Heirthia.

Yesu found favor in Kadis, but Kadis flew high in the sky and could never be captured. Valiant, Kadis flew for his prey and grasped it with his sharp giant claws. Yesu knew this, and so to capture Kadis, Yesu let out a scent of easy prey, prey which caught Kadis's eye. A beautiful deer appeared in the forest before Kadis, so Kadis soared in with such speed. He approached the unmoving deer, opened his massive claws, and let out a screech, but Yesu appeared and raised His right hand and said, "May you never soar the sky again."

Kadis fell to the ground with such force and tumbled to a stop. Again, he let out a screech, but he could not take to flight, even though he tried and tried again. He lifted his large wings, but nothing. Yesu came to Kadis, and Kadis was afraid, for he had finally been captured.

Yesu bent to His knees as Kadis lay there and said, "I am your master, and I am your friend. Do not fear me, for I will help you."

Yesu placed His right hand on the wings of Kadis, and Kadis was amazed he could move his wings again. Kadis came to his legs and stood tall, but he lowered his head in respect to Yesu.

Kadis slowly bowed. Yesu then said, "I will take one of your feathers, as your wings are strong and valiant. I will turn your feather into a bow so that the people of Heirthia can have a protector with your great strength and speed."

Kadis stretched out his right wing, and Yesu plucked out the feather. Yesu then said, "The sky belongs to you now. I hand it to you, but respect the land. My power shall one day call you."

Kadis then stretched out his wings and took to the sky. Yesu placed His right hand on the feather, and as a bright light once again illuminated from Yesu, the feather took shape and became the Falcon Bow. It had the valiant falcon embedded on it.

This was no ordinary bow. The strings that joined each end of the bow were from the hair of Yesu himself. Each piece of hair was embedded to each other to form the remainder of the bow. The bow was that of the color of gold and was capable of awesome powers through its arrows. You see, to use the bow, you would not use ordinary arrows. No, you did not even need to carry arrows in a satchel. With this bow, which was dependent on your heart and faith, you would set up your stance, lift your arm for aim, and when ready, you would simply pull the strings made of Yesu's hair, and an arrow would appear in flames of fire. Again, dependent on your heart, faith, and desire, the arrow would produce as much power as you believed was right and just. These arrows created all sorts of power. Some arrows would explode, some arrows multiplied, some arrows created fire or ice, and so on. With the Falcon Bow, arrows never ended, but if used for the wrong reason or used improperly, the fire arrows would not appear.

Yesu also granted King Jemis Seven Pearl Arrows. These arrows, if pierced through the heart of anyone, would heal them instantly. However, if any of these arrows pierced anything but the heart, the person or creature would die instantly, no matter how slight the wound. King Jemis ruled the land of Juliet, the land of the northeast. Juliet was a land of happiness and great welcome. The people here did not know how to battle and were a fragile people, but they had the talent of peace and were hard workers.

The fourth of the Quint Fey was King Jonis, "the Wise." King Jonis was the youngest of the twelve, but his wisdom was his greatest asset and talent. He stood over six feet tall, just like the others, and had light brown hair, which was short and wavy. His eyes were a bright green, and his skin was light brown. He was very handsome, just like his fellow brothers, and he always spoke so wisely. He indeed had a graceful tongue. Because of this, Yesu granted King Jonis the power of the Dragon's Claw Wand.

A wand of power, a wand of faith, it was the most powerful wand in all the land. What was interesting about this wand was that its powers were controlled by the person's or creature's emotions who handled it. Thus, dependent on the mood—love, anger, frustration, doubt, or confidence—that was the power it would produce. However, if used wisely, and if the correct spell was called, the Dragon's Claw Wand could summon the great power of Yesu himself. The wand comes from the claw of Angor, the mighty red dragon. Yesu himself confronted the red dragon in the land of Sepul, the land of fire.

As Yesu stood there seeking the red dragon, he heard in a distance the great call of Angor. As Yesu heard this, Angor appeared over a hill in flight. The dragon flew around and again came toward Yesu at a distance, letting out another scream. He circled and landed right before Yesu.

The dragon was immense, over thirty three feet tall, grand, large, and powerful. Nothing had ever defeated Angor. However, Angor was no match for the power of Yesu. Angor stood tall and inhaled a large breath to prepare to breathe fire. You could hear from his throat that fire was developing; it was the sound of fire growing stronger and stronger, rumbling and growing louder, ready to be shot out.

Angor leaned forward, and a large flame came rushing out of his mouth. It was very large. Yesu raised His right hand, and the flame came to a stop in midair. It just hung there, and Yesu held it with no effort. His face was calm and collected.

Yesu maneuvered His hand, and so the flame slowly came to Him and surrounded Him but did not burn Him. Yesu looked into the eyes of Angor, and Angor was amazed. The flame then vanished, disappeared, extinguished without a trace.

Then with one order by Yesu, "Lay down your life!" the great Angor bowed down because he was afraid. Yesu then reached toward Angor's front right arm and took from Angor a sharp claw. Angor gave a loud scream when the claw was taken off.

Yesu did this because Angor was attacking the people of Heirthia. Angor would breathe flames and destroy villages. Yes indeed, Angor had grabbed the attention of Yesu, and for this, Angor would forever be without such a claw.

Yesu ordered, "Although you have sinned, you are forgiven, my dragon, but never again return unless summoned by my power. Do not disturb the people, but go. You are free."

Angor bowed out of respect and flew into the distance, never to return. At that moment, Yesu lay His right hand over the claw, and slowly, it transformed, and he created this powerful wand. He did this as a gift to the people for all that Angor had done. It would protect them. When Yesu placed His hand over the claw, a bright light came from Yesu into the wand. There was a melody in the sky and on the ground. It was beautiful. This wand needed to be given to a most trusted king to protect as it was very powerful.

King Jonis was given this power because of his good heart and wisdom. With the Dragon's Claw Wand, King Jonis had the ability to cast spells, and if he used it with his inner power and wisdom, it could be the most powerful wand in all the land. It could produce spells for peace, spells to rebuke, spells to destroy, spells for power, and any spell that came from the true heart of King Jonis.

King Jonis ruled the land of Castillo, the land to the West. Castillo was a land of the grand hills. Here dwelt a kind people with a talent to serve and a talent of wisdom.

The fifth and last of the Quint Fey was King Phelo, "the Great." King Phelo was the smallest king but the most physically powerful; strength was his talent. He too was forty years old, but he was a very well built man. He had shoulder-length brownish-blond hair, blue eyes, light skin, and he was certainly a charmer.

Yesu granted King Phelo the power of the Ruby Stone Ring. Yesu granted this most precious stone ring because of King Phelo's small stature. He was physically powerful but too small to battle on his own. Thus, with the Ruby Stone Ring, King Phelo had the ability to utilize all the other powers to a certain limit. He was not as powerful as each but nonetheless was able to use those powers, and he could use them all at the same time.

You see, the Ruby Stone Ring was created by Yesu as a true weapon—a jack of all trades, if you will. The Ruby Stone Ring had the ability to call upon the other powers, the Sword of Yesu, the Lion Heart Medallion, the Falcon Bow, and the Dragon's Claw Wand. To create this, Yesu went to the land of Sepul, where deep in the heart of the volcano, Yesu discovered the great ruby of the land. With this ruby, Yesu gathered all the other powers and prayed over them.

Through His authority, he raised His right hand, and in an instant, the blue sky cracked open, and a beam of light came upon him, and then and there, a piece of each power went into the ruby, which became known as the Ruby Stone Ring.

Although each power went into the stone, the stone was not as powerful as each original power; nonetheless, it was very effective. Yesu created this power so that no matter when or where, the powers were all replicated and preserved through the ring. Because of this, Yesu needed to pick a very brave, honorable, and trustworthy individual to protect it, guard it, and use it for the people. For this, King Phelo was selected. He ruled the land of Flora. Flora was the land to the east and was a very spectacular land.

It was the land of the flowers, fragrances, gardens, and all kinds of plant life, and its people were small but very effective. They had the talent of physical strength, and Phelo was no exception. He was brave and strong, and Yesu found favor in him.

So then it was, so long as the Quint Fey were united with the Sword of Yesu, the Lion Heart Medallion, the Falcon Bow, the Dragon's Claw Wand, and the Ruby Stone Ring, there was nothing that could break the peace of Heirthia. Yesu summoned the Quint Fey and the other seven kings at Yesu's castle, and there, Yesu gave them their blessings and, to each, His gift of power.

As they stood there before Yesu and as the seven other kings watched, Yesu proclaimed "The great Jeinua has found favor in His eyes for you. I too have found great favor in you. You have been selected from a great number of kings. You are privileged and honored. These powers which I have granted you, you are to cherish them, to protect them, and to never give in to anger, frustration, fear, and evil. With these powers, you are to protect the people and creatures alike. Remember, no matter what you do, no matter the circumstances, stay together and never give your powers to anyone else."

Yesu then ordered, "Among yourselves, create a circle and do not face each other."

The five kings circled and took position.

Yesu then said, "Repeat after me," and so Yesu began making a trust statement, and the Quint Fey repeated it: "I, an honoree of a power of the Quint Fey, do proclaim that I shall be loyal, helpful, friendly, courageous, honorable, wise, truthful, brave, and, above all, humble in the name of Yesu. I shall use the power granted to me to protect the people at all times and to serve the great Yesu. We, together, honor the great Jeinua."

At that point, they raised their powers, and the seven kings all stood and cheered in respect. Yesu stood and was pleased. He then said, "Heirthia is yours. Although you may not see me, although I may not fight beside you, I shall be with you always." A light then illuminated from Yesu's heart, and the light surrounded him, and then the light lifted into the sky, and so Yesu was gone.

From that point on, Yesu was never been seen again, but the Quint Fey knew he would always be with them.

Since the Quint Fey were created, they were bonded so close, like a joined family to which nothing could break the core. There were many who tried to break the five, instigating battles in hopes of doing so: the Battle of Texar, the Battle of Aridan, the Battle of Kenix, the Battle of Jemzi, and the Battle of Nunii. The Battles of Jemzi and Nunii were by far the most difficult to overcome. They'd battled the army of Seitor, the evil one who desired to rule all and the true enemy of Yesu.

Seitor was created by the Almighty Jeinua as a servant and follower, and he had many talents. He could appear and disappear, he had significant strength, he had the talent of sword fight, and he was very quick. He was also a talented wizard, and he was very soft-spoken.

His words were as sweet as honey, but he used it for evil and was devious. He was indeed very convincing with his words. Jeinua created Seitor to serve others, but Seitor did not want to serve others. He wanted others to serve him, and little by little, he grew angry and developed a vengeance toward the people because they would not follow him. Just like all His other creations, Jeinua created Seitor for a good purpose.

Seitor was a very handsome man. He had very light brown hair, which was shoulder length and straight. He was very well built and had light-colored skin. He had a radiant smile. However, the most prominent feature of Seitor was his very bright blue eyes. There were no eyes like it in Heirthia. By far, they were the most beautiful blue eyes anyone had. They were the color of a radiant blue sky, the crystal clear blue waters of the ocean, or the beautiful blue streams at the base of a mountain.

Although Seitor appeared to be trying to serve and follow Jeinua, the Almighty God, he was only trying to be *like* Jeinua and Yesu, and he wanted to rule over all the land, over all the creatures, and over all the people. However, before Seitor could take any action, the Almighty God and His son, Yesu, the Living King, discovered this treachery Seitor had planned.

As it turned out, Seitor had been developing an army secretly in the land of Helum, deep in the heart of the Bar Mountains, and he planned to enter Yesu's castle in the dark of the night and enter the Wishes of Greatness to gain all the power.

So to counter this, Yesu's angels captured Seitor before he took any action. Seitor and those minions closest to him were all banished from Heirthia but not destroyed. He was to live in the depths of Helum, a place far from the kingdom of Heirthia, where he would be alone and be judged at the end of time. Seitor became strong, deceptive, and angry, and he vowed to take over Heirthia by killing all the twelve kings and taking the Quint Fey's powers.

However, he was never successful because of the power of the Quint Fey. Gathering banished and sinful people and creatures from all over Heirthia, Seitor tried time and time again to conquer the Quint Fey through battles, but he was always losing because of the talents and powers of the Quint Fey. The Quint Fey, along with the other seven kings, would battle and destroy Seitor's army's, which had no chance of victory. The Quint Fey were too powerful, and the Quint Fey's success was due in part to the help of the seven other kings. Nothing would stop them.

However, because Seitor would not stop seeking to enter Yesu's castle, Yesu blessed his castle, and anyone and everything was banned from entering. Anyone or anything that tried to enter, tried to touch, or tried to break its walls to enter died instantly. Time and time again, Seitor sent spies to try to enter, but they all ended the same way: they would vanish into smoke and disappear, never to be seen. Because Seitor would not stop, the Quint Fey would continue to defend Heirthia

There was a way to get in, but that was a secret no one knew.

To the south of Yesu's castle ran the magnificent Larena River. Its waters were crystal clear, and its powers were great. On the other side of the Larena River, to the south, were the seven great lands: Castigs, Harper, Bapti, Cain, Alpha, Isri, and Breakle. The seven other kings ruled these lands south of the Larena. The Larena River ran from east to west and thus separated the Quint Fey's lands from the lands of the other seven kings.

To the south of the seven great lands lay the massive Bar Mountains, and then to the south of that, to the depths of the land, there was the land of Helum, where Seitor lived.

The Larena River was treacherous. Death cliffs hung over the river at a great distance, and so the only way to cross was through Michael's Bridges, and there were three. There was one to the west between Castigs and Castillo, one directly south between Cain and Yesu's castle, and one to the east between Breakle and Flora. There were two other ways across, but they were prone to be deadly crossing.

The first crossing was through the Dark Forest, which was known to swallow anyone or anything that entered. The Dark Forest was known to draw young adults who sinned by gossip with their tongues and their cruel ways. The Dark Forest was the largest forest in all of Heirthia. It was dark, and no one ruled there. However, within its trees lived an unknown people—creatures, fairies, and mythical beings yet to be discovered.

Legend had it that whatever went in never came out because the ogres and giants devoured them, but there were other creatures, creatures that could speak and were said to live in the depths of the Dark Forest, and it was said that they had their own army. They were called Flamigs. They were bird-like creatures, similar to the flamingo, but although they look peaceful and graceful, they were deadly.

The second way to cross the Larena River was through the depths of Sepul, the land of fire and lava, too deadly to cross. Although no humans lived in Sepul, the red dragon, Angor, dwelt there. Angor, himself, had his army of dragons, but as long as they were not disturbed, they honored the authority of Yesu and did not disturb the people.

However, if any human or creature entered the land of Sepul, Angor and his army took them as trespassers, and they were attacked, and they were killed. No humans from Heirthia ever entered Sepul, and no creatures were said to have entered either. The only being said to visit there was Seitor. It was said that although he was banished to Helum, he had been seen gathering creatures to join his army.

These were the lands of Heirthia, to which the Quint Fey were sworn to protect. Heirthia was a beautiful land, a world full of wonder. To help and aid the Quint Fey, the seven honorable kings were sworn to serve the Quint Fey.

The seven kings to aid the Quint Fey in battle were King Bartho, ruler of the land of Castigs; King Thomas, ruler of the land of Harper; King Mateo, ruler of the land of Bapti; King James, ruler of the land of Alpha; King Thad, ruler of the land of Isri; King Somon, ruler of the land of Breakle; and, finally, King Julas, ruler of the land of Cain. Each king had his own talent and power to support the Quint Fey. Through the loyalty, bravery, and alliance of the twelve kings, Seitor could not rule. These kings were personally selected by Yesu himself.

They were not perfect, far from it, but they each had something good in them, something that Yesu saw, something that each would have to see and prove to themselves. These kings were brave, very well-built, broad-shouldered, very respectful, and very honorable men. They were loyal, friendly, trustworthy, and brave. A great army they were when together. The seven kings of the south, as they were known, were highly regarded and respected by all the people of the land. The Quint Fey themselves honored and gave thanks and praise to these kings for their service and their loyalty.

For one thousand years, Heirthia was at peace—until something happened before the Battle of Nunii.

2

BATTLE OF NUNII

S EITOR REALIZED AND discovered that there would only be
one way to take Heirthia forever, and that would be to break
the bond of the Quint Fey. Seitor conceded that he could
not defeat the Quint Fey together but realized that if he were to
take one of their powers, just one, he could defeat them all. Just
one fracture was needed.

Ultimately, by doing this, he could take the powers of the
Quint Fey one by one. Seitor devised a plan to stage his own

death at the Battle of Nunii so that the Quint Fey would believe that he was no more and drop their guard. Seitor, through his devious plans and manipulative ways, got to one of the other seven kings. He was able to reach King Julas.

King Julas was a strong follower of Yesu and followed Yesu's ways and truth for a good many years, but he was always jealous of the Quint Fey. He wanted to be a part of the Quint Fey, pleading to Yesu that he had the talent of knowledge and loyalty, but Yesu did not find enough favor in King Julas to place him within the Quint Fey.

Yesu told King Julas that although he would not be a part of the Quint Fey, he was still special, and so King Julas would rule the land of Cain for his loyalty.

Cain was a land flowing with people who were warriors, builders, craftsmen, all people of great loyalty. Cain was the land to the south with one of Michael's Bridges leading directly to Yesu's castle. Because King Julas was an honorable man, Yesu granted him the power of the Silver Sword, the quickest sword in all the land. King Julas was very pleased with this blessing.

Seitor knew that King Julas was still desperate and that he wanted to be a part of the Quint Fey, and so he made a deal with King Julas by visiting King Julas's kingdom in secret. They met in the west wing of the castle at twilight. Seitor promised that if King Julas would steal one of the Quint Fey's powers, he would make King Julas the most trusted and powerful of the Quint Fey.

Seitor would award King Julas the Sword of Yesu and allow him to rule the land of Exsul. Looking very torn, King Julas, with his heart beating rapidly, asked Seitor, "Which of the five do you seek?"

Seitor approached King Julas and leaned toward King Julas's ear and said in a most humble, quiet voice, "I only want the Ruby Stone Ring from King Phelo, and together, we will rule Heirthia."

King Julas, although uncertain as to his fate, closed his eyes and, without much more thought, returned the promise and agreed to tell the other six kings and the Quint Fey that during the Battle of Nunii, he'd come across Seitor. He would testify that he had slain the evil one and thrown him into the pits and fire of Sepul.

Seitor agreed to be pierced with King Julas's Silver Sword, so that blood would be drawn as evidence of Seitor's death. In addition, Seitor agreed and promised King Julas that he would stay in hiding for seven years in the land of Helum. In an act of confirmation and to make sure King Julas would keep his promise, Seitor then raised his wand and cast a spell, "Sanguine Fratrum!" he called, meaning "blood brothers" so that once they shook hands, the promise could not be broken and would be eternal. If King Julas broke his promise, he and his land would all perish through plague forever.

Although very hesitant and very weary, King Julas extended his hand and shook the hand of Seitor. Once their hands come together, there was a bright red light that bonded them to their promise. This red mist came upon them, and it went from their bonded hands up their wrists and arms.

Seitor then whispered, "There is no turning back now. You are part of my arm, and I am part of yours, and together, we will rule Heirthia." He let go, laughed, and spun into a black mist and was gone with the wind.

King Julas stood there for a moment and said in a faint voice, "What have I done?"

And so at the Battle of Nunii—which lasted for three days and took place between Sepul, the land of fire and lava, and the land of Breakle—King Julas came forth on the third day and announced to the other six kings that the evil Seitor had been slain during battle. To stage their pretend battle, King Julas and Seitor had met at a distance from the battle.

There, Seitor cut King Julas in various places throughout his body, and King Julas even had a broken arm, broken rib, and a laceration on his shoulder. Seitor did this to King Julas so as to make sure that it appeared they had really battled. It appeared that King Julas had indeed been in a serious one-on-one battle with the evil one.

While Seitor and King Julas were doing this, Seitor's army either died through the efforts of the Quint Fey and the Seven Kings' armies in the Battle of Nunii, or they retreated back to Helum or the Dark Forest.

Seitor then said to King Julas, "Go ahead. Cut me so you may draw my blood onto your sword. Then go to your kings and show them what you have done."

King Julas, with the quickness of the Silver Sword, swung and cut Seitor's chest, and blood was indeed drawn, and it was spilled over King Julas sword. King Julas and Seitor departed from one another, both looking back at each other, a final confirmation that Seitor would be coming back. King Julas left and joined his fellow kings. King Julas appeared before the kings.

"I am here, brothers, and I have fought, but I will die," said King Julas in a very sick and painful way.

"Brother, what has happened? Who did this to you?" said King Simon.

"Seitor, we battled, but behold, brothers and all people of Heirthia, I have killed the evil Dark King," replied King Julas. There, while on the floor, he raised his sword, and the blood of Seitor dripped from its point to the ground.

The drop of blood slowly left the tip of the sword, and it slowly fell to the ground. Because Seitor had pure evil in him, as the drop of blood fell to the ground, the ground became black, burned, and dead.

This the kings saw, and they knew it was indeed the blood of Seitor.

"I have slain him, and he has fallen into the depths of Sepul," continued King Julas.

However, King Jemis, using his discernment, came forward and questioned, "King Julas, where did this happen?"

King Julas replied, "Sepul. Near the fire."

King Jemis then asked, "And Seitor fell into the pits?"

"Yes, brother," replied King Julas while making a face as though he was in pain.

King Jemis then said, "What were you doing inside the pits alone?"

All the kings stood there, but then King Jonis said, "What does it matter, King Jemis? The evil one is dead, and King Julas has proven this with the blood of Seitor!" He then raised his sword in honor. "The evil one is dead!" he yelled, and the army cheered on.

King Simon then pulled King Jemis aside to talk with him alone and asked, "King Jemis, what is your spirit telling you?"

King Jemis replied, "You know my discernment, sire. I don't understand why King Julas was all alone in Sepul."

King Simon then voiced, "I know, but the battleground is all around Sepul, and there are soldiers everywhere."

King Jemis replied, "I understand, sire, and I am sorry to question this, but in all our battles, never has a king been left alone, especially alone with the Dark King. My spirit is weary, and I cannot understand why."

King Simon then said, "I know, brother, it does sound a bit strange, but King Julas is a loyal king, one of the twelve, and he needs us right now, or he can die from his wounds. Why would he cause himself so much physical damage and come so close to death? You do have to admit that the blood on his sword is that of Seitor's. You saw the evil blood kill the ground."

As they both looked toward King Julas, King Jemis said, "You are probably right. I guess it is odd how he was not only on Sepul but inside the volcano, enough for the evil one to fall to his death." King Jemis then walked away.

King Simon watched as King Jemis walked away. He then turned around and looked at King Julas as he was being treated. Although he too had some doubts, there was nothing he could do but give the benefit of the doubt.

After seeing the blood of Seitor on King Julas's sword, the Quint Fey together announced to the entire kingdom and world of Heirthia that indeed, the evil Seitor was dead. As it was announced to the entire kingdom, King Julas stood there with a proud smile and completed the treatment of his wounds, but in his eyes, he knew there was a very different story to tell.

However, as promised, for seven years, there was peace and tranquility throughout the land. Not one sword was raised. After so much time passed, King Simon and King Jemis felt more comfortable believing that indeed the evil one was dead and no more.

For the next seven years, the kings were able to rebuild their kingdoms and establish great lands. The people were indeed happy. Because the evil one had allegedly died, there were no more battles, no more conflicts, and a great peace blessed the land, but as quick as it came, it was quick to be gone. The eighth year had arrived, and the evil one in the land of Helum was awakened and ready to hunt.

As Seitor walked to the base of Helum and stood at the entrance of his kingdom, he looked out toward Heirthia and the twelve kingdoms. There behind him stood his new grand army, and it was grand like never before. Seitor looked on and whispered, "I will destroy you all."

3

KING JULAS'S PROMISE

I N THE EIGHTH year, on the first day, King Julas was walking the streets of Heirthia when he saw something so devastating that he could not believe his eyes. He saw Heirthia completely destroyed. From one end to the other, Heirthia was no more. Villages were burned down, and the land was dead. A big battle had surely taken place. He saw creatures of all kinds with swords, axes, and all types of weapons. These creatures were leading humans who were chained together and walking in a straight line.

He knew they were prisoners. He went toward a building and hid so as not to be seen. As these prisoners were walking, one of them fell, so one of the creatures began striking and beating the man who had fallen. Then in a distance, King Julas saw Seitor in King Simon's castle, and Seitor had complete control over all the land. King Julas looked closer, and indeed, King Simon was dead.

King Julas grew angry and drew his sword and began to charge Seitor to kill him, but as he approached, King Julas grew tired and weary, and no matter how much he tried, he could not lift his sword to kill Seitor. Seitor just stood there laughing at King Julas. Then all of Seitor's army began laughing at King Julas, and it grew louder and louder, and then all the creatures started to surround King Julas. He then looked down at himself, and he was covered with blood, and he could not understand why.

He looked up and yelled at the top of his lungs, and then he woke up. It was all a dream. He sat there for a few moments sweating and breathing at what he had just witnessed. He knew the time was coming.

King Julas got up from his bed to get a drink of water, and as he stood there taking a drink, he knew his opportunity to abide by his promise to Seitor would soon be coming, and his long hope of being a part of the Quint Fey was questionable. He was afraid, but he was not sure how far he had come. He thought to himself, *It is too late.* He was too far into the plan, and because he was known as the king who had slain the evil Seitor, the people and kings of Heirthia honored him and trusted his many judgments, including that of King Phelo, the Ruby Stone Ring king.

For all these years, King Julas had been a teacher of history at the School of Youngs. The School of Youngs was held in the land of Cain, King Julas's land, and hundreds of Youngs resided there while they trained. Here, King Julas, among the many other professors, taught the Youngs the history of Heirthia and how to be a king or queen, how to rule a kingdom, what the responsibilities in being a part of such kingship were, and how to utilize their talents and any powers granted to them.

They also trained for battle, sword fighting, and encounters with unknown creatures such as dragons, fairies, giants, and trolls. They called the students *Youngs* until they had proven themselves worthy to be called King or Queen. Once proven, they were considered kings and queens even though they may not be ruling a land, but it was up to each Young to prove his worth in the lands of Heirthia.

At the School of Youngs, King Julas preached about the Living King, Yesu, and reenacted the many battles of the Quint Fey and the importance of loyalty. During one particular session, many of the Youngs asked, "Professor, would it be possible for you to show us the actual Quint Fey's powers? We hear so much about them but have never seen them in action."

With all the students in agreement and encouraging a show-and-tell, King Julas stood there, silent, but in his mind, he knew that this was the opportunity to move on his promise.

He reluctantly said, "No, no, we must stay on track with our history lesson, and it could be dangerous as the powers of the Quint Fey must be respected."

Although true, King Julas whipped out his Silver Sword in a flash and began swinging it around as though in battle. The students opened their eyes in amazement at his speed. "When you have the opportunity, you take your opponent's weapon and have him surrender. This is Yesu's way," said King Julas. "We never kill, only preserve, as every soul is important to the Most High God," he continued.

Then one of the students asked, "When is it time for you to take not only their weapons but also their lives, sir?"

King Julas stood there for a moment and said, "You just know deep down in your heart that taking the weapon is not an option. It is the most difficult thing to do, but that is why you must allow Yesu to lead you. Never stray from his leadership and wisdom. Do not lean on your own understanding, Youngs, ever."

Looking attentive, the students continued to watch King Julas.

"If you walk astray, there are times when you can never find the path again," concluded King Julas. He continued, "It is as if you are walking a trail in the forest. It leads the way, and it shows you the path you should take. However, if you stray, there is no path. You don't know where you are going. Sure, you can make your own way, but you will run into obstacles, and challenges that could kill you if you are not prepared will confront you."

Young Iruy, a young princess, asked, "But if you don't intend on getting off track, if indeed you walk astray, how do you come back?"

King Julas thought about it for a moment and said, "You ask for Yesu's help, and He will come to you. He will always be there for you." King Julas, although he had lied and turned his back on the Quint Fey, still had the guilt of knowing what he did. He refused to continue the conversation. Class was dismissed.

Later that evening, as King Julas was preparing to go home, a warm southern wind came about into his classroom, and quickly he knew something was there.

"Who goes there?" yelled King Julas. He grabbed his Silver Sword in fear that he was about to be ambushed. As he slowly walked to the door, he could hear someone or something walking outside the door, and, with sword in hand, he reached out to open it. Nothing was there. He looked outside the door into the hallway of the school, and nothing was there except the dark evening. The wind then came to an abrupt stop.

"Nothing," said King Julas.

"Hello!" exclaimed Seitor, who was standing right behind King Julas.

King Julas, frightened, drew his sword and nearly cut Seitor's head off. "What are you doing here?" exclaimed King Julas.

"I have waited for many years for you to come to me with my prize, King Julas, and I just thought that you may had forgotten about our bargain," said Seitor.

"Of course I haven't forgotten. I'm only waiting for the right moment," said King Julas.

Seitor then said, "Right moment? I believe you had the right moment right in front of you with your students' pleas for a show-and-tell this very day."

In disbelief, King Julas said, "How do you know about that?"

Seitor said in a sneaky and evil way, "I have warriors and loyal mates everywhere now, even some of your precious Youngs." Seitor continued, "You see, although I have been waiting for seven years, I have been building my army, both young and old, and its size is like no other, and my army is spread throughout the kingdom of Heirthia ready to attack."

Seitor walked over to King Julas's window, which overlooked Yesu's castle, and said in a confident voice, "I have an army so grand that the Quint Fey will have the battle of their lives, and they won't see it coming. I have giants, wizards, armories, the strong, and so many who have been lost walking among those people in all kingdoms. I have been able to manipulate their minds to believe that I am the true and only God."

Then there was a long pause as Seitor walked to the back of the classroom, and looking outside toward the city, he said, "I have an army so great, we can take down the Quint Fey, and I can finally make you its rightful leader."

Trying to get out of his promise, King Julas said, "Well, if your army is so big, then why do you even need the Ruby Stone Ring? Go get it yourself."

As King Julas went to grab his things and walk out of the classroom, Seitor vanished into black mist and quickly went toward the front of the door. He reappeared in full fury and yelled, "Are you breaking your promise, King Julas?"

As quick as he was, King Julas raised his Silver Sword and put it to Seitor's neck and said, "Don't yell at me. Remember, I can destroy you right now with my Silver Sword."

Seitor then exclaimed, "Then what? Continue being a history teacher? Or will the Quint Fey and Yesu himself look down on you, knowing that you lied to them that I was dead! If that is what you want, then go ahead and kill me now, for you will never be anything without me!" Seitor then said, "Oh, that also reminds me, you and your kingdom will all die because of your broken promise, and this will be for generations to come!"

King Julas stood there thinking about his future and what he had gotten himself into. He withdrew his sword from Seitor, who was out of breath. King Julas walked toward the window and said, "I will do it tomorrow. I will get you the Ruby Stone Ring, but you must promise you will make me king of the Quint Fey and ruler of the land of Exsul. I want all the power to control the army. You also have to promise you will kill no more after we take over!"

Seitor, knowing that as soon as he had the power of the Ruby Stone Ring, he would rule all and would be very powerful, promised King Julas that as soon as King Simon was dead, King Julas would have his reward and his wishes. Seitor walked up to King Julas and whispered in his ear, "Soon, you will rule the Quint Fey, and together, we will take Heirthia."

Seitor then laughed in a sneaky and evil way, and when King Julas turned around, Seitor was gone. He had vanished once again into an evil black mist. King Julas was amazed, but then the reality of what he'd done came back to him, and he put his head down. He knew it was all about to begin, and he would have to turn his back on Yesu.

The next morning, while in class, King Julas stared at his students, trying to figure out which of them was part of Seitor's army, but he could not do it. He then said, "Students, I have an announcement. I will speak with the Quint Fey and attempt to have a show-and-tell."

The students cheered in excitement.

King Julas then asked, "Which of the powers do you wish to see?"

One of the students, Young Adims, who had the talent of persuasion and speed, said, "The Ruby Stone Ring."

Right there and then, King Julas knew Young Adims was part of Seitor's army. Young Adims then said, "It is such a powerful item of all the Quint Fey, sire. It would be so educational to learn of the power that can utilize all the other powers."

Another young chap, Young Ladam, voiced that he preferred to see the great sword of King Simon. He said, "It is the most powerful, and the sword can actually give its true owner a strength like no other."

Young Adims, knowing Seitor wanted the Ruby Stone Ring, said in a soothing voice, "No, we must see the Ruby Stone Ring, as its powers are more magnificent as it has the power of all the other Quint Fey. We will see the Ruby Stone Ring."

All of the students, now in a soothed state of mind, nodded and agreed with Young Adims, so, King Julas stated in a worried voice, "Well then, I can't make any promises as it will be very difficult to obtain such power for show-and-tell."

Young Adims then said in a confident voice, "Well, sir, then I propose we each sign a form asking King Phelo, requesting, for educational purposes, to have a show-and-tell of the great Ruby Stone Ring. I believe he would be most delighted to have such take place, wouldn't you agree, sire?"

King Julas then said in a most confused voice, "Okay then, prepare a form, and I shall have each of you sign it, and I will present it to King Phelo."

Young Adims said in a very clear voice, "Great, sire, then it's a *promise* that you will do *your* part, is that correct?"

King Julas said, even more worried and confused, said, "Yes, I promise."

After noticing the dialogue between King Julas and Young Adims, Young Ladam, who had the talent of discernment and ability to move objects, knew something was wrong, and that there was something more to this show-and-tell. Once class was dismissed, and after everyone but Young Ladam had signed the form, he approached King Julas and said in a quiet voice, "Is everything all right, sire?"

King Julas, who had been seated at his desk, looked up, startled, and said, "Yes, yes, everything is all right. Do you have the form, Young Ladam?"

Young Ladam hesitated and said, "Yes, I have it here, sire, but I did not sign it, sire."

Confused, King Julas said, "Why not, boy? Sign it so we can get the Ruby Stone Ring."

Young Ladam said, "Get? What do you mean by get?"

King Julas, knowing that Young Ladam was using his talent to find out the truth, stood up over him and said in a firm voice, "Young Ladam, you must learn when to use your talents and never to use them with kings who are above you. Do you understand?" He continued, "I am your professor, not your enemy!"

Young Ladam, knowing he had been caught, thought of a way out and said, "Yes, sire, I am very sorry. It's just that Young Adims seemed so insistent that we get the Ruby Stone Ring, like it was a matter of life and death. I guess it's all right then, sire." And then in a sarcastic voice, he said, "So long as we all know who is higher than us, right?"

King Julas looked at Young Ladam in shock. He knew then that Young Ladam was aware that something was wrong.

King Julas exclaimed, "Young Ladam, are you going to sign the form or not?"

Young Ladam, very hesitant, signed the form but placed a star next to his name. Young Ladam did this as he had a plan to find out what was going on. Young Ladam then left King Julas's class in haste. He was headed straight for King Phelo's castle. King Julas knew he had very little time.

"King Phelo, King Phelo!" Young Ladam knocked at King Phelo's gates after his long journey to the kingdom of Flora. "I must speak with King Phelo at once!" exclaimed Young Ladam to the guards. The guards advised King Phelo of his visitor. King Phelo had been sparring with King Mattei to continue his training.

As Young Ladam entered the castle, he was led to a sparring courtyard, where he stood looking in amazement at how

King Phelo was utilizing the Ruby Stone Ring. King Phelo, with the ring, called upon a wand and cast a spell while King Mattei shielded. King Mattei was King Phelo's best friend. The two were inseparable since being Youngs. King Mattei had the talent of flight. Thus, upon his call, his wings would expand, and he would take to the sky with a quick speed.

"Rebellis," shouted King Phelo.

A beam of light shot out right to King Mattei and knocked him back about twenty-five feet, burning his armor off. King Mattei, while in the air, called, "Expandat!" and took flight, going right for King Phelo with his sword drawn. Then King Phelo transformed into a lion and attacked King Mattei, bringing him to the ground. King Phelo transformed back and called upon the Sword of Yesu and placed it on the neck of King Mattei.

King Mattei threw King Phelo back, and the two began a sword fight to remember. King Phelo hit King Mattei's sword so hard that it shattered to pieces. Both King Phelo and King Mattei ended their sparring with a laugh.

"Good work, King Mattei," said King Phelo.

"You were spectacular as always, King Phelo," said King Mattei. The two hugged as they walked away.

King Phelo then said to Young Ladam, "Okay, what is this all about, Young Ladam?"

"King Phelo," Young Ladam said, still breathing hard because he had been running toward King Phelo's castle all the way from the land of Cain. "Sire, there is a conspiracy going on. I left the School of Youngs two days ago on foot to advise you of something I witnessed!" exclaimed Young Ladam.

"What do you mean, Young Ladam?" said King Phelo.

Once Young Ladam caught his breath, he said, "I was in class, and there was this very strange discussion between King Julas and Young Adims, and it appeared that they want to do a show-and-tell with your Ruby Stone Ring."

Confused, King Phelo said, "Well, that sounds like a great idea. Why is that a problem?"

Young Ladam said, "I don't know, sire, but…but, I, it, it just seemed that they were up to something, and I just did not feel comfortable, and you know my talent is discernment."

King Phelo said softly, "Young Ladam, your talent is still developing, and sometimes you might feel things that are not so. Look, King Julas is a highly ranked king. He killed Seitor, and there is no one else in Heirthia who is a threat. I am sure it may have sounded suspicious, but Seitor is dead, King Julas is trusted, and Young Adims is just as young as you. I am sure he is still very immature, not that you are immature. Look, don't worry, I am sure everything will be fine."

"I have a feeling the Dark King is behind this, sire," said Young Ladam in a worried voice.

King Phelo walked a bit a ways with his hands crossed. "Seitor is dead," he said, reassuring Young Ladam. "He cannot be behind this."

As King Phelo looked at Young Ladam, he noticed that Young Ladam was sincere and still very upset. Thus, he went toward Young Ladam. "Would it make you feel better that I myself will attend the show-and-tell and not release the Ruby Stone Ring?"

"It would, sire. That was the whole purpose of my visit," said Young Ladam.

"Okay then, go on, and thank you for speaking with me on this. I know you are a trusted soul, and I believe you. I just hope it is all suspicion only. Take one of my horses for your long journey home."

As Young Ladam got onto his horse and was leaving, he turned around and said, "Sire, just one more thing. They drafted a form for all students to sign, and just so you know, I did sign it, but I put a star next to my name in disagreement. And one other thing, please be careful when King Julas visits."

King Phelo, confused and realizing that something may be wrong, said, "Okay, I will keep my eye on it."

Young Ladam then went home, and King Phelo looked at the Young as he rode into the distance. King Phelo looked at the ring, puzzled, and thought to himself, *Who would want to do this to me? It's madness and impossible.*

As King Phelo stood there, King Mattei walked up behind him. "What was that all about?" he asked.

King Phelo explained, "I don't know. Something about a conspiracy being brought by King Julas. It doesn't make sense."

King Mattei then said, "You know these Youngs. They think they know it all and want to grow up in high rank quickly. Kind of reminds me of you."

King Phelo responded jokingly, "Oh yea, it kinda reminds me of you."

The two then sparred jokingly. King Mattei said, "I am sure it is not true."

King Phelo replied, "He said King Julas is apparently trying to get the Ruby Stone Ring from me."

King Mattei, in a reassuring voice, said, "I wouldn't worry. You have the ring, and no one will take it."

Still looking at Young Ladam riding away, King Phelo said, "I hope you're right, my friend. I hope you're right."

4

IT BEGINS

KING JULAS, KNOWING that he would have to act quickly, went straight to King Phelo's castle as it was a one-day journey by horse. When he arrived, King Phelo was having dinner with his wife, Lady Deena, and his son, Young Travi. Young Travi had the talent of using a dual sword. With this talent, he could overcome his enemy by using two swords at once in a very fast way during battle. Young Travi was fifteen years old, very slim, and tall.

As King Julas entered the dining room, King Phelo looked up and saw him. Quickly, he knew what King Julas wanted.

"Sire, I apologize for disturbing you. I will come at another time," said King Julas.

"No, no, come in, King Julas!" exclaimed Lady Deena. "Please join us," she continued.

King Julas sat at the table knowing that he had to be calm and act as though nothing was wrong. He knew that King Phelo would otherwise catch on quickly.

King Phelo continued to eat and stated, "What brings you here, King Julas?"

King Julas, not wanting to ask for the Ruby Stone Ring right off, said, "I wanted to know if you could come to my class and do a show-and-tell of the Ruby Stone Ring? Many of the students have been asking to persuade you."

King Phelo, a bit more comfortable because King Julas asked him to go personally, said, "Sure, I don't see why not, and I am sure it will be very educational for the Youngs."

King Julas, knowing that King Phelo would not be able to go in three days due to an engagement, said, "I need for you to go three days from now. I have arranged a special day with the school."

Lady Deena said, "Phelo, you will be out of the country at that time. You can't go."

King Julas then said, "If you are out of town, then don't worry about it. We won't do it. Perhaps another time."

They continued to eat and talk for quite some time. As they finished supper, King Julas began to excuse himself and stated, "Thank you for dinner, Lady Deena. Good day, King Phelo." He then walked away to leave.

As King Julas was in the hallway, King Phelo came up behind him, wanting to know the truth. He said, "King Julas, do you have a petition from your class wanting this show-and-tell?"

"Why, yes," said King Julas. He handed King Phelo the petition. Quickly, King Phelo saw Young Ladam's signature with a star on it.

King Phelo looked up and said, "Do you want to take the ring and conduct your show-and-tell?" He was testing King Julas for the truth.

"No, no, I prefer to do it at another time, but thank you for asking," said King Julas.

Now more confused, King Phelo took the ring off and handed it to King Julas and said, "Are you sure? You can take it now."

King Julas, knowing this was the opportunity, said, "If you insist, I will take the ring."

King Julas was reaching over to grab the ring when King Phelo suddenly closed his hand around it and said, "By the way, one of your Youngs visited me today. He said that you were going to ask me for the ring."

King Julas, controlling his nervousness, said, "Yes, and I have."

Knowing King Julas did not understand, King Phelo said, "No, I don't think you understand. The Young said you wanted the ring for yourself."

King Julas knew that he had to be very careful as King Phelo seemed suspicious, so he said, "Look, if you don't want to give me the ring, then don't. I am offended that you would even think this of me."

King Phelo, feeling more guilty about questioning King Julas, with King Julas refusing to take the ring, said, "Go ahead and take it, but it must not fall into the wrong hands, King Julas."

King Julas stated, "I will guard it with my life."

As he reached out to grab the ring, King Phelo closed his hand once more and moved closer to King Julas and said, "Promise me in the name of Yesu that you are not going to use this ring for evil."

King Mattei had just walked into the room, and so King Julas, seeing King Mattei, said in a firm voice, "Give me the ring, King Phelo."

Surprised at King Julas's demand, King Phelo said, "What did you say?"

"Give me the ring now, King Phelo," said King Julas in a sterner voice.

King Phelo, now knowing Young Ladam was right, said, "I will not do such thing, and I am proclaiming that you are hereby arrested for treason for attempting to take one of the Quint Fey. King Mattei, arrest King Julas to be taken to the Quint Fey at once!"

"Give him the ring, King Phelo," said King Mattei.

Shocked at what was transpiring, King Phelo looked at King Mattei and said, "King Mattei, brother, what did you request of me?"

King Mattei, in a battle stance now, once again said, "Give King Julas the ring now."

In an instant, King Phelo knew he was being double-crossed. As he quickly tried to put the ring on to do battle, King Julas drew his Silver Sword and forced it into King Phelo's back. The sword went through the front, piercing his heart. King Phelo had no chance of defending himself as he had taken the ring off. At that moment, King Phelo fell to the ground on his knees, and as he slowly hit the ground, he dropped the ring on the floor.

King Mattei kneeled down and reached toward King Phelo and cried in frustration, "I am sorry, brother, but you have been in the Quint Fey too long. You never acknowledged me, and you never even once lifted my name when I have been here for you. It is my turn now."

"Father!" yelled Young Travi as he saw his father killed before his very eyes. Young Travi drew his dual swords and went into battle, yelling and crying at what he had just seen. "In the name of Yesu!"

He charged and fought valiantly against King Mattei and King Julas. He swung back and forth against both foes. "Stop now," exclaimed King Mattei, "or we will kill you too. Stop now and we will let you free."

Young Travi continued to fight and swung toward King Julas, cutting his arm. At the same time, King Mattei swung at Young Travi, cutting his shoulder.

"You killed my father, your brother, your friend. He trusted you with all his heart, and you just betrayed him!" yelled Young Travi. Young Travi, battling both kings, drew back and yelled out, "King Phelo is dead, King Phelo is dead!"

King Julas grabbed the Ruby Stone Ring and put it on. Immediately, he had the power.

Young Travi once again charged the two kings and swung at King Mattei, cutting his chest. "Stop, boy, I will kill you!" The two fought. King Julas, meanwhile, tried to use the ring but could not figure it out.

Then he called for the Dragon's Claw Wand, and it appeared at his hand. He yelled, "Expellere!" toward Young Travi, and Young Travi was hit with a red light and thrown twenty-five feet back with burns to his chest and shoulders. He lay on the ground in pain and bleeding heavily.

"Leave him," said King Mattei.

"No, we must kill him for he will come back for revenge," said King Julas. King Julas approached Young Travi and said, "You are arrogant like your father." King Julas called for the Sword of Yesu, and it appeared. He then reached over and sliced Young Travi's chest, leaving a large gash on his chest and stomach.

Then he grabbed the sword as to stab Young Travi in the heart, and at that moment, both King Julas and King Mattei were taken aback in fear by the roar of King Aniser and the Lion Heart Medallion. The Quint Fey had been told by Young Ladam of what he had known. Young Ladam's discernment had continued to bother him in returning to his home, so he'd diverted his course and headed straight to advise the Quint Fey of what was happening.

King Julas, once again in position to stab Young Travi, reached over him to kill him but was then hit by a fierce white light from King Jonis's Dragon's Claw Wand.

"Rebellis!" yelled King Jonis, casting the ray.

King Julas flew back with burns on his arms. Meanwhile, King Mattei took to flight but was brought down by the giant lion, which was King Aniser. When King Mattei fell, he drew his sword and swung it toward the giant lion. He said, "The Ruby Stone Ring is ours. We have the power!"

King Mattei was then hit by the powerful arrow of King Jemis and his Falcon Bow. King Mattei knew that if he and King Julas did not get away, Seitor's plan would be destroyed, and King Mattei would not be the king of his own land. Quickly, King Mattei yelled, "Expandat!" and took to flight. He went over and grabbed King Julas, who had been knocked out, and they both flew off.

King Jonis called, "Expellere!" toward King Mattei, but he could not hit him as King Mattei was too far off and too high in the sky.

King Simon then arrived and made his presence known in the castle. He saw what had happened and ordered King Jemis to the aid of the Young Travi. King Jemis went to Young Travi, who was bleeding heavily from his wounds and at his last breath. You could hear him gasping for air, but he had blood coming out of his mouth.

"Pick him up for me," said King Jemis. King Jonis and King Aniser held Young Travi up, and then, with confidence and brilliance, King Jemis took the Falcon Bow and called for a healing Pearl Arrow and prepared to fire. At this point in time, Lady Deena was allowed to come down to her son.

As she was being escorted in by King Phelo's guards, Lady Deena cried out, "No, please don't! You will kill him. At least like this, we can try to heal him naturally!"

King Jemis said, "Lady Deena, if I don't do this, he will die in minutes. He is bleeding internally!"

King Simon grabbed Lady Deena and comforted her. "Do it King Jemis!" exclaimed King Simon. King Jemis said his prayer, reached back, and a flaming white arrow appeared on his bow.

King Jemis's eye lined up with the arrow toward Young Travi's heart, and he released. The arrow pierced the Young Travi's heart, and he fell to the ground. Instantly, all of Young Travi's wounds were healed. He had indeed been saved.

In a voice of panic, Lady Deena cried out, "What about my husband? Can you save him? Please save him!" She reached down and hugged King Phelo. King Simon reached over to examine King Phelo. "Pick him up. King Jemis, prepare another arrow!" exclaimed King Simon.

"But, sire, he has been dead far too long," stated King Jemis in a concerned voice. "It will not work."

"Do it!" ordered King Simon.

"Pick him up for me," said King Jemis.

King Aniser and King Simon picked up King Phelo, and King Jemis then reached for his bow, said his prayer, and extended his bow. Again, the flaming white arrow appeared. He lined up his eye for King Phelo's heart.

Swoosh! The arrow left the bow and pierced King Phelo's heart. He flew back, and all the kings surrounded King Phelo in prayer, hoping he would be healed, but it too much time had passed. King Phelo was dead.

The land of Flora was in mourning for the loss of its king, and news of the events were beginning to spread throughout the land.

"We must hold a proper burial and a grand ceremony for our fallen brother," stated King Aniser.

"You are right, King Aniser, but I fear the worst is yet to come, and so we may not have time at this moment. We must move quickly," answered King Simon with a tear coming down his face. "Preserve the body until we can find all who are involved in this treachery," he ordered.

King Simon was a strong king, but this was too much for him; he was crying deeply inside. "Whoever is behind this now has the Ruby Stone Ring, and if indeed Seitor is not dead, he knows how to utilize its true power." To King Aniser, King Simon said, "Gather everyone who knows anything about this."

"Yes, sire," responded King Aniser.

The Quint Fey gathered in the grand hall with Lady Deena and Young Travi, and, in addition, Young Ladam was called in.

"What just happened here? Does anyone know why King Julas and King Mattei did this?" demanded King Simon. Young Travi then explained what he had seen and what he had heard. In anger, King Simon said, "Anything else?"

Young Ladam then explained what he knew about Young Adims.

"What are we to do, King Simon?" said King Aniser.

"My fear may become a reality, my fellow Quint Fey," said King Simon. "Either King Julas and King Mattei want to rule this kingdom, or the Dark King, Seitor, was never killed," he continued. He then stood up and said, "If you recall, King Julas told us that he killed Seitor and that he threw him into the pits of Sepul, but my spirit now tells me that that may have been a lie." King Simon then said looking at his brothers, "The fact of the matter is that one of the three has the Ruby Stone Ring."

"Yes, but we are more powerful, sire!" King Jemis said.

"Don't be fooled, King Jemis," said King Simon, "The Quint Fey bond has been broken, so anything can happen now."

"If either of them opens the true powers of the Ruby Stone Ring, they could defeat us one by one," said a concerned King Aniser. He continued, "And we don't even know how many are involved, whether they have put together an army, or how many spies are out there. Young Ladam witnessed Young Adim's behavior, and so we know he is involved. Then King Mattei turned his back on his best friend. My discernment tells me there are many more spies and that Seitor is behind this, but this is only the beginning."

"What is our plan then, sire?" asked King Jonis.

"We need to inquire into who is involved in this, which of the other six kings are still on our side, and who will stand with us," noted King Simon. "King Aniser, you must go with King Jonis and visit the kingdoms of the southwest. Confirm their allegiance," commanded King Simon. "King Jemis and I will visit the kingdoms of the southeast. As we know, King Phelo's people will fight with us."

He then said, "Now go posthaste. We must move quickly before the evil spreads. We don't know who is responsible for this and what they will do next with the ring."

In a confident voice, Young Ladam and Young Travi stated, "What are we to do? We want to help."

"You must stay here and guard King Phelo's castle. Do not speak with anyone outside of this castle. We don't know who we can trust," said King Simon. "Whoever is involved in this treachery knows this kingdom is without its king. You must stay and fight if necessary. We will reunite with you as soon as possible, as soon as we have our alliance together. Have the armies ready."

"Yes, sire, we will stand strong," said both Young Ladam and Young Travi.

Then together came King Simon, King Aniser, King Jemis, and King Jonis, and together they drew their powers by proclaiming, "Faith and Honor." All the kings then rode off, watching each other ride into the distance in separate directions until they could no longer see each other.

One king would look at the other, not saying a word, and the other would look back without saying a word as well. Deep down, they were afraid, and they spoke no words. Although they had fought many battles together in the past and had been separated before, they knew this could be the last time they saw each other. This time was different. They were no longer Quint Fey. The Ruby Stone Ring was in the hands of an evil kingdom.

As the remaining Quint Fey kings rode to confirm their alliance, King Julas and King Mattei were on their way to the land of Helum, where the Dark King, Seitor, dwelled. The two kings were on the latter part of the Bar Mountains. The Bar Mountains were the largest and most grand mountains in all the kingdom of Heirthia. They completely and fully separated the seven kings' lands and the land of Helum. It was a land unexplored. The last mountain right before the land of Helum was quiet and full of snow, and there was not a soul in the land. The two kings wondered if they were even in the right place or if they were lost.

"King Mattei, are you certain we are headed in the right direction?" questioned King Julas.

"I believe so," replied King Mattei.

"Have you ever been to the land of Helum?" asked King Julas.

"No, but the Dark King told me how to get here," said King Mattei.

Then there was a pause as the two looked into the distance to find a route to follow.

"There, you see the top of those two separate hills over the ridge?" stated King Mattei. "At the end of the Bar Mountains, there is a long and high ridge that you cannot pass. If you climb over, there is a steep cliff that will surely lead to your death. At that ridge, however, there is an opening that leads to the land of Helum. It is the only way to enter the land of Helum," he continued.

"Yes, I see it," stated King Julas in a shaky and nervous voice. "What is that?" asked King Julas, pointing into the distance.

"The two hills there are in the form of two stone dragons with red eyes. We must walk through them, but there is a test," said King Mattei.

"Test! What test?" asked King Julas.

"Yes, we must walk through them and be in complete loyalty with the Dark King because if those black stone dragons sense disloyalty or an enemy, they will come to life, and you will face their fiery fire," stated King Mattei.

There was a pause, and King Mattei then added, "They may even eat you alive."

"Let's go!"

The two kings walked toward the ridge. As they grew closer, they began to see both human and animal bones, charred floors and stones, and even old swords and armor from warriors who had tried to enter.

"How are we supposed to know we are completely and fully loyal?" asked King Julas.

"You took the Ruby Stone Ring and killed King Phelo for the Dark King. I think you should know whose side you are on," stated King Mattei in a more serious and firm voice. Step by step, the two walked toward the entrance. King Mattei walked with much more confidence than King Julas. King Julas continued to look at the dragons to make sure they would not awaken. His heart began to pound. Sweat began to fall down his face, and his breathing became heavy. He was truly frightened. Right at the center point of the dragons, King Julas became even more frightened because all he could think about was how bad he felt for killing King Phelo and for turning his back on the Quint Fey.

As he walked, he heard a noise to the right. He stopped in shock and knew the dragons were coming to life. He turned, looked up at the dragon on the right, and then he saw a rat walking along the feet of the dragon. Before he knew it, they were already past the stone dragons. It was at this point in time that King Julas knew there was no turning back. He had indeed turned his back on the Living King.

As they walked up the last hill, there was still silence, and not a soul was in sight, but as they cleared the ridge, they began to hear loud noises, like metal being formed, metal hitting against metal, fire, and other strange sounds. That was when they saw what the Dark King had been doing for the past seven years: building an army of millions of warriors, creatures, trolls, giants, dragons, wizards, and so many other loyal soldiers.

They were making swords and weapons of all kind. It was truly a grand army of evil. Both kings stood in shock at what they were witnessing. In a distance, they could see Seitor's castle. Thus, they proceeded to approach.

As they approached a group of human-like creatures, one of them stared down King Julas and said in a confrontational voice, "You! You are part of the Quint Fey! You are one of the twelve kings!"

King Julas stood there confused as to how to answer, but then said, "At one time, yes, but I do not serve them any longer."

The creature, in disgust, drew his sword so fast that King Julas fell to the ground.

"Stop!" King Julas yelled. King Mattei walked back as other creatures drew their swords as well.

"We serve the Dark King!" yelled King Mattei.

"King Seitor warned us about you," one creature said. "That you would be coming to kill him!"

"Kill them!" yelled another of the creatures. In a flash, about twenty of the creatures attacked both kings. King Mattei defended himself with one of the creatures, and then three others joined in to kill him. As this happened, he took to flight and killed the first one.

As he fought the other three, King Julas got up and called upon the Ruby Stone Ring for King Simon's sword. In an instant, the ring lit up, and there was the sword!

King Julas ran toward several of the creatures and, with one swing, destroyed them. King Mattei landed in front of one of the other creatures and, in a stealthy move, got that one. Then from behind, one of the creatures jumped on King Mattei and began to bite his left arm. King Julas, seeing what was happening to King Mattei, quickly called for the Lion Heart Medallion, and he turned into a fierce lion.

King Julas, as a lion, attacked the other creature that was about to kill King Mattei from the front. He leapt on top of the creature and attacked. Then out of frustration and fear, he let out a fierce roar. *Roar!*

All the creatures stopped as they heard the roar. It was a roar strong enough to be heard for miles in the land of Helum, and then there was a clap, then two, then three. It was Seitor. He appeared in his dark evil mist with Young Adims.

"Very well done, my kings, very well done. You have fought valiantly," whispered the Dark King.

"Seitor, why would you allow this? We could have been killed!" exclaimed King Mattei.

King Julas then formed back into himself from being a lion.

"Are you not alive?" yelled Young Adims.

Seitor said, "I had never seen either of you battle as though your life depended on it. I needed to personally see how the two of you would react on your own since all you have done in the past is rely on the Quint Fey and fight against me. Although you have been in the shadows of those so-called kings, you two are warriors. Come to me!" commanded Seitor.

Both kings approached the Dark King and knelt down.

"Give to me what I ordered from you, King Julas," stated Seitor in a sinister voice.

"It is done, sire!" exclaimed King Julas. Then and there, King Julas held out his hand, and the Dark King reached to grab the Ruby Stone Ring.

Seitor grabbed the ring and placed it in his right ring finger and called out a spell, "Da mihi potestatem!"

With that spell, the ring empowered him with strength, knowledge, and the ability to control kingdoms and people of all nations. "Come, my kings, we must move quickly and take over Larena's River, the cliffs, and destroy the three bridges," stated Seitor.

"Sire, forgive my ignorance, but the Quint Fey and the remaining six kings are still very powerful, even with an army of millions. How are we to defeat them?" asked King Julas.

Seitor then stated with confidence, "If we do this and take that land, the remaining Quint Fey will be unable to battle together with the other six kings. The Quint Fey will not be able to cross, and the six kings will all be separated by our army. Remember, the six kings still do not know what is going on, so we will ambush everyone. Together, the Quint Fey and the six kings may be powerful, but separate, they are vulnerable, and we will outnumber them."

He continued, "You two will be my two top commanders."

Seitor called for the Lion Heart Medallion and transformed into a black-haired lion with a silver mane because of his dark blood. He let out a very powerful roar! It was a roar that shook the entire land of Helum. He then transformed back into himself as all his army were attentive.

Standing on top of a hill with King Julas and Young Adims to his right and King Mattei and Creature Turk (the leader of the creatures) to his left, Seitor stated, "Warriors, soldiers, and creatures of all kinds, the time has come. The time has come for us to take and rule the entire kingdom of Heirthia!"

All the army yelled and cheered in agreement.

"You will not serve any kings but me, for I will give you all, and I will give you everything you want. All you have to do is fight for me."

Again, all the army yelled and cheered in agreement.

Then Seitor continued, "Let us go and kill the kings who have kept us from their lands, and together we will rule!"

All the army yelled and cheered. The warriors raised their swords, the giants raised their clubs, the trolls let out such a loud yell, the human-like creatures screeched, and the evil dragons, wolfs, and many other creatures all roared and growled as well.

"We must fight and take possession of all the remaining powers of the Quint Fey. This must be done. Now go!" exclaimed Seitor.

5

THE ATTACK AND ESCAPE

AND SO THEY went. The remaining four kings left on a quest to find out who was behind the death of King Phelo and, ultimately, who was behind the stealing of the Ruby Stone Ring. All four raced on their horses: two to the west to the land of Castillo and two to the east to the land of Flora. The bridge to the west divided the land of Castillo and the Land

Castigs. The bridge to the east divided the land of Flora and the land of Breakle. But upon their arrival late in the afternoon, they discovered what they were to face.

King Simon and King Jemis rode quickly, and as they rode over a hill still in the land of Flora, they heard the most disturbing noise: an army of millions marching toward war. Even their horses were startled, and it was somewhat difficult to control them. "Whoa, whoa!" commanded King Simon.

They stopped, and King Jemis exclaimed, "In the name of Yesu, what is that, King Simon?"

"It couldn't be! Seitor!" King Simon peered at a figure waiting on the horizon. In a distance, Seitor was waiting, waiting with his army to battle and take the Sword of Yesu and the Falcon Bow. He was with Young Adims and many other creatures.

"There he stands, King Jemis. Seitor is alive," stated King Simon.

"We must get to the other six kings, sire, or we will never defeat them," said King Jemis.

"I am afraid Seitor already has," replied King Simon. "I am afraid he already has," he repeated.

In a distance, King Simon and King Jemis could see that Michael's Bridge to the east had indeed been destroyed. There was no way to cross to the six kings except through the other two bridges. Seitor had millions of soldiers, warriors, and creatures on the south side of the bridge and also millions of soldiers, warriors, and creatures on the north side of the bridge. There was just no way to cross. The two kings, without the remaining Quint Fey and other six kings, would be killed. They had no chance.

Shortly later, King Aniser and King Jonis rode over the hills toward Michael's Bridge to the west. There, they too were in shock as they stopped at a great distance on the land of Castillo. King Julas and King Mattei had taken control of the land of Castillo and the land of Castigs and destroyed Michael's west bridge.

There in a distance stood millions of the evil army on both sides. It was clear that Seitor's army had already taken control of the six kingdoms of the south. "My God," whispered King

Aniser. "I cannot believe my eyes. It's King Julas and King Mattei," he continued.

King Jonis, upon hearing this, became angered and enraged and, being young and brave, cried out, "In the name of Yesu!" He then rode off so quickly that King Aniser had no opportunity to stop the young king. King Aniser rode off behind to stop King Jonis, as it was a sure thing they both would die.

"Stop, King, Jonis! Stop!" King Aniser yelled from the top of his lungs. "You will get us both killed!"

King Aniser continued. It was too late. King Jonis was riding so fast that King Aniser could not catch up.

King Julas and King Mattei saw that both King Jonis and King Aniser were riding toward them, so they ordered the army to march forward. "Attack the two kings!" yelled King Mattei. All of the giants and trolls proceeded to run toward the two kings.

"Kill them!" exclaimed King Julas. Immediately the animals behind the giants and trolls were running hastily to fight.

"In the name of Yesu, in the name of Yesu, in the name of Yesu!" King Jonis yelled with anger. King Jonis raised the Dragon's Claw Wand and called out, "Magnificum lucendi!" Then and there, a bright beam of light shot out directly toward the army charging toward them. It was then quiet, not a sound was heard, and then came a loud blast as the bright beam from the wand came crashing against the giants and trolls. *Blast!*

Each and every giant and troll was thrown back. They crashed against the rest of their army, but the army of millions continued to charge. The giants were burned and severely hurt. The trolls could not even get up from the blast.

"Magnificum lucendi!" called out King Jonis again, and *blast!* another beam of light hit the army. They too were thrown back and burned.

Although very effective, the army was still so large that they continued to charge. It was becoming evident that without King Simon's sword and without King Jemis's arrows, the army would not be stopped. King Aniser continued to follow. Meanwhile,

King Jonis called out, "Expellere!" toward the animals, and several of them were hit with the spell. Some of them burned, and some were thrown back. As this happened, several of the animals from the corners grew dangerously close to King Jonis.

"Stop, King Jonis, Stop! Go back!" yelled King Aniser. King Aniser knew King Jonis was about to be killed.

King Aniser's heart began to race. His spirit grew weary and angry, knowing King Jonis was about to be slaughtered. Then from deep within his heart, he called upon the Lion Heart Medallion and transformed into the giant fierce lion that he was.

Roar!

The wave of the roar shook the entire kingdom of Heirthia. The wave was so strong that all the animals that were about to charge and kill King Jonis were thrown to the ground.

Dust was raised by the roar, and it clouded most of the land where the battle was about to take place. The roar even brought fear upon King Julas and King Mattei. All of the army stopped because they did not know what was coming.

King Aniser arrived to where King Jonis was and transformed into his human form. King Jonis had been thrown off his horse by the loud roar. King Aniser picked him up. "Get up! We must go, King Jonis," commanded King Aniser.

"No, we must fight, for those two cowardly kings killed King Phelo. They killed King Phelo! He was my friend." King Jonis exclaimed as he cried with such sentiment. He cried and cried so loudly, as he had lost his brother. Tears fell from his eyes, and he cried for his longtime friend. "He was my friend, and I will avenge him!"

Before King Jonis could charge once more, King Aniser transformed into a lion, and King Jonis grabbed on to King Aniser's mane and climbed onto his back.

"Expellere, expellere, rebellis, rebellis!" King Jonis called out as he was being carried away. The beams of light would find their way through the dust that was still in the air. Each beam would hit several of the creatures that were standing by.

Then King Mattei, knowing they needed to use their numbers to go after the two kings, ordered, "Attack!" All of the army regrouped and continued to charge.

"Get the powers from them! We need the powers!" yelled King Julas.

But there was no chance, King Aniser, as a lion, was too quick. So King Julas and King Mattei called upon the two stone black dragons, and they rode the dragons toward King Aniser and King Jonis.

"There, kill them!" ordered King Mattei. Both dragons let out a fierce fire. King Jonis then called out his wand, "Contego scuto!" There appeared a force field that protected them from the fire-breathing dragons.

As the dragons approached, both King Julas and King Mattei jumped off and drew their swords. King Mattei sliced King Aniser from behind. King Aniser, as a lion, fell to the ground with a cut to his back. All four kings fell to the ground. King Aniser transformed back as he fell. King Aniser and King Jonis then drew their swords to battle. At the same time, all four kings charged. The battle had begun.

King Jonis was fighting King Mattei, and King Aniser was fighting King Julas.

"You traitors!" yelled King Jonis toward them. A sword fight was then in play.

"Give us your powers, and we will let you go!" called King Julas.

"You have turned your back on the Living King, Yesu. He will destroy you!" stated King Aniser.

King Jonis then called his wand and yelled, "Rebellis," toward King Mattei, and King Mattei was hit in the shoulder and severely burned. He fell back and to the ground.

King Jonis charged toward him with his sword, but then suddenly, one of the dragons came and clawed King Jonis from behind. The claw ripped through King Jonis's skin as he was carried by the dragon into the air.

"Ignis!" yelled King Jonis toward the dragon's belly.

The beam burned through the dragon, and the dragon let go of King Jonis. As the dragon crashed to the ground, so did King Jonis. King Jonis landed and broke his arm.

Then King Aniser, in his fight with King Julas, swung his sword and cut King Julas's chest. King Julas was bleeding profusely. King Julas fell back and began to retreat. King Aniser knew this was his opportunity to get him. He called to transform but could not because of the large cut on his back. It was too painful. King Aniser then looked into the distance and could see how the army was quickly approaching. He went toward King Jonis and picked him up.

"We need to go! They will kill us and take our powers!" said King Aniser.

Then once again, he called to transform, and this time he did. He grabbed King Jonis, who was badly hurt, helped him on his back, and ran into the distance. Both King Julas and King Mattei retreated toward the army. King Aniser, injured, carried King Jonis north to the land of Exsul, where they would take refuge.

During all this time, King Simon and King Jemis struggled at to what to do while staying out of sight. "Must we fight, my lord?" asked King Jemis.

"Will we win, King Jemis? Please look deep into your heart, soul, and mind, will we win if we fight now?" asked King Simon.

King Jemis, looking deep into his talent of discernment, saw a vision of great control by the Dark Lord, Seitor, and much suffering by the people of Heirthia. "I see him, I see him," whispered King Jemis.

"Who, King Jemis, who do you see?" replied King Simon.

"The Dark King, and he, he, oh no, no, no!" cried King Jemis, and then with a much heartbroken voice, he said "I see the Dark King with all the Quint Fey, and he is ruling the world of Heirthia, and he is killing innocent people who will not join him."

"King Jemis, will we win if we fight right now? Will we win?" asked King Simon in a serious tone.

"We will fight bravely, sire. We will only fight bravely, but we will not win," said King Jemis. "However, I will fight to the death if I have to, sire, as I am here to serve the great Living King," concluded King Jemis.

"Do you see where King Jonis and King Aniser are?" asked King Simon.

"I cannot see them, but I see a battle, a battle that they have fought, and they are hurt," answered King Jemis. "I see the kingdom of Castings and Castillo have been taken," continued King Jemis. At this point, King Simon knew that the other kingdoms had been taken by the Dark King.

He knew very well that there was no one to help them. He knew that both King Jonis and King Aniser were hurt. He then looked at King Jemis, put on his helmet, and raised his sword to the words, "In the name of Yesu, in the name of Yesu, in the name of Yesu!"

King Jonis raised the Falcon Bow, and he too began to proclaim as the two kings set off charging the army before them, "In the name of Yesu, in the name of Yesu, in the name of Yesu!"

They looked at each other and yelled back and forth that their goal was to take back the Ruby Stone Ring from the Dark King. Their horses raced fast into the field, and as they did, Seitor spotted them and yelled, "There, my servants! There are my enemies. Kill them!"

At once, the army all charged for battle.

King Jemis pulled back his bow and, in a single moment, released his fiery flaming arrow of light. This single arrow has the ability to destroy a large area at once. The arrow flew straight toward the middle of the army that was charging toward them. The army of creatures, trolls, and giants were groaning, yelling, and screaming as they charged, but then the arrow of light released its power.

There it landed, directly at the army, and it released an explosion with a blast. The entire army were thrown back, and the ground shook before them, creating a large canyon across which most of the army could not pass. King Simon and King Jemis arrived at the edge of the canyon, and battled the army that remained on their side of the canyon. King Simon jumped off his horse while it was still running and, with all his might, swung the sword of Yesu and hit a large giant before him. The giant flew back, ramming into several other soldiers and creatures.

Then King Simon raised his left hand and used his inner power to push away many other soldiers attacking him. At the same time, King Jemis, in a speed of light, pulled the Falcon Bow and shot it, pulling back again and again. Flaming arrow after flaming arrow flew. His speed was too fast for the army charging at him. Soon, many of the soldiers and creatures of Seitor were down. Seitor then summoned a dark dragon and ordered the dragon to grab soldiers and take them over the canyon.

Clawful after clawful, soldiers were getting across. King Simon, in a speed like no other, ran and fought each soldier. Twisting and turning, he would swing the Sword of Yesu. All that was needed to defeat each soldier was one swing. Then he took out another sword so that his fierce fighting was no match. King Jemis also pulled his sword and followed King Simon so as to fight side by side.

Seitor was then taken across the canyon, and he landed right in front of King Simon. Seitor summoned his Sword of Yesu, and the two went to battle.

"You will die, King Simon," yelled Seitor.

"You are nothing to this world, Seitor. You are nothing, and you will die with no honor," replied King Simon.

The two fought sword to sword, but King Simon was much too powerful. *Crash!* The two swords met again and again, and Seitor could not take it. Seitor summoned the Falcon Bow and quickly drew his arrow and fired. The arrow struck King Simon in the shoulder, and he quickly pulled it out. King Simon regrouped and rushed toward Seitor. Seitor drew another arrow and fired, but this time, King Simon swung the Sword of Yesu and deflected the arrow. He approached and swung his sword, a blow Seitor defended with his, but the Sword of Yesu was too powerful.

Seitor fell to the ground and summoned the Ruby Stone Ring for the Dragon's Claw Wand. There it appeared, and he called "Ignis!" The wand's beam came crashing against King Simon's sword, yet he held on against Seitor's fire. Seitor's wand continued to throw the beam, and King Simon held as much as he could. Seitor then ordered his army to attack King Simon as he held on to defend against the sword.

King Jemis saw this and rushed toward King Simon to help. King Jemis drew a fire arrow while he was running because at that time, a soldier was about to kill King Simon. King Jemis pointed and fired away. The arrow flew right past the front of King Simon's head and came into contact with the solider. King Simon was saved.

King Simon then gathered all his strength and pushed forward against the power of Seitor's Wand, and he succeeded. The beam was pushed back toward Seitor, but he moved out of the way. Seitor then became angry at King Jemis, and so he called, "Ignis!" toward King Jemis, and King Jemis had no chance of moving. The beam of the wand struck King Jemis, and he was badly burned on the chest. King Jemis fell to the ground in agony.

"Jemis!" exclaimed King Simon. King Simon used his inner power and pushed with his left hand again toward the soldiers around him, and once again, he charged against Seitor. He approached Seitor, and Seitor knew he was in trouble. Seitor called upon the Lion Heart Medallion and turned into a fierce black lion. Seitor charged toward King Simon and leaped toward him.

King Simon ducked down to avoid being trampled on by Seitor. Once again, Seitor, in the shape of a lion, ran fiercely toward King Simon. King Simon tried to regain his composure but lost his footing. He fell to the ground and lost the Sword of Yesu as he fell. Seitor saw this and rushed for the kill. He leaped up and opened his wide jaws, and then *crash!* A larger and stronger lion grabbed hold of Seitor, and the two fell down tumbling and crashing to the ground.

It was King Aniser, the great golden lion. He and King Jonis had arrived in time to assist their brothers in battle. King Jonis summoned, "Procella!" with his wand, and it created a strong storm with wind and dust everywhere.

"Look there!" exclaimed King Simon. The dark dragon had carried a large amount of Seitor's army over the canyon.

"We must fight and give it all we have in the name of Yesu," said King Simon. But as they were about to reenter the battle, a horn came from the north. The Quint Fey turned around, and it was King Julas and King Mattei and the rest of Seitor's army. There, stuck in the land of Flora between two large armies, the Quint Fey were doomed, and the powers were at great risk.

"Brothers, this is our time," stated King Simon.

"We must fight in the name of Yesu, but it must come from the heart. If there is no heart, then there is no power, and the only power we need is that of the Living King, Yesu," exclaimed King Simon.

"I am in," said King Aniser.

"I am in," stated King Jemis.

"I am in," exclaimed King Jonis.

"I am in," concluded King Simon.

Then and there, the four kings went into their deathly battle. Seitor, Young Adims, King Julas, and King Mattei all prepared their army for battle. Slowly, all the kings jogged into battle. Even though they were not sure of the outcome, they knew one thing: they would fight to the death for Yesu. All four kings ran toward Seitor and his waiting army while another army charged against the four kings from behind. Seitor ran toward them, and his army charged.

King Aniser called upon his Lion Medallion, King Jemis drew his Falcon Bow, King Jonis raised his wand ready to fire, and King Simon raised the Sword of Yesu, and together they were ready, and at that moment, they put their powers together, and a beautiful melody came upon them, a light from the dark sky and clouds. It was a sweet melody, and it was everywhere, and the light shone upon them as they began to disappear.

It was an angel sent by the Living King, Yesu: Michael.

The light shone brighter and brighter, and Seitor saw this so he rushed toward the light. Right before all the kings were taken by the angel Michael, Seitor leaped toward them, and all four kings, including Seitor, were gone. The light was gone, and everything was still. Seitor's army did not know what had just happened. King Julas and King Mattei were puzzled, and the army stood there not knowing what to do. King Julas then ordered, "The Quint Fey are gone! Take Heirthia!"

6

THE NEW WORLD

"WHERE ARE WE?" asked King Simon as he and the other three kings stood in a beautiful forest, with trees and flowers. The sun was out, and the melody they had heard was still there.

"What is this place?" asked King Jemis.

"I am not sure, but are we dead?" questioned King Jonis.

"I think this is where the Living King lives. I feel so at peace and healthy," answered King Aniser. "Hey, my wounds, they're gone!"

"Mine too!" exclaimed King Jonis.

"You are in a land created by the Living King, Yesu," exclaimed the angel Michael with his hands behind his back. "He made this for you, for this day, for this hour, just for you. It is the land of Childis. Here it is all peace, tranquility, and fellowship," stated the angel Michael in a soft but deep voice.

"Who are you?" asked King Simon.

"I am the angel Michael, and I serve the Living King, Yesu."

"What happened back there? Why were we taken?" asked King Aniser.

"With time, you will know the answer to that, but first, please, let us eat, rest, and have fellowship about what is to come," stated Michael.

"Well, thank you for this, and we are very grateful, but there is a war back in Heirthia, and we must defend it," said King Simon with concern.

"I understand, but you must remember, there is a bigger plan that the Almighty Yesu has in store for you and for all the people of Heirthia," answered Michael. "Come, walk with me."

They came upon a giant tree with a wooden table underneath it. There was food for them from all imaginable countries. Fruits, meats, vegetables, bread, sweets—all you can imagine. "Please, you are a guest of Yesu, sit, eat, and rest," Michael advised them.

Without question, all four kings took a seat and prayed and gave thanks to the Almighty Yesu for his blessing and for saving them. Then they feasted, and as they ate, their bodies became strong and healthy. As they ate, other angels came to them. The kings were amazed at what they were seeing. These angels had wings and wore nothing but white. The angels came to them and attended to their needs. They filled their cups with water and offered them more food to enjoy. It seemed as though the kings had forgotten about their troubles back in Heirthia. Michael then came and joined them.

"Michael, so please tell us what this is all about and what happened back there in Heirthia," asked King Simon.

"You were going to die, and the powers were going to be taken from you. Although you were brave, courageous, and faithful, you made the wrong choice. You were not supposed to fight as you were not defending Heirthia for the right reasons," stated Michael. "Yesu found favor in you and heard your pleas, but you and the entire kingdom of Heirthia were doomed."

"I came to rescue you because you called upon Yesu and you brought all the powers together in his name. Because of this, you are here, and you are safe. You see, the powers are gifts from Yesu, gifts to protect the people of Heirthia."

"Wait, but we did not have the Ruby Stone Ring, so how did this all work?" asked King Jemis.

"Seitor did not realize that because he was at a short distance from you, it drew enough power to call upon me to save you and, ultimately, to save the Quint Fey from being taken for evil by him, and he would have succeeded," stated Michael.

"Why did we fail? I don't understand how we made the wrong choice. We were defending the kingdom. We had no other choice!" exclaimed King Simon.

"Yes, it may seem that way, King Simon, but remember, you were bonded together to fight for Heirthia and, ultimately, to keep it safe, but fighting a battle that was not yours to win was not keeping Heirthia safe. You knew deep in your hearts that you were not going to win. Remember, it is not about you. It is not about the people. It isn't even about Heirthia. It is about keeping the bond and the relationship with Yesu, who will protect you and keep you safe, and you risked that bond by allowing Seitor that opportunity to take it from you," explained Michael. "You four have done a remarkable job. You have kept Heirthia safe for thousands of years, fought bravely in battles to keep that bond and keep Heirthia safe. You have done all in your power, but Quint Fey is no more."

The kings were all shocked at what Michael was saying. They got up from their seats, and proclaimed that they could fight again and that they knew now what to do.

King Simon said, "Let us go back now. We will keep them safe. We feel reborn, and we will stay together."

Michael replied, "Yes, you are correct. You will fight again, but not as the Quint Fey. Please understand, your bond as the former Quint Fey is broken. Seitor has taken the Ruby Stone Ring, and thus, the Quint Fey is broken and cannot be fixed. Your time as the Quint Fey will be rewarded, and you have greatly pleased the Almighty Yesu, and his Father, the God of All," explained Michael.

At this time, all the angels came before the kings and together sang a beautiful chorus with no words but with a beautiful melody. Then a woman angel came before King Simon.

"You are and always will be King Simon Peuro." She then placed a necklace with the Sword of Yesu on it around his neck.

Then came a second woman angel before King Aniser. "You are and always will be King Aniser." She too placed a necklace with the Lion Heart Medallion around his neck for all he had done.

A third angel came upon King Jemis and said, "You are and always will be King Jemis." She placed a necklace around his neck with the emblem of the Falcon Bow.

Last came another woman angel upon King Jonis. She said, "You are and always will be King Jonis." She then placed a beautiful necklace with the Dragon's Claw Wand around his neck.

All the necklaces were beautifully engraved with a green emerald stone on them. Michael then came before them and said, "Oh, and I do have one more thing for you. I believe you have a friend who has been expecting you."

"What? Who?" asked King Jonis, almost with a tear in his eye.

"Well, he is standing right behind you," said Michael.

All three kings turned around, and there was King Phelo, the fifth of the Quint Fey.

"Phelo!" they all yelled. All the kings gathered and hugged their brother, whom they had lost in battle. They greeted each other and cried for what they were seeing. They then talked about the land they were in and all the good times they had had.

"I am so happy to see all of you." King Phelo smiled. "It hasn't been that long, but I already miss riding with you and feeling the wind blowing in my face," he continued.

"So where do you live, King Phelo?" asked King Aniser.

"I live and dwell here with Yesu, Michael, and a many other people, the angels, and creatures," answered King Phelo.

"Yesu, the Living King, Yesu, is here. Can we meet him and see him?" asked King Jonis.

"No, you cannot, my brother. Remember, I died back in Heirthia. You are still alive and well. Although you have been honored here, your work in Heirthia is not done yet," continued King Phelo.

Then Michael approached and said, "King Phelo, would you be so kind as to tell your brothers what is to happen now?"

King Phelo replied, "Yes, Michael, thank you for reminding me. Brothers, your powers will be taken from you."

The kings stood there, confused and almost brokenhearted. "We don't understand. Why are they being taken?" asked King Simon.

"There is a new plan with which Yesu needs your help," explained King Phelo. "Because of what has happened, the Quint Fey is no more. However, the New Faith has now been born and created by Yesu."

"New Faith? Which of the kings or Youngs is to take over?" asked King Aniser.

"Your powers will be given to the new king and queens," stated King Phelo.

"Wait, did you say *queens*?" asked King Jemis.

"Yes, a king and three queens," stated Michael.

King Phelo continued, "Yesu's plan is like no other. The Quint Fey were loyal, strong, and bonded, but throughout the battles, the intention and heart of the Quint Fey shifted because of the new evil that has loomed upon Heirthia. Because of this, the right intention and right heart are not in place."

"The new king and queens, however, are not from Heirthia," said Michael.

"Yes, the Almighty Yesu has found the new king and queens, and there are four. These new king and queens have no experience in battle and have no idea of what is taking place. They don't have the slightest idea as to what to do with Seitor."

"So why have they been chosen?" asked King Aniser.

"Because they have been tested over and over and over again in their world, and they have continued to stay bonded. Nothing has broken them, and they do not care of the material world. They live together because they love each other, and they stay together because they are one family," stated Michael.

"Are we to find them?" asked King Simon.

"No, you are to return to Heirthia in secret and gather your armies for the new king and queens to arrive. Once I find them, I will bring them back to Heirthia, and you will train them, teach them, and show them the way," replied Michael.

"What about Seitor? He will defeat us without our powers," stated King Simon.

"You need not worry about him. Remember, when I summoned you, all of the Quint Fey were brought here. However, upon arrival, Seitor was sent directly to Earth," answered Michael.

"Earth? Is that where the new king and queens dwell?" asked King Jemis.

"Yes, King Jemis," answered Michael.

Michael continued, "Seitor is on Earth right now, and he has now begun searching for the new king and queens. He is out to kill them before I get to them. Now time is of the essence because Seitor knows a new plan is in play, and thus, I will need your powers as I have a quest ahead of me. Please give me your powers."

One by one, the kings came before the angel Michael and handed their powers over. As they placed the power upon the hands of Michael, each stated, "In the name of Yesu, I surrender my power." After all four powers had been collected, each king pled farewell to Michael and to King Phelo, and they walked into the distance and back to Heirthia.

Michael walked into the distance in search of the new king and queens on Earth. He knew he had to hurry because Seitor would be lurking. In a blink of an eye, the angel Michael was on Earth. He landed in the Gulf of Mexico near the state of Florida.

The people on the beach were shocked and confused as to what had just fallen out of the sky. Michael, together with the powers in his heart, walked out of the clear blue waters and unto the sand.

He stood there as the beachgoers watched him. He was now dressed as a modern-day person. He had dark jeans and a black shirt. He was tall, very well built, and had a defined jawline and short brown hair.

He looked around, closed his eyes, and prayed to Yesu for guidance. He knelt down as the glowing sun fell on him. Behind the sound of waves and seagulls, he prayed to Yesu to make his ears sensitive to Yesu's voice, and then he heard a soft voice speak to him and say, "Gemini."

Michael opened his beautiful blue eyes, rose from the sand, and began his quest in search for the Gemini family.

7

THE NEW HEIRS

S O THERE IN the land of Orlando, Florida, lived a family that had a great faith. There were four of them, and oddly enough, they were young, with children, and with absolutely no battle experience. However, the Living King saw something in them that very few had: love, compassion, faith, forgiveness, and unselfish hearts. Could they truly be the new king and queens of Heirthia? They were the Gemini family.

There was the father, Daniel, about thirty-four years old, of Spanish background, with the strength of a lion, as majestic as an eagle, with a love so grand for his family. Daniel had short black hair, brown eyes, and a medium build, and he stood about six foot three. He was very kind and diplomatic, and he had the heart for justice. However, if crossed, if injustice was before him, he stood tall and firm and spoke with a determination and fought with honor.

If he was ever put into this position of injustice, everyone knew something was not right, and he would confront and stand before it without fear. Daniel was an attorney by profession. He was very competitive but very fair, honest, and truthful. His talent was that of making peace and offering forgiveness. There was nothing more important to him than to protect his family, provide for them, and serve his Almighty God.

Then there was Elena, the graceful gazelle with the heart of a lioness and a caring heart for her family. She too was of Spanish heritage. She was beautiful like no other. There was something about her that was so admirable. She was a fine ruby, a radiant beam of sunlight, an elegant rose, and the most overwhelming pleasing scent it gave. She was a smile that brightened the sky, the most beautiful woman Daniel had ever laid eyes on. She was his most precious jewel.

She stood about five foot three, with long straight black hair, and she was also thirty-four years old. Her eyes were in the shape of an oval, like that of an Egyptian or Arabian, and she had light brown skin. Her eyes were light brown, like that of fresh honey, and she kept her body physically fit. Elena was certainly a giver by heart. She truly enjoyed giving, seeing people smile, and serving others before herself. She certainly had the talent of giving but also had the talent of discernment.

Her spirit would speak with her and give her great wisdom as to peoples' true intentions, and she could easily read through people who were untruthful or unfair. Her faith in God was so impeccable that nothing could come between her relationship with God.

Then there was the firstborn, Katalina, the giver. She always put everyone before her, and she constantly strived to be compassionate and nurturing. Her father saw her as an elegant butterfly, moving peacefully, looking so beautiful and captivating, but when crossed, she could sting like an angry hornet. Katalina was young, fourteen years old. She had long curly black hair, small brown eyes just like her father's, and tanned skin, and she was obviously of Spanish heritage.

Katalina's heart was so grand. She loved to keep people happy and was quick to forgive, but most importantly, she would forget all the bad things people had done to her. She was truly a master healer, and her talent was that of giving off happiness, joy, love, and forgiveness. She was a crystal light. Quick to her feet, she was fast, crafty, and precise in her actions. She was very sporty, and she loved competition. She was fast with her feet and fast with her hands. Her love for God was so great, and she was so dedicated and faithful to her family.

Then there was the little precious one, Violeta or, as she liked to be called, Violet, the artist. Violet was the valiant falcon soaring through the wind, craftily moving through her ways, perfect in her every move. Violet had the strongest heart, and her faith was that of a child's, unbreakable. She certainly spoke and used wisdom beyond her years, sometimes speaking to older youth and even adults on what was right and what was wrong, what to do, and what not to do, and she always looked at the positive side of everything.

Although graceful like a falcon, she too could strike in the event of trouble or hard times. She was fierce, like a falcon, but so sweet, like the ladybug. She was the youngest of the family, only ten years old. She had straight brown hair and light brown skin, and she was very tiny. She was thin, but tall for her age. Her eyes were like her mother's.

She had the most pleasing smile and was certainly the joker of the family. Violet's talent was that of an artist. She was very artsy and had the mind of a builder, creator, and developer. She loved the Lord, her God, and loved people in general. She always looked out for others and was always fair. She always shared and always put people before herself. She always looked up to her big sister.

The Gemini family lived in the central part of Orlando, Florida. They lived in a small townhome where Daniel worked as an attorney in his small office. Day in and day out, he and Elena operated the business, helping clients get through their hard and difficult times. They constantly dealt with difficult attorneys, but somehow, through the grace of God, peace always came out of it all.

Their goal in operating a law office was to help people. More importantly, however, they wanted to show people, to show their clients, how to carry themselves, how to speak with wisdom, and how to turn every negative event or situation into an event or situation that glorified God. Violet and Katalina had attended school there, where they obtained their education, made friends, and, most importantly, learned more about their God. It was a school that was overseen by a great church, a church people called the Giving Church. The Gemini family did not have family in Florida.

All their family were in Texas, but their friends and church friends had become their family.

The Gemini family loved adventure and was always involved in activities and sports—swimming, going to the beach, boating, running, soccer. You name it, they tried it. It was their passion to be together as a family, to do things as a family, and, most importantly to grow as a family. This was a special component for the Gemini family.

They lived to enjoy life and to serve the Lord and did not live to work, which is what separated them from many other families. Their motto was to live a life of peace and tranquility, to work hard for God, and to show others that life is much more important than a career and physical things, that time with family is so precious. They did not have a purpose in life, but, rather, they lived a life full of purpose.

Then their true test came upon them. The angel Michael had left the west coast of Florida and had traveled many miles throughout the lands, forests, and wetlands of Florida toward central Florida. One night, while Michael attended to his fire, the voice of Yesu came out from the flame. The fire grew large, bright, and fierce, but did not burn.

"Michael, Michael, Michael," stated the voice of Yesu.

Michael immediately knew this was the Living King. He knelt before the flame, looking toward the ground. "Lord Yesu, it is I, Michael. How may I serve you?" asked Michael.

"You are close to the chosen ones, Michael. You are very close," Yesu said in a soft and tender voice.

"Where shall I find them, Lord. Where shall I seek?" asked Michael.

"You will continue to head east, and you will come upon a fair," answered Yesu.

"A fair, Lord?"

"Yes, a fair. This fair is in honor of the strawberry, a strawberry festival, and the family I have chosen to lead Heirthia against Seitor will be there tomorrow," stated Yesu.

"How will I know them?"

"You will certainly know them, and you must hurry as the father, King Daniel, will encounter a most difficult situation. He will attempt to protect his family, but he will be hurt, and it will be fatal unless you hurry. Seitor knows this, and he is planning the fatal event," concluded Yesu.

"But, my Lord, what shall I do to protect them? I do not even know who they are!" exclaimed Michael.

"I must go now, but I have one last word for you. You will know who they are, and your presence there will protect them. Just believe," answered Yesu.

"Lord Yesu?" called Michael as the fire grew smaller and the once bright and fierce fire faded into the night. The air and fire were silent.

Michael was very faithful and confident at all times, but here on Earth, he had taken on fear and was weary of where he was, alone and on a quest to find a family he did not know. At that point in time, Michael knew he had to hurry into the night and find the Gemini family before King Daniel would be killed. He quickly grabbed what he had, turned off his fire, and headed into the night.

8

THE FINDING
OF THE KING

THE NEXT MORNING, Saturday, Elena woke up to the bright morning sun and, for some reason, just felt like going on another adventure with the family. "Daniel, Daniel," stated Elena very excitedly, "Let's do something today with the girls."

"What are you talking about? I am already doing what we are supposed to be doing, sleeping, and I'm winning," stated Daniel in a playful voice. He looked up at Elena sitting next to him in bed. "You are so beautiful, and your dimples are so cute," said Daniel.

Elena smiled and became shy. "Stop," answered Elena.

"Really, every morning I fall in love with you all over again," replied Daniel.

"No! I know what you are doing. You are trying to buy time so you can sleep," replied Elena. Elena then began to tickle Daniel, and he laughed uncontrollably. Both Katalina and Violet heard the laughter and rushed into their parents' bedroom and jumped on the bed.

"Tickle Daddy, tickle Daddy," exclaimed Elena. "I'll hold him down. You tickle."

Both girls began tickling their father. Daniel lifted both children off the bed in laughter. He could no longer take it, and he exclaimed, "I give up, I give up! Okay, okay, we'll go somewhere today! What do you all feel like doing? Disney, Universal Studios, the movies, swim with manatees, Fun Spot, camping, the beach?" asked Daniel.

"I don't know. I feel like eating something sweet," answered Elena.

"We can eat some delicious pancakes at Peach Valley," replied Daniel.

"I want to eat strawberries," voiced Violet.

"That is a great idea, Violet!" exclaimed Katalina. "The strawberry festival is going on this weekend, Daddy," exclaimed Katalina, eager to go.

"They have rides, games, strawberries, shows, and so much more," stated Violet.

Daniel answered, "I don't know. There's going to be a lot of people, dirt, and cars. You never know what could happen in a place like that."

"They have that foot-long hot dog with onions and peppers you like, Daddy," stated Katalina in an attempt to influence her father.

"I would love a strawberry shortcake or even a funnel cake with whipped cream, sugar, strawberries, and vanilla ice cream on top," said Elena with her eyes wide open.

Daniel sat there for a moment looking at his three girls, processing all of it. He then replied, "You had me at foot-long hot dog!" The girls were very excited.

Elena responded, "Okay, let's get ready and get out of here. We're going to the strawberry festival!"

The Gemini family got ready and was off to the festival for some food and fun, but what they did not know was that Daniel would be in danger.

A few hours' drive after breakfast, the Gemini family arrived at the festival in their red Dodge Durango. Daniel was certainly correct; there were lots of people and cars everywhere. Nonetheless, they found parking and were off to the fair. They entered the fair and went straight for some fun rides. It was a great carnival. While in line for the roller coaster, the four were talking about all the events, and they could smell the cotton candy, the grilled onions and hot dogs, and all the sweet goodies.

Then a light west wind came, and no one really noticed, but Elena felt something. She thought the wind was strange, different, odd, because it was a beautiful sunny day with no clouds or wind. The wind blew through her hair, and her beautiful black hair was lifted upward.

"What is it, Elena?" asked Daniel as he noticed her looking concerned.

"I don't know. I just felt something in my chest like something is wrong or something is about to happen," answered Elena using her discernment.

"Do you have any idea of what it could be? Something happened to the family back home?" asked Daniel. He became a bit worried as he knew his wife had great discernment.

"No, well, I don't know. It is probably nothing," answered Elena.

The four of them then got on the roller coaster, as it was their turn. Daniel sat with Violet, and Elena sat with Katalina. The roller coaster moved and began its climb upward. Elena grew weary. "Hold on to Violet!" So Daniel grabbed hold of Violet's arm.

The coaster grew higher and higher, and as it reached the top, *swish*, the coaster sped up in a haste as it rolled around the tracks. It was a great ride, without incident, and they bumped back and forth through all the turns. As the ride ended, Elena got off the coaster a bit dizzy, exclaiming, "Thank God that is over. I felt so uncomfortable."

The family then went off to enjoy more rides, and Elena felt a bit better. When they were done and exhausted after all the rides, especially the tilt-a-whirl, they headed for the food. Daniel headed for the hot dog stand, with the others right behind. "I can smell the grilled onions. They're around here somewhere," he voiced. "They're calling my name," he continued jokingly.

The girls just laughed at their father's persistence in finding his precious hot dog. They finally found it. They placed their order, and while they were waiting, Daniel was looking at the three girls with a smile when he felt someone looking at them. He just got this vibe that he was being watched.

He quickly turned his head and saw a man in a distance looking straight at them. Right when he looked at the man, the man turned and walked behind one of the concession stands. It was odd, but he ignored it. Once they got their orders, they sat down on some benches to enjoy their hot dogs and sweets.

Of course, Daniel had his fully loaded hot dog, as did Elena, and the girls ordered corn dogs: one with mustard and the other with ketchup. They really enjoyed their food. After eating, they enjoyed their sweets. Elena had a sweet funnel cake, Violet had some pink cotton candy, Katalina had a grape snow cone, and Daniel had a strawberry milk shake.

It was indeed turning into a great day.

Again Daniel felt someone looking at them. This time, he turned to his left and saw the man again, but this time, he got a good look at him. He had dark brown hair, blue jeans, and a black shirt. He had something of a beard and looked very suspicious.

Daniel, while eating, was slouched, but when he saw the man, he knew something was wrong. Daniel sat straight and lifted his head and chest, looking straight at the man.

"What's wrong, Daniel?" asked Elena.

"That man, this is the second time I have seen him staring at us," replied Daniel.

"What man?" asked Elena.

As Daniel turned to look at the man again, he was gone. "He was standing right over there looking at us," stated Daniel.

"There are a lot of people here. He could have been looking at anyone."

"It just looked weird," Daniel said.

Nonetheless, the family ignored what had happened, finished their sweets, and moved on to play some games. They headed toward the dart game, where both Katalina and Violet won prizes. It was a lot of fun. Then they came upon the basketball game. Make two, win the big prize. Daniel, being the competitive one, took up the challenge.

He shot the first one. *Swoosh!*

"Yes!" Elena exclaimed.

"One more, Daddy!" said Violet, excited to get the giant fairy.

Daniel lifted the ball and took the shot, but out of nowhere, another basketball came flying and hit Daniel's shot. Daniel turned in shock. It was the man. This time, he was within a few feet. Daniel quickly noticed that the man's eyes were red, but not just red, dark red, to where the man looked like a demon.

Daniel said, "That wasn't very nice."

The man replied, "What are you doing to do about it?"

The man looked violent and confrontational. Daniel approached the man with chest up, but Elena got in front of him. "It's not worth it, Daniel. It is just a game."

Daniel's face was visibly upset, his eyes were squinted, and his eyebrows were lowered. Elena then said in a very soft voice, looking at her husband, "Daniel, Daniel, sweetheart, let it go."

Daniel took his eyes off the ma, and looked at his bride's beautiful honey-brown eyes. Her voice was so sweet and calm.

"Let's go," said Daniel. He took hold of Katalina and Violet and walked away.

"Is that the same man you saw earlier?" asked Elena.

"Yea, that's him. Did you see his eyes?" asked Daniel.

"I did," answered Elena. "We need to leave. I'm getting a bad feeling about this," she continued.

Daniel then turned around, and the man was following them at a distance.

"Let's just go," stated Elena in a nervous voice. At that same time, the angel Michael was running in a haste as he knew he had very little time.

He ran with such speed and strength, and nothing was going to stop him. He knew that Seitor was already there, possessing people to come against the family.

"Quickly, girls, we need to leave," stated Daniel.

"Who was that man, Daddy, and why did he do that?" asked Violet.

"He's a bad man, Violet," answered Katalina, who was becoming visibly scared at what was happening. The four moved through the crowds of people, and as Daniel looked back, the man was gone.

"Keep moving," exclaimed Daniel.

The angel Michael moved quickly and found the festival. He stopped for a moment and prayed for guidance. He quickly continued to run through the crowd but could not see any sign of the family. Daniel, hand in hand with Katalina and Violet, and Elena right beside, came to the end of the festival and upon a curb to cross a double-lane street. Michael was really focusing, and he looked around but could not see anyone who stood out. What he did not realize was that the evil man was just a few feet from the family at the curb facing the opposite direction.

Daniel looked both ways and did not see any car coming. Thus, they began to cross the street. Then as they were right before the center of the street, an old Ford truck came racing toward them.

At first, Daniel did not see this, but then he looked left and saw the vehicle racing right toward them. Right away he noticed who was driving. It was the man with red eyes, and he was in a rage to kill Daniel's family.

Daniel quickly turned to his children, and because he was holding their hands, he pushed his hands forward so that both Katalina and Violet would cross the other side of the curb. As the truck was within ten feet, Daniel twisted and grabbed Elena's right hand with his right hand and jerked her toward him and toward the other side of the curb to place her out of harm's way. Daniel knew the evil man was after him. As Elena passed Daniel, they looked at each other eye to eye with fear and sadness. Right as Elena stepped on the curb, the truck was within five feet from Daniel and going very fast.

Daniel had absolutely no way of moving out of the way without putting his family in danger. He immediately lifted his chest, stood tall, put his chin down, lowered his forehead, and leaned his left shoulder forward for what was about to happen.

Crash! All you could see was a flash of bright light, and all you could hear were the sounds of horror and grief as the truck slammed into Daniel. There were people screaming in the background because of what had just happened. Crowds of people gathered, and the innocent Elena, Katalina, and Violet were screaming at what they had just witnessed: their father's death. Katalina and Violet were crying as Elena stood there and fell to her knees in disbelief, with tears falling down her cheeks.

But something was odd. Smoke was coming out of the truck. It sounded as though the radiator was spilling hot water, and the truck, now twisted metal, was at a standstill right where Daniel had been hit.

"Daniel!" yelled Elena.

When the crash happened, the angel Michael turned around in grief. He was too late. He knew Daniel had been killed.

But there he was, Daniel, standing right where he'd been when the truck hit him, unharmed and not a scratch on him.

Daniel stood there and appeared to be stronger and bolder, and he looked as confident as ever. And there in a distance stood the evil one, Seitor. Seitor looked from the forest in disbelief. The truck had been smashed in and had significant damage.

The front end of the truck was smashed in as if the truck had run into a large steel pole. Daniel walked toward the driver's side to confront the man with red eyes. Daniel opened the door, and the man was sitting there unconscious and bleeding from a gash to his forehead.

Daniel dragged him out and onto the floor, and the man awoke, but he no longer had red eyes, and he looked confused.

"Who are you?" Daniel yelled. "Tell me who you are, and why did you try to kill me and my family?"

"What happened? Where am I?" replied the man. "Who are you?" the man asked Daniel.

"You have been following us at the fair, and you just tried to kill us!" exclaimed Daniel.

"I don't remember any of this," pleaded the man. "I am a peaceful man. I have my own family, my own children. Why would I want to kill you?" he asked. "I don't remember any of this. I just don't know what happened. I am so sorry!" said the man as he began to cry.

Daniel let him go in confusion as the paramedics, police, and fire personnel arrived. Daniel just did not know what was happening. Elena and the girls came to Daniel in disbelief and hugged him very hard.

"Are you all right?" exclaimed Elena.

"Daddy, Daddy!" yelled the girls. They were still crying from what they had seen.

Violet then said in a shaky voice, "I thought you were dead."

"I am okay, sweetheart. I am okay," stated Daniel with a knot in his throat.

The paramedics came and checked Daniel, but there was nothing wrong with him, not a scratch. Then a police officer came and asked, "What happened here, and what happened to the truck?

Was there another vehicle that hit it, or was it already dented before he hit you?"

Daniel replied, "No, well, I, I don't remember really. It just came out of nowhere, and the man driving the truck looked like he wanted to kill us. The truck came and rammed into me, but, well, I don't understand."

The police officer looked confused. Daniel then said, "It just bounced off me."

The officer now looked even more confused. He then said, "Well, whatever happened, your guardian angel must have been with you because no one should have survived that accident."

The police arrested the man on the spot and took him in for questioning. As the police escorted him away, he resisted and said, "Please, please, don't arrest me! I didn't do this! All I remember was getting to the fair and then waking up after the accident."

Daniel then intervened, "Officer, I don't think this man did this on purpose."

"Daniel, what are you doing?" asked Elena.

The officer then replied, "I understand, sir, but this man tried to kill your family."

Daniel responded, "I just don't think he tried to do anything. For whatever it's worth, Officer, I am not going to press charges. This man has a family and children and must go to them. Bless you, sir."

The officer then said, "Well, we already checked him for alcohol and drugs, and he came out clean. If you're not going to press charges, then we will just give him a ticket for reckless driving."

The man replied, "Thank you, Officer, and thank you very much, sir. I don't know what happened, but I am sorry for what I have done. I pray for blessings for your family."

Daniel and the man shook hands, and Daniel turned and walked away with his family.

"Daniel, what happened back there? How did you do that?" asked Elena in a very confused and concerned tone.

Daniel continued walking, but Elena went to him and grabbed his shoulder. "Daniel, what happened?" She began to cry again.

"He hit you with his truck, but it bounced right off you. You should be dead. What happened?"

Daniel put his right hand on his head and nodded as he said, "I, I really don't know, Elena. All I remember was feeling this enormous amount of strength, faith, and confidence. It felt as though I was indestructible," replied Daniel.

"I don't know what happened, but God was with you today," replied Elena with tears coming down her face. She then hugged her husband with so much force as she was grateful that her husband was still with them.

"Let's go home, sweetheart. We have had enough events for today," concluded Daniel.

Seitor continued to look at what was unveiling and said to himself, "So that is why you have chosen them, Yesu, a humble family indeed. But be assured, I will kill them and rule Heirthia. But why, why did that man survive? You must be behind this, Yesu, as no human could have survived this. He is nothing, his family is nothing, and I will kill them." Seitor then placed his black hood over his head and walked into the forest and to the distance.

Although unsuccessful, Seitor was determined to kill the family. It was he who had possessed the man to kill the family. Earlier, when the man arrived at the fair, Seitor took control over the man and made him evil. Seitor had called upon the Dragon's Claw Wand with the Ruby Stone Ring and cast, "Memor Imperium!" and in an instant, the man was controlled by Seitor, and that was why he had red eyes, the eyes of evil.

Once the man was under Seitor's spell, Seitor commanded, "Kill the Gemini family. There in a distance, you will see a man with his wife and two children waiting." Although no one could see Seitor in his black gown—he'd made himself invisible—he was right behind the man, and he pointed over the man's right shoulder toward the roller coaster, where the Gemini family had been waiting.

"Go. Follow them and then kill them!" Seitor commanded.

Seitor had indeed failed in this attempt to kill them, but he was determined to follow them.

Still the angel Michael stood there. He knew that was the Gemini family and the new chosen heirs to the Heirthia kingdom. Michael realized that because the Sword of Yesu was so close to Daniel, it automatically gave Daniel the strength of a true king, and that the sword itself had chosen its new king.

As the Gemini family was in the path of the deadly truck, Yesu's Sword had lit up like the bright morning star, which gave Daniel power, strength, and confidence to destroy that truck. As Daniel and his family drove away from the accident, Michael stood there and looked at Daniel. At that moment, Daniel looked at Michael too and their eyes met.

There was a connection, and Daniel, deep in his heart, knew there was much more to this event than what actually occurred. Michael felt peace, knowing Heirthia had a chance. Michael watched Daniel and the family drive away into the distance and smiled in relief, knowing he had found the family.

All that was left to do was to get them to believe that their destiny was in Heirthia.

9

THE QUEEN'S TEST

THE EVENT AT the fair was on a Saturday and thus throughout the following week, the Gemini family rested and went on with their lives, with no other events taking place. Although they became busy with school, the law firm, and everyday life tasks, the events that unfolded still crossed Daniel and Elena's mind.

Daniel and Elena were working in the office one morning, and Elena asked, "Daniel, what was that all about this past weekend? I mean, the truck hit you," Elena spoke in a confused voice.

"I still don't know. I have thought about it so much, but I just don't know," replied Daniel.

"Well, all I remember was that there were people everywhere, and that man was just following us. I remember feeling afraid, and right when you saved me, right when I passed you, something just told me that it was going to be okay," said Elena.

Elena then moved from her desk at the office and went right up to Daniel's desk. Daniel opened his arms, and Elena sat on his lap, and the two embraced and shared a small but romantic kiss. Daniel lifted his right arm and gently touched the right side of Elena's face and said, "I am just glad to still be here with you, mi amor."

Elena then leaned forward and hugged Daniel with such an embrace, and as a tear fell from her eye, she said, "I love you so much. God sent an angel to be with you Daniel, and He has a plan for us because He is not done with you. Daniel, my heart is telling me that God has something for us, something really big, a special mission that He wants us to handle."

She paused for a moment, looking into Daniel's eyes. She then said, "He will be with us."

Daniel smiled and replied, "I know you are right. You have a special gift, Elena, and I believe God is speaking through you. Elena, I am ready for whatever God has for us, and I want you to know that I will be here for you, I will defend you, and I will never let you or our girls go. If God is for us, then who can stand against us?"

Daniel and Elena then sat there for a few moments and prayed. They held hands and prayed together for God to lead them into the right direction and to make their ears sensitive to His voice. They prayed that if God truly had a mission for them, they would be ready to follow Him. Once they were done praying, Elena got up and said, "You know what? All this tension and thinking has to stop. I say we go to the Central Florida Zoo on Saturday and have some fun."

Daniel then replied, "You know what? I think it will be good for the whole family."

What Daniel and Elena did not realize was that it was God who had put this into Elena's mind. It was He who granted Daniel and Elena this new mission to save Heirthia. Daniel and Elena did not realize that the trip to the zoo was solely to test the new queen Elena, and tested she would truly be.

On Saturday morning, the great outing arrived. Daniel prepared ham sandwiches for the girls to eat for lunch while at the zoo, and Elena prepared small snacks, drinks, and extra clothes in case the girls got wet at the water park. As the girls got into their red Durango, the angel Michael was at a distance watching them, making sure they were okay.

Michael knew that it was time for them to know the truth and time for them to understand their mission. However, also at a distance was Seitor, watching their every move. As they drove off, both Michael and Seitor knew that this would be the day that either the Geminis would die, or they would know the truth. In haste, both Seitor and Michael quickly followed the Geminis' path.

Seitor and Michael already knew where the Geminis were going, and so, as quickly as the Geminis entered the zoo, both Seitor and Michael were already inside waiting to fight and to defend. It was a beautiful sunny day at the zoo for the entire family.

The family arrived at the zoo and were indeed having great family time. They visited the bird exhibit, the reptile cages, and even saw the elephant show.

The Geminis were watching the elephants, and they were in the stands under a shaded area. Daniel pulled out the kids' sandwiches, and they all began to eat. At that time, the angel Michael sat right next to Daniel.

Michael smiled as the show went on and then said, "It was pretty amazing what happened with the truck last Saturday, wasn't it?"

Daniel had just bitten his sandwich, but he immediately stopped, and goose bumps filled his entire body.

He turned his head to the right and looked directly at Michael. "Excuse me?" Daniel replied.

Michael, continuing to look at the show, said, "I said it was amazing what happened with that truck the other day. You know, the one that hit you."

"I am sorry, but I don't know what you are talking about," replied Daniel in a most confused voice, even though he knew exactly what the gentleman next to him was talking about.

Then and there, the angel glanced over at Daniel and said, "I am the angel Michael." He then looked over at where the elephant show was going on. He continued, "I am here on behalf of our Almighty God, and He has called you."

Daniel grew concerned because he did not know who this person was and did not even know whether this man was evil or good. All Daniel knew was that so many strange things had already happened to him.

"Look, I don't know who you are, and I don't know what you want, but you need to stay away from my family!" Daniel said with such a straight face, his tone very determined.

At this point, Elena heard what was happening and looked over at the man sitting next to Daniel.

Feeling uncomfortable, Michael said, "I am sorry. I must have the wrong person. My apologies for disturbing you."

Michael then began to walk away, but then Daniel said, "Who are you really?"

Michael stopped where he was and just stood there. He then turned his head and part of his shoulders and looked at Daniel and his family, who were staring at him. "I am the angel Michael, and I am here to serve you, Your Highness." He lowered his head and walked away.

"What was that all about, Daniel? What did he call you?" asked Elena.

Daniel, looking very concerned, said, "He said he was the angel Michael and that he was here on behalf of God."

Elena giggled nervously and said, "The angel Michael? Like the archangel Michael?" she voiced. "He is probably just some crazy, lonely man. He has probably been in the sun too much."

Daniel then said, "He knew about the truck incident."

Elena turned to Daniel with a surprised look, goose bumps everywhere. She said, "Let's just get out of here."

The Geminis left the elephant show as it was coming to a close. As they were on their way to the exit of the zoo, they came to the lion's den area. To calm down, Daniel stopped and held Elena's arms and said, "It's okay, sweetheart. This is all just going too fast right now. Everything will be okay. I promise."

As they continued to talk, Violet said, "Mommy, look at the big lions."

Of course, Daniel and Elena were talking, trying to comfort each other and trying to understand everything that was happening. As they did this, there was a worker giving a presentation about the lions and lionesses. The woman presenter was telling the audience there that the lionesses are the hunters of the den and that the lions are the protectors of the land and territory.

She then explained how the lionesses either hunted very early or late in the evening. At the time of the presentation, it was a little after noon. The announcer said, "At this time of day folks, the lions and the lionesses rest and mostly sleep. It is really hard to get them to come out of their den, so you can't really get a good look at them."

The structure of the den area had giant boulders, rock formations, and large trees to provide shade for them. As Daniel and Elena were discussing what to do, whether to go to the police or authorities with all that was happening, Katalina came to her parents and said, "Look at the lions, look at the lions!"

Daniel was continuing to say things and talk about what was going on.

"Daddy, look at the lions. Look at what they are doing."

Again, both Daniel and Elena were so focused at their discussion.

Then Katalina spoke again, this time tugging at her mother. "Mom, look!"

Elena finally turned her head to the right and just left Daniel talking by himself. She couldn't believe what she was seeing. Elena approached the den, which was surrounded by a fence, and she was amazed. In the distance, all the lions and lionesses were looking toward them.

Slowly, the alpha male lion looked at Elena and began walking toward her. The announcer said, "Oh, look, ladies and gentlemen! If you're lucky, the lion may approach, so get your cameras ready as this doesn't happen very often this early in the afternoon."

At a distance, the angel Michael looked on, and he smiled. He knew what was about to happen.

The lion then stopped, still at a distance, and let out a roar. This call was different, though, because he continued to make a specific call, as though he was calling the other lions.

Then out of nowhere, six other lions, lions and lioness both, came out of the den. The lion that had made the call approached the front of the gate, where all the people were standing. As the lion drew closer and closer and closer, its eyes were fixed on Elena. Then right before the gate, the lion stopped and would not take its eyes off Elena.

As this lion stopped, all the others then followed. As Elena stood there, all seven lions stood before Elena and would not take their eyes off her. They all then sat down, but they were still staring; their eyes were fixed on her.

The announcer woman then said, "Wow, ladies and gentlemen, this is very extraordinary. I have never seen such a display of affection!"

Elena then moved to the side so as to allow people to have a look, but the lions all moved their heads and eyes toward Elena.

Several of the people, although they were taking pictures, were amazed at what the lions were doing. Feeling even more uncomfortable now that people were looking at Elena, she moved about ten feet to the left, though still in front of the gate, so as to completely get out of the way.

All seven lions got up and moved to the left to once again be right in front of Elena. Elena was amazed at what was happening. She moved side to side, and the lions and lionesses moved with her. Elena just smiled and giggled a little bit, not knowing what was happening. Daniel looked on in absolute amazement.

"I can't believe this," he whispered to himself, but then he smiled with such excitement.

"Why are they looking at you?" he asked.

Elena was smiling and just so amazed, and she then looked to the right, and everyone was looking at what was transpiring.

The announcer said, "I…I don't know what is happening. This is very, very rare. I have never seen this before. They are honoring you, ma'am. I don't know why, but they are welcoming you to their den."

Daniel got closer to Elena and just looked back and forth between Elena and the lions. He then put his arms around her as he was so proud of her, but the head lion stood up, quickly went to the gate where Daniel and Elena were standing, and growled so as to protect Elena. It growled so loud that Daniel was startled and took his hands off of her. The angel Michael reached for the Lion Heart Medallion, and behold, it was glowing. The Lion Heart Medallion had found its queen, and it was Elena.

Therefore, because the Lion Heart Medallion was so close to Elena, it gave her the power within it, and it was enough for even the lions to see through Elena and see the inner lioness in her. It was indeed amazing. Even the angel Michael was amazed at what was happening, and he was so joyful that he had indeed found the new king and queens of Heirthia.

"I don't know, Daniel, but I feel something inside of me, like this energy or power. I feel so strong."

As Daniel let go of Elena, he stepped away, and the lion again sat down and fixed his eyes on Elena. Daniel and Elena both looked at each other, then at what was happening, but then the lion stood up and growled again.

Daniel then said, "Okay, big boy, I will get farther away."

Crash!

A man came from behind and grabbed Elena. Daniel immediately grabbed the man from the shoulders and pulled him off Elena, who had fallen down.

All seven lions stood up, and all began to roar, angry.

Many of the people there began to scream and run away. Daniel got into a fight with the man. As the man stood up, Daniel realized the man had red eyes, just like the man who had been driving the truck. The man then charged at Daniel and tackled him.

Then three other bystanders came in and charged against Daniel as well. All four men were dressed in regular clothing, as though they had been visiting the park. Elena was on the ground. She got up and tried to help get the men off Daniel, who were choking and hitting Daniel. Unfortunately, they were big, and so she could not get them off.

Daniel was able to get up as he fought them off, and he began fighting with each of the men. All four had red eyes.

Daniel looked at them, and each of the men had a twisted, animalistic expression on his face. They looked at Daniel and Elena like they were meat. Daniel yelled to Elena to get Katalina and Violet out of there. Both girls were scared at what was happening. The announcer called the police, but Daniel and Elena were in trouble.

Daniel went at them, bravely trying to defend his family, but they were so strong as they were being manipulated by Seitor. Daniel swung his fist at one of them and hit him so hard that he got knocked out. Then the others hit Daniel so hard that he fell to the ground. Blood spewed from Daniel's mouth.

One of the men went toward Elena with a knife, and he raised his hand so as to strike, but Daniel came from behind and hit the guy to the ground near the cage, making him drop the knife. The lion inside the cage was able to stick its claws outside the cage and get ahold of the man. The lion, being ever so strong, began to bite the man on his shoulder and would not let go.

"Get out of here, Elena!" Daniel yelled.

"No!" she yelled back. She would not leave her husband. Elena then instructed the girls to run to the main office and get help. Both girls listened and ran off.

Elena then went to help Daniel. One of the men was on top of him, hitting him, and another was trying to crush his head. Elena went and grabbed the man on top of Daniel and pulled him off from behind. He turned around and grabbed Elena by the neck. Daniel could not help her as he was being choked by the other man from behind. The third man went toward Elena to kill her, but Elena, in a state of frustration, tried to scream for help. Instead, she gave a loud growl, her eyes beginning to change. Her hands began to change too, and claws were beginning to come out. She drove her claws into the man holding her neck, which caused him to immediately let go.

Daniel was finally able to get lose. He got up and hit another one of the men toward a wall. Daniel realized his wife was about to be killed. Daniel grew angry and gained an incredible strength.

He ran toward the two men who were fighting Elena, and as he did, he raised his right hand with such confidence. As he did this, both men were lifted into the air.

Daniel was amazed at what he was doing. Daniel closed his eyes and concentrated on what he was doing. The men were helpless in the air. He moved his hand to the right, and both men were thrown to the ground. The third man was finally able to get free from the lion's claws and jaws, and he and the fourth man came at Daniel and Elena, and again, Daniel raised his right hand, and the two were thrown to the ground. He then placed his hand over them. They could not get up.

"Fulgur!" called Seitor with his wand, and Daniel was thrown a few feet away, hitting the ground hard. Seitor then revealed himself and called for the Sword of Yesu. He quickly swung the sword toward Elena, and she was cut on her stomach. Elena stood there in shock, holding her stomach as blood began to spill.

Daniel whipped his head around and saw his wife being attacked. Elena screamed and fell to the ground, bleeding heavily.

Daniel got up and screamed, "Mi amor, no!"

Daniel ran toward Seitor in anger, and Seitor once again called, "Fulgur!"

Daniel was thrown to the ground, but this time, he fell and got right back up and then ran toward Seitor again in a rage.

"Fulgur!" but this time Daniel moved so as to miss the flame from Seitor's wand. Daniel leaped toward Seitor and swung his fist toward Seitor, but Seitor was too fast. Daniel fell to the ground.

"I will kill you now!" Seitor exclaimed to Elena. He raised his sword, but Daniel raised his right hand, and Seitor was lifted up. Daniel, with all the strength in him, swung Seitor hard to the ground away from Elena. After Seitor had fallen, Daniel ran toward Elena. Daniel ran calling for his love, but Elena just lay there heavily bleeding. She was still awake, but she was losing consciousness, and Daniel's voice was becoming an echo.

Seitor got up and raised his wand. "Mors Mortis!" he called, and a red beam came out toward Elena.

Daniel leaped into the air, and the spell hit Daniel on the chest, knocking him to the ground. He was hit so hard, he could not even move. He was awake, but he just could no longer move. Seitor again raised his wand, and Daniel raised his hand and motioned something.

Seitor put his wand down and said, "What, peasant! You think you are a king? A king of Heirthia? You are nothing, and you are no one! You have no power. You think you can move your hand and move me!"

Daniel, barely awake, then said, "I was not trying to move you, but I did move the gate." Daniel then passed out, holding on to Elena.

Seitor then questioned, "Gate?" and then out of nowhere, the head lion leaped onto Seitor's back and drove its jaws onto Seitor's neck, knocking him to the ground. Seitor screamed as the lion bit into his flesh. Two other lionesses grabbed on to Seitor's legs, and they too drove their jaws deep. Seitor once again yelled in pain, but then he motioned with his wand and turned into mist and disappeared. The ordeal was over.

Light voices began to come about as Elena woke up.

"Where am I?" asked Elena as she woke up.

"You're at the Arnold Palmer Hospital, dear," said a nurse.

"Where's my husband?" exclaimed Elena as she tried to get up.

"Take is easy, dear. You had a big ordeal at the zoo today," said the nurse.

"Please tell me where my husband, Daniel, is, and my two girls," asked Elena again with a more anxiety and worry in her voice.

"Your husband is right next door. He is fine too. It appears you two fell down pretty hard."

Elena replied, "How bad is my cut?"

"Cut?" the nurse questioned in a puzzled voice as she turned and looked at Elena.

Elena then looked down below the gown she was wearing, and her cut was gone. "I was cut during the fight," stated Elena.

"Fight? Sweetie, you and your husband had a heat stroke, and you both fell down, hitting your heads," replied the nurse.

Elena was even more puzzled. "No, we were fighting these men with red eyes, and then this man came from nowhere, and he waved this wand at Daniel…" Elena began to cry.

"Sweetheart, honey, don't worry. There were no other men. The only witness to this said he saw you and your husband fall down."

Elena replied, "But all those people saw the lion, and then they saw this guy attack me. They all saw it," replied Elena in a more frustrated voice.

"Well, yeah, the police took their statements, but no one said anything about a fight," replied the nurse.

"What about the lions? They got out," said Elena.

"Wow, you must have really hit your head hard for you to think about these things," said the nurse. "Look, dear, you fell and hit your head, and nothing else happened. Let me check on your husband. Maybe we can get him over to see you," reassured the nurse.

Daniel then walked into Elena's room. It was a breath of fresh air to see each other. The two embraced. They cried and cried so much over what had just happened. They didn't say a word, but they were very emotional and very grateful to God for taking care of them. Elena then said, "Please tell me you remember what happened at the zoo."

Daniel then said, "I do, mi amore, I do. The nurses say we both fell down and hit our heads, but I know what I saw. It was a wizard or something."

Elena then became emotional and cried. She said, "I also remember. I remember the lions and the men with red eyes, and then that wizard came out and hit you several times with spells. I remember."

Just then, Katalina and Violet walked in with the doctor. Daniel and Elena really didn't pay attention to the doctor as much as they welcomed their children, and they were just happy that they were all okay. The doctor was looking at Elena's chart.

Daniel whispered, "Girls, I am going to ask you something, and Mommy and I need for you to be honest and truthful. Do either of you remember what happened at the zoo today?"

Katalina then said, "I do, Dad. The lions were following Mommy."

It was at that moment that both Daniel and Elena realized all that had happened was true. Everything they remembered was indeed a reality.

"Then what happened, sweetheart?" asked Daniel.

"You and Mommy were fighting the bad guys," said Violet.

"Then what happened?" asked Elena.

"Then you both fought the Dark King, Seitor!" exclaimed the doctor.

Both Elena and Daniel were stunned at what the doctor was saying. The doctor then turned around, and it was the angel Michael. "You both did very well. I was truly impressed on how neither of you would leave the other. I really did see true love," said Michael.

"So all that you were saying was true?" asked Daniel.

"Yes," Michael responded.

"Then why doesn't anyone remember or know what happened at the zoo?" asked Elena. "The witness says we fell down," she continued.

"I was the witness," replied Michael.

"Why would you do that? Those men need to be reported and arrested," said Daniel.

"It is very complicated. No one in this world can know about Seitor or myself, which is why I did not help you during your battle and everything must continue as it should. Seitor and I are not from this world." He continued, "After you too were out, I used my powers to put the lions back into their den, and I was able to restore the men whom you battled to their natural states, and they simply walked away not remembering anything that happened."

Michael continued, "They were possessed by Seitor. With my healing hand, I then healed your wounds, Elena, as you were bleeding to death, and I then healed your severe burn marks, Daniel. All you two really had were bumps on the head. Once everyone came back, I was able to use my power and put their minds at ease and make them forget what had actually happened. I reported that I was the only witness and that you two had just fallen because of the heat."

Elena then cried out, "Why have these things been happening to us, and who was that wizard?"

"Well, allow me to explain, but we need to hurry, as he will be lurking to find you."

10

KING AND QUEENS OF HEIRTHIA

"**Y**OU HAVE TO understand, we are from another world, another dimension," said Michael, still in the hospital room with Daniel and his family.

He continued, "I am the angel Michael, and I serve the Almighty King, Yesu, and I serve the Almighty God, Jeinua. We come from the world of Heirthia."

Katalina, being so intrigued at what the angel was saying, asked, "What is Heirthia?"

Michael smiled, walked up to Katalina, knelt down, and said in a fascinated voice, "It is a most beautiful place, a beautiful land where the Living King, Yesu, lives. It has so many wonders, so many creatures, and it truly is a heaven. There are kings and queens, sword fighting, and giant castles."

Michael then stood back up and said, "Yesu's father created Seitor to serve and protect the people of Heirthia, along with the many other kings and rulers, but he grew jealous, angry, and did not follow the path of Yesu. Instead, he went his own way trying to obtain all the power of Heirthia through Yesu's kingdom. He never understood that Yesu is Jeinua's son, and Yesu alone is our Lord, our Savior."

Daniel, still in disbelief as to what was happening, asked, "This all seems so unreal. If this is all so true, what are you doing here on Earth? You should be back in your world helping them."

Michael answered, "It's not that simple. There is a purpose. I have come as an order from Yesu. You see, in Heirthia, we have—had twelve kings of honor and protection. Five of those were separate and distinct and much more powerful. They were known as the Quint Fey, rulers and kings of greatness, and they controlled all evildoers in Heirthia, and each one received an extraordinary blessing from Yesu, powers granted by Yesu."

Violet replied, "What did they get? Like powers to make things move and make unicorns?"

Michael smiled at the young child's heart. "You have a great heart, little one. I already see greatness in your heart, power to maintain peace, power to utilize strength, and power to defend the people of Heirthia and beyond."

Michael walked over to the window and as he looked at the land in the distance, he said, "But the Quint Fey were broken. It has been broken forever." He turned and looked at Daniel and Elena with a sadness in his face.

Daniel replied, "What happened?"

Michael responded, "Well, there is much to tell you all: the seven other kings, the kingdoms, the powers, and your destiny."

Elena, looked shocked. "Our destiny? Our destiny? What do we have to do with any of this?"

Daniel quickly interrupted, "Look, I don't know what is going on, and I am still not even sure what we have to do with all of this, but we have already been attacked by what I can only see as an evil person, and my family is in danger and apparently continues to be in danger. We would like to help you, but we can't."

Daniel paused for a moment and then said, "You need to leave us and get far from us so that that crazy man does not come to us. You got the wrong people. We are a young family. You need an army."

"King Daniel, the faithful, the defender, the righteous. Yes, this is what they will call you," Michael exclaimed.

"Michael, Angel Michael, you need to leave us alone. I'm sorry, but you need to go," said Daniel with more authority.

Michael walked up to Daniel and said in a most humble voice, "It is not I who has chosen you. It is the Living King who has found favor in you." Michael then raised his right hand and pointed toward Daniel's heart, saying, "He knows the heart of you and your family. He and He alone chooses, and it is because of this, it is because you are the chosen ones, that Seitor will not stop."

Elena voiced, "I know, Michael, but you have a married couple with two small children, and you want us to fight?" She continued, "We appreciate this, but we cannot accept this honor, and certainly not this responsibility."

Michael went to her and said in a frustrated voice, "Don't you understand? This is why it must be you. You desire no power, you desire no rule, and you don't want any glory. Most people would jump at the opportunity to have such power to control a whole world, but your family is not like that. You are a family of justice and a family of love."

Michael then quickly turned around and walked to the other side of the room, looking outside the door to see if Seitor had yet found them, then he continued, saying in a stronger and more forceful voice, "And he will continue to hunt you. Whether you accept this task or not, he and his army will not stop looking for you and trying to kill you and your children. He craves your blood. It has become an obsession."

Michael quickly walked up to Daniel and said, "Do you understand, sire? He will stop at nothing to kill you! He will never stop, ever, until you and your family are dead and until your blood is drawn on his sword! There is no other way. There is no escape. He will find you, and he will kill you and anyone who gets in his way!"

The room went silent.

Both Katalina and Violet went to their mother and embraced her at what they were hearing. Daniel and Elena looked at each other in disbelief but realized this was all a reality. They indeed knew that Yesu was calling upon them.

Daniel, still in denial, said, "I know what you are saying, but this puts my family in danger."

Michael said, "Either way, they are in danger, but by believing in Yesu and accepting his mission, you too will gain great power. Accepting this mission means you will become kings and queens of Heirthia, that you will inherit a kingdom of your own. You will have great power and great authority over many. You will rule Heirthia, and this means having all the gold, all the riches of the lands. It will all be yours, and you will be honored for it."

Daniel responded, "Again, I know what you are saying, and I know that you need our help, but with all my heart, no."

Michael walked up to Daniel and said, "This is why it must be you, it must be you. Even with all the riches, honor, and authority, you deny this. This is why Yesu has chosen you and your family, because you humble yourself. You are not looking to your own interest but the interests of others."

Daniel, knowing that this was their destiny, responded, "What does Seitor want?"

Michael replied, "Seitor has stolen one of the Quint Fey's powers, and his goal is to take the other powers one by one. It is what he has always wanted: all the power. Once he has taken each power, he will take Yesu's castle, and if he succeeds, Heirthia will be lost forever."

Elena said, "Well, if this Yesu is mighty and all powerful, why doesn't he just kill Seitor? I mean, Jeinua created Seitor. Why doesn't He just kill him and end this all?"

Michael responded, "Heirthia was created for the people to rule, for the people to decide its future. Jeinua created Heirthia because He wanted for all the people and all creatures to rule it, to manage it, and to protect it. It belongs to the people. Yesu and His Father will not stop what the people have chosen. Yesu and His father want for the people to honor them, to believe in them, and to have faith in them for all they have done, for their blessings."

Elena nodded her head in understanding and said, "And so Yesu and Jeinua want for the people to decide what happens to it. Free will."

Michael responded, "Yes. Jeinua is a kind God, and Yesu loves the people with passion. Yesu will not help and will not intervene unless the heart calls for him, unless the true faith of someone believes in him and knows that he is there. This is when Yesu presents himself."

Daniel then asked, "Is this why he created the Quint Fey's powers?"

"That is absolutely correct, Daniel," said Michael. He continued, "The powers are like no other."

Daniel also asked, "What should we expect of Seitor next?"

Michael answered, "The powers Seitor has obtained are grand, and he obtained this power by stealing one of the Quint Fey powers. He will continue to control people here on Earth, or worse, if he knows the correct spells, he can call upon the Dragon's Claw Wand and bring his solders from Heirthia to your world one by one, and if he does this, your planet will turn into a battlefield."

Michael continued in a worried voice, "We can only pray through the goodness of Yesu that Seitor does not summon the Blakers, which is what I believe he will do."

Elena said in a questioning voice, "Blakers?"

Michael responded, "They are giant creatures, creatures of pure destruction. They stand twenty to thirty feet tall. They stand on two feet, they have great strength, their arms are large, and their goal is to hunt and kill."

Daniel asked, "What? Are they like ogres?"

Michael said, "They are ogres but of a massive scale—giants—and in Heirthia, they are all under the spell of Seitor."

They all stood there for a few moments, and Daniel then looked at his family, and it appeared as though they were ready once again for another adventure. Daniel then asked, "What do we need to do?"

Michael looked at Daniel closely and then looked toward his family next to him and said, "I need to prepare you for Yesu's Four Questions of Faith. It is through these questions that Yesu will decide if indeed you are ready, if indeed your heart is pure, and if indeed you have faith. Remember, it is a test, you could fail, and if so, you will no longer be pursued for this mission. You will not inherit the powers, you will not become the king and queens of Heirthia, and I can no longer protect you from Seitor killing you and your family. However, if you pass, Yesu's glory will be on you, and you will become the king and queens of Heirthia." He then asked, "Do you accept this?"

Daniel looked at his family, and they all looked at him in agreement. Daniel looked back at the angel Michael and said, "We accept the challenge."

Michael walked over to the door of the hospital room and closed it. He stretched out his right hand, and the door became sealed so as not to allow anyone in. It was magical. He turned his head and shoulders around, looking at the Geminis and said, "Let's begin."

He turned around and faced them, and he looked up. Then he stretched out both his arms, and he began to grow into his true angel body.

His arms became large, his chest became broader, he grew taller, and overall, he became more muscular. He then knelt on his right knee with a force, cracking the floor, and lifted his hands slightly upward in a very calm manner.

He said a small prayer with his head down. "Yesu, bless me with the guidance and grace to test your chosen ones this very moment. They have accepted your Questions of Faith, and as a family, they pray for your divine favor. In Your name, I pray."

Michael then lifted his hands higher, his eyes closed, and then a beautiful light began emanating from his chest. The angel Michael's beautiful white wings then appeared, and they spread outward. His wings stretched out twenty feet. The room was filled with a beautiful scent of freshly baked sugar cookies, and there was a sweet melody. It was the sound of angels singing.

It was the most beautiful thing the Geminis had ever seen or heard. The light from Michael's chest illuminated even more to where even the Geminis had to slightly look away, but they still could not take their eyes off him. Then from the light came a woman's soft voice, "Do you believe, do you believe that although you have not seen the Almighty Yesu, He is there?"

Daniel looked down at Elena, who was still on the bed with Katalina and Violet, and he reached over and embraced them. He hugged them with such passion and gave a kiss to each on their foreheads.

Katalina then looked at her father and said, "I believe, Dad."

Violet also looked up at her father and said, "I also believe, Daddy."

Elena took her right hand and touched Daniel's chin and said, "I believe."

Daniel stood tall, and with a tear running down his cheek, he said, "We, as a family, believe."

The light continued as a sign of acceptance. The voice then came again and said, "You have answered honestly. Now your second question is, do you wish to rule the land of Heirthia?"

Daniel looked at his family and already knew the answer. He said, "No, we do not wish to rule the land of Heirthia, as the purpose of servants is to serve. We wish to solely serve Yesu and accept his will."

The voice came again and responded, "You have wished wisely, for it is not up to you what you rule. It is the Yesu's choice."

The voice came again. "Your third question, what is the greatest gift anyone can give?"

Daniel, looking a bit more challenged with this question, looked to his family. He looked at his two daughters and his beautiful wife. Elena motioned for him to get closer, and she whispered the answer in his ear. Daniel looked at her and agreed. Elena then looked up at the angel Michael and responded to the voice, "It is the gift of giving."

The voice came back and said, "You have answered with a pure and giving heart." The voice continued, "As for your last question, you and only you, Daniel, can answer it.

"Imagine you are in a boat in a raging river with your two children and your wife. However, the boat is sinking, and Yesu speaks to you and orders that you must stay afloat so as to prepare for battle, but the only way for the boat to stay afloat is for you to either throw off both your children or your wife, which would end in death. Which would you choose to stay afloat with you? Be wise in your answer."

Daniel stood there in the room, knowing he could not ask for help from his family. He stood there for just a moment and tried to think it through. He closed his eyes and imagined both scenarios. He could not decide what to do.

The voice then came again. "You must answer now, or you will fail."

Again, he continued to try to avoid imagining the scenarios, and in doing this, he looked up, and he knew the answer.

The voice came louder. "Answer now, or you fail!"

Daniel closed his eyes as he continued to sweat, and at the very last moment, he yelled, "I stop imagining!"

The room went silent, and the voice would not come. Again he said, "I stop imagining."

The voice then came and asked, "Why do you answer like this?"

Daniel said, "You said, 'Imagine you are in a boat.' There was no real-life question. There was no real-life threat. It was not a matter of life or death. It was a riddle. It was a trick question, and I refused to choose the option of death. If I accept defeat, I will get defeat, but if I believe there is a way, then God will make a way. Instead, I chose to look at the question as a whole, a way out to save all my family, and therefore, I would stop imagining it."

The light was silent, but then in a distance within the light came the woman who had been speaking. On each side of her were two tall and strong angels, making it a total of four angels in front of the Geminis. They each carried a large sword, and each had wings spread out. They were truly remarkable. The woman came closer and closer until she was nearly standing in the room, though she was still in the light shining from the angel Michael's chest.

She said, "You have answered correctly. You chose not to accept any scenario of death, but, rather, your faith was so strong that neither your children nor your wife needed to die."

She continued, "My name is Wisda, and I am the protector of the Quint Fey powers. I am here as a messenger from the Almighty Yesu. He has found favor in you as a family. You are strong together, you pray together, and you have faith together. Yesu has seen your hearts, and nothing can break you, no matter the circumstances, and this is why he has chosen you. You think of others before you think of yourselves, and you honor, respect, and protect each other always. For this, Yesu has chosen you, the Gemini family to rule Heirthia."

Wisda also had wings, and although she was not very tall and her wings not very big, she was a beautiful dark-skinned woman with a soothing voice.

Wisda then looked at Daniel, and with the light shining brighter and the four angels looking on in respect, she said in a peaceful voice "Now Yesu hereby names you the king of Heirthia. He has named you King Daniel, 'the Righteous.'" The Almighty Yesu grants you the Sword of Yesu."

The light then shone upon Daniel to bless him. From behind Wisda came King Simon Peuro. King Simon stood before King Daniel and said, "I am King Simon, and I say to you that you will be a great and mighty king. I am here to pass on to you the Sword of Yesu. It is the most powerful sword in all of Heirthia or anywhere else, but you must use it solely with your heart and never in fear, never in anger, and never in greed. It gives you great strength, wisdom, and courage. Because of your heart, you will lead and rule Heirthia. I will help you learn its ways, and I will fight beside you always."

From the light, King Simon then reached out with both hands for the Sword of Yesu and lowered his head, and King Daniel reached out both his hands and accepted the Sword. King Daniel then said, "I accept this gift from you, and I will honor it and protect it always."

"When you need it, call for it with your heart, and it will come to you. When you do not use it, it will fade into your heart, and there it will stay safe." King Simon extended his hand, and both he and King Daniel shook each other's hands in honor and respect. King Simon then walked back into the light and went into the distance.

Wisda then said, "Elena, please stand next to your husband, my dear."

Elena got up from the bed completely in tears and stood by Daniel, and with the light shining even brighter and the angels looking on in respect, Wisda said, "For this, Yesu hereby names you the queen of Heirthia. He has named you Queen Elena, 'the Giver.'" Because of your giving pure heart, Yesu grants you the Lion Heart Medallion." A light from inside shone upon Queen Elena to bless her. Then from behind Wisda came King Aniser.

King Aniser stood before Queen Elena and said, "I am King Aniser, and you are but a rare beautiful rose in a field. However, with the Lion Heart Medallion, none should touch this rose as it has its sharp thorns. With it, you can become a great and grand lioness. Your roar will be mighty, and your speed will be unmatched. With this power, you can only transform with your heart. Your heart will direct your path and transformation. Let it be known, Elena, if strong enough, and with the right faith, you can also change those trusted around you. Do not worry, I will teach you its deepest secrets, and we shall run together."

Queen Elena, shaking a bit nervously, leaned forward as King Aniser placed the Lion Heart Medallion around her neck. Queen Elena then said, "With this medallion, I shall honor and protect the people. I shall use it wisely, and only to protect and never in anger. This I promise."

King Aniser then bowed once more, and walked back into the light.

"Now, Katalina, go and stand next to your mother."

Katalina did so.

The light, for a third time, shone, and Wisda said, "For this, Yesu hereby names you as the princess of Heirthia. He has named you Princess Katalina, 'the Light.'"

A light then shone upon Katalina, and she too was blessed. From behind Wisda came forth King Jemis. King Jemis knelt before Princess Katalina and said, "I am King Jemis, and it is truly an honor to have a beautiful and gracious young lady and princess to rule Heirthia. I must now say: a light indeed you are as I can see your heart, and it is truly a radiant beautiful light, a light that no darkness can ever extinguish. In times of difficulty and grief, shine your heart, and all will see it."

King Jemis then reached out with both his hands, bowed his head, and said, "It is my honor to pass onto you, a true Young, the power of the Falcon Bow. For as it did great things for me, it will serve you well. Just like the Sword of Yesu, when you need the bow, call for it, and it will come to you. Otherwise, it shall stay safe in your heart."

Princess Katalina looked at her father, and King Daniel nodded in approval for her to accept such a gift. Princess Katalina then reached her hands out and received the Falcon Bow.

King Jemis said, "To use this bow, to receive its arrows of fire, you must be pure of heart, and never seek to use it in anger. Each time you reach for it, every time you will use it, Yesu must be the purpose for its power, and indeed, it will give you power. I have seen your beautiful heart, and I know you will serve it well."

Katalina then said, "Thank you, King Jemis. You are a very nice and graceful knight, and it will be an honor to train with you."

King Jemis replied, "The honor is mine, Princess."

Katalina looked down. She became shy and felt very special. King Jemis walked back into the light.

Violet stood next to the bed and said, "What about me? My name is Violeta, but you can call me Violet."

Wisda smiled and answered, "Oh yes, how could I have forgotten little Violet? Go, my dear. Stand next to your father."

Violet, in a rush to receive her blessing, ran over to her father and embraced his left arm. For the last time, the light shone, and the angels bowed down at the little princess, and Wisda said, "For this, Yesu hereby names you as the princess of Heirthia. He has named you Princess Violet, 'the Faithful.'"

The light then shone upon Violet, and she closed her eyes. She then became emotional and cried.

King Daniel asked, "What's the matter, sweetie?"

Violet said, "I don't know. I just feel happy. I feel like something is hugging me and comforting me." Then and there, with the light, she was blessed by Yesu. Just then came King Jonis.

Just like King Jemis, King Jonis came to little Violet, held her hand, and knelt before her, and said, "I have the greatest honor of meeting you, little Violet. You are a beautiful little girl, your hair is so beautiful, and your sweet smile cannot go unseen as it fills any room with love and tranquility. The words you use are beyond your years, and they are sweet, graceful, peaceful, and like no other. For this, I am honored to pass on to you the Dragon's Claw Wand."

King Jemis raised his hands and offered the Dragon's Claw Wand, and Violet, looking at her father, moved forward and extended both her tiny hands and received the wand. King Jemis said, "It is the most powerful wand in all of Heirthia. There is none like it, and none can match it. With your wisdom of choice words, you will be able to cast spells of all sorts to bring peace, love, tranquility, power, and, yes, maybe even make a unicorn."

Violet smiled.

King Jemis smiled and continued, "I will be with you and help you to learn to use your heart and deepest emotions to use this wand. For the words you use will determine the power that is used."

Violet then said in a shy voice, "Thank you, King Jemis. You are my knight in shining armor, and I am thankful that you will help me to learn how to use my wand."

King Jemis then said, "I will be waiting for you, my dear." He then turned and walked into the light.

Wisda looked at all the Gemini family and said, "And so it is done. You are now the king and queens of Heirthia. You have been empowered, and you have been blessed by Yesu. What you do with the time and powers given to you are completely and absolutely up to you. But remember, no matter where you are, no matter what you are doing, no matter how you feel, Yesu is watching you, and he is waiting for you. You are now the New Faith. The Quint Fey are no more. May you be blessed always."

The Gemini family all said, "Thank you, and may you be blessed always."

Wisda turned around and walked back into the light. The angels followed right behind her, and the light slowly dimed and disappeared. Then just as quickly as it came, it was gone.

The angel Michael was still kneeling on one knee, but as the light went away, he slowly raised his head, and his wings went back down. He then stood up, but he was tired from opening the portal from Heirthia to Earth. As he stood there, he then became weak and fell to the ground.

King Daniel and Queen Elena quickly went to help him, but right before they got to him, there was a loud horn. It sounded as though a ten-story horn was blown right next to the hospital. It was loud. As it sounded, it felt like an explosion. It shook the hospital room.

Both King Daniel and Queen Elena lost their balance, but then they finally reached Michael. "Michael, are you okay? What happened to you?"

Michael then said, "It has begun."

11

THE RETURN TO HEIRTHIA

KING DANIEL AND Queen Elena tried to help Michael up, but they struggled.

"Michael, what has happened to you?" asked Queen Elena.

Michael responded in a soft voice, "I have lost my power here on Earth. There is only so much power that one from Heirthia can have while on Earth. I held open the portal and, therefore, it is my time to die."

Michael, trying to keep himself up, fell back to the ground. Slowly, one by one, his feathers began to fall, but it was very slowly. Princess Violet looked at one of the feathers and picked it up.

She voiced with a very sad tone, "Mommy, he's dying."

Both King Daniel and Queen Elena looked at their daughter and knew they had to hurry.

At this point in time, the room once again shook, and once again the horn sounded. It sounded as though something was being announced, that something had arrived, and indeed the horn was loud. Both Princess Katalina and Princess Violet got scared, and so they went with their father.

"What is that sound, Dad?" yelled Princess Katalina.

Princess Violet then went with her mother, who was on the floor with Michael.

"Michael, what is that? What is happening?"

Again, the hospital room shook, and the horn sounded.

"Are we in an earthquake?" asked King Daniel.

"No, Seitor has done it. He has summoned the Blakers. Giant, twenty-foot ogres with large hands and claws. Their teeth are like fangs of a dragon, eyes like red amber, and they destroy everything in sight. For every horn blown, a Blaker enters your world," said Michael.

Princess Violet then said, "I have heard three horns, Mommy."

The room grew silent in disbelief, and they all looked at each other. King Daniel got up from the floor in shock. He slowly moved away from Michael and his family, walking backward toward the window. He then slowly turned around and took a look outside. He peeked out the window to the left. Nothing.

He peeked out the window to the right, and nothing was there. He turned to look at the others in the room and said, "There's nothing—."

Crash!

There was a big crash at the window, and King Daniel was thrown to the other side of the room. It was a Blaker.

Michael yelled, "Run, King Daniel, and take your family!" Michael, with all his strength, got up from the floor, opened his wings, and leaped onto the giant ogre at the window, grabbing his right shoulder. There were people outside screaming and running at what they were seeing.

King Daniel quickly grabbed Queen Elena's hand, as she was still on the floor, and helped her up.

"We have to go!" King Daniel yelled. Queen Elena stood there, scared, with both her hands to her mouth in disbelief. She and the girls were very scared.

King Daniel again yelled, "We have to run!"

Queen Elena was just in shock and could not move. King Daniel quickly grabbed on to her waist and ran toward the door with the girls right behind, but the door was sealed.

At this point, the angel Michael drew his sword, yelling, "In Nomine Yesu!" He raised his sword above the Blaker's head. He drove his sword through the Blaker's neck. The Blaker screamed horrendously and quickly raised its large left hand and grabbed Michael.

The Blaker lost its balance, and the two plummeted to the ground. Both Princess Katalina and Princess Violet were terrified and screamed at all that was going on. King Daniel turned around at the now silent room and put his family behind him. He attempted to look at the ground outside for Michael and the Blaker and leaned forward but saw nothing down there.

Crash!

Another Blaker had destroyed the next room. *Roar!*

King Daniel moved back close to the wall and called for the Sword of Yesu to defend his family, and it appeared instantly. It was a shining light, and King Daniel was amazed at the power it was radiating. He raised the sword high as to strike the Blaker but then quickly turned around and struck the door where the frame was, and it sliced the door in half. It cut so easily and so smoothly it was like cutting a freshly picked tomato.

King Daniel quickly pushed his right shoulder against the door, and it opened. He pushed his family and ran down the hall to get away from the Blaker. Queen Elena, Princess Katalina, and Princess Violet quickly followed. Doctors, nurses, and patients were all running away too, frightened at was going on. As everyone ran down the hall, Queen Elena turned around and saw that the Blaker continued to destroy the room, and then it leaped into the hallway floor.

"It's coming!" she yelled.

The Blaker saw the Geminis running down the hall and let out another loud roar. The chase was on. The Geminis continued and cut a corner to the left. King Daniel was looking for the stairs or elevator. As they cut the corner, they were running very quickly. The Blaker was so large that they could hear its footsteps behind them at a distance. People were running in all directions. The Blaker was smashing everything, even the people it was passing. Then in a distance, the Geminis saw the sign for the stairs.

"We need to take the stairs!" yelled Queen Elena. King Daniel, leading his family, headed straight there. People were everywhere. King Daniel then pushed the door open with great force and led his family down the stairs. The door closed behind them as they continued down the stairs. They had been on the seventh floor. Floor by floor, they continued down, but by the fifth floor, the Blaker that had been chasing them caught their scent.

Crash!

They heard the loud crashing sound above them. In a distance, they could hear its roar. The Blaker was now above them. Then suddenly, they heard another crash, but this time it was below them.

"Another one!" yelled Princess Katalina.

There was indeed another Blaker below them on the fourth floor. The Geminis stopped for a second in fear of being crushed in. The Blaker above them was crashing toward them, breaking the stairs. The Blaker below then continued to climb, and it broke the stairs as well. The Geminis were moving as quickly as they could to get to the fifth floor to enter back into the building, but the Blakers were moving quickly.

King Daniel picked up Princess Violet and held on to her as Queen Elena and Princess Katalina held hands to stay together. As the Blaker below them saw them, he roared again and reached out for them, but King Daniel, Queen Elena, and the girls leaped toward the door at the fifth floor and just made it out in time to escape the grasp of the Blaker below them. The Blaker fell to the ground given the Geminis time to escape. The hospital lights were flickering on and off because of all the damage that had been done.

There were not many people on the fifth floor, but random medical personnel and patients were hiding and moving around from room to room.

Quickly, King Daniel remembered what King Simon had told him, that the Sword of Yesu was the most powerful sword in all the land. King Daniel called for his sword, opened the door back into the stairs. He could see the Blaker just below beginning to stand up, and he could hear the Blaker right above getting near. King Daniel drew his sword, took a deep breath, and swung the sword toward the stairs right above him where the top Blaker was nearing.

Clank! Nothing happened. The sword hit the concrete stair just above his head and didn't even scratch it.

"Daniel! You're not going to make it. We need to get out of here!" yelled Queen Elena.

Again, King Daniel swung. *Clank.* Again, nothing happened.

The Blakers got even more angry as they continued to approach the Geminis.

King Daniel then remembered what King Simon said, "You must use it solely with your heart, and never in fear, never in anger, and never in greed."

King Daniel then closed his eyes and began to pray. He grew calm even though he could hear the Blakers nearing.

Queen Elena then yelled, "They're coming," and at that moment, he felt something in his heart. His heart felt as though it was talking to him and guiding him. He felt his heart say, "Protect!" when he heard his wife yelling in fear of being harmed.

King Daniel opened his eyes and immediately swung the Sword of Yesu again toward the concrete stairs, and like a piece of paper, the concrete sliced in half. The sword made a cutting sound, but it was so graceful and clean. The concrete split in half, and the Blaker came crashing down. The floor where the Blaker was below was already coming apart because it had partially destroyed it.

Thus, when the top Blaker came crashing down on the floor where the Geminis were, the floor caved in. The top Blaker came crashing down on the Blaker below. It was a loud crashing sound of twisting medal and bricks breaking. Dust filled the air everywhere, and it became silent. Because of the crash, King Daniel was thrown back toward where his family was crouching on the floor.

"Are they dead?" whispered Queen Elena.

"I don't know. I think so," replied King Daniel.

Crying and scared, Princess Violet said, "Let's go, Daddy."

King Daniel got up from the floor and walked very slowly over to the stairway. He slowly stepped toward the door and peered down to see the rubble.

"What do you see, Daddy?" asked Princess Katalina.

King Daniel looked down and saw much rubble and dust and what appeared to be a dead Blaker under the concrete.

"I see one. It's dead," replied King Daniel.

"Do you see the other one?" asked Queen Elena.

"I'm not sure, but I think so. There's concrete everywhere, so I think they are both dead!" exclaimed King Daniel in a happy and relieved voice. He turned around to look at his family and said "Yes, they're—"

Roar!

Before King Daniel could finish his sentence, a Blaker came crashing through the door. The ogre's fall had been cushioned by the Blaker below it, crushing it, and it had then used the twisted staircase to clamber back up. The Blaker that was alive then reached out and grabbed King Daniel with his massive hands and claws. King Daniel yelled in pain as the Blaker began squeezing him to death. Although the Blaker was doing this, he was bleeding from his head from the fall, but it wasn't enough to stop him.

Queen Elena got up in fear at what was happening, screaming and yelling for the Blaker to stop, but the Blaker was determined to kill King Daniel. King Daniel lifted his sword and swung toward the Blaker's head, but it was too far. King Daniel then raised his sword downward and rammed the sword into the Blaker's hand. The Blaker yelled in pain but would not let go.

At this point, King Daniel was beginning to lose consciousness from being crushed. Princess Katalina got up and called for her bow, but nothing would happen. Princess Violet, in a deep fright, also got up.

"Get your wand, Violet," yelled Princess Katalina.

"I can't! I can't! I'm scared!"

Princess Violet fell to the ground, feeling hopeless in not helping her father. Queen Elena, seeing what was happening, looked around and saw a firefighter's water hose. She ran over to it and saw a firefighter's ax. She grabbed the hose and broke the glass to grab the ax. She reached for it and ran toward the stairway.

With one swing, she cut the Blaker's wrist, and the Blaker finally let go of King Daniel.

King Daniel fell into the stair shaft where the other dead Blaker was. The live Blaker then reached for Queen Elena, but out of nowhere, the angel Michael came flying through the top of the stairway shaft with his wings out. He fell onto the Blaker's neck, raised his sword, and stabbed the Blaker down into the neck. The Blaker reached out for Michael and grabbed him and swung him to the ground where King Daniel was.

The Blaker lost his balance and grip on the doorframe and came crashing into the floor, barely missing King Daniel and Michael. The Blaker, still moving, was lying on the ground.

He reached for Michael, who was on the floor. The Blaker began to squeeze Michael, crushing him. King Daniel, seeing his opportunity, yelled, "In the name of Yesu," swung his sword, and drove it into the Blaker's heart. The Blaker immediately died. Michael was finally released.

Both King Daniel and Michael fell to the ground in exhaustion and pain, and Michael was very weak. King Daniel went over to where Michael was lying. Queen Elena yelled, "Daniel, Daniel! Are you okay?"

"They're dead, *mi amor*. They're dead." King Daniel then said, "Michael, are you okay? What can we do to help?"

Michael said, "I need to get you out of this world and into Heirthia."

Roar! They heard the sound from a distance.

King Daniel looked at Michael and said, "What happened to the other Blaker?"

Michael replied, "He's not dead yet. We need to get out of here and out of the hospital right now!"

King Daniel got up and then helped Michael to his feet. Michael, still very weak, grabbed hold of King Daniel and flew them to where Queen Elena and the girls were.

"Michael, are you—" said Queen Elena.

Michael interrupted and said, "I'm fine for now. I will make it."

Right then and there, Princess Violet ran toward her father and hugged him, saying, "I love you, Daddy. I thought you were going to die," she said this with such a sentiment.

Queen Elena turned to Michael and said, "Thank you for saving us."

"It is you who should be thanked Queen Elena. King Daniel would have been crushed had it not been for your bravery," he responded. "Now quick, we need to get you out of here. Let's go."

The five then ran down the hall to find another way out.

Crash! Again, they heard the sound, and they knew the last Blaker was in the hospital. They ran down the hall and found an elevator.

"We can't take this. It's too dangerous," said Queen Elena.

"We need to move, and there is no other way out as the stairway is destroyed. Get in!" replied King Daniel. The five got into the elevator and pushed the button for the first floor. The doors closed, and it was silent.

Floor by floor, they got closer to the first floor. The light in the elevator showed 5, 4, 3, 2—

Crash!

The elevator shook and stopped between the second and first floors. King Daniel and Michael quickly attempted to pry open the doors. As they opened the doors, there was about a foot of space to get into the first floor, but not enough space for any of them to fit through.

Bump! The elevator moved to the side.

"The Blaker has grabbed the elevator cords," Queen Elena whispered.

"Don't move," whispered Michael. Again, *bump!* The elevator moved as though something was moving it.

Another crash was heard as the Blaker jumped onto the elevator.

Crash! The Blaker rammed his hand on the roof. With all the weight of the Blaker on the elevator, the elevator moved another foot down.

"Get the kids out!" yelled Michael. Queen Elena quickly motioned for Princess Violet to be the first to get out as she was the smallest. Princess Violet got on her knees and was out onto the first floor.

"Come on, Katalina, you're next!" yelled Queen Elena.

Meanwhile, the Blaker reached down and tried to grab a hold of King Daniel, but it missed as King Daniel dodged its massive hand. At that point, Princess Katalina got on her knees and was slowly lowered to the first floor. Although Queen Elena was glad to see both her children out of the elevator, she was alarmed and yelled as the Blaker grabbed her.

"Ahh!" she screamed in fear.

The Blaker lifted his hand so as to pull her out of the elevator, but King Daniel quickly raised his sword upward and lifted his arms as the blade cut through the elevator and went right into the Blaker. The Blaker roared in pain and let go of Queen Elena. The Blaker fell onto the top of the elevator, but it was still alive.

King Daniel then moved Queen Elena toward the doors to get her out of the elevator.

"Get out, mi amor!" yelled King Daniel.

Again, although very weak, the Blaker reached out again for Queen Elena and grabbed her leg as she tried to get out.

Michael then jumped onto the Blaker's arm and said, "Both of you get out of here!"

King Daniel quickly swung his sword toward the Blaker's arm and sliced its wrist. The Blaker roared yet again and let Queen Elena's leg go. Queen Elena quickly moved and was lowered by King Daniel to meet her children on the first floor.

"Get out of here!" yelled Michael toward King Daniel, and King Daniel said, "As king, I will not leave you."

Both King Daniel and Michael raised their swords, and at the same time, both lifted their swords upward and drove them into the ceiling of the elevator. The Blaker roared in pain and was finally dead. Both King Daniel and Michael quickly got out of the elevator safely onto the first floor.

The battle was finally over.

King Daniel went to his family, embraced them, and began to cry.

"Are you all okay?" King Daniel asked his girls. They all hugged each other and were glad it was all over. The Geminis then looked over at Michael, who was leaning against a wall with one hand.

Michael looked at them and said, "This is why Yesu has favor in your family. There is a great love," he then smiled.

"What's that, Michael?" asked Princess Violet.

The Geminis looked down toward where Princess Violet was pointing, and there were several of Michael's feathers from his wings on the floor.

"I'm dying," replied Michael. The Geminis rushed over to help him.

"What can we do, Michael?" asked Queen Elena.

Michael replied in pain, "It is not what you can do for me. It is what I was meant to do for you, and I must get you to Heirthia." Then and there they all heard the police arrive, and the people began to come out of hiding.

Queen Elena and King Daniel looked at each other knowing the authorities would find this man with wings. "Michael, the people are coming—the police. You need to hide your wings, and can you get rid of the Blaker's bodies?" asked Queen Elena.

"I will try," replied Michael. Michael knelt down and attempted to pull in his wings.

"I can't," said Michael. "I don't have enough power."

King Daniel then motioned Queen Elena to help him get Michael out a back door. "Come on, girls, we need to hide Michael, or they will take him away," he said. The Geminis, with Michael in arms, walked away posthaste from the sound of the sirens.

"There's an exit!" exclaimed Princess Violet. They went toward the exit door.

As they exited, they were relieved to find themselves outside. King Daniel quickly noticed a forest at the back end of the hospital. "We need to hide in there," exclaimed King Daniel. Without being noticed, they rushed Michael into the forest.

"We need to hurry. I feel Seitor's presence near," said Michael. They must have walked and stumbled far into the forest until they could no longer hear the sound of people and police cars. They finally came to a stop at a small river, and they placed Michael down on the bank.

King Daniel and Queen Elena fell to the ground in exhaustion.

"We did it. We are safe," said Queen Elena.

"You are not safe until you return to your army in Heirthia," said Michael. Michael looked up. The day was starting to cool as the sun was setting. He then stood to his feet and said, "Come together, Gemini family," he requested. The four gathered together, and Michael began to speak, "I am already proud of you for your courage. You have been through your first challenge, and already you know the true value of family, love, and bravery. For this, I commend you."

Michael then began to cough in pain. He finally continued, "You each were given powers by the kings of Heirthia. It is a great honor and something that the people of Heirthia will never forget, something you will never forget. When you enter the kingdom of Heirthia, it will be the most beautiful place you can ever imagine, and your army will be waiting for you. Remember, your responsibility is to keep the powers of Yesu together and to never compromise its power through anger, frustration, or revenge. You must follow its power, its love, and the guidance of Yesu always. He will show you the way through your hearts. Before I send you off to Heirthia, I must warn you, never put the powers together."

King Daniel replied, "What happens if we do?"

Michael responded, "Well, if you do, you will be taken back to Earth, but if not done properly, and a power stays in Heirthia, and a power comes to Earth, you will never be able to return, and Heirthia will be lost as we know it."

Michael then looked at the Geminis with a kind and serious face and said, "And also, in order for me to take you back to Heirthia, you need all the powers together." The Geminis got close together. King Daniel raised his sword. Queen Elena raised her medallion. Princess Katalina raised her bow, and Princess Violet raised her wand, but nothing happened.

Michael said, "I'm sorry, Your Highness, for what you are about to go through, and you must remember that you need *all* the powers to take you back, all *five* powers."

Blast! King Daniel was hit from behind. He flew forward a few feet, and they all came crashing down on the floor.

"You are nothing!" exclaimed Seitor with a deep and evil voice.

Again, he raised his wand, and exclaimed, "Expellere!" He blasted King Daniel, who was laying on the floor, now almost paralyzed.

Seitor walked up to where King Daniel was and was very angry. He put his foot on King Daniel's chest, and said, "You think that just because you defeated my Blakers that you are the great king!" he yelled. "You are nothing!" he screamed at the top of his voice. Seitor raised the Ruby Stone Ring and called for the Sword of Yesu, "Gladius Yesu!" and there it appeared.

He quickly raised his sword and was going to kill King Daniel by ramming the sword through King Daniel's chest, knowing it would kill him instantly. King Daniel had suffered significantly and could not move, but he could see. Queen Elena was embraced by the girls and yelled, "Leave him alone!"

All the girls then began to yell, "Leave him alone!"

Michael was still on the floor and could barely move. He tried to get up but did not have the strength. Seitor, looking at the girls, swung his sword and cut Daniel's chest, but just barely. King Daniel yelled in pain, and this brought great pain to his family.

"What, you think you can save him? Nothing can stop me, not you, not Michael, and not Yesu," said Seitor, looking at the girls. Once again, he raised his sword, this time looking down. Princess Katalina was so scared, but she could no longer take seeing her father suffer, so she ran toward Seitor, but Seitor grabbed her by the neck and held her up.

Seitor looked right at Princess Katalina's eyes and was about to say something when he then yelled in pain. He looked down, where Princess Violet was hanging on to his leg and was biting him hard. Queen Elena then came from behind and put her arms around Seitor's neck.

At that very moment, as King Daniel was lying there, he knew what the angel Michael had done. He had trapped Seitor and lured him into his plan.

He remembered what Michael had said. The only way back to Heirthia was for all five powers to be together. To do this, Seitor needed to be tempted, and it was now the right time and right place. King Daniel regained some power, raised his sword toward the other powers, and yelled, "Michael, now!"

Michael, who had been on the floor in pain, came from behind Seitor, opened his wings to surround and embrace the Geminis and Seitor, and lifted his arms and said, "In Nomine Yesu! Through the powers created by the Living King, the powers have joined, and the people shall be free. Take these powers back to be bold and return its new king and queens to Heirthia so the story will unfold!"

As Michael said this, dark clouds covered the forest. The river became raging. The trees were blowing side to side with all the wind, and in an instant, a bright light came forth from the sky, and it became brighter and brighter, and they were all gone.

Michael, Seitor, and the Geminis were nowhere in sight, and all was calm in the forest once again. They indeed had been taken back to Heirthia.

12

THE NEW HEIRTHIA

FLASH! BLAST! IT sounded as the Geminis found themselves in another world.

Michael was not with them, and Seitor was nowhere to be found. Each of the Geminis came to a stop, kneeling on one knee. They all had their heads bowed down and their eyes closed.

They were all holding hands. King Daniel was holding Princess Violet's hand to his left. Queen Elena was holding King Daniel's right hand with her left hand, and Princess Katalina was holding on to Queen Elena's right hand. King Daniel slowly opened his eyes.

"We're alive," he whispered.

Slowly, Queen Elena opened her eyes, and then Princess Katalina followed. King Daniel looked toward Princess Violet and said, "Sweetie, you can open your eyes."

Princess Violet said in a small child's voice, "No, because I think we're dead."

"Sweetie, we are alive. Open your eyes," said King Daniel, but she was still so scared, and would not open them.

"Where are we, Daniel?" asked Queen Elena.

"I believe we are in Heirthia," responded King Daniel.

"How do you know, Daddy?" asked Princess Katalina.

At that point, Queen Elena, Princess Katalina, and Princess Violet were all facing King Daniel, and behind King Daniel was a forest. King Daniel was looking behind them all and pointed behind them and said, "Look at that. Where else could we be?"

Queen Elena and Princess Katalina both turned around, and they beheld the most beautiful sight they had ever seen. King Daniel went to Princess Violet and knelt before her. He then graciously held her hands and said, "Sweetheart, princess, I am here with you. You are well. Behold, Princess Violet, your kingdom."

Princess Violet slowly opened her eyes and whispered, "Wow, Heirthia."

From Earth, they had landed on a high mountain at the edge of a forest in Heirthia. Following the forest was a beautiful cliff, and a raging waterfall was coming down. The water was a beautiful blue crystal clear color. The trees and flowers beside the waterfall were all in bloom and of amazing colors. The air was so fresh.

Beside the cliff was a valley, and that valley had the most amazing colors of flowers and beautiful trees, and there was wildlife all over. There were creatures they recognized, such as deer, bears, birds, mountain lions, and others. They could see beavers working on their dams and so much more.

But they could also see creatures that they had never seen before. There was this one animal that had the body and look of a zebra, but it had wings. Then all of a sudden, the zebras took flight and were high in the sky.

There were many like this one and so many more other amazing creatures. The Geminis were truly amazed. There was another creature, very large, as it must have stood fifty feet tall. It was a man with the body of a bear. However, all the creatures were not afraid of it. As the Geminis looked closer. The man seemed to be a gentle giant and was engaging with the other creatures. He sat at the bank of the river and lay back into the forest beside it.

In amazement, Princess Katalina pointed out what appeared to be an upright walking elephant. It was not as large, but it walked on two feet. It looked like an elephant, and even had its trunk. However, it was of a brown color. There were several of them walking along a trail.

"What is this place?" voiced Queen Elena.

Then above the Geminis came flying several birds, but they were different. They appeared to be white eagles, but they were enormous, at least ten to twelve feet tall, and the wings spanned over twenty feet wide.

There were seven of them, and they were in formation, beautiful birds and so graceful. There were three of them on one side and another three on the other side between one larger eagle with red stripes on its side, almost like the leader.

"How beautiful they are," said Queen Elena.

They flew with authority. The Geminis smiled as the eagles were graceful and peaceful birds.

"Mommy, why are all the animals leaving and running away?" asked Princess Violet. Suddenly, the Geminis looked to the ground and knew something was wrong. Even the giant took refuge into the forest. The seven birds quickly and swiftly began flying downward toward where the animals were, and all the creatures on the ground began to run.

"They are attacking the creatures on the ground!" exclaimed King Daniel.

As the Geminis looked on, Queen Elena exclaimed, "Why are they doing this?"

The eagles then separated as each targeted a creature. Deer, a mountain lion, beavers, the bird-like zebra, and even a bear were all swooped up from the ground by the giant and fierce claws of the eagles. All the animals were screaming for help, but nothing or no one came to their aid.

"Dad, isn't there anything we can do?" exclaimed Princess Katalina in a frustrated voice.

"Unless you get that bow to work, sweetie, there is nothing we can do at this point and from this height," said King Daniel.

"Can't you do something with your hands like you did on Earth?" she asked again.

King Daniel then raised his right arm and closed his eyes. He could feel something moving within him, but they were too far. He could not reach them.

"I can't, sweetie. There is nothing there."

Princess Katalina turned around and put her body in a stance. She called for her bow and held the bow firmly. She drew back its beautiful strings, but nothing would appear. "Why won't this work? They are getting away," she said as she began to cry. "Daddy, it won't work," she again said as she cried. Again, she pulled the strings back, but nothing happened.

"This doesn't work. Why would I be given a bow if there aren't arrows? It doesn't make any sense," said Princess Katalina again. She then fell to her knees and cried as she felt so sorry for the animals as the white eagles flew into the distance and disappeared.

Princess Violet went to her mother and embraced her as she too felt bad. King Daniel knelt down and went to Princess Katalina's eye level and said, "Katalina, sweetheart. With all my heart, we will find out what happened to them, and we will get them back, but first we need to find out where we are, and we need to find this army that Michael said would be waiting for us. I promise, God Almighty is with us always, and so is Yesu."

She then hugged her father with such force and said, "Thank you, Daddy, I love you." King Daniel looked up at Queen Elena, and she gave him this smile, a smile so full of love. She was proud of him.

"Okay, girls, we need to get moving and find a camping spot and make a fire before it gets dark."

To the side of them, there was a trail that led down the mountain they were on.

"Let's go, girls. You lead the way," said Queen Elena. As the girls began to walk, Queen Elena followed them, but then King Daniel reached down to take Queen Elena's right hand, and pulled her back toward him. Then and there, he wrapped his left arm around her waist. He gently placed his right hand on her chin, and he gave her a soft kiss.

It was one simple kiss, but a kiss that she knew meant he was there for her, that he would protect her, that he would serve her, and that he would never leave her. He then slowly moved his lips from hers and said, "I will always love you, mi amor. You are everything to me. You are the reason I live, my queen."

Queen Elena looked at him, and a tear came down from her right eye. "Thank you, mi amor. Thank you for leading us. We need you more than ever," she whispered. It was a beautiful moment for them both.

They embraced so tight, as though they were never going to see each other again. As they hugged, Princess's Katalina and Violet looked at them. They were both smiling. Princess Katalina asked, "Need some alone time?" but Princess Violet replied, "I think it's beautiful."

King Daniel and Queen Elena both looked at the girls and smiled, and King Daniel said "Hey, girls, are you ready for another adventure?"

All three girls looked at each other and said, "We're ready, Daddy."

King Daniel, standing tall, said, "Let it begin."

All four continued to walk down the path that led deeper into the forest. As it turned out, they were in the far west side of the land of Castillo headed east, but still, they did not know where they were going.

Meanwhile, the white eagles arrived at their lair and dropped the animals as they landed. They went to the land of Cain, where King Julas ruled. But there, a land that once was so green, so beautiful with plants, flowers, and creatures of all kind, was now dead. The trees had been cut down, the grass was gone, and even the land looked plagued.

King Julas had indeed destroyed his land to serve the Dark King. As the animals landed on the floor, the eagles stood next to them and guarded.

"Who are you?" yelled King Julas.

None of the creatures moved.

"I will ask you again, who are you?" he yelled again. "Where did you find these?"

The while eagle with red stripes known as Kanel then spoke and said in a firm and intelligent voice, "In the land of Castillo. There were more, but these were the most vulnerable."

King Julas then looked at them and said, "Where are the Quint Fey powers?"

He walked very fast toward the deer, drew his sword, and again said, "Where are the Quint Fey powers, or you will die!"

He put the sword to the neck of the deer, and because he did not respond, he raised it, and as he swung his word to strike, the deer spoke in fear, "They have left this world." The other animals then looked at the deer.

The bear said, "Darel, no, don't say more."

King Julas then said, "Darel, is it? I knew you animals could talk."

King Julas then walked back to his chair and said, "So, Darel, what world have they gone to. Is this a world you have made up?"

The bear, beaver, and the other animals looked at Darel, and looked at him as though not to say anything, but Darel, still in fear, said, "Yes, it is a real world, or so that is what is being said."

King Julas said, "And what is it that is being said, Darel?"

Darel just stood there but would not say more.

"What is being said, Darel?" yelled King Julas. Still, Darel would not speak.

King Julas once again rushed toward them, but this time, toward the bear. He put his silver sword to the bear's neck and said, "Darel, tell me what is being said, or I will kill your friend. I will cut his head off!"

As King Julas was about to cut Brady's head off, Darel spoke again. He said, "Earth. The powers were taken to Earth to find—" He paused.

"To find what?" yelled King Julas.

"The powers were taken to find its new kings—the new family, they are being called."

King Julas stood there for a moment. "A new family?" he questioned. "What does this mean?" he asked.

Darel turned away.

King Julas went toward Darel and struck him with the handle of his sword and said, "Tell me!"

Darel, now angry, said, "A new family from Earth. They have been granted the powers by Yesu himself, and they are now here on Heirthia, and they will destroy you and the Dark King!"

All the creatures, white eagles, and even King Julas were shocked at what they were hearing.

Darel continued, "They are the chosen ones, and Yesu has found favor in them, and they are coming for you and your army!"

The room went completely silent.

All the evil creatures were looking at King Julas in shock, and no one knew what to say.

Slash!

The room became silent.

"You think you're brave don't you?" said Darel. Darel began bleeding as King Julas, out of anger, swung his silver sword and cut the brave deer's chest. It was a deep laceration.

"It does not matter what you have done to me. I will die proud, knowing that you know your doomed fate in all of this. In the end, I know where I will be going: to the Father, the Creator. But you, you know exactly where you're going," whispered the deer.

Cut!

King Julas stabbed Darel in the chest and ended his life. Amazingly, the deer smiled but then slowly fell to the ground. All the other forest creatures were in shock, and tears were coming down from their faces as they lost their friend. Darel would always be remembered for standing up to the Dark King's allies.

"Take the rest to the dungeon and lock them up. We will kill them upon the Dark King's return," exclaimed King Julas. As the forest animals were being taken away, King Julas sat on his chair.

Kanel voiced, "What is this all about, King Julas? Are they really coming for us?"

King Julas then said, "Don't listen to them, these peasant forest animals. They know nothing."

"Well, the deer sure sounded like he knew what he was talking about," replied Kanel.

"I tell you the truth. There is no such thing!" yelled King Julas.

Flash! Blast! A loud sound was heard, and King Julas, Kanel, and the other creatures around all fell to the ground.

"It's true!" yelled the Dark King as the room became dark, and there was black mist all over.

Seitor then appeared, kneeling from being transported from Earth to Heirthia.

"Seitor!" exclaimed King Julas. All that were there knelt before him.

"You have returned, Dark Lord," said King Julas once again.

Seitor then stood up and walked toward King Julas, and as King Julas tried to embrace and welcome Seitor, Seitor swung his right arm and bashed King Julas over the face. "Where is my army! Where?"

King Julas fell to the ground and said, "They are ready for you, Lord. They are placed all around the land waiting for your orders."

Seitor questioned, "Waiting? Waiting? There is nothing to wait for! Destroy and kill everything and everyone!" Seitor then walked toward King Julas's chair and sat down.

"Don't you understand? The new family has been chosen, and they are now here in Heirthia," exclaimed Seitor.

Kanel moved his head back in even more shock that indeed this new family was real. "Yesu has granted them the Quint Fey, and they will build an army. That is why we must kill everything and everyone who is not loyal to us."

Seitor got up and walked with King Julas to the edge of the cliff, where they stood at King Julas's castle, and said, "We must take the Quint Fey, or they will destroy us one by one."

Kanel came forward toward Seitor and said, "Lord, what is your command? My fleet is ready."

Seitor turned and looked toward Kanel and said, "Go, my loyal warrior, take all of your fleet and find them! They are a father and mother and two young children. Although they know nothing of the powers of the Quint Fey, be cautious as there is a great love between them."

Kanel yelled, "Eagles, unite!"

Then from inside the castle came forth twenty-one white eagles. They all gathered, and Kanel said, "We shall fly, and we shall find the Earth humans. They are a father, mother, and two young children. Find them and kill them. Be sure to bring back the Quint Fey powers they possess."

Kanel then turned toward Seitor and asked, "What do they call them?"

Seitor then turned toward Kanel and said in a firm and very deep voice "Geminis."

Immediately after that, Kanel screamed out as eagles do, leaped into the air, and took flight. His enormous army then followed, and all the white eagles were on the hunt. Seitor looked on as he stood next to King Julas and whispered, "Yes, find them and kill them," and he then gave an evil smile as his blue eyes shone.

The Geminis, slowly but surely, were still walking in the forest. Exhausted from their many miles of trekking, the girls said at the same time, "Can we stop already? It's getting dark!"

Princess Katalina then said, "I'm hungry too Dad."

Princess Violet joined in, "Yeah, and my skinny arms and legs aren't helping."

King Daniel stopped and looked over at Queen Elena. She nodded her head. "It is getting late, sweetie."

King Daniel looked at the girls. "Okay, let's camp here. Can you girls gather wood so we can make a big campfire?"

The girls were just excited to stop and camp for the night. There was still some daylight, but the sun was fast fading into Heirthia.

"Sure, Dad," the girls exclaimed as they began looking around together. Together, the Geminis went and gathered lots of wood. Queen Elena cleared an area next to a very large tree.

She and Princess Violet gathered leaves and grass around the camp area and placed it on the ground so that it would be at least somewhat padded and more comfortable than hard ground. Princess Katalina was helping her father with some of the larger pieces and branches.

While helping her father, Princess Katalina asked, "Daddy, do you think we are ever going back to Earth?"

King Daniel looked at her as though he knew the answer, but in reality, he really wasn't sure. King Daniel responded, "Look, I can tell you for sure that with all my heart, I believe we will go back."

Princess Katalina looked down and asked, "Do you think we will survive here?"

King Daniel looking even more puzzled at the questions his daughter was asking. "Of course we will. Remember, we always stay together. God is with us, and the family that prays together—"

"Stays together," Princess Katalina said before he could finish. She then smiled and went to her father, and they gave each other a hug. King Daniel and Princess Katalina rejoined Queen Elena and Princess Violet with all the wood.

"Okay, it looks like we have what we need," said King Daniel.

"Do you have matches or a lighter?" asked Queen Elena.

"I didn't think about that, but as the good Boy Scout that I am, let's try it the old-fashioned way." King Daniel gathered a flat piece of wood and turned it so that the center was facing up. He then got one strong branch that was thin but strong enough to use to perhaps start a fire by rubbing the two pieces together.

Time after time, he tried and tried and tried, but the fire never started. He got a bit of smoke, but the fire just wouldn't light. Even the girls and Queen Elena took turns, but the fire never started. "So much for being a Boy Scout," voiced King Daniel.

Queen Elena said, "Girls, let your dad continue while we look for something to eat."

The girls then set out around the camp, not too far, and began looking for anything to eat. While they were doing this, King Daniel continued with the wood rubbing. While out looking, Queen Elena found a berry tree, and so she called the girls over to help her.

"Girls, anyone want berries?"

The princesses came rushing over to where their mother was. The tree was high, but that was not going to stop the girls from getting those berries. Thus, all three girls began to climb high up on the tree and immediately began to eat.

"I am so hungry," voiced Princess Violet.

As they were eating and gathering all the berries they could carry, which was quite a ways from camp at that point, Queen Elena heard something walking in the woods.

"Shh, girls be quiet, I hear something."

As the girls listened, there was nothing except the wind hitting against the trees.

Growl.

It was not a loud growl, but they clearly heard a growl in the distance opposite of where King Daniel was back at camp. Although they could not see what it was, they knew something was out there. The girls waited for several minutes, but then whatever was there was gone.

"Okay, we need to get back to Daddy," whispered Queen Elena. The girls climbed down with the berries and quickly went the opposite way from where they heard the growl and went toward camp.

Arriving back at camp, King Daniel had his sword in hand and was trying to rub it against some rocks he had gathered in the hope of making fire.

"Daddy, look what we found," said Princess Violet.

"Awesome, girls, thank you for bringing me some." King Daniel began to eat some of the berries.

"Yeah, but we also heard a growl out in the woods," said Princess Katalina in a worried voice.

"A growl?" asked King Daniel. Queen Elena then explained what had happened.

"We heard it, but we never saw what it was. Besides, it walked in the opposite direction of where we were. I don't think it will come this way."

By this time, the sun had gone down. It was dark, and still they had no fire. "Violet, do you think you can maybe somehow wave your wand toward the wood and make a fire spell?" asked King Daniel.

"Daniel, she has no idea how to use that thing. It could be dangerous," said Queen Elena.

Princess Violet replied, "I can try, Mommy. I'm not afraid."

The little one took the Dragon's Claw Wand out and said, "I mean, how hard can it be?" She raised her wand and flicked it forward, but nothing happened.

"I think you have to say something, Violet," said Princess Katalina in a witty voice.

Again, Princess Violet lifted the wand and this time said, "I want fire."

Again, nothing happened.

"Fire," she tried again, but the wand would not do anything.

"That's okay, Violet, you tried your best," said her father.

"I think it's broken," commented the little one.

"I think you just need to learn the spells, sweetheart," assured King Daniel.

Princess Katalina then said, "Yeah, remember what King Jonis told you. You need to use it with your heart."

Princess Violet thought about that for a moment and then looked back at the wood that was gathered and began to concentrate. She tried looking deep into her heart. Queen Elena then suggested and said, "Say it in Latin, sweetie. Say 'ignis!'"

Princess Violet then closed her eyes, prayed with her heart, raised her wand, and whispered, "Ignis." She then quickly flicked her wand toward the wood, but nothing happened.

She visibly became disappointed in herself as she felt she had failed her family.

"You see, it doesn't work even if I say *ignis!*" she exclaimed with such emotion as she motioned her wand forward, and as she did this, a small light came out of her wand and hit one of the branches! The light was so small, very tiny, very slim, smaller than a hair. The Geminis were all taken back and shocked that Princess Violet had cast her first spell, and it worked. Smoke slowly came out from the rubble.

"Smoke!" exclaimed King Daniel.

He quickly went to the wood and began blowing into it. The smoke grew larger and larger, and, as all three girls watched on,

King Daniel continued to blow toward where the smoke was coming from.

He quickly turned to the girls. "I need dry grass," and he continued to blow.

Queen Elena quickly grabbed some dry grass that was near her and went to help her husband. She placed it where the smoke was coming from, and with one more big blow by King Daniel, fire was born.

"Fire!" the girls all yelled. "We have fire!" Princess Katalina quickly turned to Princess Violet and yelled, "You did it!"

Queen Elena went toward Princess Violet and gave her a big hug. "You did it, sweetheart, you did it. You gave us fire with your wand!"

Princess Violet was so happy and joyful that she had helped her family to stay warm throughout the night. Princess Violet began jumping and dancing all around at what she had done. Lifting her wand, she yelled, "It works! I am Princess Violet, the great small wizard!"

King Daniel went to his daughter, gave her a big hug, and lifted her into the hair as he stood and said, "My little wizard."

"I'm a wizard?" asked Princess Violet in a more serious voice.

"Yes, sweetie. You have your wand that has chosen you, and you have accepted it. Through your good heart, your brave soul, and your pure spirit, you will be a great wizard for the glory of God," said her father in a very compassionate voice. He continued, "Yes, you are a wizard. Your sister will be a master archer and healer, and your mother is a courageous lioness."

"What about you, Daddy?" asked Princess Katalina.

King Daniel stood there, not really knowing what to say.

"A king. A brave king, knight, and leader," replied his bride.

The four then gathered together, and they gave one big family hug. The Geminis then tended to their fire and made it somewhat large. They sat together and cuddled up and began eating their berries. They sat there for a while and talked about their new adventure.

Princess Katalina asked, "What do you think will happen to us tomorrow?"

Her mother looked at her and said, "I'm sure we are going to find the army that has been made for us. There will be thousands of soldiers, and we will be ready to lead, right, Daddy?"

King Daniel responded, "Oh yeah. I think it will be a grand army, and they will find us tomorrow. They are probably already looking for us now."

Princess Violet then said, "What about Yesu?"

"What about him, Violet?" replied King Daniel while looking at the fire in the dead of night.

"Well, I'm not too sure, but he sounds like a great man, a great person who cares about Heirthia. I mean, for him to come to Earth to find us when he doesn't even know us means a lot."

Queen Elena added, "Well, sweetie, from the great power and love he has for his people, he reminds me of someone close to our heart."

Princess Katalina then said, "Yeah, he does remind me of him. He has so much love, and he has given all of this to his people. I am glad he chose us because we are going to do everything to protect it, right, Dad?"

"Right, you are absolutely correct. We will indeed serve."

As they sat there and prepared for the night, in the distance, they heard the sound that they never wanted to hear: the howls of wolves.

King Daniel quickly sat up at the horrid sound. Queen Elena soon followed.

"Is that—" Princess Violet began to ask, and King Daniel finished her sentence, "Wolves."

"How far are they?" asked Queen Elena.

"Maybe a mile or so?" he responded.

"We need to make the fire bigger," said Queen Elena. To their feet, they tended to the fire that was slowly dying down. They added both small and large pieces of wood. King Daniel grabbed several large branches and placed the top portion of the branch on the fire so that in the event the wolves showed up, they could use the sticks with fire on them. Queen Elena sat next to the girls as King Daniel continued. Both girls were very frightened.

"I'm scared, Dad," whispered Princess Katalina.

Princess Victoria was embracing her mother in fear of the wolves.

The howls continued, and there were many. King Daniel then grabbed hold of his sword and sat next to his bride and his two girls. Soon the howling was slowly but surely gone.

Queen Elena asked, "Do you think they can smell us?"

King Daniel responded, "I hope not. They will probably get scared with the fire anyways."

They sat there for awhile without a sound, but the girls were very much frightened. Queen Elena rested her head on her husband's shoulder, and she held his right arm. Queen Elena tried to comfort the girls, but they were still visibly frightened.

All four were in a huddle, leaning against some brush for cover. Although Queen Elena looked visibly okay and confident, she too was indeed very scared. She worriedly looked at King Daniel and said, "What do we do?"

King Daniel began to quietly sing a song as an act of love toward his family. He knew that his family needed to be comforted.

> You are safe now
> You are safe now
> Don't you worry, my children
> I am here, and I will make my voice loud for all to hear so
>   that you will not fear
> You are safe now
> You are safe now
> And now you can sleep
> You can dream a good dream, and you will wake to a
>   brand-new day
> For I will never say good-bye
> Just because of the watchful eye of the Most High, you
>   are safe now

You are safe now because I love you, because I adore you
I will stay and watch while you pray with your heart
Believing and trusting that nothing will bring us apart
You are safe now
You are safe now
So go to sleep
Have full trust in me as I shelter you, and I will care for
        you,
And so, you are safe now

As King Daniel quietly sang this to his three girls, they were comforted, and they fell asleep in peace. As King Daniel looked upon the warm fire, and with no noise in the forest, he too fell fast asleep, resting for a good long while.

Growl!

King Daniel opened his eyes and quickly sat up. It was still dark. Right behind the fire across from them at about twenty feet away was a massive black wolf. It was about five feet in height on all fours.

Growl! Again the wolf growled as it stood ready to attack.

Queen Elena opened her eyes and screamed in fear. Both Princess Katalina and Princess Violet woke up, not knowing what was going on. They both saw the wolf, and they too screamed in terror. King Daniel was on his feet with his sword drawn, and he quickly reached for the branch that was on fire.

All three girls got behind King Daniel, and King Daniel yelled at the top of his lungs, "Get out of here!" Again he yelled, "Get out of here!"

He took the branch on fire and began waving it in front of the wolf. The wolf began to hiss, and it opened its mouth and showed all its sharp teeth. This wolf was not going anywhere. King Daniel then pushed the branch forward, and the fire got really close to the wolf, and so the wolf, feeling the heat, moved back. King Daniel, little by little, was moving forward, and little by little, the wolf was moving back.

Again there was a growl, but this time it came from several places surrounding the Geminis' camp. King Daniel looked to his right and saw three other wolves, just as large, standing there ready to pounce.

The girls then looked to their left, and there were five more wolves standing there, also growling. The Geminis were surrounded. Queen Elena then moved forward and grabbed another branch that was on fire and began swinging it toward the five wolves to the left.

Princesses Katalina and Violet were very scared, and Princess Violet was crying uncontrollably in fear at what was happening. The wolves one by one began to move closer. As this was happening, the alpha male, the black one that King Daniel was facing, began to move closer as the fire on the branches were starting to extinguish. Daniel, unsure as to what to do, got close to his family and held them behind him.

"Stay behind me!" he yelled.

"You're the chosen ones, aren't you?" spoke the alpha male.

The Geminis were in shock at what they were hearing. The animal was talking. King Daniel replied, "You can talk! Animals don't talk! What kind of place is this? Leave us alone!"

"Daddy, please make the wolf stop talking. It's freaking me out!" cried Princess Violet out of fear.

Katalina voiced in a soft but most confused voice, "It's a talking wolf. I'm looking at a talking wolf."

"You are. You are the ones Yesu chose," the alpha male continued. "Now I will kill all of you."

King Daniel yelled, "Who are you, and what do you want?"

"I am Cauffa, and I am the alpha male of the Wind Pack. All we want is your head," said Cauffa as he growled in a very deep voice. "Your head!" he said again.

Then one of Cauffa's wolves leaped toward King Daniel, its mouth and massive jaws open, and with one swing of his sword, King Daniel yelled, "In the name of Yesu!" *Swoosh!*

The head of the wolf was severed, and its body fell to the ground. Cauffa was amazed at what had just happened and said, "That is the Sword of Yesu! Wolves, kill the family and get the powers Seitor wants!"

Right then and there, the seven wolves leaped forward so as to ambush the Geminis, but then small bright lights came from the trees behind the wolves. These lights moved very quickly and flew in front of each wolf, and behold, each of the lights was a small fairy, and each fairy put its own two hands together, and as it separated its two hands, a blast came out toward each wolf. When the blast came out, a blue circle glowed, and *blast!*

The wolves were thrown back into the forest, and they cried in pain. Between the wolves and the Geminis, the lights hovered and waited for another attack.

"Fariets!" yelled Cauffa.

Fariets were about five inches in height. They had wings, and they always glowed with light.

"You are banished. You are not to interact with humans!" Cauffa commanded.

He growled as the other wolves came back. Then twenty-one wolves appeared in the forest. They were everywhere. There were eyes everywhere staring at the Geminis from the dark night, and then they all began to howl loudly.

Then one of the Fariets spoke, "You are not hunting for food. You are hunting to kill in vain. Therefore, we shall defend these humans. Go, Cauffa, you are not welcome in our forest."

Cauffa, even more angry, said, "This is not your forest, Lizzet. This is the Dark King's forest, and we will kill you and the humans and take the powers. This is not your battle, so move!" he yelled.

All of the massive wolves then began to completely surround the Geminis, so then Lizzet raised her tiny head, closed her eyes, and put her hands together. She then separated them. Strings of blue lights went everywhere into the forest and made a special call out into the woods, and over one hundred Fariets came from the trees, and quickly the night became as bright as day as the lights of the Fariets illuminated the forest.

The battle began, the wolves leaped into the air, and the Fariets counterattacked.

Crash! Blast! Growl! Snap! were all that could be heard.

Cauffa attacked, and the other wolves were attacking as well.

Blast!

Cauffa was thrown back as Lizzet blasted him with her magical powers. One of the wolves came through and grabbed King Daniel by the arm, and as he did this, Queen Elena was thrown to the ground, where she hit her head against a fallen tree. King Daniel yelled in pain, but Princess Katalina quickly grabbed her bow and hit the wolf with the corner of the bow.

As the wolf let go, it stared at Princess Katalina, and so King Daniel swung his sword, and he stabbed the wolf, and it fell to the ground dead.

"Take them to the trees!" ordered Lizzet as they continued to fight the wolves.

Quickly, about thirty Fariets came and lifted the Geminis into the sky. The Geminis were amazed at what was happening but knew that the Fariets were on their side.

"Where are you taking us?" asked King Daniel.

"To our home, where nothing can hurt you," said one of the Fariets. Queen Elena looked back at their campsite. The battle was still raging, but little by little, she could see no more. Queen Elena looked on, and she slowly began to become unconscious from her blow to the head. As she faded into a sleep, she could hear them flying through the forest and into the sky, and then she was out.

Then from a far distance, Queen Elena could hear a very light whisper.

"Elena? Elena, Elena."

As she began to wake, the voice got louder and louder, and it was King Daniel calling her name. "Elena, mi amor, are you okay?" asked King Daniel.

Queen Elena was still very dizzy and sleepy, and her eyes were very heavy, but she said, "Hi, mi amor." As she lay there in bed looking up at her husband, she said, "Yeah, I'm okay. My head hurts a bit, but I had this strange dream. We were like this chosen family, and we had these powers. It felt so real. Then we came to this place called Heirthia, and we were in a big fight with these wolves. And then these fairy-like creatures came out of nowhere and saved us. It was crazy."

King Daniel looked at Queen Elena like he was holding something back, and then he looked off to the side of her.

Queen Elena then looked over to where her husband was looking, and about twenty of the Fariets were looking at her.

"You're very pretty," said one of the child Fariets.

Elena quickly sat up and said, "Oh my, this is real! This is all real! They are real! They're everywhere!" Queen Elena looked around where she was. She was in a room and was lying on a soft bed. There were Fariets everywhere looking and smiling at her.

King Daniel smiled and said, "Elena, these are the Fariets. They are the fairies of the forest, and they saved us from the wolves."

Queen Lizzet then came forward and said, "Hello, my queen." She bowed, and all the Fariets bowed down to honor their new queen. Queen Lizzet continued, "I am Lizzet, and I am the queen of the Fariets. We have brought you to our home."

Queen Elena was just in shock at what she was seeing and said, "Where are we?" Then and there, Queen Lizzet raised her little hand and pointed toward the window of the room.

Queen Elena slowly got up, looking at her husband, and went to the window. As she got up, she noticed she was wearing a white gown, and as she looked out the window, she saw the most amazing sight—an entire city of Fariets built on the treetops of the forest. The entire city was lit up, and it was beautiful.

"This is Quintus Shallow, home of the Fariets," whispered Queen Lizzet.

13

THE FARIETS

"WOW!" SHE EXCLAIMED as she looked out the Fariet's window. It was still nighttime, and the Fariets were up and alive at the visit of their newfound friends. Among the treetops, the Fariets had built an entire city. There were homes built on each tree, and massive stages, decks, and walkways everywhere, and there were large homes, buildings, and walkways large enough to hold a human. There must have been hundreds of trees all interconnected with bridges and more and more homes and halls. There were no lights, but the entire city was lit up as each Fariet glowed.

Queen Elena turned to her husband. "The girls?" she questioned.

King Daniel, with a smile on his face, walked up to Queen Elena, stood behind her, and pointed into the distance. "There," he whispered. Both Princesses were with some of the Fariets. Princess Violet was playing with many of them as Princess Katalina smiled and laughed on. They were indeed friends.

"It's amazing, isn't it?" said King Daniel to his bride as they stood there looking out the window. "I am in awe at what God has done. Never in a million years would I have known or even wondered whether there were other creatures from another place."

Queen Elena then asked, "How long have I been out?"

King Daniel responded, "Two days."

"That long?" she responded.

They both turned around, and King Daniel asked Queen Lizzet, "Please tell us more about Heirthia."

The Geminis were taken to a giant and grand hall where the thousands of Fariets would meet to discuss their affairs. They were treated with a fine meal of fruits and vegetables. As the Geminis ate, the Great Council of the Fariets came forth and took place.

There were seven of them who would discuss and have dialogue with other Fariets to talk about issues, decisions, and their future. Queen Lizzet then came forth and addressed the Fariets.

"Great Fariets!" she projected her voice. The room then became silent. She continued, "As you know, for the last one hundred years, our kind was but a myth, a legend, as we were banished from the society of Heirthia and were to stay away from the humans. The kings of that time were honorable, respected, but the people would not accept us, and therefore we moved away into a land where we could raise our own families, our own children, and that we have done."

All the Fariets cheered on and clapped as they were truly proud at what they had accomplished.

The Geminis looked on as Queen Lizzet continued, "But today, our lives may have changed forever. Maybe it is for the good, maybe for the worse. Two days ago, we came out of the shadows for the first time in one hundred years. We came out because we were needed once again. We came out, and we fought bravely against the Wind Pack of Wolves, and we did it to protect the humans."

The Fariets once again cheered on at what they had done.

"However, we have discovered something about these particular humans that you all are not aware of. Behold, they are the new chosen king and queens of Heirthia, the Geminis!" Queen Lizzet exclaimed.

The entire hall burst into cheers and excitement. It was indeed a happy and proud moment as they had indeed defended the new king and queens.

Queen Lizzet continued as she then faced the council, "Council members, as your queen, I address you with a decision that must be made for the Fariets to move forward. We have indeed saved the new king and queens of Heirthia as they have been honored and granted by the power of Yesu with the Quint Fey powers. However, a decision must be made as the wind has been carrying voices that claim the evil Seitor is after them and will kill and destroy anything that gets in his way."

All the Fariets became fearful at this, and there were many that gasped for air.

She continued, "Two days ago, we fought the wolves, and the battle ended with many of our own dead, but the true worry is that they know where we live. They know we are still here, and they know we have the Geminis. The question now remains, what do we do with them?"

Throughout the room there were many with different feelings. Some yelled for the Geminis to be removed so that their lives would not be affected, but there were many that yelled for the protection of the king and queens.

The council then addressed the Fariets, "Hear, hear!"

The room slowly went silent. One councilman continued, "We have a dilemma before us. King Daniel, please stand."

King Daniel stood, and the councilman continued, "Please know that we do not regret assisting you and your family against the wolves. Our kind is truly kind at heart, but please know that we must make a decision as to our own future."

King Daniel responded, "Your Honorable Council, on behalf of my family, we are very grateful to your entire kingdom for saving our lives. However, we do not want to put your family in danger of any kind. We are grateful for your hospitality, for your food, and for your protection, but we are at a stage where we must join our army and the past kings to face the Dark King."

The councilmen then discussed what King Daniel had said. The councilman stood and said, "The council has discussed Your Highness's wish, and we grant you your journey."

Queen Lizzet then stood and said in a firmer voice, "Your Honorable Councilman, thank you for your decision, but I must stress that we have to help the Geminis with greater care than just letting them go and granting their wishes. You know very well the wolves will be back, and only Yesu himself knows what other creatures or evil spirits are out there waiting to kill them. Therefore, we must do much more for them. They are the key to our future in Heirthia."

"We hear your dilemma, Your Highness, but we must also think of the future of our hidden homes. For over one hundred years, we have never been found or rediscovered by Heirthians, and therefore, we do not want to put our own lives at risk."

Queen Lizzet replied, "Understood, Council, but as your queen, I must say this"—Queen Lizzet then turned around and faced the Fariets—"for over one hundred years, we have been in hiding. For over one hundred years, we left civilization because we were not accepted. For over one hundred years, we have built our homes and stayed hidden. Now I ask you, is this the way we want our legacy to be remembered? As a hidden race?"

Many of the Fariets clapped and cheered in agreement.

She continued, "But I ask you why? Why? Why did we leave Heirthia? Because we were brave? Because we wanted to? Because we wanted our own lives? No! No, I tell you. We did these things because we were not accepted. We were not wanted because we had no purpose. But now we have an opportunity. An opportunity to make a difference, to be accepted for who we are, to be accepted for what we can do, and that opportunity is to help our new king and queens defeat the Dark King and his army."

An alarming sound came from the crowd, some in agreement, but many were not so happy.

"Your Highness, please, we are already at risk. The wolves have gone back already and alerted Seitor of our whereabouts. It is best that the Geminis go now and that we have no involvement in this. As it is, I am afraid Seitor will be sending the White Eagles for us," said the councilman.

Immediately, the Fariets became afraid. The small children all hid under the tables because the Fariets were truly afraid of the White Eagles.

"You're afraid?" replied King Daniel in a firm and loud voice. "You're afraid?" again he asked.

"My family was visited by an angel in our world, and then Seitor himself continuously tried to kill us when we had no involvement in your world. He drove ordinary people, ordinary humans to come against us and try to kill our family. Then we are told that the entire world of Heirthia is in our hands. We were told that we would have to leave our world and go into another world and that our family, children and all, must fight an entire legion of creatures and evildoers that want to kill us. And in the end, we didn't have to do it. We could have just said, 'It's not our problem.'"

As Daniel walked around the Fariets, he continued, "But what did we do? We said yes! We said, 'We will go and fight for a world that we do not even know.' Why? Because we believe and because we have faith in Yesu for what he is planning. We did this because Yesu is love, and therefore, who He loves, we shall love, and where He goes, we shall go! Will you join us?" he exclaimed.

The entire hall jumped in excitement and in agreement. Fariets from all over proclaimed, "I will follow, I will follow, we will follow!"

King Daniel once again faced the council, and said, "So once again, I ask you, are you afraid? I have a ten-year-old child, a fourteen-year old child, and my wife in a world we have never known. All we know is that there are wolves out there that so desperately want to kill us, and you're afraid? Do not be dismayed, Councilmen. Be courageous, and join our kingdom to protect yourselves, your home, your children, and your kingdom."

Again, the Fariets jumped in agreement and proclaimed, "We will fight!"

Another yelled, "We don't want to hide anymore!"

Queen Elena then stood up and said with passion, "Dear Councilmen, we don't want to impose, and we are sorry if indeed the White Eagles are coming, but any help we can get from your kind will greatly impact what happens to the future of Heirthia. Today, this very moment, you can make a difference. Our family is already indebted for what you have done for us, and if there is nothing more you can do for us, then we understand, and we leave with no animosity. I just want you to know that, as the new queen of Heirthia, you will always be accepted and welcomed into the land of Heirthia. We will always accept you as our friends, as our new family."

Queen Elena then reached out for her girls hands and said "Girls, we need to get going."

"Queen Elena!"

Queen Elena then turned around, and as she did, each of the seven councilmen stood up and gave her a respectful bow. One councilman then said, "We are very grateful for what you have just said. It has taken over one hundred years, but Yesu is so great and almighty. He has answered our prayers. For this, we will help you and grant all that you need."

All the Fariets then cheered on and clapped in excitement. Queen Lizzet mouthed the words *thank you* to the councilmen and then said, "Your Highnesses, we will send with you five hundred of our bravest Fariets, and we will give you food and water for your journey. The Fariets will show you the way to King Simon's castle. They will lead you all the way. We will also give you weapons and many other necessities. It is to King Simon's castle where you must go and find your army."

Queen Elena then walked up to where little Queen Lizzet was flying, and she gave her gratitude. Queen Lizzet said, "Fariets, we must hurry and begin to prepare for the journey, and we must also begin to prepare for the arrival of the White Eagles. Let us begin!" The Fariets cheered, and all began to fly to prepare.

As morning came, the Geminis and Fariets knew that they did not have much time. Quickly the Geminis gathered their few belongings, and the Fariets set up a selection grid for the five hundred Fariets. There was a mixture of men, women, and even young adult Fariets selected to go on the journey to make sure the Geminis would make it to King Simon's castle. Many fruits and vegetables were provided in a sack to each of the Geminis. Canteens full of water were also provided.

Queen Lizzet then met with the Geminis and introduced to them the Fariet warrior that would lead them. His name was Ut.

"King Daniel and Queen Elena, this is Fariet Ut. He is our best and strongest warrior, and he knows all the lands between Castillo, Demble, and Exsul, where you will ultimately need to go."

Fariet Ut was also small, but a little bigger than the rest. He was about seven inches in height, but he was very well built and very fast.

"He is the one who first defended you against the wolf that leaped for you."

King Daniel then said, "Thank you, Fariet Ut, for your courage and bravery."

Fariet Ut replied, "My king and queen, I am honored to lead you to your destiny, and I lay down my life if need be to protect you and the princesses."

"Okay, everyone, we have one last item to take care of," exclaimed Queen Lizzet. "King Daniel, take this with you."

Queen Lizzet showed King Daniel a large shield. "Although you have the most powerful sword in all the land, this is Fariets' Shield of Honor, which will protect you always. Its powers are not grand, but its structure is unbreakable. The Fariets built it out of silver and with a touch of our magic. Nothing can penetrate it. We initially built it for King Simon, but when the people banished us, it was never presented. Now we present it to you."

King Daniel looked at the shield, and it was beautiful. It was oval and all silver but very light. It had an image of an angel on it with a sword. In the background were two massive hands that looked as though they were guiding the angel. Queen Lizzet then called, "Queen Elena, come forth."

Queen Elena came to where Queen Lizzet was.

Queen Lizzet continued, "We gift to you Fariet's Touch of Healing."

Queen Elena reached out for the small bottle and looked inside. It was a cherry-red liquid and had a pleasant fragrance to it. Queen Lizzet continued, "When needed, drink it, and it will take the complete fear from you, and it will give you or whoever drinks it bravery, courage, and strength like you have never seen. Choose wisely, though, as it can only be used once."

Elena bowed in respect and said, "Thank you, my dearest Queen Lizzet. I will honor and protect it."

"Now, Princess Katalina, come forth," said Queen Lizzet. She continued, "To you my dearest Princess Katalina, we give you the Fariet's Dagger. It is a small weapon, but with much power. Princess, this dagger is not to be used on anyone. Remember, do not use it on anyone. It is to be used during great need, when you have nowhere else to go or when you are trapped. When needed, you shall drive this dagger into the land, and you will see its great protection. Keep it safe. If used against a person, great harm will come to you, but if used wisely, it will help you."

Princess Katalina responded, "Queen Lizzet, I shall keep it safe. That is my promise." Princess Katalina looked at the small dagger. It was very shiny. On the dagger were the words *Vade Cum Deo*. One of the small Fariets went to Princess Katalina and whispered to her, "It means 'go with God.'" Princess Katalina then went with her father and mother.

Queen Lizzet then called, "Now where is little Princess Violet?"

Princess Violet then came fourth before Queen Lizzet and said, "I am here, Queen Lizzet. What do you have for me to protect the people with?"

The crowd laughed. Queen Lizzet said, "You have a good heart, my dear Violet. Your first priority in life has always been to serve and protect others. For this, we grant you Fariet's Dust."

Queen Lizzet placed the small pouch over Princess Violet's head as it had a small band around it, like a necklace. Princess Violet then opened it and noticed gold dust inside. "It's dust," she answered.

Queen Lizzet smiled and said, "Yes, sweetheart, it is dust, but not just any dust. It is Fariet Dust, and it comes from our wings."

Queen Lizzet then knelt on one knee before little Violet and said, "With this dust, you can do anything. All you do is take a pinch, just like this." Right then and there, Queen Lizzet pulled some out of the pouch and poured it over Princess Violet's head. "You take it, and you sprinkle a little on what you want to do."

Princess Violet, a bit puzzled, asked, "What did you want to do with me?"

Queen Lizzet then said, "You're already doing it, little one."

Princess Violet looked at her parents and noticed they were gone, but she then looked down, and they were all below her. "I'm flying. Mommy, Daddy, I'm flying." Indeed, Princess Violet was flying, and she began maneuvering all over the room. She then said in excitement, "Katalina, look at me!"

Princess Katalina was amazed and really wanted to join her, so Princess Violet flew toward her sister, grabbed just a pinch of the Fariet Dust, and poured it over Princess Katalina. Princess Katalina closed her eyes, and then all of a sudden, she too was up in the air.

"Oh my! I'm flying, I'm flying!" exclaimed Princess Katalina.

All the Fariets and the Geminis were laughing at what they were seeing.

Crash! came a loud sound through the roof of the hall.

"It's the White Eagles!" yelled a Fariet guard. The entire room nearly caved in.

Crash! Crash! Crash! Four White Eagles had crashed into the hall with their massive claws. Both princesses were thrown to the ground. The eagles were yelling out a loud eagle scream.

"Get the royals out of here!" yelled Queen Lizzet.

Fariet Ut then yelled, "Fariets, form a line. Keep the line!"

Around one hundred Fariets made a line, and they waited patiently for the eagles to return. Fariet Ut whispered, "Hold it, hold it, hold it now!" and as the eagles once again came crashing into the hall, all the Fariets individually put their hands together, and together, they opened their hands.

Swoosh! A loud powerful blue band was thrown from the Fariets, and it shot the eagles out of the hall and onto the ground under the trees.

"That will hold them off for just a few minutes!" yelled Fariet Ut. "How many were there?" he asked.

One of the guards yelled, "It is just the four of them, sir."

Fariet Ut then asked, "Was Kanel among them?"

The guard responded, "No, sir. The flock split into several groups when they left the land of Cain."

King Daniel and Queen Elena then went to find their daughters. "We need to get out of here!" exclaimed King Daniel.

Queen Lizzet then ordered, "Fariets! Take the Geminis now!"

Quickly the five hundred Fariets went to the Geminis and held on to them, and they all took flight away from the colony. The thousands that stayed behind went down the trees to create a distraction from the White Eagles. As they were being flown away, King Daniel looked behind, and all he could see were bright lights going down the trees to attack the White Eagles. Soon, all the trees began to cover the lights, and they were soon gone.

At this point in time, the Geminis were flying high in the air along the treetops. In the distance, the Geminis could see beautiful trees, forests, mountains, and the entire world of Heirthia. It was truly breathtaking. Each of the Geminis was being carried by many Fariets.

Little Princess Violet didn't need that many, but the Fariets were extraprotective of her and Katalina, the two princesses. Then within twelve miles of flight from the Fariets' home, they began to descend.

"What is happening? Why are we landing?" asked King Daniel.

"Sire, we can no longer fly," exclaimed Fariet Ut, attempting to catch his breath as he was landing. "We only have so much strength and magic in us before we can no longer fly. At this point, sire, we must walk."

Still in the forest, all the Fariets came to a safe landing in a clearing in the forest. "That was fun!" exclaimed Princess Violet as she was let down by the Fariets that were carrying her. "Thank you kindly," she said to one of the Fariets.

"You are welcome, Your Highness," said the Fariet to Princess Violet.

"It is our pleasure to protect and defend the new king and queens of Heirthia," he continued.

"You are very nice. What is your name, dear Fariet?" asked Princess Violet.

"Fariet Elliot, at your service," replied the Fariet as he bowed down. He was a brave little Fariet. He had shoulder-length brown hair and an accent, as though he was from Ireland on Earth.

As the others regrouped, Princess Violet continued talking with Fariet Elliot. "I'm Violeta, but everyone calls me Violet."

"Okay then, I shall call you Princess Violet."

"How old are you, Sir Fariet Elliot?"

Fariet Elliot, not really sure how to answer, said, "Well, in Fariet years, I'm about one hundred years old, but I guess in human years, I'm about thirteen. What about you, Your Majesty?"

"I'm ten, but I'll be eleven in November," she replied in a happy and excited way. Princess Violet, still curious about Fariet Elliot, inquired, "And what do you do for the Fariets?"

"Let's get walking, everyone," commanded King Daniel. He continued, "We need to get moving into the forest before we are seen by the White Eagles."

The Geminis began their journey with the five hundred Fariets into Barrens Forest, still in the land of Castillo, heading east.

As they walked, Fariet Elliot flew next to Princess Violet at the level of her head and answered, "Well, I am what you call a multi-tasker. My primary duty is to protect the outskirts of the colony."

Princess Violet, intrigued at what he was saying, replied, "Oh, so you're a warrior?"

Fariet Elliot, feeling more proud of what he did, smiled and said, "Yes, I guess you can see it that way. My job is to stay watch on the outskirts, and if any intruders are approaching, I warn the colony."

Still walking, Princess Violet asked, "What type of powers do you have?"

Fariet Elliot replied, "Well, all Fariets have just about the same power, but others have it much stronger than the others. You see, when I put my hands together, the inner power within my wings come together and join at my hands. It's like the power is being preserved there. Well, when we open our hands quickly, the power has nowhere else to go. So when we open our hands quickly and shoot them outward, that power is cast out, and it shoots a very powerful energy which can—"

Violet then interrupted and said, "Blast anything you hit."

He replied, "That's right. And we can use that energy to do other things. We can cast spells, make things move, make things fly, and so much more."

Princess Violet voiced, "Wow, I wish I was a Fariet."

Fariet Elliot then looked at Princess Violet and said, "No, you are beautiful the way you are."

Princess Violet, feeling very shy at what Fariet Elliot said, replied, "Thank you," and put her head down.

Fariet Elliot continued, "Plus, you have the Dragon's Claw Wand. You realize—"

Then another Fariet came along and said, "It is the most powerful wand ever known, and it is in the hands of a child."

Fariet Elliot responded, "Fariet Bert, you don't have to be so negative about it. Princess Violet, this is Fariet Bert. He is one of the high leaders of the Fariets. He is in charge of all the watchmen, just like me." Fariet Elliot then whispered, "He's always grumpy."

Fariet Bert then said, "I am not grumpy, I just take things seriously, with great importance, and I speak the truth."

Princess Violet then said, "It's nice to meet you, Fariet Bert."

Fariet Bert, not too happy that a child had the Dragon's Claw Wand, flew forward with the others.

Fariet Elliot continued, "Don't mind him. He's always like that. But in the end, he's really a great Fariet and would die for any of us."

Princess Katalina was then walking close to her sister and Fariet Elliot, and Princess Violet said, "Katalina, this is Fariet Elliot, he is a watchman warrior."

Princess Katalina then looked at Fariet Elliot and said "Hi, nice to meet you."

Fariet Elliot, being the gentleman he was, said, "The pleasure is all mine, Princess."

Suddenly, King Daniel and several of the Fariet leaders ahead stopped. King Daniel raised his hand and signaled for everyone to get down. Princess Violet, very afraid, began to get nervous. "What is it? Is it the wolves?"

Fariet Elliot went to her and said, "I am here, Princess, I am here to protect you." Fariet Elliot got in front of Princess Violet.

Then all of a sudden, there were creatures about forty yards ahead of them crossing their path. There were sixteen of them.

"What are they?" asked Princess Katalina.

Fariet Elliot whispered, "Teaks. They are called Teaks. They serve the Dark King."

Princess Katalina whispered back, "What are they doing here?"

"They are looking for you, my princess," replied Fariet Elliot.

Teaks were human-like creatures with dark red eyes. They had the bodies of humans and all the characteristics of humans, but they had three very small and short horns growing out of their heads. They had no hair on their heads, and they had dark brown skin. Their bodies were very muscular, and their hands had sharp claws.

All they wore were garments that covered their hip and thigh area and straps around their shoulders crossing their chests. Their feet were that of a Falcon, with sharp claws.

Princess Violet, a bit too scared, began to cry, but was holding it in. Then she could hold it no longer and let out one small whimper. The Geminis and the Fariets turned around.

"Stop!" yelled one of the Teaks. "What was that?" he yelled again.

Another Teak came forward and said, "I heard nothing, sire." He then began walking slowly toward where he heard the cry. As he looked down into the forest, he could not see anything. There were large trees and knee-high grass. He took a few more steps and continued looking. He then took in a deep smell with his nose. Another Teak then approached, "What did you hear?"

He replied, "I thought I heard a cry." But the forest was silent, just a small breeze.

"There's nothing here." Hearing nothing more, he walked back where the others were, and they continued walking and left. The Geminis and Fariets all waited for several minutes until they knew it was clear.

"Who were they?" asked King Daniel.

"Were they looking for us?" asked Queen Elena.

Fariet Julip, the Fariet leader, said, "They are Teaks, and, yes, they are looking for you."

"How do you know?" asked Queen Elena.

"The Teaks are from the pits of Helum, and they only live to serve Seitor. If they are this far into the forest, they have one thing in mind: the Quint Fey powers," continued Fariet Julip.

King Daniel ordered, "Get three of your Fariets to follow them and report when they are clear of this area. If there are sixteen here, there are certainly more out there. We will continue walking. Have them catch up."

Fariet Ut replied, "Right away, sire."

Fariet Bert then pointed to two Fariets and also selected Fariet Elliot. "You three, go and follow them for one mile, and make sure they do not return to our path. If so, you must warn us. After the mile, return to us. We shall be heading northeast toward King Jonis's castle, which is where we are headed. Fariet Ut, I need you to stay with the group for protection."

Fariet Julip and the Geminis then turned around so as to continue walking.

"No." Fariet Elliot made no move to go. Fariet Julip and the Geminis turned back around.

Fariet Bert replied, "Excuse me?"

Fariet Elliot, flying, said, "No."

"Fariet, you better have a good explanation for this, or I will banish you," demanded Fariet Julip.

"Forgive me, sir, but, I, well, I can't, I—" Fariet Elliot then looked at Princess Violet and said, "I wish to stay with the child."

"Fariet Elliot, you have no choice! You are ordered as I commanded, or you will be banished," said Fariet Julip.

The Geminis looked on at what was happening.

"I am sorry, sir, but I must stay with the child."

Fariet Julip, getting more frustrated, said, "Fariet Elliot, you are not to be disobedient. I am the power and leader of the Fariets in the absence of our Queen Lizzet, and I order you the duty of watchmen.

Fariet Elliot looked down and said "Sir, I cannot go for I have given Princess Violet my heartsdust."

All the Fariets were in shock at what he had done. They all gasped for air at what was happening.

Fariet Julip then yelled, "You have given her your heartsdust! This is forbidden, Fariet Elliot!" Fariet Julip yelled again.

Princess Violet, still kneeling on the ground, slowly looked up, and as she did, a light illuminated from her neck. She was wearing a beautiful glass ball with dust in it.

"What is that?" asked King Daniel.

One of the women Fariets that was leading the Geminis said, "He has done what every Fariet is forbidden to do. He has given his life to serve your daughter."

Both King Daniel and Queen Elena looked at each other and then looked at Princess Violet.

Fariet Burt exclaimed, "I will—" but King Daniel quickly said, "You, quiet."

King Daniel then walked over to Fariet Elliot and said, "Why did you do this?"

Fariet Elliot, intimidated at King Daniel's presence, said, "She was afraid and was about to cry much louder. The whimper she let out was much greater. It was a scream, sire."

King Daniel questioned, "A scream?"

Fariet Elliot continued, "Yes, sire, a scream. As she was to let it out, I made my declaration and swore that I would never leave her side, that I would protect her to my death, and that I would serve her always. At that point in time, sire, my heartsdust was automatically removed from me, and it went to her."

Fariet Elliot stayed quiet for a moment and continued, "If it pleases Your Majesty, I shall stay with the child to honor and protect her as her guardian always."

"What happens if he doesn't?" asked Queen Elena.

Fariet Julip answered, "Fariet Elliot will automatically be banished for not serving his purpose, and he will die."

"No, Daddy!" exclaimed Princess Violet. She ran to her father and continued, "Daddy, please don't banish him. He has given his life to protect me."

King Daniel looked at his daughter and said, "I know what I want, Violet, but what do you want?"

Princess Violet looked at her father and then looked at Fariet Elliot and said, "I want him to be my guardian because that is what he wants."

Fariet Bert then exclaimed, "But he has no choice, and he has broken the forbidden law of the Fariets, so therefore, he must die for what he has done." Fariet Bert then went to Fariet Elliot so as to take action against him and banish him.

"Stop!" ordered King Daniel.

Fariet Bert stopped and looked at King Daniel and said, "Your Highness, this is not any of your business. This is a dealing with the Fariets' kingdom and its law." Fariet Bert went to Fariet Elliot, put his hands together, and was about to banish Fariet Elliot.

"Stop, or I shall banish you and your kingdom from the land of Heirthia forever!" said King Daniel as he raised his sword toward Fariet Bert. Everything went quiet. King Daniel continued, "As king of the entire world of Heirthia, I will never deny anyone the gift of giving. This law Yesu commands, and that law is above all else. The honorable Fariet Elliot has given his life to serve the princess, and therefore, I shall grant him his deepest desire, and no one shall take that from him."

Fariet Julip then went to Fariet Bert and said, "The king has spoken."

Fariet Julip then went to Fariet Elliot and said, "You have done something that has never been done before. It is honorable and a selfless act to protect someone you care for."

Fariet Julip then paused for a moment and continued, "Therefore, I too grant you your wish. By the power vested in me, Fariet Elliot, the guardian protector, you shall honor, serve, and protect Princess Violet at all times."

Fariet Elliot then looked at Princess Violet and then looked back at Fariet Julip and said, "I will protect."

Fariet Julip continued, "Then it is done."

Blast! Everyone was thrown as a large explosion came upon them.

14

THE SEPARATION

“WHERE ARE WE?” Princess Katalina slowly came to from being knocked out, only to find out that both her hands and feet were chained to a wall. Her hands were chained upward, and her feet could not move more than a few inches.

“Katalina, Violet!” yelled Queen Elena.

“Mommy, Mommy, Mommy!” yelled Princess Violet, who was also chained to the wall.

"Violet, I'm right next to you," replied her sister. Princess Katalina could see Princess Violet with the little light that was upon them from a ceiling hole.

"Girls, I'm right over here, but I can't see you. My hands and feet are chained to the wall," voiced Queen Elena. Queen Elena had realized that they were prisoners chained in a dungeon somewhere mysterious.

Princess Violet then began to cry, "Mommy, I'm scared. I need you!"

Queen Elena, feeling that her daughter needed comfort, said, "Sweetie, I am right here not far from you. I can't see you, but please know that I am here for you. Daddy is on his way to help us."

Then there was a whispering voice. "Daddy's coming for you, Daddy's coming for you." Something in the darkness laughed in a very deep and evil way. Then two other laughs came from the darkness in the room.

Queen Elena could not figure whether they were persons or creatures because they sounded like hyenas.

"Daddy's not coming for you because you are mine!" said the voice in the darkness of the room. It was silent for a moment.

There was a little light shining upon Queen Elena, but she could only see a few feet around her. "Who are you, and what do you want?" she demanded.

"Who are we? Who are you to ask your master questions?" the voice came.

"We are the new—" said Princess Katalina.

"Nobody. We are nobody but peasants on a travel," Queen Elena interrupted.

"The new nobody?" questioned the voice. It then continued, "You are not peasants. You were with Fariets, and Fariets stick with their own. For them to help you is because you are someone worth protecting."

There was another slow and evil laugh. Then Queen Elena could hear footsteps coming toward her, and it was not of one person but of three, and she knew they were watching her.

Again the laughs came from various directions, and Queen Elena began to get very nervous from what was coming from the darkness, but she could not see. She began to sweat.

Princess Violet then pleaded, "Please, just please let us go, and you can have all our money."

The room went silent. Princess Violet was crying very softly, afraid.

"Quiet!" yelled the thing in the darkness so loudly that it echoed through the dungeon they were in.

At that point, Princess Katalina began to get very nervous, and so tears began to run down her cheeks as well.

The voice then returned and said, "Mother and daughters, what shall I do with you?"

Queen Elena, in a state of panic, yelled, "Please, just leave us alone, and you will get what you want."

The voice responded from the dark, "I want to know who you are."

"We are nobody. Just peasants!" responded Queen Elena.

Again the room went silent.

"Hello?" replied Queen Elena. All of a sudden, Elena caught a shadow to her left, but it was too fast, so she could not see what it was. Again she caught another shadow, but this time to her right. She squinted her eyes so as to see better into the darkness, but she could not see anything.

As she peered into the darkness, she could hear one step of something getting closer, then another step, then another, but still she could not see.

Growl! Out of the darkness came a creature yelling at the top of its lungs, and Queen Elena could finally see it. It was a creature that had the head of a hyena, with large sharp teeth, but the body structure of a human. Queen Elena was afraid and closed her eyes.

"Elena, Katalina, Violet!" yelled King Daniel back in the forest.

Slowly but surely, all the Fariets were coming to from the blast. As soon as Fariet Elliot was awakened, he knew what had happened. He had failed his first duty to protect Princess Violet.

"Elena! Katalina! Violet!" once again King Daniel yelled with all his might.

"They are gone, sire! We have looked within the last mile in diameter," said Fariet Ut, who had already gathered many Fariets to search the area.

"Was this the work of the Teaks?" asked King Daniel.

Fariet Bert responded, "I believe not. The Teaks are more brutal. You would not have been spared, sire. They would have tried to kill us all to take the Quint Fey." Fariet Ut then added, "No, I believe this is the work of the Prosecs."

King Daniel questioned, "Prosecs?"

Fariet Julip continued, "Yes, Prosecs. They are catlike creatures, like hyenas from your world, but with human-shaped bodies. They are simply thieves, and I assure you, they know not what they have in their possession. We have little time, though. We must hurry and find them before it's too late."

King Daniel, even more concerned, said, "Before it's too late for what?"

Fariet Julip, looked at King Daniel, then looked at Fariet Bert and Fariet Ut with great concern and said, "Before they are eaten."

King Daniel stood there with the shock of his life and yelled, commanded, and declared, "We must find them now! Every Fariet, spread out by ten feet and create a circle. We must enlarge this circle and continue on until we find them. They are our priority, and we will stop at nothing until we do find them. Remember, the attack did not happen too long ago, so they should have not gone far. If you find a cave, gather another with you and search it!"

The Fariets and King Daniel created a circle and began their search, but meanwhile, Queen Elena was still being interrogated in the dungeon.

"I ask you again, who are you, and what were you doing with the Fariets?" demanded the creature that had finally come out of the darkness. All of a sudden, Queen Elena heard something above her. It was another creature, but it was climbing and holding on to the wall with its claws.

"Let's eat her."

Then another one came but this one climbed and held on to the wall to her right. That creature was slowly moving close to Queen Elena, and so Queen Elena closed her eyes and moved her head to her left so as to get away from the creature. Slowly, the creature to the right got close to Queen Elena and put its nose against her neck and took a deep smell of her.

"Her flesh is fresh. It is different from the others, Laris." Then the creature stuck its tongue out and licked the side of Queen Elena's cheek while her tears came down. It then said, "I say we eat her now."

"No!" exclaimed Laris, the creature that was standing in front of Queen Elena, clearly the leader of the Prosecs. "You," he ordered a Prosec at the entrance to the dungeon, "go and let the Dark King know of our findings. I have heard the Dark King is searching for something, and these peasants may be it."

The Prosec quickly went and gathered five other Prosecs, and in a hurry, they left to advise the Dark King of their findings.

"Maybe you are the ones he seeks. If so, then I will be rewarded."

Laris made an evil laugh and as he walked out of the room, Princess Violet whispered in fear, "Just give it to him, Mommy."

Laris stopped in his walk. "Give me what?" he asked.

Princess Violet, knowing she had said too much, replied, "Well, all that we have, so we can be let go." Laris approached little Violet and got very close to her and made a fearful growl.

"Give me what!" he yelled.

"Leave her alone, you animal!" yelled Queen Elena from the top of her lungs.

Quickly Laris went to Queen Elena's right, extended his left hand and claw, and grabbed Queen Elena by the neck. He grabbed it so tight that blood began to slowly drip.

"Oh, the blood, it is warm and fresh," he exclaimed.

"Please let us eat her now!" yelled the other Prosec.

Laris then exclaimed, "Tell me who you are, or I will let them eat you!"

"We are no one. Now let us go!" she yelled but in a forceful way as she was being choked. Laris then raised his right hand and, with his claw, forcefully stabbed Queen Elena on the chest and slowly began to cut her open. Elena yelled in pain.

"Stop, stop!" yelled both Princesses Katalina and Violet, crying even harder now.

"Take a bite," he ordered the Prosec to the left. Queen Elena yelled in pain even louder as the Prosec to the left bit into her left shoulder.

"All you have to do is tell me who you are, and he will stop."

Being the brave, strong, and valiant woman she was, Queen Elena would not budge.

However, Laris said, "Well then, if you will not talk, maybe your daughters will."

Laris then walked over to where Princesses Katalina and Violet were, and the two Prosecs that were with Queen Elena followed him there. Queen Elena could barely see her two girls' faces, as the room was pitch-dark.

"No!" Queen Elena yelled. "Leave them alone. They are just children."

"Mommy, he's coming to me," yelled Princess Katalina.

Laris then went toward Princess Katalina, and with his left hand and finger, he lifted his claw. He didn't stab Princess Katalina, but he placed his claw on her left arm and began to slowly cut it downward. Princess Katalina began to scream in pain as the claw began to cut her flesh little by little. Laris then placed his right hand and claw on Princess Violet's right arm and did the same thing. Princess Violet then began to cry and yell.

Queen Elena let out one last scream, "No!" and she cried profusely in frustration as she was helpless. Looking toward Princesses Katalina and Violet, Laris threatened "Tell me or I will—"

Then there was a bright light for a split second.

Laris turned toward the back of the room, but there was nothing there. "What was that?" he asked.

One of the Prosecs responded, "What was what?"

Laris once again asked, "That, the bright light?"

The other Prosec answered, "I don't know. I didn't see it, master."

Deciding his eyes had been playing tricks on him, Laris once again looked at Princesses Katalina and Violet and said with an evil voice, "Tell me or I will—"

Growl. A long but faint growl was heard in the room with them.

"Stop growling in my ear," ordered Laris to his other Prosecs. Laris looked at the Prosec on the right and said, "Wasn't that you?"

Swoosh! Quickly the Prosec on the left was gone.

Laris and the Prosec on the right looked toward the left where the other Prosec had been, but he was gone.

"Guards!" yelled Laris, and as he did, five others entered the room with torches, and so there was little more light. "What is it?"

Swoosh! The Prosec next to the leader was then pulled away.

"What is going on?" yelled Laris. The other Prosecs gathered with Laris, and they walked toward Queen Elena, and as they approached her chains, she was gone. Her chains just hung there, broken off.

"Where is she?"

Then again, a very slow but intimidating growl came from the dark part at the end of the room.

"What is it?" asked Princess Violet as she looked at her sister.

The Prosec heard this and looked at Princess Katalina as she slowly replied, "Mommy."

Then came a very loud growl toward the Prosecs.

Swoop! One of them was taken into the darkness, and a struggle was heard. Two of the Prosecs went toward the struggle to attack and help, and there was more growling, fighting, and tearing of flesh. Then a scream, but it was one of the Prosecs. The struggle and noise was all over the room.

Laris stood there next to Princess Katalina with the other two Prosecs, and he ordered in a scared voice, "Go and kill it."

The two Prosecs slowly went into the darkness, and one of them was taken. The last one stood there and began to whimper.

He turned around and looked at Laris, and *swoosh*, he was gone, and he let out a scream. He continued to scream, but then you could hear a bone breaking, and there was no more sound.

The room went silent.

Laris stood there next to Princesses Katalina and Violet, and the three of them peered into the darkness. The three squinted their eyes, and behold, two bright yellow eyes were looking back at them. The three became very afraid at what they were seeing, but then the eyes were gone.

Slowly, they could hear steps coming closer and closer to them. In a last-ditch effort, the leader ran toward the door, but then *swoosh*, he was lifted to the air, and there was a faint scream, a bone breaking, and then the room became silent.

Princesses Katalina and Violet stared into the darkness in front of them, and they could hear something coming toward them.

"Mommy!" said Princess Violet with such peace and relief when she saw her mom.

"Mommy, are you okay?" asked Princess Katalina.

Queen Elena looked bold and confident in what had just happened. She had a bit of blood dripping at her mouth.

"Mommy, is that your blood on your mouth?" asked Princess Violet.

Queen Elena looked at them as she wiped her mouth with the back of her hand. She squinted her eyes at where Laris lay and said in a serious voice, "You can do what you want with me, but do not touch my children."

Queen Elena then reached back toward the creature and found the key to the locks and helped her children down. The three then went out of the dungeon and noticed that they were in a cave.

They saw light in the distance, and they escaped into the day. Quickly they realized they were still in the forest. Not really knowing where to go, Queen Elena took the route less traveled and walked into the woods with her girls.

Meanwhile, the Prosecs arrived at King Julas's kingdom, where Seitor awaited word on the whereabouts of the Geminis. Because of the Prosecs' quick speed, they had arrived very quickly.

"What do these creatures want?" asked King Julas. "They are worth nothing to us. Get rid of them," he continued.

Seitor then interrupted and said, "King Julas, why are you banishing our friends. They are not worthless creatures. They are creatures we honor. Tell me, why are you here?"

"Your Majesty, we come with good news. We have captured a woman, and we have heard that you are seeking her," said the Prosec.

"Woman, well, I am looking for more than that. Was she alone?" asked Seitor. Everyone in the room stared and waited for the Prosec to respond.

He then spoke, "No, she is with her two daughters."

Seitor responded, "Who else was she with?"

"They were with a man and the Fariets," responded the Prosec.

Seitor then got close to the Prosec and said, "Where is the man?"

The creature, looking afraid at Seitor's demeanor, said, "We left him in the woods, sir."

"What?" yelled Seitor. "You left him in the woods alive?"

"Yes, all we wanted were the girls. We have the three of them in our cave."

"Gather the army, King Julas. Kanel, gather your eagles now, and go before us to the Prosecs' cave. I want the three females dead, and take the powers. Go! Now!"

Quickly, Kanel let out an eagle's scream. He then took to flight while the other White Eagles each grabbed the five Prosecs and headed toward their cave. Cauffa and his pack were there, also waiting for orders.

"Cauffa, now is your chance to get the father. This time, the entire kingdom of Fariets won't be there to stop you. Take your pack and head north toward that region. Find the man's scent!"

Cauffa, in his human body form, bowed his head, and he and his pack leaped and transformed into their wolf forms and headed northwest. They cried bone-chilling howls. Their search had begun. Seitor quickly got on Rasier, his black horse with red eyes, and took off onto the trail toward the land of Castillo.

"We battle now!" yelled Seitor. Soon his entire army were off. They had finally found the new King and Queens of Heirthia.

"Girls, quickly, we need to hurry!" whispered Queen Elena.

"But, Mom, we don't even know where we are going," replied Princess Katalina.

"I know, sweetheart, but we have to go in the opposite direction of the trail. We must follow where the sun is setting. That will lead us east, where your father was headed. Those creatures will likely be on the trail. We must go the opposite way and move quickly away from them."

Princess Violet, feeling very scared and emotional, said, "I miss Daddy." She then began to cry.

Queen Elena knelt down on one knee and comforted her daughter. "I know, mi amor, I know. We will find him. But that is why we need to keep moving." She embraced her daughter so she would calm down. They then continued on their journey through the unknown. Quickly, night began to fall as the three walked.

"Mommy, I am so tired. Can we please stop and sleep?" asked Princess Violet.

"Well, it is kind of late, Mom, and we haven't heard anything following us," continued Princess Katalina.

"Okay, we need to stop and find a safe place to sleep. We need to move quickly, girls, before it gets too dark," said Queen Elena.

The three walked a little more until they came upon some trees that were next to a hill with boulders.

"Here, girls. I think we can hide between the boulders for the night."

"This is great, Mommy. Let's start a fire!" exclaimed Princess Violet.

"We can't, Violet," replied Princess Katalina.

"Why not?" asked Princess Violet in a confused voice.

Princess Katalina said, "It's because those creatures, the wolves, and even the White Eagles will be looking for us. They will stop at nothing. If we have fire, they will be able to see this at night."

Queen Elena, looking very proud of her daughter's quick thinking, said, "That's right, Violet, not tonight. Once we are with Daddy, then we can. For now, we just need to rest so we can be ready to keep walking in the morning."

"But I'm cold," added Violet.

"I know, I know, and that is why the three of us are going to cuddle up so we can stay warm," replied Queen Elena. They then squeezed between the boulders and settled close to each other.

"Mommy, can I ask you a question?" asked Princess Violet.

"How did you do it?"

"How did I do what?" asked Queen Elena, although she already knew what Princess Violet was talking about.

"You know, turn into whatever it was that you turned into back at the cave," she asked.

"Well, remember the angel Michael?"

"Yeah, I remember," replied Princess Violet.

"Well, remember I was given the Lion Heart Medallion."

"I know, but, well, how did you change? Like, did you just tell it to turn you into a mama lioness?" the little child continued.

Queen Elena lay there with her daughters and smiled.

"Well, sweetie, I guess when I knew that you and your sister were going to get hurt and when I heard your cries, something inside of me just grew. I mean, my whole body got really hot, and my heart grew stronger and stronger, urging to help you, and when this happened, all I remember was the medallion lighting up, and then…"

"What?" asked little Princess Violet, looking very intrigued.

"Well, my whole body changed. My body grew larger, my muscles got bigger, and I remember claws coming out of my hands, and then my whole body just followed," replied Queen Elena.

"Did it hurt?" asked Princess Katalina.

"No, not at all. All I remember was feeling very hot. I guess my mind and heart were focused on you two," replied Queen Elena.

"Mommy, I know it's called the Lion Heart Medallion, but did you turn into a regular lion or what?" asked Princess Violet in a curious voice.

"Oh, I was a lioness all right, but I turned into a very big lioness. Not like they are on Earth. Maybe two times as big."

Princess Violet, looking even more curious, asked, "And when you were the mama lioness, could you recognize us?"

Queen Elena, looking at her daughter and running her hand through Princess Violet's hair, said, "Yes, sweetheart. My mind and heart did not change. Only my physical body did, and it only changed to protect you."

At that moment, Princess Violet felt at peace. She closed her eyes, and she was fast asleep. Princess Katalina soon followed after she whispered, "Thank you, Mommy. I love you."

The three were tired from the adventures of the day, and as Queen Elena lay there with her daughters, she prayed, "Lord, please keep us safe tonight. Please bless us with sleep, and please take us back to Daniel. Thank you for all these opportunities. We know you are protecting us. In your name, I pray." Queen Elena, knowing Yesu was protecting them, fell fast asleep.

About ten miles east from his girls, King Daniel camped with the Fariets. They had searched high and low for their queen and princesses but had had no luck. King Daniel, feeling and looking very frustrated and saddened at not knowing how his girls were doing, paced the campsite. The Fariets Bert and Julip continuously reminded their king that there was nothing more they could do for the night. King Daniel, in a very low moment, broke into tears. He sat down by the campfire, and tears came running down his cheeks.

He then said, "I have never left my family alone like this—ever. Please understand. I live, breath, work, and love them. They are my world. They are my everything. Without them, I have no purpose to live."

Fariet Julip asked, "How long have you and the queen been together, sire?"

King Daniel smiled a bit and said, "Well, back on Earth, we have been together for twenty-one years, and we have been married for sixteen years."

Fariet Bert responded, "Wow, and you look so young, sire. That long! When did you first meet?"

King Daniel, looking much calmer, answered, "She was fourteen years old, and I was fifteen. We actually met at a basketball game in high school."

Both Fariet Bert and Julip, looking confused, said, "Basketball? High school?"

King Daniel let out a small smile.

Fariet Bert then exclaimed, "And he smiles!"

King Daniel replied, "I'll explain those things later. When I first saw her, she was and continues to be the only girl I have ever met that has truly taken my breath away. As I sat at that game, I was actually waiting for a friend of mine to show up. I then spotted my friend, and behold, the most beautiful girl was right behind her. I could not keep my eyes off her. I noticed my friend walking up the bleachers—you know, chairs—and that girl behind her, with her beautiful radiant smile and light brown eyes, she was perfect just the way she was. She had braces, and, oh, I remember that beautiful mouth full of metal. It was wonderful. Even the football players all turned around and followed her with their eyes as she walked up the stairs. As it turns out, she was with my friend, and so she was both our friends, and they sat right behind me. My friend introduced us, and for the first time ever, I was nervous around a girl—a perfect girl, I might add. Both girls kinda turned around to meet and greet other friends of ours, but I just stood there looking at her. I could not keep my eyes off her." King Daniel paused as he continued to stare at the campfire.

"Go on," said Fariet Julip.

"Well, as I stood there, I looked at her eyes and smiled, and even though I had just met her, I wondered what it would be like to be married to her. The day she said 'I do' was the happiest day of my life."

King Daniel had been staring at the campfire so long that he actually did not realize he had a crowd of Fariets listening to his story. Even Fariets Elliot and Ut were there. They were all intrigued. One of the Fariets, a woman, said, "That is a beautiful story. That, Your Highness, is a true love story. Love her, keep her, be there for her."

Ending the evening, Fariet Julip said to King Daniel, "I promise, sire, we will find them. We will find them."

15

THE LAND OF CASTILLO

HOWL!

Queen Elena was awakened by the howling of a wolf pack. It was very early in the morning, and the sun was just beginning to come out. It was at a very far distance, but she knew they were going to find her scent eventually.

Again she heard a howl in the distance.

"They're at the cave," she whispered. "Katalina, Violet, we need to get moving."

Neither girl woke up as they were exhausted.

"Girls, the wolves are coming," she said in a very worried voice. When the girls heard this, they quickly woke up.

"The wolves, the wolves, the wolves!" voiced Princess Violet in a trembling voice, and in a haste, they were back to walking in the forest.

The White Eagles had arrived at the cave with the Prosecs. They all entered into the cave only to find the massacre of Prosecs. The Prosecs went into their cave and immediately began to mourn at the death of their leader, Laris. Kanel quickly realized the queen and princesses had escaped. Cauffa and his pack arrived at the cave sometime thereafter. Kanel, walking out of the cave, said, "Cauffa, the woman and children are gone. Can you find their scent outside?"

Both Kanel and Cauffa walked outside, and Cauffa immediately caught the scent. "I found it!" Cauffa exclaimed.

"We are also going for the hunt!" exclaimed the remaining Prosecs. "They killed our leader. We now fight for Seitor. We will gather all of our fellow brothers to fight." Then an army of twenty Teaks arrived.

Kanel looked on, and he greeted Dawson, the commander of the Teaks. "Dawson, we are on the trail for the human women and her children. The Dark King has ordered their deaths. Kill them and do with their bodies as you wish, but you must recover their powers, the Quint Fey."

Dawson replied, "We will join the hunt and kill all."

Kanel ordered, "Prosecs, go with Cauffa and find them. I will alert the Dark King." Kanel took flight with the other White Eagles. Their wings were useless in the forest. Cauffa and the Prosecs went on the search for Queen Elena and the princesses at a fast run. Trailing them were the one hundred Teaks.

Queen Elena and the girls quickly walked in the forest. They walked and walked and walked. After some time of walking, the sun had finally begun to rise.

"Mommy, can we take a break?" asked Princess Violet.

"Sure, but just a few minutes," said Queen Elena.

Princess Katalina added, "I'm so hungry."

In the distance they heard several wolves howling. All three became afraid and, in haste, began to run. The wolves were still at a distance, but they, with the Prosecs, were growing closer. The wolves and Prosecs were gaining quickly on them.

"They're coming, Mommy, they're coming. Please turn into a lion!" yelled Princess Violet.

Queen Elena, being so tired, tried to concentrate while she was running, but the medallion would not work.

The girls continued to run, but they were growing tired. Again they heard the howls of the wolves.

Princess Katalina then turned around as she was running, and in the very far distance, she caught a glimpse of the wolves. "I see them, Mom, I see them! They're coming!" she yelled.

There was nothing they could do. The wolves and Prosecs were too fast, and the three had walked and run all they could. Queen Elena stopped the girls and placed them behind her as they awaited the attack. Queen Elena placed her right hand on the medallion and called for her transformation.

"I call the Lion Heart, I call the Lion Heart, I call the Lion Heart!" but nothing happened. Fear was getting in the way.

Princess Katalina called her bow out and closed her eyes. She pulled back on the strings, but nothing happened. She tried over and over and over again, but it would not work. She then began to cry in frustration. So did Princess Violet. They were too afraid and knew they were about to die, and there was nothing Queen Elena could do about it.

Cauffa and the Prosecs saw the three girls in the distance, and Cauffa and his pack let out one last howl before their final attack. All twelve wolves and five Prosecs grew closer and closer as the Teaks trailed right behind. As they approached, a wolf leaped toward Princess Katalina and opened its massive jaws, but right before it bit into Princess Katalina, she lifted her bow and, in one last effort, pulled back the string! *Swoosh!* An arrow came flying through the air and struck the wolf right in the forehead, but the arrow did not come from her bow.

The wolf came crashing down on the floor.

"In Nomine Yesu!" yelled Young Ladam to the other Youngs with him, all young and handsome youth with British accents. Several arrows then came flying through the air toward the wolves and Prosecs. Two more wolves were struck by arrows and one of the Prosecs, killing them instantly.

Queen Elena did not know what was happening, but she knew they had indeed been saved. Princess Katalina watched as Young Ladam drew his sword and went swinging toward the wolf pack. Seven Youngs, including Young Ladam, were on the attack with their swords. Quickly the wolves and Prosecs went into attack against the Youngs. The Youngs swung their swords back and forth to keep the giant wolves from attacking.

Queen Elena once again tried to call upon the medallion, but she was too exhausted. Young Ladam stood in front of Princess Katalina and fought one of the wolves. The wolf came flying through the air, and Young Ladam struck his sword upward and drove the sword through the wolf. It came crashing to the floor, dead. Young Jason ran forward and swung his sword toward a Prosec. The Prosec moved back screaming, and as the sword swung by, the Prosec leaped forward and grabbed Young Jason.

It then bit Young Jason on the shoulder, and he yelled in pain. Young Joey went toward Young Jason and pulled the Prosec off of him. The Prosec turned around to attack Young Joey, and then *swoosh*, Young Jason cut the Prosec.

At this point the Youngs were fighting bravely, but then the Teak warriors were coming, and they were armed with swords and axes.

Young Ladam looked up and knew they were outnumbered. Little by little, the Youngs and the queen and her princesses were moving away.

"Get them out of here!" yelled Young Ladam to the others.

Young James went to the queen and said, "We need to get you out of here. The Teaks are coming."

Young James and Young Joseph began to lead the way in the opposite direction of where the battle was taking place as Young Ladam, Young Jason, Young Joey, Young Jeremiah, and Young John continued to fend off the pack and the Prosecs. With the Teaks right behind, it was going to be a difficult battle. Someone or something would certainly die.

However, as Young James and Young Joseph were treading away, Young James saw in the distance what the Teaks had done. They had formed a circle around the battle area. They all were surrounded. There was no way out, and so they all would have to fight to the death. Queen Elena saw this and had this look in her eyes, as though she knew their fate.

Meanwhile, King Daniel and the Fariets were searching a distance away to the east. As they searched through the forest, several Fariets came into contact with King Daniel and his group of Fariets.

"Sire, a battle to the east of here has begun," said a Fariet, reporting to Fariet Julip and Fariet Ut.

"Are the queen and princesses there?" asked King Daniel. The Fariet turned and looked at King Daniel and was very hesitant to answer.

"Please, are my wife and children there?"

The Fariet looked down and said, "Yes."

Fariet Julip looked at King Daniel and went toward him. Fariet Julip raised his hands to hold King Daniel back. Worry left King Daniel, and he took on a battle stance. His forehead wrinkled up with determination, his eyebrows lowered, and his eyes focused.

Fariet Julip said, "Now, King Daniel, let's make a plan of action. Don't react with anger, sire."

King Daniel began to walk east to where the battle was taking place.

"Sire?" called Fariet Julip, but King Daniel would not answer.

"Sire?" Called Fariet Ut, but King Daniel would not answer. He was focused, and nothing was going to stop him, and all the Fariets there knew this. Fariets Julip and Bert got in front of King Daniel so as to stop him.

The two put their hands on King Daniel's chest.

"Fariets, come help us!" exclaimed Fariet Julip. Fariet Ut and many of the Fariets got together in front of King Daniel and laid hands on him to stop him from reacting this way, but it was no use. King Daniel was focused and determined to save his family. King Daniel, looking straight toward the east but not saying a word, stopped.

"Thank you for stopping, sire. We will go, but we need to make a plan of attack," said Fariet Bert. King Daniel, still looking toward the east and not saying anything, slowly reached with his right hand and called for Yesu's Sword. Fariet Julip saw this and said, "We're making a plan—" But then the sword lit up, and Fariet Julip and all the Fariets knew there was nothing that was going to stop King Daniel. King Daniel burst into a very fast run. All the Fariets flew after him, but they could barely catch up.

"He is going to get killed!" yelled Fariet Ut.

Fariet Bert continued, "Do I shoot in front of him to stop him, Fariet Julip?"

Fariet Julip was hesitant but responded, "Just don't hit him."

Fariet Bert flew as fast as he could to catch up to King Daniel and quickly put his hands together.

Blast! A shot was fired in front of King Daniel. The blast caused dirt to fly up in the air, and a cloud was lifted in front of the Fariets. As the air cleared up, King Daniel was still running. Fariet Bert was amazed.

Again, Fariet Bert shot out, and *blast!* Again the dirt shot up, and a cloud came up. King Daniel was still running. Fariet Bert was about to shoot again for a third time, but Fariet Julip yelled as they continued to fly, "Stop! It's no use. He will not stop, and we cannot stop him. He is our king, and we must help him!"

The Fariets gave up trying to stop King Daniel from running into battle. Instead, all the Fariets came together right behind King Daniel, and they all were flying with him in support. All the Fariets were flying, and they knew the battle was approaching.

The Teaks were quickly approaching Queen Elena and the princesses. The Youngs continued to fight off the wolf pack and Prosecs. Young Ladam and the others got together with the queen and princesses and surrounded them.

"Fight to the death, Youngs!" yelled Young Ladam.

The wolves and Prosecs began to close in, and in a strategic move, all the wolves leaped toward the Youngs at the same time. The Youngs continued to fend off the wolves, but one of the wolves grabbed hold of Young Joey's leg and dragged him into the forest.

"Young Joey!" yelled Young James.

One of the Prosecs jumped onto Young Joey and bit into his neck. Another wolf came and leaped onto Young Joey and bit into the side of Joey's chest. There were just too many for the Youngs to handle. Young James freed himself from being cornered by the wolf attacking him and went toward Young Joey. He approached and swung his sword toward the Prosec and stabbed him right through the heart. The Prosec died instantly. James then swung backward, and cut the neck of the wolf biting Joey's chest. The wolf too died instantly.

The other wolf let go and backed up. The wolf crouched and slowly moved forward. Young James held his sword toward the wolf and began to drag Young Joey toward the others. Young James looked up and saw that the Teaks were running toward them.

As the Teaks were running and approaching the Youngs, they pulled their swords for battle. The Youngs knew they were outnumbered and were going to die. Young Ladam looked at his mates and said "Gentlemen, fight bravely and don't hold back. Either way, live or die, you will go home."

As they stood there waiting for the Teaks, exhausted, they held up their swords. The Teak in the front line went straight for Young Ladam. A wolf leaped at Young Ladam as the Teak swung his sword so as to make certain Young Ladam would be killed. Just then, just in time, King Daniel arrived and leaped over Young Ladam from the boulder behind them and drove Yesu's Sword right into the wolf's back, killing it instantly. King Daniel fell to the ground, rolled forward, and, in the same motion, got up, and swung his sword from left to right and held up his shield to the Teak that was there. The Teak fell as it was cut badly. King Daniel ran forward and again swung his sword with such power, this time from right to left, and hit another Teak.

Another wolf leaped toward King Daniel from his right side, and a Prosec ran toward King Daniel's left side while three Teaks ran with their swords forward toward King Daniel. King Daniel swung Yesu's Sword with his left hand, catching the wolf in midleap. Then he whipped it so hard toward the Teak that when their swords met, the Teak's sword was shattered.

King Daniel's hand swung toward the ground, and the wolf fell with such force. After shattering the Teak's sword, King Daniel twisted around and swung his sword toward the Prosec, hitting him. King Daniel continued turning and swinging Yesu's sword forward, killing the Teak. All the Teaks, wolves, and Prosecs watching were amazed.

"Kill them!" yelled Dawson, leader of the Teaks. The Teaks, afraid, would not move.

"I said kill them!" said Dawson once more. The Teaks finally gathered enough courage and ran toward King Daniel. All the Youngs went and joined King Daniel in a battle stance. There were many Teaks coming toward them. The Youngs began to move forward toward the Teaks, but King Daniel raised his hand and said, "Wait, do not do anything. Do not move."

Young Ladam responded, "They are coming to kill us. We must attack."

King Daniel looked at Young Ladam and said in a sincere and confident voice, "Do not move."

Seconds passed, and as the Teaks were approaching, they raised their swords. Young Ladam, looking very afraid and worried, said, "Now?"

King Daniel yelled, "We need not do anything!"

Young Ladam looked forward and said, "But we will die!"

King Daniel whispered, "5, 4, 3, 2, 1," and he then yelled, "Fariets!"

Blast! Blast! Blast! Blast! From all around came many blasts toward the direction of the Teaks. The Fariets had been waiting for the command of their king, and indeed they were loyal!

The Teaks knew not what was happening, but they indeed were being overtaken by the blasts. All of the Fariets powers had overcome the enemy. With the blasts, the Teaks, wolves, and Prosecs were thrown everywhere, and many were killed.

"Now!" yelled King Daniel, and in a courageous act, King Daniel and the Youngs went swinging into battle, and it was too much for the Teaks. Fariet Elliot and some of the other Fariets guarded the queen and princesses. When Fariet Elliot saw Princess Violet, he grew happy and regained his strength as he was weak from being away from Princess Violet, but he began to cry. He'd thought he had lost her forever.

"I'm okay, Fariet Elliot, don't cry."

"I thought I had lost you and that I had failed you, my princess."

"Well, you're here now, and you have found me, and that is all that matters. I am just glad you're alive. I thought you would be dead by now by being so far away," said Princess Violet.

Soon, the Teaks, wolves, and Prosecs were overwhelmed, and they retreated back to the cave to gather their army and the White Eagles.

The celebration began as the Youngs and the Fariets cheered for their victory, but it was quickly silenced as the Youngs went to Young Joey. As the others approached, Young Jason knelt Young Joey's side. He looked at the others and said, "He's dead."

The Youngs became silent, and they mourned their fallen brother. Young Jason, still kneeling there by his brother was crying brokenly, and he embraced his fallen brother and would not let go.

King Daniel turned around and went to his bride. As they approached each other, the two began to tear up and cried, thankful they were still alive. They finally embraced each other and gave each other a beautiful love kiss. King Daniel fell to his knees and held on to her. He then looked up at her and said in a soft and loving voice, "You are the reason I live. You mean so much to me Elena. You captivate me, and you take my heart where no other can. You are my everything."

King Daniel began to cry as the Youngs and Fariets looked on.

"You are my life, and I will always love you because I know you are there for me when I need you. Thank you for saving us," said Queen Elena as she cried and went to her knees. The two embraced again as though they were never to see each other. Both Princess Katalina and Princess Violet joined their mother and father, and the four embraced.

King Daniel then went to his feet and went to the Youngs. He went to them and said, "I am King Daniel. Thank you for protecting my family, but I am truly sorry for the loss of your brother."

The Youngs put their heads down in respect. Young Jason said, "The pleasure is all ours, sire. We are here to protect at all costs. On the contrary, thank you for coming and saving us." King Daniel gave a small smile and then introduced his family. "This is my wife, Queen Elena, and my two daughters, Princess Katalina and Princess Violet."

Young Ladam stepped forward and said, "I am Young Ladam, and these are my brothers in Yesu." Each of them introduced themselves and shook the hands of the family. Young Ladam continued, "We are grateful to you, King Daniel, for saving us as well. Without you and your—what did you call them?"

"Fariets," answered King Daniel.

"Yes, Fariets, thank you all for coming to our aid."

King Daniel responded, "You're welcome. These are our friends, the Fariets."

Fariets Julip, Ut, and Bert flew forward and shook the hands of the Youngs. King Daniel then said in a very sympathetic way, "Again, I am sorry about your brother's death. He fought bravely to save someone he did not know. The Good Samaritan, we call him on Earth."

Young Ladam then said, "Thank you." He turned his head so as to see where Young Joey was lying and watched the other Youngs mourn their lost brother.

"He is actually not my brother. All the Youngs there, they are actual blood brothers. I am their leader, and I am their friend, but I am their brother in Yesu." He turned back to King Daniel and asked, "Where did you train to fight like that?"

King Daniel said, "I have never trained."

Very puzzled, Young Ladam looked at him. Even Queen Elena turned and looked at her husband and said, "Yes, where did that come from?"

King Daniel looked down and said, "I don't know. All I remember is the Fariets telling me that there was a battle and that you and the girls were in the middle of it." He paused for a moment and took a few steps. He then turned around and said, "It was like my body was on fire, and my heart was full of passion." Again, King Daniel paused and then said, "Nothing was going to stop me."

Young Ladam then responded, "But you were using your sword as though you were an expert in swordsmanship."

King Daniel turned and looked at Queen Elena and said, "It was the sword. It just took over me."

Young Ladam, even more puzzled, began to question his new-found friends, "Who are you, and what land do you rule?"

"He rules no land," said Fariet Julip.

"No land?" responded Young Ladam. "Well, if you're a king, then which of the twelve lands do you rule?" he asked again.

"He rules all of the lands, now," responded Fariet Bert.

Young Ladam, more offended and defensive, responded, "No, the other kings rule the other lands. I don't understand."

The other Youngs then approached where Young Ladam and King Daniel were talking. Young Ladam and the others then pulled their swords against King Daniel and said, "Are you preparing an invasion? If you rule no land here, then you are an enemy trying to take something that does not belong to you!"

King Daniel, knowing the immaturity of the Youngs, said, "We are the new Quint Fey. Yesu has created a new era. We are now called New Faith."

"The new Quint Fey? How is this possible?" questioned Young Joseph.

Young Jeremiah then said, "We apologize for our rudeness, King Daniel, but we were told that four men were to be the new kings after the fallen. There must be a mistake."

Young John then spoke and said, "What they are trying to say is that the Quint Fey are not—with all due respect, ma'am—women, let alone children."

King Daniel then raised his hand, and Yesu's Sword appeared.

Queen Elena then followed by pulling out the Lion Heart Medallion. Princess Katalina proudly called the Falcon Bow, and Princess Violet, with a big smile, raised the Dragon's Claw Wand. The Youngs were amazed and lowered their swords.

"You are the Quint Fey. New Faith. I don't believe it," said Young Ladam an more astonished expression. "But why would Yesu call upon you?" Young Ladam continued.

"Enough talk. We need to get moving out of here right away," said Fariet Julip. "The Dark King is drawing near with his army, and his watchful eyes in the sky will be looking for us."

"Fariets Julip, Bert, and Ut, can the Fariets fly us out of here?" asked King Daniel.

"We could, but the White Eagles will be flying high above the trees."

"Okay then, we need to get moving on foot right away," exclaimed Queen Elena.

The New Faith, the Fariets, and the Youngs took to their feet, and began the hike posthaste.

"We know these woods by heart. There is a secret passage down the mountain to the east. We can take you there to find refuge," said Young Ladam.

As the Youngs began to lead the way, King Daniel asked, "And what will we find when we get there?"

Young Ladam turned around and said with a brilliant smile, "King Jonis's castle, of course."

16

THE WITCH

BACK AT THE Prosecs' cave, anther storm was brewing.

"Where are your prisoners?" asked Seitor in a deep evil voice.

The Prosec stood there, not really knowing what to say. "I don't know, King Seitor. I was at your castle. Right before we left to find you, the three females were imprisoned here, chained." The Prosec then led them into the dungeon where the queen and princesses had been jailed.

"The older women was there, and the two younger ones were there," said the Prosec.

Seitor, with his Ruby Stone Ring, called upon the Dragon's Wang Claw and said "Lux!"

The entire dungeon was lit up. The room looked bright as day, and at that point, they saw what remained. There all over the cave lay the bodies of the Prosecs, mutilated.

"What could have done this?" asked Young Adims, the young wizard.

"The Lion Heart Medallion. The woman found out how to use it!" exclaimed the Dark King.

"What do you mean she learned how to use it? What can you do with it?" asked King Mattei.

The Dark King responded, "She turned into a lioness." He continued, "We must find them, and we must kill them before they reach the kingdoms."

At that point, Cauffa and his wolf pack got to the cave with several of the Prosecs. Right behind them were Dawson and the Teaks. Cauffa entered the cave and transformed into his human body.

"Tell me, Cauffa and Dawson, why are you not showing me the queen or princesses?" questioned Seitor.

"There was a battle, my lord," responded Dawson.

"Yes, and there were many," continued Cauffa.

"Where are the queen and the children?" Seitor demanded to know.

"We attacked, but then several Youngs came and defended the Queen and her children," said Cauffa.

"And you could not take care of them, even with you and your Teaks, Dawson?" said Seitor sarcastically.

"We would have killed them all, but then the man with the sword came and fought like a king," said Dawson.

"*I am the one and only king!*" yelled Seitor as he reached out and grabbed Dawson by the neck and slammed him into the wall.

"The man had Yesu's Sword, my lord," said Cauffa.

"He also had the help of the Fariets," voiced Dawson in a very scratchy voice that barely came out as he was still being choked.

Seitor then released Dawson, and Dawson fell to the ground, coughing to catch his breath.

Seitor walked away and said, "Fariets? They were banished."

Cauffa continued, "Yes, my lord, that was what I thought, but there were hundreds of them, and they worked together with this man."

Seitor responded, "So the so-called new king has accepted them and is now using them as allies. Where are they headed?"

"Not sure, my lord. We retreated before they left. They must be heading east, though," said Cauffa.

"We will find them and kill them, my lord. We need to take the White Eagles, the wolves, and the army and attack them!" yelled out Dawson.

"No!" commanded Seitor. "They have gone into the woods. The eagles cannot find them, and you alone will be killed, Cauffa."

Seitor then walked toward the woods and said, "But one among them would tell us everything." Seitor then raised the Ruby Stone Ring, called out for the Dragon's Claw Wand, and then called out a spell. "Cum hoc annulo, ego voca in mons pythonissam!"

The wind grew stronger and stronger. Dark clouds were everywhere, and the forest was moving as though a hurricane was passing through. There were leaves everywhere, so much one could hardly see into the distance of the forest. A rainless storm was brewing. Then the Dragon's Claw Wand lit up, and then it was quiet and calm. From within the forest came a dark shadow, a cloud of black smoke. As it grew closer, a shape began to form. It appeared to be a woman, but she was still in the dark cloud form.

"Seitor," called the dark smoke in a woman's whisper.

"Yes, come to me, Ruka, for I have called upon you to serve me," said Seitor with his wand still lifted up in the air.

You could tell that the dark figure was staring at Seitor in a very curious way. "What do you want?" asked the voice again in a woman's whisper. "What do you seek?" she continued.

Seitor responded, "I am the new king of Heirthia, the ruler of all, but there are four that are enemies."

The woman asked, "And what do you want with me?"

Seitor commanded, "You will go and find them, and you will tell me what they are doing, who they are with, who is helping them, and what their plans are."

Ruka responded, "And if I don't wish to serve—"

Immediately, Seitor, with his wand, began to squeeze Ruka's throat.

All that were around could hear her gasping for air. Little by little, the dark smoke began to disappear, and she began to appear. The dark smoke was then gone. Seitor finally let her go, and she fell to the ground coughing and trying to regain her breath. Ruka was a mid-aged woman, dirty blonde, thin, and had evil, devious eyes. Ruka was the witch of the east and accompanied no one. Seitor had indeed summoned her with his spell. She was a loner and truly had no heart. Ruka's strongest gift was that she was a shape-shifter. She could change into anyone or anything that was not in her presence: dark smoke, a man, another woman, a child, an animal—nearly anything.

"You could have just told me!" she yelled as she stood up.

"Anyone that crosses me or gets in my way will die!" said Seitor in his evil voice for all to hear. "Now that we have an understanding, Ruka, the great witch, I want you to find them. They are headed east, but they are in hiding with some Youngs and Fariets."

Ruka, now gathered, asked, "Why don't you send your bloodhounds? They can find them and kill them."

"Oh, kill them we will. That is of no concern. But first, I need to know how many allies there are. I want to know who is helping them. More importantly, I want to know where the people of Heirthia are hiding. There is no point in killing my enemies if I don't know who is on their side. Once we find out, I will unleash death upon all of them," replied Seitor as he circled and walked around her.

"How big is your army?" asked Ruka, then corrected herself, "Your Highness."

Seitor smiled, and with his big blue eyes looking up, said, "Let me put it this way: for every warrior they have, I have ten thousand." He continued, "Your job is to find them and spy on them. Walk with them and follow them. You will then report to me, and I will decide when it is time."

Ruka looked up at Seitor, who was staring down at her. He had this evil eye in his face.

Ruka smiled back and said, "Who am I looking for?"

"There are four: a man, his wife, and two children," explained Seitor.

"You're fighting with children?" Ruka laughed.

"They are the new Quint Fey," screamed Dawson.

"I am after the new rulers of Heirthia? Do they have the powers?" exclaimed Ruka with a voice of fear.

One of the Teaks said to her, "What, are you afraid of the little children?" He and the other Teaks began to laugh.

Ruka quickly raised her wand, got into a stance, and called, "Crepitus!" A beam of fire came bursting out toward the Teak who had taunted her, hitting him in the chest. Nearly his whole chest was blown away. Another two of the Teaks behind her came with their swords. Ruka raised herself into the air and again chanted, "Crepitus," toward both Teaks, and they too where hit in the chest.

Ruka then called upon the strong winds again, and clouds began to come. She called for lightning, "Magnificum Lucendi!" and it began to strike, hitting several of the Teaks that where there. The other Teaks were getting ready to attack her. The Teaks raised their bows, and they fired all the arrows toward her.

But then suddenly, the arrows stopped in midair. The Teaks and Ruka did not know what was happening.

"Enough!" exclaimed Seitor as his wand was raised to stop the arrows. The arrows then fell to the ground. "If you kill each other, then I will have no one to serve me. You are a powerful witch, Ruka. You have proven yourself."

Ruka then came down from the air and said, "You have saved me, and you are the Dark King. Therefore, I now serve you." Ruka bowed down. As did the other warriors, the Teaks, the Wind Pack, the White Eagles, and the Prosecs. Seitor looked at all of them and then looked to the east and whispered, "We will find you."

Ruka got up and raised her wand. She whisked it around her, and she turned into dark mist and went toward the east.

"Come, let us gather the army for our war." Seitor and the others began their descent back toward the land of Cain.

Once the Youngs buried their fallen brother, the Geminis, the Fariets, and the Youngs were all en route to King Jonis's castle, walking through the forest.

"It's not too far from here. Come on," said Young Jason.

As they walked, Young Ladam went to where Princess Katalina was walking. "Hey," he said.

Princess Katalina, not very impressed with his arrogance while speaking with her father, said, "Hello."

Young Ladam, just about the age of princess Katalina, and knowing why she was acting cold with him, said, "Look, I am really sorry about what happened back there, you know, with your father."

Princess Katalina stopped for a few seconds and said, "Look, I know it is difficult for you to trust anyone because of all the things that have happened in your world, but you have to remember, we were brought here from our world, brought here to serve you, to help you. My father saved your life back there, and that is how you show him respect?" She continued walking.

But Young Ladam, looking at Princess Katalina, was very impressed with her sassiness. He followed her in a persistent manner and said, "I know, and that is why I want to tell you that I am really, really sorry."

Princess Katalina looked over at him.

He continued, "I am really, really sorry, but I know now that you all are the true and rightful kings." He then looked at her with his bright blue eyes and smiled at her in a friendly manner.

Princess Katalina said as she continued to walk, "That's okay. Just don't do it again," and she gave him a smile.

"Trust me, I won't. I learned my lesson. So what is your world like?"

"Well, it is very similar to yours, but much more modern."

"What do you mean 'more modern'?"

Princess Katalina, intrigued with Young Ladam's curiosity, said, "Well, we don't live in castles and fight with swords or fight with talking animals."

Young Ladam responded, "You don't live in castles? No swords? What kind of world is that?"

Princess Violet then responded, "And you forgot to mention 'no talking animals.' That's a big one."

"Wow, that is very different. What did you think when you heard the first animal speak here?"

Princess Katalina stopped and said, "I don't really remember because that animal wanted to kill my mother. To be honest, I was pretty scared." She then continued to walk. Young Ladam gave her a blank stare, not knowing what to say. Princess Violet then continued, "In our world, we have fast-food restaurants, where food is ready for you. We have music and video games, phones, electricity, and Disney World."

Young Ladam looked even more confused.

Fariet Elliot, flying right close to Princess Violet, asked, "What is Disney World?"

"Well, it is a magical place with rides, shows, food, and so much fun. They even have Tinker Bell. She's a fairy, just like you."

"You have fairies in your world too?" Fariet Elliot responded.

"Well, not exactly. They aren't real."

"But you just said that Tinker Bell lives in the land of Disney."

"She does, but she is a made-up character."

"Why would you do that?" he asked.

"Well, because it's fun."

"So in your world, you make things up to have fun?" again the little fairy asked.

"I like you, Fariet Elliot, you make me smile," Princess Violet continued to walk, and Elliot followed her as they continued on their journey.

As they walked, Young John, one of the oldest of the brothers, came to where King Daniel and his bride were walking as they held hands.

"Sire, I wanted to ask you. Does anyone in Heirthia know you're here?"

"Just you and your men, the Fariets, and all the evil creatures that have tried to kill us," responded King Daniel.

"So none of the allies know you're here?"

"No," answered Queen Elena. "Why do you ask?"

"Well, we don't exactly know where they are," answered Young John.

King Daniel and Queen Elena stopped in their tracks. King Daniel said, "Then where are you taking us?"

"Well, no worries, Your Majesty, we are taking you to King Jonis's castle. This would be the best choice and closest castle of them all. It's hard to say because after the original Quint Fey disappeared, there were battles all over Heirthia. Of course, Seitor was gone too, so there was no power on Heirthia, just fighting. All the evil creatures and army of Seitor just attacked everyone and everywhere."

Queen Elena asked, "Did anyone win? I mean, what happened?"

Young John continued, "Well, after the Quint Fey left, there was no direction, so the people held up the army. It was the people who fought for their own lives. There was no one there for them. They had nothing or no one to look up to to save them."

King Daniel then asked, "When did all of this happen?"

Young John continued, "Not long ago. It's about seven months now when all the powers vanished. Immediately when they left, everything just went up in the air. The castles were attacked. No one knew who was on whose side, and so everyone just went into hiding to wait for the Quint Fey to return."

Queen Elena then inquired, "But I thought that once the Quint Fey turned their powers over to us, they returned to Heirthia."

"Oh, they did, but their powers were gone. They fought, but because all the kingdoms were separated, no one has ever been able to find out who was alive and who was dead. It was nearly impossible to get from kingdom to kingdom. You see, what made the kingdoms strong was the unity of the kingdoms. Alone, a kingdom could not survive a battle, let alone a war, but together, they were unstoppable."

King Daniel then added, "So because the kingdoms are so separated and Seitor's army is in between, no one has been able to reach out and unite."

"Right. Only a few brave have been able to escape and move about, but remember, this just began not too long ago. This is why we were around in the forest. Just trying to find answers and find allies."

Queen Elena then asked, "Where are the original Quint Fey now?"

"We are not too sure, but when they returned, they were not together." Then in a more serious tone and almost in fear, Young James said, "You see, what is defeating us is that no one, not even the original kings, knows where anyone is right now. Therefore, we cannot fight because we are alone."

Young Joseph then said, "All we have been able to do is pray that Yesu would return."

Princess Violet then came to her father, and King Daniel lifted her into the air. She then said, "And Yesu now sends you, Daddy, to help."

Young John replied, "Oh yes, he did indeed send a warrior who can use a sword."

Little Princess Violet then said, "My daddy has never used a sword before, you silly." All the Youngs and Fariets stopped, and they all turned around.

Fariet Julip asked, "King, Your Majesty, you have never used a sword before?"

"That is what I was telling you all back there. Never," answered King Daniel.

Then in a curious voice, Young James asked, "We thought you were being modest and humble, Your Majesty. Please forgive my ignorance, but you fought like a true experienced knight. Where did you learn this?"

King Daniel took a few seconds and then replied, "Our true faith, our true character, and our true talents come not in times of training but in times of tribulation. My family is my life, and therefore, my true talent came out. You see, our courage, bravery, and love come from inside our hearts. Open your hearts, and God will show you wonders."

"There it is, sire, the castle! The castle! We made it!" yelled Young Jeremiah.

Indeed, they had finally reached the end of the forest and had made it to King Jonis's castle. From a distance, it was a beautiful sight. They had finally reached the first castle in their journey to meet their army. Immediately, all the Youngs ran to the castle. The new king and queens and the Fariets were all joyful. They continued walking and soon reached the giant gates of the castle, but soon, they knew something was wrong. There was no one there.

They hurried inside and went directly into the center court of the castle. "Hello!" yelled Young Ladam. Again he yelled, "Hello, is there anyone here?" There was not a sound.

However, around them, there were arrows, swords, armor, and even a few skeleton soldiers who clearly had died in battle.

"They took the castle. Seitor's army was able to breach Jonis's castle, the great wizard's castle," said Young Jeremiah. "Without his wand, he had no power, only that of his body. They were doomed," replied Young John.

17

IGNITE

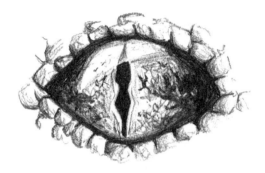

T HE GEMINIS, THE Fariets, and the Youngs were now at the heart of King Jonis's castle and empire, or at least what it used to be. This was a good land with people of good heart. It was very welcoming at the entrance gates. As you entered, there were people all gathered in a market buying, selling, and trading goods and services. They were indeed in unity.

Now, however, it was abandoned and clearly there had been a battle. It was gone, and everyone in it were gone. Still, the Geminis were determined to find anyone.

"It doesn't matter. Go through the entire castle and look through every room, dungeon, and anywhere someone could hide. My spirit is telling me there is someone alive here!" ordered Queen Elena.

Therefore, all the Fariets and Youngs went into the depths of the castle. The Geminis also searched high and low. Room by room, corner to corner, they searched.

"Hello, is anyone here!" they all yelled out.

"We are the Youngs of Yesu who have come to rescue you," yelled Young Ladam. Still not a sound.

"We are the new king and queens of Heirthia!" cried out Princess Violet.

Then there was a sound.

"Did you hear that?" asked Princess Violet.

"I heard it, Princess," replied Fariet Elliot.

Princess Katalina, listening attentively, said, "I did. Say it again!"

Again, in a young child's voice, Violet called, "We are the new king and queens of Heirthia. I am Princess Violet, the queen of the Dragon's Claw Wand!"

Again, they heard what sounded like a door closing. Together, Princess Katalina and Princess Violet yelled, "Daddy! Something is over here!"

Quickly he came along with a few Youngs. "Where?" he asked.

Princess Katalina pointed to a back room in the castle. King Daniel slowly walked over to the room. It was dark, and there was a cold chill.

"Hello," he called. "Hello," he said again. "I am King Daniel, ruler of Yesu's Sword. I am here to protect you."

Still, he could not see anything. Then there was a thump behind him in the corner of the room. King Daniel quickly turned around with his sword drawn, but he still could see nothing. "It's too dark. I can't see," he called. Young Jason and Young Ladam came into the room.

"Please, Your Highness, I have the talent of light. May I?" asked Young Jason.

King Daniel nodded his head, not really sure what to expect.

Young Jason stepped into the room and closed his eyes. He took a deep, slow breath and spread out his hands. *Flash!* He opened his eyes, and light was illuminating from them. The room had been dark, but it was now bright as day. King Daniel was amazed.

"What is this place?" asked King Daniel. "I don't understand. You have powers within you. How is this possible?"

Young Jason, still with his eyes lit, said, "Yes, Your Majesty. Many of the people, and even creatures of Heirthia, have been blessed with a talent. Out of all my brothers, only three of us have been able to find our talent that Yesu blessed us with."

Queen Elena, intrigued, asked, "How do you find your talent?"

Young James said, "It just comes naturally when you need it the most. It seems as though if you try to find it, you never will, but when your heart calls for it, it comes."

Thump! A sound was heard, distracting them from their discussion. Quickly, King Daniel noticed a hatch on the floor of the room. He and Young James approached the hatch with swords drawn. They knew something was there, and although very nervous, Young James opened it. King Daniel quickly peered in, and there were two small children inside with their older sister, alone with just a few fruits to eat and a few blankets.

"Hello, little ones. Please do not be afraid. I am King Daniel, and this is my wife, Queen Elena."

"Hello, girls. Are you all okay?" asked Queen Elena as she looked in.

Still, the children and their older sister were afraid.

"We are not here to hurt you. We have come to help you," said King Daniel.

"They are traumatized at what happened here," said Queen Elena.

"Katalina, Violet," called their father for them. Quickly, the princesses came.

"Little girls, don't be afraid. This is Princess Violet and Princess Katalina," said Queen Elena.

"Hi, I'm Violet, and this is my guardian, Fariet Elliot. What's your name?" said Princess Violet as she climbed down to where the young children were.

"Wow, this is a great hiding spot when you're playing hide-and-go-seek," she continued.

"Violet, I don't think they know what that is," responded Princess Katalina.

"I want to play," said one of the children in an eager voice.

King Daniel and Queen Elena were happy that one of the children had finally broken the ice.

"Yea, we can play," replied the other little girl.

"How do you play hide-and-go-seek?" replied the first little girl.

Then Princess Violet, in a more sophisticated voice, said, "Well, you have to use your best thought and judgment and find the best, most glorious place to hide so that the other person won't find you."

The two girls just stood there staring at Princess Violet with absolutely no idea why.

"Oh, we have played this game before," said the second little girl in a quiet, more serious tone, and she continued, "But only, well, we don't hide from the other people."

This caught the attention of everyone in the room. King Daniel turned to his wife, wondering what she was referring to. Then Princess Katalina, though a bit hesitant nonetheless asked, "Then what do you hide from, sweetie?"

Before the child could answer, there was a loud screech, but not from a human, it was from a creature outside the castle.

Then the little girl turned toward the others and answered with a fear in her voice and her eyes wide open, "We hide from Egwaks."

Quickly, the little girls went into the corner of the small hiding room, and the three hugged. Princess Katalina and Princess Violet, along with Fariet Elliot, quickly went with them. Young Jason closed his eyes to stop illuminating light. King Daniel and Queen Elena, along with Young Jason and Young Ladam went into the hatch, and closed the small door.

Meanwhile, across the castle, all the Fariets went into hiding along with the other Youngs. Everyone was quiet and still.

Then they could hear the Egwak walking toward the castle, and they were loud steps.

King Daniel whispered, "What are Egwaks?"

The older sister whispered "Giants!"

Young Jason then whispered, "These creatures live in the forest, and they roam between all the castles looking for the people. They have been doing this since the Quint Fey left."

As the Egwak grew closer, it shook the whole castle. Then there was another screech that was clearly from a second Egwak.

Queen Elena then whispered, "But why are they roaming from kingdom to kingdom?"

Young Jason replied, "To keep the people from the different lands from communicating with each other and joining forces."

King Daniel, looking concerned, said, "To keep the kingdoms from working together and making a rebellion?"

"Exactly," replied Young Jason. He continued, "A kingdom alone cannot withstand a battle against the Dark King and his army, but with the kingdoms joined, there is a chance."

Indeed, the two Egwaks were now in the center of the castle.

"They are here somewhere!" yelled a voice as King Daniel and the others listened.

"The Egwaks smell something," said another voice. King Daniel slowly looked through a crack in the wall and saw the two who had been speaking. It was King Julas and Young Adims.

Shortly thereafter, King Mattei flew into the castle as he had the talent of flight with his massive wings.

"Where are you?" Young Adims yelled.

"Come and show yourself, Your Highness!" yelled King Julas.

King Daniel looked, and he was shocked at what he was seeing. The Egwak were human-like creatures but massive in size, about fifteen feet tall. Their eyes and skin were like that of a reptile's. Each had four massive arms and claws like a sloth's. Their nose was like a pig's, and they had tiny ears. However, their teeth were not tiny. They were sharp and large like that of a great white shark's. Again, both creatures screeched. Quickly, the Egwaks went into the castle, tracing their prey's scent.

"We know you're here. The Egwaks can smell you!" yelled King Julas.

The Egwaks went from corner to corner attempting to follow the smell. Back in the small hiding room, the children and others stayed quiet. Then a loud sound came near the room. It was one of the Egwaks smelling the wall. King Daniel motioned to the others with his finger to remain quiet.

Princess Katalina, shaking uncontrollably, put her hand on her mouth, and tears began to fall. Young Ladam, the brave soul that he was, went to Princess Katalina and embraced her. Although the Egwak had been smelling that area, the Egwak moved on, and it became quiet. King Daniel, not knowing where they were, stepped forward back to the crack in the wall and looked out. He could not see anything, and there were no sounds. It was very quiet. King Daniel looked at Queen Elena and made an expression as though he did not know what was going on.

Meanwhile, the Fariets and Youngs were in a bottom room of the castle, but they could see what was happening outside.

"That is Young Adims," whispered Young James. "He is the traitor. He is the one who conspired with Seitor and King Julas. Young Ladam saw it all happen," he continued as he whispered.

There was a loud crash in the room where King Daniel and his family were hiding. The Egwak had slammed his snout into the wall, creating a big hole. It screamed very loud, and there was panic. The children were all crying, and King Daniel fell to the ground. The Egwak came back as if to take King Daniel into its mouth. Young Jason put his hands together and closed his eyes. With all his might and force, he opened his eyes, and a very bright light came out, blinding the Egwak.

King Daniel got to his feet and yelled to the others "Run!" All the children and those who were with them leaped out of the hatch and began to run down the hall of the castle. The Egwak regrouped, and the other Egwak also came.

"Kill them!" yelled King Julas.

The Geminis continued to run through the halls, and as they did, the massive Egwaks were smashing through the hall right behind them. The roof and walls were all crashing in, and the windows were bursting as the Egwak broke through. Princess Violet was so frightened that she was crying as she was running. Fariet Elliot quickly flew backward and let out a massive force with his hands.

The power was very strong, and it blasted toward the Egwak that was closest to them, sending shattered glass toward it.

Although they ran with all their might, the Egwaks were getting closer and closer. As they approached the end of the hall to enter the center of the castle, Queen Elena yelled, "Faster!" The children entered the room along with Young Jason Young Ladam and Queen Elena. King Daniel was trailing right behind them, but right before he entered the room, he was lifted up into the air. One of the Egwaks had grabbed him by the leg. He yelled as the Egwak lifted him up and took him out of the hall.

"Daniel!" yelled Queen Elena in desperation, knowing her husband was about to be killed.

"Daddy," cried Princess Violet.

The Egwak held King Daniel by the leg, and King Daniel was upside down. The Egwak, standing in the courtyard of the castle with King Daniel in hand, lifted his arm high, and the other Egwak approached, and as it did, it let out a roar. The Egwak lifted its hand as to punch King Daniel. The Egwak swung back, and King Daniel knew he had to do something.

He quickly called for Yesu's Sword, and right before the Egwak was about to punch and kill him, King Daniel forced his sword downward and quickly swung it up to the hand that was holding him. The sword cut through the hand of the Egwak that was holding him and sliced it like a piece of paper.

Blood immediately covered King Daniel, and the Egwak screamed and let him go. King Daniel came crashing to the ground and landed on his back, his fall taking all his air.

As King Daniel stood up still trying to gasp for air, the other Egwak came toward him and swung his fist toward King Daniel, hitting him on the side and sending him through the air and crashing against the castle wall. King Daniel was badly hurt.

King Julas then approached King Daniel with his sword drawn and said, "So this is the new king!" He continued, "You are nothing, and you will die."

I will fight you, you coward!" yelled Young Ladam with his sword drawn.

"Young Ladam, always the hero, always so stupid," said King Julas. "You are absolutely no match for my silver. Stand back, or I will kill you," commanded King Julas as he pointed his sword at Young Ladam.

Young Ladam, although knowing he was outmatched, knew he needed to stand his ground and defend King Daniel.

"Well then, die!" King Julas swung his sword, and the two began to battle.

Quickly, Young Ladam fought back, and their swords met at every angle. The first touch of their swords created a bright light. King Julas swung his sword, turned around, and swung it the other way. With King Julas's back to Young Ladam, King Julas swung his right elbow and smashed it into Young Ladam's face, immediately causing Young Ladam's nose to bleed. Young Ladam fell back. King Julas swung his sword and cut Young Ladam on the arm.

From behind, Young James swung his sword, striking King Julas in the back but only slightly cutting him. The Egwak came toward the battle and was about to strike Young James, but then Queen Elena yelled, "Fariets."

All at once, the Fariets went into battle. Fariet Bert and Fariet Ut yelled, "Fariets, fire up!" With its massive size, all the Fariets flew together right before the Egwak, and together they put their hands together and released a grand power. *Blast!*

The Egwak was sent flying back many yards. It hit the ground so hard, the land shook. It yelled in pain, badly hurt.

"Exitium!" yelled Young Adims as he raised his wand toward the Fariets, sending a destruction spell.

All the Fariets scattered as they all flew in different directions. Some were hit with Young Adims's spell, including Fariet Julip. Fariet Julip fell to the ground. Again Young Adims yelled, "Exitium!" and a powerful spell came crashing toward the Fariets, even destroying part of the castle wall that was behind them.

The rest of the Youngs summoned their bravery and went into battle. Soon thereafter, there were six Youngs with swords drawn, and they all went toward King Julas and Young Adims. King Mattei then flew toward the Youngs who were charging. King Mattei attacked from above, raising his sword.

Young Adims yelled, "Ignis!" causing his wand to shoot a massive beam of fire toward the Youngs.

Young John pulled his wand and yelled, "Murus!" Immediately, his beam created a wall that stopped Young Adims's fire. King Mattei flew in and swung his sword toward the wall created by Young John, and he broke it.

Again, Young Adims yelled, "Ignis!" and again he shot a massive beam of fire, and right before it hit the Youngs, the fire stopped in midair and would not move. The Youngs turned to see who had saved them, and it was King Daniel, with his hand up in the air as Yesu's Sword gave him power. Up on the roof of the castle, Queen Elena, the princesses, and the three young girls were watching the battle take place.

As King Daniel was holding on, King Mattei went toward him and swung his sword. King Daniel lifted his sword with his other hand to defend himself. The two swords collided, but King Mattei had the advantage. The Youngs went to help King Daniel, but they were met with King Julas's Silver Sword. King Julas's sword was so fast the Youngs could not go past him as they battled him one by one.

King Mattei pulled back and swung harder toward King Daniel, and King Daniel defended again, but King Mattei continued to strike King Daniel's sword repeatedly, and King Daniel was growing weak.

As King Daniel was holding on to Young Adims's spell to keep it from hitting the Youngs and, with the other arm, trying to defend himself against King Mattei, he saw the Egwak that he had cut charging at him. King Daniel looked to his right and saw that King Julas was holding the Youngs back, keeping them from helping. The Fariets were attacking the other Egwak, who was swinging his massive arms, trying to kill them. They were trying to keep the Egwak from attacking the others.

King Daniel looked up to his left on the rooftop and saw his children looking down directly at him. He knew he could very well die in front of his family. King Daniel went down on one knee. He could not hold any longer. He looked at his family, and a tear came down his cheek.

Queen Elena yelled, "Daniel!" and Violet was crying uncontrollably, yelling, "Daddy!"

Then he looked at his daughter Katalina, who was in disbelief. She reached for the Falcon Bow and, in a state of panic, pulled back, but nothing happened. No arrow appeared. She began to cry out of frustration.

She yelled, "Daddy!" and again she pulled back on her bow, but again, nothing came out. She was sobbing harder now, and King Daniel saw this.

Still, he looked at Princess Katalina and mouthed the words, "I love you, sweetie."

Then he mouthed the word *ignite*.

Princess Katalina was trying to see what he was saying. Again he mouthed the word *ignite*.

Princess Katalina concentrated on what he was saying. As the Egwak drew closer, he then yelled in a soft voice, "Ignite!" The Egwak was dangerously near, and so King Daniel yelled in a louder voice, "Ignite!" as a tear fell from his face. Princess Katalina heard this but was not sure what he meant.

As through asking if she'd heard him right, she yelled, "Ignite?"

The Egwak let out a screech, and so King Daniel shouted desperately, "Ignite, Katalina! Ignite, ignite, ignite!"

Princess Katalina opened her eyes wide and got this feeling in her stomach. It felt as though a fire was building inside of her. She felt a storm brewing within her entire body, and she felt as though she was on fire but would not burn. She dropped her head slightly, looking directly at the Egwak now. Her eyes were fixed on him, and she took a deep breath, and for the first time, she felt in control of her bow.

Then a voice whispered to her, "Ignite by faith, ignite by sight, ignite your bow, and fight with right."

Princess Katalina slowly drew her bow, and as she did, its strings became inflamed, and a fiery arrow appeared. She drew back and closed her eyes. She said her prayer, "Blessed is He who gives me strength," and she released.

The arrow flew swiftly through the air in a flame. The Egwak drew his hands up to kill King Daniel. The arrow came, but then the flame grew larger and larger, and all of a sudden, it split into seven arrows, and each arrow grew large.

One arrow went toward Young Adims and struck him in the shoulder, giving him a severe burn. One arrow struck King Mattei in the arm, causing him to fall back and drop his sword. Another arrow struck King Julas in the leg, and he yelled. The remaining four arrows struck the Egwak directly in the heart. It was as though Princess Katalina had guided each arrow to strike exactly where she wanted.

The Egwak made no sound but came to a stop right before King Daniel. It fell to its knees and then fell to the ground. It was dead. Princess Katalina had indeed saved her father and wounded the other enemies. Seeing their opportunity, the Youngs went into attack.

Although they fought back, King Julas, King Mattei, and Young Adims quickly began to retreat.

"Kill them, Egwak!" ordered King Julas to the other Egwak.

As the three retreated, the Egwak became enraged and charged the Youngs. The Fariets soon gathered together and began attacking the Egwak with their powers.

Princess Katalina, knowing now the power she had, raised her bow, but nothing happened. The power was gone. The Egwak looked up at her and knew she had killed its brother. The Egwak swung its massive hand at the Fariets, and they went flying everywhere. The Egwak ran toward the walls of the castle and leaped into the air toward Katalina.

As it leaped, Young Ladam grabbed the Egwak's back and held on. The Egwak, focused on killing Princess Katalina, did not pay attention to Young Ladam on its back. As it reached the roof of the castle where Princess Katalina was standing, she continued to focus and once again pulled her bow, but nothing happened because she was afraid.

The Egwak reached out for her and grabbed her by the leg. She yelled in panic.

King Daniel yelled, "Katalina!"

Young Ladam then gathered himself and, on his knees, pulled out his sword, forced it downward, and drove it directly into the Egwak's back. The Egwak yelled in pain and fell off the roof It slammed onto the floor with Princess Katalina in hand. As it fell, it released Princess Katalina. She quickly crawled backward away from the Egwak.

Young Ladam, visibly in pain from the fall, tried to pull himself away from the Egwak. The Egwak turned its massive head and saw Young Ladam moving away. The Egwak reached over with its right hand to grab Princess Katalina. As it approached, Young Ladam quickly got up and swung his sword, severely cutting the giant's wrist.

Young Ladam grabbed ahold of Princess Katalina by the waist and helped her move away. King Daniel ran toward them with his sword and placed himself in front of Young Ladam, who was holding on to the exhausted Princess Katalina. Princess Katalina fell to the ground. Young Ladam looked down at her, gently holding her head. With her eyes gently open, she looked up at Young Ladam.

He then asked, "Are you okay?"

Princess Katalina whispered, "Thank you for saving me."

Young Ladam, feeling something within him, went down to her, looked her in the eyes, and immediately fell in love with her. He slowly looked down at her and gave her a soft kiss. His lips barely touched hers, but they did. She looked up at his blue eyes and immediately fell in love with him too. She felt safe, protected, and loved by this young man.

The Egwak got to his feet and stared down King Daniel. Young John lifted his wand and yelled, "Expellere!"

His spell hit the Egwak, but it did not move! The Egwak charged and let out a roar.

King Daniel held his sword high at an angle. When he did this, the other Youngs raised their swords, and they formed a line. with their sharp swords facing the Egwak. They all knew something was going to happen but did not know whether it was good or bad. As the Egwak grew closer and closer, it raised its arms and swung them toward the line of warriors. All of a sudden, "Eliminare!" was yelled out.

The Egwak came to a stop and lifted its head. It had been struck and shocked from behind. The Egwak appeared to be paralyzed, and it was surrounded with this glow. The glow lifted the Egwak from the floor. King Daniel and the others were amazed at what was happening.

As the Egwak was lifted into the air, King Daniel and the others saw what was happening. Behind the Egwak, there was an older man with a wand who had cast a spell on the evil giant. He was clearly a wizard. There was much wind blowing, and the Egwak was being lifted higher and higher by the spell. The wizard had his wand up in the air, and his other hand guided the Egwak through the air. The wizard had his eyes focused on the Egwak, but then he looked at King Daniel and the others and put both his hands down. The Egwak fell to the ground and was dead.

"Who are you?" demanded King Daniel, still with his sword up.

"Are you really going to threaten a man who just saved you, Your Highness?" replied the wizard with a surprised tone.

"How do you know he is the king? There has been no indication of this," questioned Queen Elena.

"He who holds the Sword of Yesu is the king of the land. Isn't this so?" replied the unknown wizard.

"We are grateful that you have spared our lives from this beast, but what is to say you did so in order to take the sword for yourself? Clearly, you know enough about this sword," said King Daniel.

"Fair enough. I am Jities Holmes. I am the Wizard of the East. I do come in peace."

"Wizard of the East? We have lived here our entire lives and have never heard of a Wizard of the East," replied Young Jason.

"What brings you here, Mr. Holmes?" asked King Daniel.

"The same thing that brought you here: hope. Ever since the Quint Fey left, all the people have left, all the kings are gone, and there are creatures just like this all over the place. I have been alone, and I am just looking for refuge," said the old wizard.

All who were there continued to stare at him, not really knowing what to believe. They still held their swords toward him.

"Please, if I wanted to fight you, I would have already lifted my wand or let that beast kill you," he continued.

Jities Holmes was an older wizard. He had a long black beard, a brown gown, and a small hat. Knowing they were still not convinced, he continued, "I have lived in the Dark Forest. Ever since the falling, every piece of land has changed."

The old wizard went and sat on a boulder and continued, "It seems that all creatures, both human and land creatures, are in hiding, afraid to come out. Then you have all these Egwaks and Blakers between all the kingdoms. The people are afraid to leave wherever they are hiding because of these beasts, the wolves, the White Eagles, and the wrath of the Dark King."

"Where are you headed?" asked King Daniel.

The old wizard responded, "Well, this is King Jonis's castle, in case you didn't know. The next castle is King Aniser's in Demble. Since all have left here, I will head there. My best guess is all the people left here to get away from Michael's Bridges, the border of the river that is being controlled by the evil one."

At this point, King Daniel put his sword down, and so did the rest. Although they did not trust the old wizard, they knew he was no threat at that time.

"Are you a good wizard or a bad one?" asked Princess Violet.

The wizard smiled and said, "What do you think, little wizard?" he replied.

"Well, you killed that monster that was trying to kill us, so I would say a good wizard," said Princess Violet.

"I certainly hope so," he replied.

"How do you know I am a wizard?" she asked.

"Oh, I can spot one a mile away. You have a good heart and a very special spirit. Plus, your wand is on your side," he replied.

Princess Violet gave a big smile.

"Well, I can't say with certain who you are, but what I can say is on behalf of my family, thank you for saving us," said Queen Elena.

"You must be the queen. It was my pleasure ma'am." Mr. Holmes went to the queen and bowed before her. He then stood tall, put his hat on, and said, "Well, very nice to meet you all, but I am off on another adventure."

King Daniel replied, "It was a pleasure to meet you, sir. We are off in that direction. You are welcome to tag along. We could certainly use your wand."

The old wizard, with a great big smile, looked at Princess Violet and said, "I guess it's our adventure then."

18

THE CURSE

I T WAS NOW the new king and queens of Heirthia, the six
Youngs, the many Fariets, the two small children and their
older sister from Yesu's castle, and the Old Wizard on their
way to the land of Demble to reach King Aniser's castle.

Before they'd left, they'd gathered the bodies of their com-
rades. Many of the Fariets had lost their lives during the battle
with the Egwaks. Then and there, many of them were buried by
their brothers and sisters. The Geminis stood with respect as they
said their farewells to their fallen.

"Fariet Elliot, I'm sorry for your losses," whispered Princess Violet.

"Thank you, Your Highness. I know one thing for sure: they died with honor protecting what Yesu wanted all along, for the people of Heirthia to rule this land." He then smiled and embraced the little princess.

As they were preparing to leave, Queen Elena went to the two small children and their older sister and asked, "Sweeties, we are going to another castle to find all the good people. We really, really want for you three to come with us. We will take care of you and protect you. Do you want to come?"

The older sister said, "Well, I'm the older sister, and I vote we go. My heart tells me that is the way to go."

Queen Elena then asked, "What about you, sweeties, ready for an adventure?"

One of the little ones said, "You're pretty. I love you." She then went to Queen Elena and gave her a hug. Then the second little girl when to her and also hugged her. They were truly comforted by the queen. Queen Elena looked up and smiled. She was very touched by the little girls, and her eyes teared up.

Queen Elena then said, "By the way, what are your names?"

One of the younger girls said, "I'm Jesila," and the other said "I'm Miala." The older sister said, "I am Donia."

"I'm Katalina." The princess had been nearby, watching the girls talk to her mother.

Donia then said, "No, ma'am, you are Princess Katalina."

Princess Katalina smiled and said, "That is very sweet, but please just call me Katalina."

Queen Elena then said, "Okay, girls, remember, we need to stay close to King Daniel. He will protect us."

"All right everyone, we need to get moving before more trouble comes," said King Daniel. The entire group then began their journey north to the land of Demble. Their goal? King Aniser's castle. It was their hope to find the army that angel Michael had told them was waiting for them.

They were soon on their way up the region of Castillo and toward the beautiful plain lands of Demble. It was their hope that indeed their army was waiting for them there. However, King Daniel knew from the depths of his heart that there were more enemies waiting for him on the way.

"Fools! Idiots! You let them get away!" yelled the Dark King to King Julas, King Mattei, and Young Adims. All three stood there, tired, and hurting from their wounds from battle.

"My task to you was to find them, kill them, and get the powers from them. But you did not take charge and complete this task!" he continued to yell.

"Sire, we did everything we could. Even the Princess with the bow was able to use the Falcon Bow," replied King Mattei.

"She used it?" questioned Seitor as he looked back at them with an evil stare.

King Mattei nodded his head in the affirmative.

"And you did not kill her?" Seitor continued.

Seitor then lifted his hand with anger, and King Mattei felt his throat close. There was nothing King Mattei could do. Seitor was choking him without even touching him.

"You failed me, all of you. You are not worthy of serving me," exclaimed Seitor. All who were in the room were afraid. King Mattei was turning red and slowly dying. King Mattei was slowly lifted up in the air, and then Seitor released him. King Mattei fell to the ground, gasping for air and grabbing his throat.

"Kanel, what do we know?" asked Seitor.

The Great White Eagle came forward and answered, "We have control over the seven lands: Castigs, Harper, Bapti, Cain, Alpha, Isra, and Breakle."

Seitor asked, "These are all the lands south of the Larena River?"

Kanel nodded his head in the affirmative. "Our prisoners include all the kings from these lands, except, of course, King

Julas. He is our ally. We also have a majority of its people under our control."

Seitor responded, "Go on."

"All the people and the original Quint Fey are in hiding. These are the people from the north, but there is no trace of them. We have absolutely no idea where any of them are."

Young Adims asked, "Get Cauffa to follow their scent."

Cauffa, in his human form, responded, "We have gone over all that area. There are no scents. It's almost as though everyone disappeared."

Young Adims questioned, "Everyone?"

Cauffa responded, "Everyone. There is nothing there."

"Sire, we must attempt to take Yesu's castle," said King Julas.

The Dark King replied, "You don't understand the power of that castle. Its powers are great, and the power I can obtain from it is never ending, but we cannot get in without all the Quint Fey. Its doors and walls are impenetrable. And now I have to deal with this new king and queens. Even if we did get in, I do not know the secrets of the Seven Wishes of Greatness."

Seitor walked over to the window and looked beyond the river and, in the distance, could see the magnificent castle. He continued, "When Yesu built this world, this castle was made for refuge for all the people, but unless all the powers he created come together, there could be no peace, and therefore, there could be no one to enter the great castle. So I say, no, King Julas, we cannot take the castle, but what we can take are the powers, and that is why it is time that my army rises."

Seitor walked toward the middle of the room, and he continued with a confident and rebellious voice, "We must rise. Our kind must rise up against the powers and take this world for our own. I, the great Dark King, call on you, Kanel! Are you and your White Eagles ready for battle?"

Kanel came forward and bowed before the Dark King. Seitor lifted the Ruby Stone Ring and called upon his wand "Sanguine

Fratrum!" chanted Seitor, and there was a red glow that brought both Kanel and Seitor together.

"And you, Cauffa, are you and your wolf pack ready to serve me?"

The large beast came forward and bowed. "We are ready, my lord."

Again, Seitor raised his wand and chanted, "Sanguine Fratrum!" and Seitor and Cauffa were united together.

"King Julas, King Mattei, and Young Adims, are you ready to take back what is ours?"

All three came forward and knelt down on one knee. "We are ready our king," they said.

Seitor raised his wand and for the third time chanted, "Sanguine Fratrum!"

The red glow brought them all together.

Seitor then walked up to the window, pointed his wand outward, and yelled, "Sanguine Fratrum!"

The red glow burst and radiated from the wand, and the red spell and curse surrounded the entire castle. It grew like weeds in a field, and it was covering everything. It went to the guards, the Blakers, the Egwaks, the entire Teak army, the Turk soldiers, and all of the Prosecs. Immediately, everyone was overtaken by it, and they were as one with Seitor and under his power and control.

Slowly but surely, the red curse was everywhere. Under the castle was the dungeon with all the other kings and the people who had been captured. Among them were King Bartho, King Thomas, King Mateo, King James, King Thad, and King Somon.

They were all brave and courageous kings, but their kingdoms had been overtaken by surprise when the Quint Fey were gone. As they sat there in their cells, the red spell and curse began to come inside.

"What is that?" said King Thomas.

"Close your eyes, and deny it, brothers!" yelled King James. Although they all did this, the red curse came to them and tried to take them over.

"Whatever you do, don't open your eyes, or it will consume you!" yelled King Somon.

The curse was everywhere, but the only way for the curse to enter the body was through the eyes. It is said, the eyes are the windows to the spirit.

All the kings resisted and kept their eyes closed. The red curse knew this and was pulling and tugging at them to see. Seitor closed his eyes and could see the kings resisting. Seitor raised his wand and shouted, "Sanguine Fratrum!"

King Thad was resisting, but then it became all very quiet for him, and he felt peace.

"Thad, Thad, sweetheart," he heard the voice of his beloved wife. King Thad slowly opened his eyes, and right before him was his wife. He fully opened his eyes and went to her and embraced her. He looked at her again, and the red curse took over him.

King Thad yelled as he was taken over, and King Thomas and King James opened their eyes to see what was happening. They too were taken over by the spell and curse.

"Daddy, Daddy, please help me!" yelled a young boy's voice.

King Bartho yelled back, "Jacob! Jacob!" He knew that voice was the voice of his son.

"Daddy, please help me!" King Bartho opened his eyes, and although he saw his son, he knew it was the curse. "Jacob, my boy. I love you."

"Dad, come to me," the boy responded. King Bartho looked at his boy and gave a very big smile and said, "Oh, how I love you, my boy, but I cannot come. I know you're the curse. I know you're Seitor. I opened my eyes, but what you don't know is that my boy was killed when you took over. He was killed, and I thought I would never see him again. I opened my eyes freely right now knowing I would be taken over, but in the end, you lose, because I see my boy again through the gracious blessing of Yesu. Yesu tuned your evil act into something good."

The curse revealed itself in anger. Seitor yelled, "It was not Yesu. It was I who has done this for you."

"No, Yesu is with me."

King Bartho raised his hands and went and embraced his son and was overtaken by the curse. King Mateo and King Somon could no longer resist. They opened their eyes and walked with their brother King Bartho, knowing they would not win.

"For the love of Yesu, I surrender," said King Mateo.

"And for the love of Yesu and all of Heirthia, I too surrender," said King Somon.

The Dark King was furious at their proclamations but overtook them as his own.

"Sanguine Fratrum!" yelled Seitor.

The entire south region of the Larena River was cursed.

"It is over!" yelled the Dark King. "Everyone is now serving me! Nothing can stop me!"

Still unsure of everything that was happening, the Geminis continued to walk through the lands of Heirthia in search of their army and their people.

"We have been walking for days, Mommy," voiced little Princess Violet with little Fariet Elliot by her side.

"Look on the bright side, Princess, we will soon be with all the people who love you and your kingdom," replied Fariet Elliot.

"Have you ever seen it, Fariet Elliot?"

"What, the people and the kingdom?"

"Yeah, you know, where we are going."

"I did, but a long time ago. I know the people are good, and with the new princess by my side, I know they will be excited."

Princess Violet then asked, "But what about my wand? I don't even know how to use it. They will all be embarrassed about a wizard princess that doesn't even know how to use her wand."

"Oh ye of little faith," said Jities Holmes. "A wand is only good as the wizard holding it."

Princess Violet stopped for a moment and said, "I know, my dad is always saying that I need to believe and that I am in charge of my happiness."

"And he is right," said Jities Holmes.

"He's always saying, 'Violet, who is in charge of your happiness?' and I'm always like, 'I am, Daddy.' He makes me happy when he says that."

Jities Holmes replied, "You will be a great wizard, Princess. You know what, can I borrow your wand?" Jities Holmes asked.

"Well, sure," Princess Violet reached out her wand, and—

"Stop! Stop! Stop!" said Fariet Elliot. "The law is as follows: the Quint Fey powers or now the New Faith are only to be used by the one who it has chosen. Anyone attempting to take or use these powers is a direct enemy of the Holy One."

Jities Holmes, knowing he had just met his newfound friends, said, "No, no, I do not wish to violate anything, young man. Thank you for reminding the young child of this. Princess Violet, hold on to your wand and never give it to anyone." Jities Holmes put his hand on Princess Violet's hand and moved it closer to her.

"Wizard Holmes, will you show me?"

"Show you what, my dear?" replied Jities Holmes.

"Will you show me how to use my wand?"

As the whole group walked, they finally came to a clearing. They had finally left the dense forest and entered the lands of Demble, the country of King Aniser.

"When we rest and camp, I will show you a few tricks. How about that?" He then lifted his wand, motioned it in a circle, and beautiful stars, rays, and colors appeared before her.

Princess Violet gave a big smile, and said, "That would be great!" She went to Jities Holmes and gave him a hug. She then ran off toward her father.

"Daddy, Daddy! Wizard Holmes said he would show me how to use my wand!"

Jities Holmes smiled at the child's excitement.

King Daniel stopped and looked at Fariet Julip. King Daniel turned around and went right up to the old wizard and said in his face, "I don't know your intentions, old man, and I still don't truly know who you are, but to play it safe, stay away from my family. Do you understand?"

"Your Highness, I don't want anything from anyone. I am simply trying to find out what is happening to this place I once loved. I am very grateful that you have allowed me to come. I am here solely to serve you. I will honor your word, and I will stay away from your family."

Jities Holmes bowed his head down in respect to the new king.

"I smell something in you," said King Daniel.

"I promise, it is my robe your majesty. I will wash it right away," the old wizard replied.

"My spirit tells me it is not your robe. It tells me it is your spirit."

King Daniel then looked straight into the old wizard's eyes, and said, "Jities Holmes, I am going to say something to you, something very important. It is a matter of your life and your death, and I am only going to say this once. If you hurt my family, I will kill you, and I will do it with no hesitation."

The old wizard continued to keep his shoulders down in submission.

Queen Elena then went to her husband and said, "Sweetie, come with me." She then walked with him. "Look, mi amor, I know he is a little creepy, but he did save our lives, and he has been following us for quite some time now. He has the power to take us out with his wand, but he doesn't. Look, you're tired, and so are all of us. Fariet Ut tells me there is a beautiful river just at the end of the clearing up ahead. Let's rest there for the night."

King Daniel, looking at his beautiful wife's eyes, said, "I love you so much, mi amor. You are everything to me. As you wish. We shall stay there for the night."

Queen Elena looked at her husband, and he looked back at her. He whispered to her, "I will always be here for you." The two drew closer and shared a beautiful romantic kiss at the edge of the forest.

Princess Katalina looked at her parents and smiled.

"Hey, I'm sorry about what I did back there," said Young Ladam to Princess Katalina.

"You should be sorry. Why did you kiss me?" asked Princess Katalina.

"I don't know. There was something about how you protected your father with your bow, and then when you just lay there, you, you, you—"

"I what?"

"You looked so beautiful. I couldn't resist how beautiful your eyes looked."

"Well, next time, resist. I'll let this one go."

Princess Katalina was walking away when Young Ladam said, "You don't know you're beautiful."

She went back into the forest and went behind a tree. As she stood there, she felt something in her stomach, like butterflies, and she smiled. She was falling in love with Young Ladam, but she did not know how her father would react.

The entire group hiked just past the clearing and went toward an area with a few trees next to the river. They all got comfortable and built a campfire for the evening.

Seitor sat at his castle with his eyes closed. He whispered, "Ruka, where are they?"

She spoke to him in his mind. "They have entered the land of Demble, my lord," said the evil witch, Ruka. "I have seen them in the forest, and they have just left the land of Castillo. They have stopped for the night at the river that meets the lands. Come quickly, as they may find refuge soon."

The Dark Lord opened his blue eyes and stood. "It is time! Let our armies go forth and cross the Larena River. Let us begin our takeover!"

The Dark Lord's army all rose to their positions, and the entire evil nation began its march across the river. Along with them were the people and the kings who were under the curse. They too were ready to battle.

"Ruka, keep following them, but do not intercept. Report to me when the people and the other kings are found. I must know where they are hiding," commanded Seitor.

Back at camp, it was early in the morning. Most of the group was still asleep, including the king and queen. It was a beautiful land where they had camped. To the west was a massive volcano, which was known as Arenal Volcano. It had had not erupted in hundreds of years. There were forests all around it. Princess Violet had woken up early with Fariet Elliot and was sitting on a rock along the bed of the river.

"What are you doing?" asked Fariet Elliot kindly. Princess Violet had her wand in hand and was motioning it toward the floor.

"I'm casting spells, but I'm not doing such a great job."

Rock by rock, she would zap them. A very small zap would come out of the wand. She knew no spells and knew no commands, and so she solely went by her heart. Princess Violet, even more frustrated, closed her eyes, and Fariet Elliot said, "You can do this, Princess. Just concentrate on a big spell or light."

She motioned with her hand again, hoping something would happen, but again, only a small light illuminated from her wand and hit the small pebbles on the floor, and they would jump up, like popcorn.

"It's pointless. I can't do this," she said.

"You can, my sweet princess. You just have to believe."

They then heard noise just down the river and as they turned and looked, it was Jities Holmes, the old wizard. Violet quickly got to her feet and went to him, followed by Fariet Elliot.

"Wizard Holmes, good morning!"

"Good morning," he replied.

"Please, can you show me what you said you would?"

"No! Now please go away."

With a confused face she replied, "But you said you would—"

He interrupted, "I know what I said, but your father is king, and he does not want me near you, so go!" he said with a bit of frustration in his voice.

She turned with a sad face and slowly walked away. Fariet Elliot went to the old wizard and said, "You made a promise. Bad or good, you have knowledge that can help her. She really believes in you, but you let her down."

Fariet Elliot flew away toward the little princess and consoled her as she returned to the rock she had been sitting on. With her little heart broken, she sat on her rock, a tear going down her cheek.

"Princess, please don't cry. You're a very special little girl. You have great potential to be a great wizard. You'll see."

Princess Violet looked at Fariet Elliot and said, "I don't know why I can't do this. I try to concentrate, but nothing happens. My dad knows how to use his power, my sister just saved the whole family, and my mom already used her power. I'm the only one that can't use my power. I think something's wrong with me."

"Princess, why don't you use what you feel inside to fuel what you can do with your wand?" said the Fariet.

The little princess looked at Fariet Elliot and said, "You think it will work?"

"It's better to try than to never try at all," said the Fariet.

Princess Violet stood up and closed her eyes. She took a deep breath and began to concentrate. She raised her right hand and felt someone touch her hand.

"Take another deep breath, my dear, and concentrate." She opened her eyes, and it was Jities Holmes. "Close your eyes," he said.

Princess Violet closed her eyes again and breathed in deeply.

"Listen to everything around you and take it all in. As you take it in, feel the energy and the power around you. It develops inside of you, inside of your heart. It will build to a point that you cannot hold any longer, and so you have to just release it all back. The difference, my dear, is that you are sending that energy to someone or something, and that is what makes you good or bad." He then whispered, "In the end, you must believe."

He let go of her hand, and she continued to breathe. She continued to feel everything around her—the trees, the morning sun, the early birds, and the wind. She slowly raised her hand, opened her eyes, and motioned her wand with such force toward the river. Fariet Elliot looked upon her and was so excited as he felt it was working, but the same little light came out and zapped the water. A small sprinkle came out.

She was devastated.

She turned and looked at the old wizard, and he replied, "Practice, my dear, practice. I promise. You will get it. I see it in you."

With such sadness in her heart, she continued to motion her wand, and the same light came from the wand and moved pebbles. It was no use. She was too young to understand. From around the tree, her father appeared.

"What a shot, sweetheart!" he exclaimed.

She went to her father and began to cry, heartbroken, "I tried, Daddy! I tried to be brave like you, but it doesn't work."

King Daniel was kneeling down, embracing his daughter. He looked over to the old wizard, but the wizard kept his head down. The old wizard looked visibly afraid as to what was to come for not staying away from the king's family.

"I promise, sweetheart, Yesu will show you the way. He will guide you, and he will teach you. Go. Go be with your mother as we will be leaving soon."

Princess Violet went as her father told her, and Fariet Elliot went with her.

Still looking down, the old wizard said, "Your Highness, I am so sorry. I told her to go away, but she persisted in my helping her, and I felt so bad not helping her as she wanted to learn." The old man broke into a few tears.

King Daniel placed his hand on the old wizard's shoulder and said, "Thank you for trying to give her confidence. I am watching you, but thank you for trying." King Daniel walked away with nothing more to say, but for the first time, the old wizard was afraid. However, he was humbled at the King's reaction. He felt peace and was very pleased at how King Daniel had accepted the situation.

Jities Holmes felt something in his chest and made a confused face, not knowing what it was but knowing that something was tugging at him and telling him that he had finally found his home. He stood there for a moment and smiled.

King Daniel joined his family, and they gathered themselves to continue their journey to King Aniser's castle.

"Sire, sire! Your Majesty!" Fariet Bert and Ut came flying.

"What is it?" replied Queen Elena.

"A red glow, a red evil, is far into the distance to the south. A group of us were looking for food, and we saw it in the early horizon to the south, and it's coming this way!" he continued as he yelled in fear. "It's Seitor!"

"All right, everyone we need to move now!" yelled King Daniel. "Gather all you have, and we leave now," he continued.

"Sire, we have a bigger problem," Fariet Julip spoke in wisdom.

"Go on, Fariet Julip," replied the king.

"We have left the cover and safety of the forest canopy of Castillo. Although there are trees and some forestry, the majority of the lands in Demble are mountains and clear lands. I fear the White Eagles."

"We have no choice at this point. If that red curse is headed our way, we cannot backtrack into the forest. We must move quickly before the White Eagles find us. May God be with us," said King Daniel with a worried tone.

The group began their hike immediately. It was King Daniel leading the way, with his Queen following, the two Princesses, and the three young girls. The Youngs surrounded them with their swords drawn, and the Fariets were scattered among them all.

The land of Demble was indeed a beautiful land. A great mountain stood to the north and wrapped around the northeast, but at the base, it was all grasslands and lands filled with flowers. King Aniser's castle was more toward the northeast side, with the mountains in the back. Directly to the east of King Aniser's castle was a valley that led to the grand land of Exsul, King Simon's castle.

There were a cluster of trees, but for the most part, it was open land, with many hills. Thus, one could clearly see up until the next hill. However, once leaving the land of Demble to the east and entering the land of Exsul, there was the great Backbone Desert, where the sun burned with the wind, and there was nothing for miles but dry wasteland.

19

HOMECOMING

THEY WALKED, AND they walked, and they walked. The entire group was growing very tired very quickly. They had not eaten much and had not rested sufficiently, and with the children, it was getting more and more difficult. King Daniel carried Princess Violet for a long part of the journey, but there were the other three children, and they too were tired.

"Sweetheart, we need to stop and rest," said Queen Elena.

"Yeah, there is a small stream over there by that clutter of trees. Let's head down that way," replied King Daniel. The entire group headed for the water, and perhaps there, they could find some food to nourish their bodies.

When they arrived, they all went for the water. It was a small stream, but the water was clean and pure. As they drank the water, it was a nice and sweet taste. It was cold and refreshing.

King Daniel, seeing the dejected faces around him, said, "I'm sorry, guys, but I can't take it anymore. It's so hot." The king leaped into the stream to refresh himself. *Splash!*

All the Youngs smiled, and the children were truly tempted. Soon enough, they all jumped in. They were splashing in the water and having a good time.

"Thank you, sire, I believe we all needed this," said Young James.

The queen stood there and nodded her head to her husband. She smiled as she knew he would do something like this. She then said, "Enjoy your time, children, including you, adult children. I am going to look for some food, but we must leave soon."

The queen then went off not too far away to look for food.

Ruka again called to the Dark King. "They are at the base of Arenal Volcano in a small stream to the east. There is still no sign of the others."

Seitor was riding his black horse when he received this message. He called, "Kanel, the family is in the land of Demble, near the stream of King Aniser's castle at Arenal. Go and capture them, and take with you the wolf pack."

Queen Elena and a few of the female Fariets went searching, and they were truly blessed as they found a patch of fruit trees and bushes with berries.

"Those look so delicious. Gather as many as you can," said Queen Elena to the eager Fariets. Quickly, they gathered as much fruit and berries as they could for the others.

As Queen Elena was gathering some of the berries near the floor, she heard a noise in the batch of trees just up a small hill. She looked up, but there was nothing there. She continued picking the berries and thought nothing more of it. Again, she heard a twig break. This time, it was a little louder.

Again, she looked up, and this time she voiced, "Is anyone there?"

There was not a sound, just a light wind blowing. Feeling a bit uncomfortable with this area, she backed off and went toward where the other female Fariets were.

"Do you all know if anything lives in these woods?"

Fariet Margaret answered, "Oh yes, dear, all types of critters, even bears, deer—you know, regular wildlife. Is something the matter?"

"Well, I thought I heard something walking in the woods right over there," she replied.

"Yes, you probably heard a squirrel or something."

Queen Elena, a bit confused, said, "But I though everything was gone, vanished?"

Fariet Margaret opened her mouth to speak but then made a facial expression and realized the queen was right.

"I'm sure it was nothing, but let's just get going. I think we gathered enough food," said the queen. They made their way back to where the others were. As they were walking, Queen Elena felt as though something was watching her. As she walked, she turned around and looked into the forest and quickly thought she saw a shadow in the distance.

She looked forward to ignore it but then looked back again. By the time she looked back, what she thought she saw was gone. She stopped and continued to look back curiously.

"Are you okay, my dear? Did you see something?" said Fariet Margaret.

"There in the trees, I thought I saw—" But then she stopped.

"Saw what?" Fariet Margaret replied.

"I thought I saw...I saw nothing." Queen Elena turned and looked at Fariet Margaret and said, "I think I'm just tired and hungry."

Fariet Margaret smiled and said, "Well then, let's get back and feast."

The group walked away and paid no more attention to the woods. Then from within the dark woods, something appeared from behind a tree. Indeed, something had been watching them. Was it the evil witch, Ruka? Was it an evil spirit? Was it a troll or goblin? They would soon find out.

"Mommy!" Princess Violet saw her mother coming to them with food. All the Youngs and the children went to the queen and the Fariets. Soon enough everyone was eating and sitting on the floor. King Daniel stayed in the stream by himself and prayed. "Dear God, I don't know what this is all about, and I don't know why you are using us, but I'm grateful for what you have done for my family. We are here to serve you, and we will follow you."

"Sire, it is in your best interests to have some food in your body. Please come join us," said Fariet Julip.

King Daniel stood up and went with them to eat. They were all smiling, and they ate for some time. As they were finishing their meal, they suddenly heard the scream of an eagle. All froze. Princess Katalina's eyes were wide open.

"Don't anybody move," whispered King Daniel. "Not a movement. Not a sound," he continued. King Daniel slowly looked up, and in the distance, there was one eagle.

"It's only one," replied Queen Elena. "Do you think it's them?"

Then out of nowhere, there were several flying high above in the distance. "They found us!" said King Daniel. "Quick, run!"

Together, they all began to run north in the hope they would reach someplace they could hide. They continued to run hill after hill, but there was nothing to hide in for quite some distance. Again, the cry of the eagle grew closer and closer.

"Run! They are tracking us!" yelled Young Ladam. Young Joseph picked up little Jesila, and Young John picked up little Miala so that they could move faster. King Daniel was carrying little Princess Violet.

Although they continued to run fast, they were growing very tired. They reached another hill, and as they reached the top, they saw another hill in the distance, but they were still in open land. The Youngs carrying the children fell to their knees in exhaustion. Young Jason picked up Jesila, and Young Jeremiah picked up little Miala. King Daniel, looking very exhausted but still carrying little Princess Violet, yelled, "We need to keep moving. They're coming!" He took a few steps and fell to the ground.

"Let me carry her!" yelled Jities Holmes.

"No, I got her!" yelled King Daniel.

"Please, there is no time. I can help you. Let me carry her!" again pleaded Jities Holmes, who looked visibly worried for the child.

King Daniel tried to get up, but again he fell in exhaustion.

Queen Elena went to her husband and said, "Daniel, please trust him. He means no harm. Let him carry Violet."

King Daniel, knowing he was in trouble as his legs began to cramp, said, "Be careful with her."

Jities Holmes reached for the little Princess and carried her. "Nothing will take her!" the old wizard yelled as he took out his wand and yelled, "Crepitus!" and fired a spell to the sky. The beam hit two of the eagles as they approached everyone. King Daniel got up, and they all continued to run.

The next hill was a high one, but they continued to run up the hill. Harder and harder it became as they grew closer to the top, and once they reached it, it was a beautiful sight. "King Aniser's castle! We made it! It is King Aniser's castle!" yelled Young John.

Swoosh! An eagle came out of the sky and, with its massive claws, took Young John high into the sky. The others were just reaching the top.

"John!" yelled Young James. Young John reached for his wand. "Ignis!"

The giant eagle was hit with a fiery spell. It yelled in pain and let go of the young wizard.

Young John was then falling from the sky and headed for the solid ground.

"Mr. Holmes!" yelled King Daniel.

Jities Holmes looked up and raised his wand, "Aranea telam!" and a white spell came out and burst into a massive spiderweb. It spread out and caught Young John as he fell. Young Ladam went to Young John and took out his sword. Quickly he cut the web, and Young John was released. All the Youngs went to him, and they embraced as they'd thought they had lost their brother. Soon, they all reached the top, and they all saw the massive castle not too far away.

"We made it. We made it!" yelled King Daniel.

Screech! Again the sound of the eagles announced they were returning. Young John, visibly upset that his life was nearly taken, raised his wand and waited. One by one, the White Eagles appeared again. But this time, there were twelve of them, and they were headed toward the group. Young John waited patiently as the rest of them looked on.

"What are you doing? Shoot them!" yelled Young Ladam.

Still, Young John would not fire, but rather, he just stood there with his wand raised and stared at the giant birds.

Screech! All the eagles yelled, and as they reached just above the group, all were afraid as to what was about to happen. The giant eagles opened their sharp massive claws, and then, "Magnificum Lucem!" yelled Young John, and a very bright light spell came out, and it lit the entire region. The eagles were immediately blinded.

The group rushed to the side, and all the eagles crashed onto the ground because they could not see where they were headed. They crashed into the side of the hill where everyone was standing, and a large cloud of dirt and dust went into the sky. The eagles stood up, but still they could not see. They screamed loud in frustration.

"Run!" commanded King Daniel, and the entire group continued to run toward the castle.

Then a sound that brought chills to the back of everyone's head: the howl of a wolf pack.

"It's the wolves, they found us!" yelled Princess Katalina.

"To the castle!" yelled King Daniel. Quickly, they all continued to run.

"Run, run, run!" yelled Young Ladam. The howls grew closer and closer. The wolves had found them with the help of the eagles.

Then the loud scream of an eagle was heard. Princess Katalina looked up, and sure enough, a giant eagle came and swept her off her feet as it grabbed her with its massive claws.

"Ignis!" yelled Young John with his wand, and it was a direct hit to the eagle. The eagle quickly dropped Princess Katalina, who was about fifteen feet off the ground. Young Ladam went and broke her fall as he caught her. They both fell to the ground.

Young Ladam pulled her up, and the two ran together holding hands. The eagle regrouped with the other eagles, and soon they all came in an assault. Together, all seven let out screams. It was a very chilling sound, and it was loud.

"The eagles are coming!" yelled Princess Katalina. As one of the eagles came again for Princess Katalina, Young Ladam leaped and turned around in midair. As he turned around, the eagle was stretching its massive claws toward Princess Katalina. Young Ladam swung his sword, cutting the massive bird in its chest, killing it. The bird fell to the ground along with Young Ladam.

"Ladam!" yelled Princess Katalina.

Young John let out a spell, "Murus!" and quickly a spell came out and made a wall of stone, to which the eagles crashed and fell to the ground. They quickly took flight to regroup in the sky.

King Daniel heard this and turned around. Princess Katalina was at Young Ladam's side. She was trying to pull the dead eagle off.

The sounds of the wolves' howls was getting closer. Finally, Young Ladam and Princess Katalina managed to get the bird off him. He was covered in its blood. They continued to run.

"Come on!" yelled King Daniel as Princess Katalina and Young Ladam caught up with them. Just over the last hill that the group had passed, the wolves appeared. King Daniel looked up, and there were three wolves.

"There are only three, sire. We can take them," said Young Jeremiah.

"No, my son, there is never just three in a pack," King Daniel replied.

Then on the hill came two more wolves, so now there were five, but then, more and more appeared on top of the hill.

"Oh my, no! We can't take them, sire," replied Young Jeremiah. In total, there were thirty-one wolves, with Cauffa in the middle as the alpha male. Young Jeremiah turned around and ran as fast as he could.

King Daniel turned around and yelled, "Wolves!" Immediately everyone turned and continued to run toward the castle, which was not too far.

Cauffa let out a loud chilling howl, and immediately all the giant wolves ran toward the Geminis.

Fariet Julip yelled, "Fariets. We are to protect the Geminis! Turn and stand your ground! We must use our powers!"

King Daniel said, "No, Julip, do not sacrifice. We must stay together and get to the castle and get help."

"Forgive me Your Highness, but if we don't do this, none of us will reach the castle." Although King Daniel did not want to sacrifice anyone, he knew this needed to be done.

"In Yesu's name, fight bravely," said King Daniel.

All the Fariets gathered, except Fariet Elliot, who was to stay with the young Princess Violet, and made a line, and each put their hands together, ready for battle. Little by little, beautiful purple-and-white lights began to glow from the Fariets. There were colors everywhere.

As the wolves grew closer, Fariet Julip said in a sad voice, "Be brave, my Fariets. Some will make it, some will die, but just know, either way, you will be home. If you live, we will live to serve the New Faith and go home with them, but if you die, you will go home with our Lord. Don't hold back! Let all of your powers out!"

The lights, magic, and colors little by little began to grow.

The wind and air began to swirl faster. The trees and bushes began to move side to side as the powers grew. Surrounding the Fariets were leaves that had fallen from the trees, and the leaves began to fly around the Fariets. The magic was completely surrounding them.

The wolves grew closer and closer, but because of all the leaves, they could not see what was happening. Then when the wolves came within ten feet of the line, Fariet Julip yelled, "In Nomine Yesu!" and together they let out their hands.

Blast! What an amazing blast it was. The entire region shook as though an earthquake had rocked the land, and when this happened, there was a loud boom.

The wolves were blasted with such power that they were thrown back. Several were thrown into boulders and trees. They were hurt badly, and five were killed instantly.

"Regroup, Fariets!" yelled Fariet Ut.

Again, the Fariets line regrouped, this time with a little less power because they had used so much the first time.

Again, the wolves, although hurt and visibly shaken, charged toward the Fariets, and again the Fariets put their individual hands together, and *blast*, the wolves were again fired with a blast and thrown back. Several of the wolves were killed with the hit.

Many of the Fariets could no longer hold the line. One by one, the Fariets slowly fell to the ground with no power.

Cauffa saw this. "Their powers are weakened. Get the family!"

With much frustration, Fariet Julip fell to the ground with no more power, but he knew he and the other Fariets had stopped the wolves in their tracks long enough for the Geminis to get

254 ◆ *David Jimenez*

closer to the castle. The wolves ran past the Fariets as they lay there with no power.

"May Yesu be with them," whispered Fariet Margaret.

"They're coming!" yelled Princess Katalina.

The Geminis ran as fast as they could. King Daniel had Princess Violet by the hand, and Queen Elena was right next to him.

"Daddy, I'm scared!" cried Princess Violet. She ran but was so scared that she was crying. Queen Elena looked to her left toward the forest as they got closer to the castle. She turned and looked because she could see something with a cape and hood running in the forest next to them. It was a dark shadow.

"There's something in the forest! Run!" Queen Elena yelled in fear.

Again she looked to the left and again. She could still see the shadow in the forest running parallel with them. She then looked back, and the wolves were gaining on them. King Daniel looked to the left as Queen Elena yelled, and he too saw the thing running next to them.

Jities Holmes held on to the two little girls. "Run, little ones! The wolves are coming!"

The two little ones were crying hopelessly. "Please shoot them, Mr. Holmes. Shoot them with your wand," yelled Donia, the older sister.

"I cannot, my dear. I am tired and cannot concentrate. We need to get to the castle!" he replied. Even though tired, Jities Holmes turned around and yelled, "Ignis," shooting a ball of fire toward the wolves, but being that he was tired, the wolves dodged it.

Queen Elena looked to the right, and there too, she saw another something with a cape and hood running in the forest. It was also a dark shadow. She became very terrified. They heard a loud cry from the sky. It was the White Eagles. The Geminis were no more than fifty yards from the entrance of the castle.

"The gates are open!" yelled Young Ladam who was holding on to Princess Katalina's hand.

From a distance, King Daniel looked inside and could tell no one was there. There were no guards, no people walking around. The castle was abandoned. His heart sank. He knew they were doomed.

King Daniel could feel the wolves right behind them and knew they were running for nothing. There was no help at this castle. He pulled Princess Violet ahead along with Queen Elena and all the others as they ran. He looked back, and Cauffa was right there. He peered up and saw Kanel in the sky with the other White Eagles soaring down to grasp them, and to both sides, the dark shadows were following them.

He looked at his family and did not know what to do. He called out his sword and looked back only to find Cauffa in the air with his jaws wide open and all the eagles within feet of his family.

Then out of nowhere, the dark shadows left the forest and attacked. It was not two shadows. It was many, and now that they were out of the shadows, King Daniel could finally see they were warriors.

Crash! The many shadows came and tackled the giant wolves with their swords. Many wands were raised, and spells were cast toward the White Eagles. Everywhere, "Magnus Igne!" could be heard from these warriors, and the eagles were blasted out of the sky.

The wolves were pounded to the ground as there were many warriors. Queen Elena and the others turned around, only to see they had finally found their army. They had finally made it home. It was the original Quint Fey and many other loyal warriors, kings, and Youngs.

"Protect the New Faith!" yelled King Simon Peuro.

In a line, with their swords drawn, it was King Simon Peuro, King Aniser, King Jemis, and King Jonis. Along with them were their loyal servants, and many Youngs who that had made it into hiding after the fall of the original Quint Fey. They all had their weapons, swords, bows, and wands. Cauffa and the wolves let out a chilling growl. The White Eagles and Kanel landed on the ground with their massive claws, and so, the two groups faced each other for a potential battle. However, the wolf pack and the White Eagles knew they were outnumbered.

"The Dark King is coming, and nothing can stop us!" yelled Cauffa.

Kanel then spoke and said, "Surrender the New Faith now, and the Dark Army will leave you alone in your forest. We now know where you live and where your families are."

"You want the New Faith? We are all the New Faith," replied Queen Elena.

"Queen, you appear to be brave, but you are nothing," said Cauffa.

"You trust these so-called kings Your Highness, when they are the enemy. They left their people out of Heirthia like cowards!" yelled a giant White Eagle.

"We do not trust them, and they do not trust us—" replied Queen Elena.

Then King Daniel stepped forward and continued what Queen Elena had been saying, "but we all trust the Living King, Yesu." King Daniel then raised his sword in a battle stance.

"Fall back!" yelled Cauffa, and the wolves ran into the distance, and the White Eagles went into the sky.

King Daniel turned, and King Simon looked at him.

"Hello, old friend," said King Daniel.

King Simon gave King Daniel a very big smile, and the two embraced each other, and all who were there cheered and rejoiced. They all began to hug, and there was true fellowship for the Geminis and, for once, true relief.

The king and queens of Heirthia had finally arrived home, and they had finally found the army Yesu had promised.

"We are so glad to have finally found you all," said Queen Elena.

"It is good to see you, my queen," replied King Aniser.

"Where have you all been hiding? We thought you would have been in one of the castles," asked the queen.

"There was no way, Your Highness," said King Simon. He continued, "Once we got back to Heirthia, everything had changed. We arrived at our castles, but by that time, everyone was gone because the Dark Army had taken over everything. All the people went into hiding into the forests, which was the only place they could find refuge. The Dark Army is afraid of the forests because of the unknown. So because of this knowledge, the people knew they could find a safe haven in the forests."

Queen Elena then asked, "Why are they afraid of the forest? I don't understand."

King Jemis continued, "They are afraid of the legend of the Dark Forest. Inside the Dark Forest lurks creatures that are unknown. People and creatures have gone in and have never come back. Well, although that forest is to the west of everything, it still connects with all the land. Therefore, they are afraid, and that is why we have lived in the forest ever since."

"Ever since? It's only been a few days since we last saw you on Earth," said King Daniel.

"Well, not exactly. That may have been two days of Earth time, but here on Heirthia, it has been two years. Every one of your days is one year of ours," said King Aniser.

King Daniel slowly walked away and said in a shocked voice, "You have been in refuge for two years?" He continued, "Why haven't you fought? Come out and taken what is rightfully yours?"

King Simon responded, "The Dark Army came many times, and they came in large numbers, but without the protection and power of the New Faith, it was not the right time to fight. Today is the first time we have come out of the forest. We actually saw your queen back at the stream."

"That was you in the forest! I knew I had seen something hiding," she answered.

King Simon answered. "Yes, my queen, and I'm sorry for startling you. We just wanted to make sure you were the actual New Faith. There are many false wizards in this land that have deceived in order to lure us out of the forests and find the people. Once we saw the wolves at your feet, we knew it was time."

"It is time?" replied Princess Katalina.

King Simon replied, "Yes, time for the true people and creatures of Heirthia to come out and take back their land."

"Come out of where?" asked King Daniel.

King Simon smiled and pointed behind the Geminis. The Geminis turned around, looking into the forest, and then they saw it. The forest began to fade away as that portion of the forest was made by a spell of the wand of Bazar, the good wizard.

Behind the fake forest, a large village magically appeared. This was where all the people and creatures had found refuge for those two years.

"You made a fake forest because you knew they would never enter," said Queen Elena.

"That's right, my queen, well, except the wolves, but they all fear, and with so much forest, it would take them years to find this little place."

King Daniel and all the others walked closer to the village, and all the people and creatures looked upon them, and they were excited and joyful that the New Faith had finally arrived.

King Daniel embraced his wife. He then looked at her eyes and said, "I love you with all my heart, and I will always be here for you. You are my light. You are my stars. We are home, my love, we are home."

Queen Elena gave her husband a beautiful kiss, and they embraced. The New Faith had finally come home, and as they walked into the new land, the forest closed in to once again hide their new land.

20

THE CITY AWAKES

"THE FARIETS!" YELLED Princess Violet.

"We are here, my little princess," replied Fariet Julip behind them all.

"Fariets? We have not seen a Fariet for so many years," said King Simon with a surprise tone.

"Fariet Julip, are you and your family well?" asked King Daniel as he went to help his friend.

"We are fine, Your Majesty, very tired and weary, but we will recover," replied Fariet Julip.

All the people and creatures that were there came and welcomed the New Faith and the Fariets to the new world they had created. With Bazar's spell shielding and protecting their hiding place, the people and creatures could live their lives in peace and quiet, and so they did.

The New Faith, the Youngs, the three small children, all the Fariets, and Jities Holmes went into the crowd, and there were smiles of hope. King Simon came to the New Faith and invited them back to the main meeting building so that they could shower, clean up, and have a warm meal.

"Thank you for having us in your kingdom, King Simon," said King Daniel.

"The pleasure is all ours, Your Highness. After all, you are the new king of Heirthia."

After walking some distance toward the meeting building, King Daniel asked, "So how many people are living here?"

"How many people?" replied King Simon as he smiled. He stopped right where he was and said, "Just look over the hill."

King Daniel continued climbing the small hill they had been walking on to get to the main building, and as he cleared the top, he whispered "Oh my lord!"

Queen Elena joined him, and she too was surprised. "Wow," she whispered.

There were thousands of people, creatures, and all types of critters in their little city. Children of all ages and elderly people were there. Even the creatures were looking at them, and they too were talking.

"Your Majesty, I am here to serve the Almighty Yesu. Therefore, I am here to serve you," said a giant tiger.

"What is your name, tamed tiger?" asked Queen Elena.

"I am Teimur," the giant cat replied.

"Teimur, 'the Loyal,' is what we call him," said King Aniser. King Aniser walked up to the big cat, which was bigger and much larger than him and began scratching the back of his ears.

"That's not fair. You know I love it when you do that," Teimur voiced as he lowered himself to the ground, enjoying the scratch. Teimur completely fell to the ground on his back as King

Aniser continued to scratch, and he began to move his leg in a quick motion.

"Well, Teimur, we will certainly need your size and weapons to help serve Heirthia," said King Daniel.

Teimur got up from the ground and opened his massive jaws, showing all his sharp teeth. "My teeth are craving the blood of the Dark King," and then he raised his paws, and all his sharp claws came out instantly. "And these will help me." All that were there began to laugh.

"King Daniel, Queen Elena, meet all the citizens of Heirthia. Well, at least the people who found this refuge. There are millions more, but they are still lost."

As they looked on, the people would turn and look at them with a smile, knowing Yesu had come to save the people. As the Geminis looked on, they saw the people, young and old, and they saw all types of creatures—deer, bears, birds, panthers, leopards, horses, gorillas, and many other types of animals they had never seen before—interacting with the people as they all lived together.

"Your city is too small for so many people and creatures. How do you get by?" asked Jities Holmes.

"Sir, with no disrespect, I don't recall ever knowing you, and so, I don't know your intentions and do not trust you, especially with you being a wizard," replied King Simon.

"This is Jities Holmes. He is a wizard from the land of Castillo. We met him at King Jonis's castle, where he helped save our lives. We trust him," replied King Daniel.

Jities Holmes responded while keeping his head down, "King Simon, I am sure I will impress you with my actions. I have no ill intentions. I only want to find a home. The new king and queen and their family have embraced me, and I am here to serve them and Your Highness in any way I can."

Staring at him was the wizard Bazar, and he approached Jities Holmes and shook his hand. "You say you're from the area of the Dark Forest."

"That is correct, sir. I lived there in my hut, but then came the army, and they drove me into the forest. I have stayed there alone ever since."

"I have never heard of you. What clan are you from?" asked Bazar.

"I come from the wizards of Larena, the River Wizards. I lived there up until I was a youngster until my parents were killed long ago," said Jities Holmes. He then asked "How about yourself?"

Bazar answered, "I have always served King Simon. I came to him as a child, and I don't remember where I came from. My family is his."

Jities Holmes then replied, "And that is what I seek—a new beginning, a new home."

Bazar seemed to carry a nice conversation with Jities Holmes and the rest of the kings felt it was okay. "Well then, if my wizard brother accepts you, then I accept you," exclaimed King Simon.

"Are there any other wizards here?" asked Jities Holmes.

Bazar answered, "Well, yes, there are many others, but most do not possess sufficient powers or knowledge. We did find one just days ago lost in the forest. A young man who says his family was killed by the army, but he managed to escape. He is still very timid and won't talk much."

"You brought him here, and you don't know him?" replied Jities Holmes.

"Well, yes, he was so young, and he was so in shock at every-thing. Even today, he does not say much."

Both wizards looked upon the young wizard as he looked on at the celebration of the arrival of the New Faith. "His name is Jaysade."

King Simon and the other kings showed the Geminis the main building.

"Please accept this as your new home for now. We expect to build a special home for you and your family soon," said King Jemis. The Geminis, the other Youngs, and even the Fariets were shown the places where they would be staying. After showering and cleaning up, the Geminis and all the leaders gathered for a nice dinner.

As they sat at the table, King Simon spoke, "I want to thank you all for being here this evening. I consider every person, creature, and critter in this world of ours as special. I especially consider everyone at this table as needing to be here to enjoy the fellowship of our new king and queens and to further discuss the future of our city. Before we feast, please allow me to make a toast and say, in the name of Yesu, thank you, Geminis, for joining us on this journey, but more importantly, thank you for accepting the mission Yesu himself has placed upon you. Cheers!"

All that were there lifted their cups of wine and water, and they all cheered and greeted each other.

"Enjoy!" yelled King Aniser.

Together, all the people at the table began to eat. At the table were the Geminis; the original Quint Fey and their families; several of the Youngs, including Young Ladam and his brothers; the two wizards; some of the elders; Fariet Julip, Ut, Bert, and Margaret; and several other warriors.

As they were just about finished eating, King Daniel spoke and said, "King Jemis, I wanted to ask you about something interesting that you said earlier. You said a special home would be built for us soon. I wanted to know where?"

"Well, we are thinking about the western end of the city," replied King Jemis.

"What concerns you?" Queen Elena asked King Daniel.

"Why here in this city?" King Daniel questioned. All who were there became quiet to listen.

"Well, this is where we live, sire. Where else do you want to live?" replied King Jemis in a confused manner. King Daniel paused for a moment and then went to his feet and slowly walked around, thinking.

"Heirthia, I want to live in Heirthia."

"This is Heirthia, sire," replied Wizard Bazar. Bazar then stood up and motioned with his wand in the air, he drawing a map of Heirthia that showed all of the kingdoms. It was magical. As Bazar did this, his wand left a trail of bright light, which marked where he intended to write. Slowly, but surely, the entire kingdom was on his map.

"You see, here is Yesu's castle and, of course, all of the other kingdoms."

"I'm listening," replied King Daniel.

"Well then, yes, you see here?" He pointed to the northern end of Heirthia and then continued, "Well, this is the unexplored area of Heirthia, an area that was never developed. Our plan is to build our new kingdom here." The wizard Bazar then looked at King Daniel and smiled, as though he was pleased with their plan.

"I understand, but this is not the real Heirthia, the Heirthia granted to you, the people, and creatures of all kinds by Yesu himself. I know this is your home now, and it's great, but that out there beyond your spell of a home, that is your real home, your land, and the home these people and creatures deserve and know," continued King Daniel. "To make matters worse, you have thousands, if not millions, of souls still lost out there.

King Simon then replied "Out there? You want to take them out there? And do what? Risk their lives? Because surely they will die. Your Highness, I know you are the king of Heirthia now, and I respect you as our leader with Yesu's Sword, but this would be suicide for all the people to go out and try to reclaim their land. The Dark Lord has control over all the land—all of it. There is just no way. His army is larger than all other armies put together."

"You did it before. You controlled the land, and you had the power just as we do now," continued King Daniel.

"When we had control. We had all five kings, thus the word *quint*, meaning "five." We had the Ruby Stone Ring, and we also had the other seven kings. Without those elements, we don't have the power to overtake the Dark Lord and his army," exclaimed King Simon.

"Seven kings? Who are they?" asked Queen Elena.

King Simon explained, "We were twelve kings—twelve tribes, if you will—all chosen by Yesu the Great. He then selected five of the twelve to serve as the original Quint Fey. It was myself, King Aniser, King Jemis, King Jonis, and King Phelo. It was King Phelo who was the fifth of the Quint Fey with the Ruby Stone Ring." King Simon paused.

King Aniser continued the story. "Whenever we battled, all of the twelve kings worked as a unit. We were like brothers, and we fought like brothers. No doubt the Quint Fey were the stronghold of our army and the power behind it, but with all the twelve kings together, we were unstoppable."

King Jemis added, "And that all ended when King Phelo was killed by one of the twelve, and that was King Julas. He and King Mattei, King Phelo's best friend, got together and they ambushed King Phelo, killing him and taking with them the Ruby Stone Ring, and they gave it to Seitor."

King Simon then concluded, "And that is why we no longer have the power. They have taken everything."

"I have even taken King Phelo's widow and child, Young Travi, as part of my family. I will not put them in more danger. They have been through enough."

Young Travi, sitting at the table, stood up, and said, "Well, I will fight for my land, the land my father died for." He then became emotional and began to tear up. He continued, "My father did not die for nothing. He died for Heirthia, he died for you, and he died for Yesu, and I will fight in his honor."

One of the elders then voiced, "Young Travi, I am sorry for your loss, and you are absolutely right, but they have even taken some of our families' lives as well. We cannot risk any more of our lives or our children's lives to be lost."

King Daniel looked at them in amazement. "What little faith you all have. I am going to tell you something, and I am only going to say it once. They will find you. Eventually, they will find you, and they will have no mercy on you, and you will have no opportunity to fight. The wolves and the eagles already know the general area, and they went back to get the rest of their army."

King Daniel then slammed his fist on the table and said, "And when they find you, they will kill you! They will kill your families! It's not about if. It's about when! But if we fight now and we train and prepare now, we, at the very least, have that opportunity. The New Faith is here, and we will fight for you."

King Simon then said, "New Faith? The New Faith isn't here yet. It's just you. With all due respect, Your Majesty, Queen Elena, you have not mastered your power, and the children have no idea how to utilize their powers. It's at best spontaneous right now." He continued, "They will take our lives and everything we have. Don't you understand!"

King Daniel then yelled, "They can take your things, they can take your home, and they can even take your very lives, but there is one thing they cannot take, and that is your faith in your Lord." He then paused for a moment and continued "Never, never, never! They cannot take the very thing that believes in you, the very thing that lives in you."

King Daniel then walked toward the door so as to leave but stopped for a moment and said, "The only question you have to ask yourselves is whether you have any faith in you. Remember, when you believe, you have trust, but most importantly, when you trust, you have faith. The question is, where does your faith lie?"

He then walked out of the main hall building where they were eating, and all who remained there did not say anything. Some even felt a bit ashamed.

King Daniel walked into the city, looking at all the people there. It was close to sundown, and the people were all beginning to put their things away and getting ready for the evening time. He looked at the frail people. Some were elders, but then there were many young there as well. There were children, Youngs, and many adults, and he could see in their faces that they were scared.

"Daniel!" called Queen Elena.

She caught up to him, and he looked at her, his disappointment in the former kings still clear in his eyes. Elena looked at her husband and said, "I am so proud of you." She then put her hands around his neck and looked at him in his eyes. She then slowly reached over and gave him a romantic kiss.

King Daniel, still a bit frustrated, closed his eyes, and put his head down. Again, Queen Elena looked at him and said, "You know, you're cute when you're angry. You put your lips together and make them small. You then put your eyebrows together."

King Daniel could not hold it any longer. He smiled and gave Queen Elena a big hug.

"I'm sorry I got frustrated back there. You know I mean well, and you know I am not afraid of anything," said King Daniel.

"Sweetheart, I know, I know. You know that you and I are go-getters. We face the problems, we face our enemies, and we fight for what we believe is right."

"Am I wrong? Am I wrong in trying to encourage them to fight?" asked King Daniel in a confused and unsure voice.

Queen Elena looked at her husband and said, "You are so brave. You are a man of courage, a man of honor, but most importantly, a man of peace. You are not trying to be right. You are trying to do what is right. I have never known another person who wants peace more than you do."

She then paused for a moment and looked toward some small children playing nearby, and she continued, "You are not wrong, my love. You are not wrong at all. You are encouraging them to face their fears, to face what will come one day. That is exactly what these little children need. You are their leader, and it is up to you, my king, to encourage them always to be the best they can be, to be the bravest they can be, and to live a life of courage, trust, and faith. The problem the kings and these people are facing is that they believed too much in the Quint Fey rather than believing in themselves and believing in Yesu."

King Daniel smiled and replied, "This is why God gave me you." He lifted his right hand and gracefully touched her jawline.

He leaned closer until he was within inches of her, looked into her eyes, and said, "Thank you for being my bride." He leaned and gave her a soft kiss, and then the two embraced.

"Seitor! Seitor, my lord."

Seitor and his had just moved into the land of Castillo to the west and into the land of Flora to the east, and a massive army it was.

"Go on, Ruka," commanded Seitor as he rode Rasier, the dark horse, full of armor. Even his horse had armor, and the horse was enormous, with red eyes, very aggressive.

"I have seen the people," she reported.

"Where are they?" exclaimed Seitor with such enthusiasm and interest.

"You will go north into the land of Demble and just west of the castle of Aniser. They are in the woods behind a spell."

"Ruka, the forest is grand. Where exactly?" replied Seitor.

"Your wolves and eagles know where as the original Quint Fey saved the New Faith from a fatal battle. They shall lead you there." As she concluded, Cauffa and his pack arrived.

As they arrived, the wolf pack turned into their human bodies. "Sire, we have found them," stated Cauffa. Kanel then landed with his other eagles and continued, "The original Quint Fey are there, and they are living in a secret spelled land behind the forest."

Cauffa added with a smirk, "We can take you there right away."

"Ruka!" called Seitor.

"Yes, my lord," she replied.

"What are they planning?" Seitor asked.

There was a pause for a few moments, and then she replied, "The new king wishes to prepare and fight, but all are afraid."

Those around Seitor smiled at the news that the people were afraid. However, Seitor looked very displeased.

"Ruka, why did you call him the new king?"

Everyone there went silent. Ruka stayed quite for a moment. "My apologies, Dark Lord, this is what they are calling him, but it means nothing to me. I serve you."

"Let it be the last time you or anyone else refers to that nobody as the new king!"

Ruka replied, "Yes, my lord."

All that were there bowed their heads and knelt down in fear.

"Remember this!" Seitor exclaimed. "I am the only king of this world. I am the new king. I am the power of Heirthia, and the New Faith will be no more. Only I shall rule!" he yelled.

"All hail the Dark Lord, Seitor!" yelled all of his army.

"Cauffa, take your pack and lead us on the ground. Kanel, take to the sky and report to me any ambush they may be planning."

Seitor and commander of the Teaks, Dawson, and the grand army moved forward through the land of Castillo and Flora. They headed north right toward King Aniser's castle. The glow of the red spell illuminated the sky as they moved forward. Battle was looming.

***

Back in the secret forest, King Simon and the other kings were still at the dinner hall debating what to do.

King Simon voiced, "It would just be so difficult to put our people in a position to fight into the dark."

King Aniser added, "They outnumber us one thousand to one. There are thousands, maybe even millions of soldiers that would be coming toward us at once, not to mention the Dark Lord has the Ruby Stone Ring."

King Simon replied, "As your former king, it is my advice to stay where we are and let them find us. Once they near, we can ambush them at the narrow entrance of our city, and we can fight them one by one."

Fariet Julip then said, "May I take a moment, Your Highness? I have a question. So it is your plan to wait for the thousands,

270

maybe millions of soldiers to come to your front door, and the four of you will fight them one by one?"

King Jemis replied, "It will also be King Daniel and perhaps several of the brave Youngs."

King Simon added, "We understand it is not the best plan, but we have no other choice."

They all sat there looking at one another in shame, knowing their plan would surely fail. Fariet Ut responded and said, "I know you mean well, but at one point or another, you will grow tired, and you will grow weary. There is just no way for us few to fight them at your door. It will take the entire city to help and to do something. That is the Fariet way."

Fariet Bert then spoke, "Now correct me if I am wrong, Kings of Heirthia, but didn't you all always used to fight the battle as King Daniel has just advised?"

"It's not that simple anymore," voiced King Aniser.

Then King Simon continued, "Before, it was very different. We were five strong kings, and the powers were in full force. The seven other kings always fought with us, and together, we were unstoppable. This is a very different situation now, Sir Fariet. Out of the five powers, we have four, and of the four, only Yesu's Sword is of any controlled power. Not to mention, we don't have the other seven kings. We don't even know where they are, but we can only assume they were either taken or killed by the Dark King."

Fariet Julip then spoke, "We'll let me encourage you. King Daniel and his family have fought far more than we have ever expected, and what do they get out of this? With what, you ask? Nothing! They just have the faith that is needed to fight, and that is the Fariets' way!"

King Simon replied with much frustration and stood up, "Yes, but this is not the Fariet world. We love those people. How can we possibly ask them to risk their lives knowing they will surely die!"

Then among them all, an argument broke out as to what to do. Some of the elders were of the opinion that they should fight. The Youngs yelled and voiced that they were ready to battle, with

Young Ladam leading them. "We can fight, and we will fight. We should all be brave!" yelled Young Ladam.

Then little Princess Violet stood up, frightened. She put her hands to her ears at all the arguing that was going on and became very frail. Fariet Elliot saw this and became concerned over all that was happening. The argument was becoming very heated, and so he put himself in front of the young princess and put his hands together.

He put his head down and closed his eyes. *Blast!* He opened his hands with a force that ignited a blue wave of power that sent all who were arguing, flying through the air and falling to the ground.

Princess Katalina yelled, "Stop fighting with each other!"

All were quiet. She continued, "You must use that power and energy against the Dark Lord. The closer they get to us, the closer the evil takes over you. Can't you all see this? You are all acting like animals, and you are no better than Seitor! My father is always asking us who is in charge of our happiness. If the answer is anything but me, then I am not in charge, and I have let them take over my happiness! I will have then let them take over my life!"

Princess Katalina paused for a moment as she'd begun to cry, and then she concluded, "The question is, who is in charge of your happiness?"

All that had been arguing stood there, ashamed at what they had been doing. Then little Princess Violet went to them and said, "In my world, Jesus Christ is my Lord and Savior. My heart tells me that Yesu is the same person, the same God." She became a little emotional, and it was heard in her sweet little voice as she looked down. She then raised her head to look at them and said in a very light child's voice, "The Lord is the everlasting God, the Creator of all the Earth. He never grows weak or weary. No one can measure the depths of His understanding. He gives power to the weak and strength to the powerless. Even youths will become weak and tired, and young men will fall in exhaustion, but those who trust in the Lord will find new strength. They will soar high on wings like eagles. They will run and not grow weary. They will walk and not faint."

The Kings, elders, Youngs, wizards, and even the Fariets were all silent, staring at the small child. None there knew what to say to a child of such faith.

Princess Katalina then said in a very light voice, "If God is for us, then who can be against us?"

"No one!" exclaimed King Simon.

"No one!" exclaimed King Aniser.

"No one!" exclaimed several others there.

"In Nomine Yesu," stated one of the elders.

"We shall fight for Yesu," said another one of the elders.

"In Nomine Yesu!" exclaimed all who were there.

Crash! The door was opened by King Simon, and all who were in the dinning hall went outside. King Simon went straight to where King Daniel and his bride were standing. They both turned around at what was going on behind them.

King Daniel asked in a serious voice, "What's going on?"

"Your children are truly beyond their years," said King Simon.

He continued, "The two have spoken true words of wisdom and have voiced true encouragements that have motivated our lives."

King Simon then looked at all the kings around him and at all the people there. He then exclaimed, "We will fight, and we will fight for faith and honor for the glory of Yesu!"

Queen Elena then spoke and said to all, "And I admire your courage and bravery. The people of Heirthia will retrieve what is rightfully theirs."

All who were there then looked at King Daniel. King Daniel exclaimed, "I will fight for you, and we will fight together. No matter what happens, people of Heirthia, life or death, either way, you will be home. If you find yourself near death, then behold, you shall be home with your Lord. However, if you are closer to life, then behold, you shall be in your rightful home of Heirthia!"

All the crowd yelled and cheered in enthusiasm and excitement. The people were ready to fight back. King Daniel then yelled, "In Nomine Yesu!" and all the people responded, "In Nomine Yesu!"

With no time to waste, everyone in the city began to gather all their weapons and things they could use in battle. Unbeknownst to the kings, many of the elders were wizards, and they took out their wands. King Simon approached one such elder and said, "Sir, you're a wizard?"

The elder responded with a big smile, "I may not be the best, sire, but I know a few good spells that can blast anything from the sky."

Right then and there, the elder got into a stance and yelled, "Crepitus!" but his wand did nothing. "It's perhaps a bit rusty."

King Simon crossed his arms and gave a smirk, as though the elder had no idea what he was doing. "Honestly, I went to the School of Youngs as a young man. I didn't finish, but I do remember a thing or two."

The elder man cleaned up the wand and again got into a stance. King Simon said, "Sir, with all due respect, you don't have to—"

"Crepitus!" yelled the elder, and *blast* came the spell from the wand. It hit a nearby tree, completely destroying it, and it went up in flames.

"I told you, I told you!" exclaimed the old man as he jumped up and down. "I told you, I told you!"

"Ignis!" yelled another elder wizard, and a bright blue-and-purple light illuminated and directly hit a large bush next to King Simon. The two elders began to laugh as King Simon took cover from all that was happening. King Simon then looked up at the two elder wizards and said, "King Daniel can truly use you."

King Simon and King Daniel met, and King Daniel asked, "I need for you and the original Quint Fey to show us how to truly use the powers. We need for you all to train us."

King Simon replied, "We will show you, and you four will be the most powerful subjects in all the land." Both kings reached out to shake hands, and they grabbed each others' forearms and shook. And so, the training began.

"Seitor," called Ruka in the blowing wind, "They are beginning to train. Come quickly as they are preparing for battle."

Seitor and his army were speeding toward the kingdom, and Seitor asked, "What are their numbers?" Ruka replied, "Not many. Your grand army will overtake them, but do not underestimate the—"

Remembering not to call King Daniel the new king, she paused, but then continued, "The weak king. They are spreading much work, and they are gathering all that can fight. Come quickly."

"So this so-called king will try and defend Heirthia." The Dark King's blood boiled at the thought. "Not if I kill him first. I'm going to start with his family so he will regret coming against me. Then, I will take his life before all of Heirthia so that they will never forget that I alone rule."

21

THE POWERS WITHIN

"**Y**OUR MAJESTY, ARE you ready?" King Aniser asked to Queen Elena.

Queen Elena gave a big smile and nodded her head. "Yes."

"Okay, so, have you ever been able to use the Lion Heart Medallion?"

Queen Elena responded, "Well, yes, one time."

"And what did you become?"

"A lioness, a big lioness, but I don't remember how I did it. It just happened when my girls were in danger," she responded.

In amazement, King Aniser said, "Interesting, the medallion changes to the character of the person. With me, I transformed into a lion, but with you being a female, you changed into a lioness, the hunter, the brave. I'm impressed." King Aniser then continued with a smirk and a bit of sarcasm, "Well, I guess we'll just have to settle for that then," and he walked past her.

Queen Elena, looking a bit surprised, turned around toward him and said, "What do you mean 'settle for that'?" She then crossed her arms.

He replied, "Well, I'm just saying that a lion is much more powerful than a lioness, and so theoretically, that would have been better." He walked away again, turning his back on the queen.

"Don't turn your back on me. I'm talking to you. Why are you saying such a negative thing?"

Again, he stopped and turned around and said, "Look, I'm sure you'll do fine. A lioness is okay. You'll be strong."

The queen was becoming very upset at what he was saying, feeling so horrible at the position he was taking. She felt so discriminated against. With even more frustration, Queen Elena replied, "Well, Yesu gave me the medallion and took it from you for a reason. Maybe you weren't good enough."

She quickly walked away from him, and he then said in a very sarcastic voice, "Oh, you'll be good—for a woman, of course."

Without turning around, her back to him, the queen stopped where she was and replied in a very quiet voice, "What did you say?"

King Aniser stood there and crossed his arms together and said, "I said, your lioness transformation will be good, for a woman. For a man, however, you will never make it, and you will never be as powerful. Thus, you'll be good for a woman."

The queen just stood there with her back turned. She had her eyes closed. King Aniser then continued, "Trust me, I'm wasting my time teaching a woman how to use a man's power." He then turned around and began walking away again.

Queen Elena heard this and quickly opened her eyes. Her eyes had changed color to a light honey yellow, like that of a lioness's. Trying to keep calm, she turned her head around, and he turned his head as well. He added sarcastically, "Oh, and by the way, your husband, the so-called new king? He's a nobody and a worthless example of a man!"

When she heard this, her eyes opened wide. "You can talk about me all you want, but never, ever talk or touch my family." She let out a growl, quickly turned her body around, and leaped into the air, immediately turning into a fierce and massive lioness.

She let out a strong and powerful roar that sent King Aniser flying to the ground. She leaped again toward him with her massive jaws open and landed above him.

She roared again as she stood above him, and he yelled, "Yes, my queen, yes! Do you feel it? Do you feel it? Look deep inside yourself. Feel what is in your heart! That is what you need to feel so you can control when you change! Feel what is going through your entire body, Your Majesty. Memorize it, feel it, control it, so that you know what you need to feel in order to change!"

The Queen Lioness stood and moved back in confusion. Her fur was bristling, and she was still very angry.

King Aniser quickly stood up and voiced, "Your Highness, concentrate on what you are feeling. Understand the power inside of you. It is very important for you to take in what your heart is feeling. Feel the blood going through your body and digest that power within you. Control your mind and focus on staying as a lioness. Try to feel that power not in anger, but in justice and righteousness."

King Aniser pulled out his sword and swung it toward the queen so as to entice her. Again, she let out a growl. "Yes, like that, like that. Come on, you big cat, you're nothing!" Again, he swung his sword toward her, and she moved back and crouched down.

He swung his sword toward her, and again, she dodged the sword by less than an inch.

"Watch my sword at all times. Never take your eyes off it. You can focus on me, but watch my sword because what I do with it will determine your opportunity of attack," he continued.

He quickly kicked a rock that was on the ground toward her. As he did this, he attacked her, swinging his sword. The rock hit her on the face, and she roared. His sword came close to her as she was focused on the rock, and so she stumbled for a moment and fell to the ground.

She quickly got up. Her eyes and facial expressions were still in much confusion as she was still trying to feel all that was happening inside of her, but she quickly realized that he was teaching her all along.

"Good, my queen, good. A little stumble now, but I would prefer that you do it now rather than in battle."

Then he kicked the rock again, but this time with some dirt and dust. He charged with his sword and swung from left to right. She quickly made a small leap to the right side, avoiding the rock and dirt, and because he had swung his sword so quickly and missed, the sword was away from her. She saw the opportunity. She could hear her heart beating rapidly, and she could feel the power within her racing, but it was being controlled. She lowered her eyebrows, raised her snout, and then quickly leaped toward King Aniser, and with her massive paws and claws, she pushed him to the ground.

"Very impressive, Your Majesty. You have done well," whispered King Aniser. The giant cat walked backward and then turned, pacing around King Aniser as he sat there. "What you need to learn now is how to turn yourself back into your human self, but be ready to transform back in a split second."

Queen Elena stood there for a moment, breathing just like a lioness but trying to control her lioness within.

He whispered, "Breathe slowly. Take long breaths. Close your eyes and concentrate on something you absolutely love, something very dear to you. When you do this, feel all the lion power within you slowly be taken out of you, and put back into the medallion where it will stay until you need it. Breathe, Your Majesty, breathe."

Slowly, Queen Elena's breathing was becoming more and more controlled and much slower. She could feel the power slowly moving through her body and into the medallion. It was truly magical. She then began to change, and she was changing back into her human body, becoming smaller and smaller. As she grew into her human self, her clothing began to reappear, and within moments, she was exactly as she was prior to changing into a lioness.

"You did it, Your Majesty, you did it!" remarked an excited King Aniser.

Queen Elena gave a big smile and was very pleased at what she had done. King Aniser went toward her to congratulate her. He extended his hand to shake hers, and as she raised her hand, King Aniser swung his forearm, hitting her on the shoulder, knocking her to the ground.

"Come on, Your Highness, can you do it again or not? You can't keep up with me, great lion!" he yelled in a sarcastic voice, smiling at her tauntingly. She had fallen backward, but she'd broke her fall with her left hand and twisted around, staying in a crouched stance. She stayed there with her eyebrows lowered and gave a very small smile. She quickly leaped toward him, changing into a lioness in midair.

As the giant lioness landed, she let out a loud roar, showing all her sharp teeth.

King Aniser stood there for a moment looking at the giant cat, and as he looked at her staring down at him, he was truly afraid. He got out of his fight position and voiced, "Your Majesty, you changed without anger. That is the key to your success. You changed with passion, with your heart, with the blessing of Yesu." As he looked at her, he concluded, "You are ready."

Out in the south end of the city, near the woods, there came several figures. It was King Daniel and Queen Elena with their daughter, Princess Violet.

"Violet," called her father as he squatted to speak with her, "are you ready to train as a young wizard?"

She looked at him right into his eyes. The little ten-year-old glanced at her mother. Queen Elena smiled back and nodded her head in approval. She then said in a sweet voice, "I'm ready, Daddy."

Her father smiled at her and said, "You are a very brave young lady, and I am so proud of you. Remember this, my sweet little one, you are everything to me, and I will always protect you. Whatever you do, no matter what situation you are involved in, do everything in the name of your Lord."

Little Princess Violet smiled and said, "Thank you, Daddy. You always make me smile."

He continued, "I want you to concentrate when you are training with Fariet Elliot, Wizard Bazar, and Wizard Holmes. They will teach you what you need to know. If you don't succeed now, I promise you will succeed later. With patience and persistence, you will be all you want to be, my little baby. Remember, you are my super girl, my hero, and my courageous little girl because of your young and brave heart."

They smiled at each other, and Princess Violet went to her father and hugged him around his neck. He smiled with such peace, and he kissed her on the cheek.

All who were there smiled. Jities Holmes stood there, and a small tear came down his cheek.

"Mr. Holmes, are you all right?" asked Queen Elena.

"Yes, yes, I'm fine. A bug must have gotten in my eye.

"Why are you crying?"

Being a bit nervous, he responded, "No, no, I just, I just…He loves her very much, doesn't he?"

Queen Elena looked at Princess Violet and King Daniel embracing, and she looked back at Jities Holmes and said, "Yes, she means the world to him. She is his little girl, and he will fight the world for her. She has, like, a very special place in his heart."

"I see," the big wizard replied. "It's nice to have a father who cares so much about you."

Jities Holmes walked away, looking a bit depressed at what he was seeing. He then turned around toward the queen and gave her a little smile. She smiled back and was concerned at what Jities Holmes was feeling. She thought to herself that he must have had a hard life without his father.

"Princess," called Fariet Elliot. Violet turned around to see the Fariet flying next to her.

"The first step in being a wizard is knowing that you have the power within you to cast spells and, more importantly, to create power from within you to come out. Does that make sense so far?"

"Well, kind of. You mean like the power comes from my heart, right?"

"Yes, pretty much. The wand is a tool. It's just a tool."

Princess Violet responded, "So its like a hammer. The hammer is strong and hard, but without me using it, pushing it, and swinging it, it won't do anything, right?"

Fariet Elliot was nodding his head as she was saying this and then responded, "What's a hammer?"

"You silly, it's like a stick with a hard rock at the end of it, and you use it to build things," said Princess Violet.

"Oh yes, I know what you mean. That is exactly right. You can't use a hummer unless you use your inner strength to swing it and make it do something."

Princess Violet, giggling, responded, "Hammer, not hummer. A hummer is a truck."

Fariet Elliot, making the most confused face, responded, "What's a truck?"

Princess Violet, smiling, said, "Oh, this is going to take all day."

King Daniel and Queen Elena stood there and began to laugh at the dialogue Fariet Elliot and Princess Violet were having.

"In all seriousness, Princess, I care about you, and I only want to protect you. However, there will be times when I may not be there, nor your father or mother, and so I want for you to have the courage, power, and ability to create power from within you to face anything." Fariet Elliot slowly flew backward away from Princess Violet, and he closed his eyes. He then faced the forest, lowered his head, and slowly raised his hands. All who were there were watching.

The wind came to the area, and it began to blow. Little by little, the wind began to pick up. The trees branches began to move side to side. It was as though a strong storm was brewing. Fariet Elliot motioned his hands to a battle stance, and the leaves began to lift themselves up from the ground, and soon enough, all the leaves were flying around them in a circular motion, all moving so gracefully. He then motioned his shoulders side to side, and the rocks and small boulders began to rise into the air. A light then began to emanate from Fariet Elliot. Princess Violet looked at what he was doing, and she was amazed.

She whispered, "He has special powers!"

Wizard Bazar came to her and whispered back, "No, he has nothing more than you do, my dear, but what he does have is the ability to control that power within him and use his hands as his tools to take that power out, and ultimately, he has the faith in our Lord to believe in that power."

The wind got stronger, and the leaves, rocks, and boulders were moving fast. Fariet Elliot then put his hands together and yelled, "Rebellis!" and when he did this, all the power within him and all that was flying around him exploded forward into the forest, and there was a great blast into the woods.

Everyone there was startled. As the dust began to clear and the wind slowed down and died away, Princess Violet could see what he had done. He had cast a spell that blew a large portion of the forest completely away.

She turned and looked at Fariet Elliot, and he was on the ground.

"Fariet Elliot, Fariet Elliot!"

"He is fine, my dear," said Jities Holmes. "Remember, he is a Fariet, and their bodies are so small and fragile, they lose all their energy and power within them. He just needs some time to rest."

Princess Violet looked down at him and said, "Fariet Elliot, I am so proud of you. You showed me so much, and you showed me the true power of the heart. Thank you." She reached down and gave him a kiss on his forehead. "Besides, you blew up part of the forest."

As he lay there, he opened his eyes. "Thank you, Princess. Just remember, when you feel that power at the tip of your heart, let it all out, and Yesu will show you his true power."

"Come, Princess, let him rest," said the wizard Bazar. Jities Holmes, Bazar, and Princess Violet went into the field to train further. Bazar then said, "Well, Princess, let's see what you got. Have at it."

Princess Violet then reached out for her wand and said, "What do you want me to do?"

"You see that boulder over there?"

Princess Violet nodded her head.

He continued, "Break it in half."

Princess Violet, looking a bit intimidated, said, "You want for me to break that giant rock in half?"

Both wizards Bazar and Jities Holmes nodded their heads in agreement. Princess Violet then squared herself, facing the boulder, and concentrated on her heart. She closed her eyes and moved herself to a battle stance. She opened her eyes, extended her hand with the Dragon's Claw Wand, and yelled, "Expellere!"

Zap! A small light illuminated out of the wand, and it hit the boulder, creating a small burn mark. She immediately put her head down in disappointment.

"You see, no matter how much I try, it's always a small zap and not a blast."

The wizard Bazar went to her and said, "No, my dear, that was good."

She looked up at him and said, "How is that any good? It's only good to burn ants."

He smiled and said, "The good thing is that there is something there. I would be more worried if nothing came out, meaning you have nothing inside of you. But here, you were able to take something out. You just need to dig deeper, look harder into yourself."

Jities Holmes, felling bad for the little wizard, said, "What he is trying to say is, let's try something easier for you, and we can build you up from there." Jities Holmes went to the big boulder and put a smaller rock on top of it.

"Your job, just hit the little rock off the big rock. Here, you will learn several things, little wizard. One, you will learn to aim, and two, you will learn to use the power that you do have instead of frowning on what you can't do." He smiled at the little apprentice.

Wizard Bazar, a bit bothered with Jities's suggestion, interrupted and said, "Well, I did not mean that. I believe a young wizard needs to look deeper and be more challenged than to just use what they got."

Jities Holmes, getting very close to the wizard Bazar's face, responded, "Well, you'll certainly have your chance to show her something, but right now, this is what I am showing her. You have a problem with that?"

The wizard Bazar looked at him and raised his wand. His wand lit up like a star, and he positioned himself into a battle stance. Jities Holmes raised his wand in the same gesture, but then Princess Violet went between them and said, "Stop it, you're scaring me!"

Jities Holmes looked at the small child and lowered his wand. He then looked back at Wizard Bazar and voiced, "You are not worth fighting with."

Wizard Bazar put his wand down and then walked away to watch what Jities Holmes was teaching her.

Jities Holmes continued, "Okay, now that he is gone, let's move forward, my dear. Princess, remember, when you are using your wand, I want you to pretend it is like a toy, a fun thing you are playing with. I don't want you to take it so seriously, okay? That is okay, and that concentrating will come naturally when you are using your wand, but right now, I want you to feel comfortable with the wand, especially with the wand that you have. It is a tool, but that is a big and powerful tool. Does that make sense?"

"I like you, Mr. Holmes. You're a sweet man, and from my heart, thank you for being nice to me." Princess Violet then gave Jities Holmes a smile, went toward him, and hugged him around the neck as he crouched down.

Jities Holmes, feeling uncomfortable with all the emotions, replied, "Yes, yes, well, let's continue, young princess."

Princess Violet then positioned herself about twenty feet in front of the boulder and stared down the boulder. She kept her eyes fixed on the smaller rock on top, and with all her heart, she wanted to cast the rock off.

"Focus, Princess," replied Jities Holmes.

Princess Violet closed her eyes and prayed. "Dear God, please let me hit that rock. There are a lot of wizards out there, but I want to be a good wizard for your glory, Lord."

Fariet Elliot, just waking up from regaining his power, leaned over as he sat on the ground, and saw what Princess Violet was doing.

"Look deep into your heart and let it all out, my princess," said Fariet Elliot.

Princess Violet, with even more confidence that she could do this, got into a battle stance, and with her left hand extended, she yelled, "Expellere!" while her right hand motioned forward with her wand.

Zap! A beam came out, but it did not hit the smaller rock. It actually hit the giant boulder. Princess Violet was devastated as she failed again.

"Good, Princess, good," replied Jities Holmes, wanting to encourage the little wizard.

"I missed, Wizard Holmes, I missed, and I can't seem to get anything bigger than just a small spell."

Wizard Bazar went to the princess and said, "You have done well. You have focused, and you have explored this powerful wand! Why don't we go and join some other Young wizards at the school so you can see what they are all doing? Good?"

Princess Violet, still very disappointed in herself, nodded her head in agreement. Wizard Bazar, the Princess, Fariet Elliot, King Daniel, and the queen all went up the hill toward the school to join some of the younger children.

Jities Holmes stayed behind just a little bit, and he saw them all walking away. He put his head down, feeling a bit bad for the Young Princess. He looked back at the boulder where Princess Violet had hit the boulder. All that was there were two small black marks where she had created a burn. Jities Holmes smiled with a bit of a smirk and laughed a bit and began to walk away.

Crack!

There was a loud breaking sound that came from behind him. He was greatly startled, putting his shoulders up in fear and raising his wand in a battle stance as he turned around. Standing there with his eyes wide open, he was in amazement. "What is this?" he whispered in confusion.

The boulder had completely shattered. It did not crack. It did not break. It completely shattered. The once-giant boulder was a rubble of rocks and pebbles. Princess Violet had completely destroyed the boulder. He was speechless.

"Princess Katalina!" yelled Young Ladam as he approached her in the field where she was preparing to practice with King Jemis, the original Falcon Bow king. "May I join you in the art of archery?" he asked with a bit of a smile.

"Yeah, sure, that would be nice if you're going to be nice," she kindly responded.

Young Ladam, looking pleased, said, "Great! Maybe I can show you a thing or two."

"I'm watching you, and don't think your blue eyes help any," said the princess with a smile.

"Let's focus, Princess," said King Jemis. "Remember, this is the Falcon Bow, no arrows, and nothing more, only what is in your heart."

Princess Katalina listened tentatively, and Young Ladam looked on. "Your father tells me you used it back at King Jonis's castle. He says you tried many times and failed, but on one instance, you pulled back, but you pulled back with a passion. What happened?"

"I really don't know," she said as she walked away. "I tried and I tried, but nothing would happen, but then I saw that look in my dad's face, and he needed me."

As she said this, she was looking down. She then looked up at King Jemis and said, "He cried out for me. He cried out to me as I cried out to him when I was a little girl. I love my dad." As she concluded, she became teary eyed. "I really thought my dad was going to die."

King Jemis looked on and said, "That's the passion I need from you, Princess. I need for you to dig deep into your spirit and remember what you were feeling when you pulled the bow for your father. Close your eyes."

Princess Katalina closed her eyes and tried to concentrate. As she did this, several Youngs approached the archery field. They all looked on as they began to prepare for practice. King Jemis went to them and said, "Okay, Youngs, you know the drill. Although this is practice, your concentration and focus is vital and very important."

Young Caster, a Young from the school and about sixteen years old, replied, "Yes, Your Majesty. May I help the young princess with her concentration?"

Young Ladam, hearing what Young Caster had said, replied, "Well, with all due respect King Jemis, I saved the Princess from the wolves, and so I would be honored to help in her concentration."

Young Caster, seeing Young Ladam was a bit wary with him being around the princess replied, "I understand, Young Ladam, but your expertise is in sword fight, and mine is in archery. Thus, it would only be best for her to get a prospective from an experienced archer."

King Jemis, noticing the debate between both Youngs and knowing their true intentions to be beside the Princess, said, "How about both of you train on your own, and I will work with her. Young Ladam, you must head on over to the sword chambers. King Simon is expecting you."

Young Ladam looked over at Young Caster in a bit of embarrassment, and Young Caster gave a smirk of a smile, nodded his head over toward the sword chambers, and made a clicking sound so as to direct Young Ladam to leave like a horse.

Feeling a bit out of place, Young Ladam said, "Yes, Your Majesty, I will train. Thank you, Young Caster, for looking after the princess."

Young Ladam then went to Princess Katalina and said, "I am very sorry for this little incident. I just want to make sure you're okay."

Princess Katalina, admiring his intentions, said, "I know, Young Ladam, and thank you for caring."

He replied and said, "I will go now to train to protect you."

Princess Katalina immediately felt something in her stomach and was not sure what she was feeling. She became a bit nervous. "Thank you," she replied, and he then turned and walked away.

"Enough of that, Princess. Let's get back to your concentration. Close your eyes, and I want you to go back and remember the day you used Falcon Bow for the first time. Now you're back at the castle."

When he said this, Princess Katalina made a facial expression as though she was actually seeing it.

"Now everything is fine. Your family is with you, and you're getting ready to leave, but then, all of a sudden, there are enemies in the castle. They are looking for you and your family, and they want to hurt you."

Princess Katalina was clearly becoming visibly upset. "No, stop," she whispered.

"They are coming, Princess!" he raised his voice.

Princess Katalina, still with her eyes closed, raised her bow toward the array of targets. She quickly pulled back on the string, but the arrow would not come out.

"Concentrate, Princess. Your father needs you. Dig deeper!" Again, he raised his voice.

The other Youngs were training, but at the same time, they were looking at Princess Katalina.

"I can't, I can't," she voiced, still with her eyes closed.

"Yes, you can, Princess. You did it before. Focus! Your family is in trouble," he tried to encourage her.

"It's not the same," she replied. Again she pulled back the bow, and a very small spark of fire came out.

"Yes, Princess, I see it. Focus and concentrate. They are coming, and they are looking for you."

Princess Katalina, still with her eyes closed, continued to focus on her family. She pulled again and again, and every time, a small fire illuminated out of her bow, but the arrow would not appear.

She was beginning to become frustrated and could not continue. King Jemis saw this and stopped her, "That's okay, Princess. Take a break, take a break. You need it."

Princess Katalina opened her eyes and gave a small smile with a small tear coming out of her eye.

"You did well. It just takes practice."

She replied, "I can feel something there. There is something deep in my heart that wants to come out."

King Jemis, admiring her ambition, voiced, "Princess, many times it takes emotions and incidents to take place in order for that deep fire in you for the arrow to come out. It is difficult to practice with the Falcon Bow. After all, Yesu created it to protect, not to practice with."

"For now, why don't you practice on your aim with a regular bow? It would do you good," recommended King Jemis.

Princess Katalina put down the Falcon Bow on the small table beside her, and King Jemis handed her a wooden bow. She took the bow and a few arrows.

"My dad used to be the executive director for the Boy Scouts of America, and I used to love using their bows and arrows when I was a little girl. My dad showed me how to use it. He would take me out to the woods and show my mom and me how to shoot. Even my little sister practiced."

King Jemis smiled and said, "What are Boy Scouts?"

"Well, they are kind of like the Youngs from your world, and in our world, they are very admirable because they learn good morals and values, and they learn to be independent, strong, and knowledgeable in so many areas."

"Well then, let's see what you learned from the Scouts."

Princess Katalina positioned herself sideways as her father showed her and took an arrow and placed it on the bow. She pulled her shoulders back and took aim. She released, and the arrow flew uselessly a few feet away.

"Oops," she commented.

Many of the other Youngs were looking at her, and a few made fun of her. They giggled a bit. Again she took the bow and shot, but this time the shot was very wide.

"This is strange."

"What is, Princess?"

"Every time I take aim, it just doesn't feel right. It's like the arrow has no control."

"Just take aim and breathe," he responded.

She tried a few more times, but every time she shot, the arrow would not reach the target. One of the Youngs there commented a bit sarcastically, "Maybe we should set it closer, sire, and get a much bigger target." He, along with three other Youngs, laughed, making fun of her.

King Jemis looked at the Youngs with a serious face, and they went back to shooting their targets. Young Caster voiced, "Have more respect for the woman that will rule over you one day."

The Youngs, respecting Young Caster and hearing the tone in his voice, went on and continued their training. They were good sharpshooters.

"That's how you do it, Princess," said one of the Youngs after hitting a bull's-eye. A bit more irritated, Princess Katalina again took an arrow and really concentrated on the target.

She breathed deeply and released. The arrow was on track and had the right speed, but again fell short of the target.

Again, several of the Youngs smiled, and some laughed.

"At least she hit the air," one commented.

Young Princess Iruy, an excellent archer herself, voiced, "Stop it. That's not funny. She will be queen one day, and she will rule. Show more respect." She went to Princess Katalina and apologized for the comment.

"That's okay. I'm sure they don't mean wrong," said the frustrated Princess.

"I'm Young Iruy. Nice to meet you."

"Thank you, and it's nice to meet you too."

Young Iruy continued, "Look, don't impress anyone. Be yourself and be genuine. No matter what you do, it is between you and Yesu." Young Iruy was about Princess Katalina's age. She was slim and of an Asian background. Princess Katalina felt more comfortable with what Young Iruy said. She looked over at the other Youngs, and still they were laughing at her. She still felt what they were doing was wrong. One of the Youngs mouthed the words, "She'll never make it."

Princess Katalina dropped the wooden bow, and it hit the ground. She reached over to the Falcon Bow, stretched out her shoulders, and pulled back. She was still feeling and remembering the comments they had just made. The Falcon Bow then became completely and fully enflamed, and a fire arrow appeared.

She aimed the bow toward all the Youngs who were laughing at her, and they all became very serious and quiet.

They froze and could not move. She quickly turned toward all the targets and yelled, "Expandat Ignis!" She released the arrow, and it burst into seven arrows, all on fire. The arrows flew swiftly, and all seven arrows hit all the targets of the Youngs who had been laughing, and their targets were completely destroyed. The Youngs ducked down at the blasts that had come out from the impacts. King Jemis cheered into the air and jumped up and down. "You did it, Princess, you did it!"

She smiled and was very excited at what she had done. "I felt it, King Jemis, I felt it. It was like a fire that came out, and now I understand the bow. The purpose is not to fight but to protect and to do justice. That is why you just can't practice with it. It can only be used when you are absolutely ready to use it."

"Were you angry at what they were saying?" asked King Jemis.

"No, I wasn't. I just felt that they needed a scare, but what I did feel was that justice needed to be done."

"Well, I believe they got the message," he replied with a big smile.

Princess Katalina looked over at them and said, "That's the way you hit a target."

Young Caster approached Princess Katalina and said, "That was amazing. I was very impressed, Princess. You looked wonderful."

Princess Katalina looked at King Jemis, and as King Jemis walked away, she replied, "Well thank you, Young Caster. You're also very good at the bow."

"Well, I'm okay. I'd practice more, but you would just put me to shame."

"That's sweet, but I think I'm done here. I'll see you later."

Young Caster looked at her and said, "Your beauty would put me to shame is what I meant to say."

She looked at him feeling very shy at his sweet words. He then reached for her hand, raised it, and gave it a small kiss on the top of her hand. Princess Katalina smiled and then walked away.

"You were great, Princess," voiced Young Iruy, catching up to her. They gave each other a small hug.

"Thanks for talking with me. Hey, do you want to go get something to eat?" asked Princess Katalina.

"That sounds great. I'm starving," answered Young Iruy.

Young Sebastian came to where Young Caster was and said, "You are really impressed with her."

"Like, you have no idea. She is so beautiful and magnificent."

Young Sebastian then said, "Yea, and her hair smells so good."

The two watched as she walked away with Young Iruy. "You know you can never have her, right?" commented Young Sebastian.

"Why do you say such a thing?"

"Well, for one, her father is the king of Heirthia, and two, Young Ladam already has her favor."

Young Caster responded, "Remember something, brother, nothing is certain until she has chosen for herself, and until she does this, I will never give up."

Standing at a distance was Young Lielgab, a wizard and sword fighter. He watched all that was going on and took interest in the Young Princess but was too shy to even approach her. It was certain that several of the Youngs took an interest in the Princess, but right now was certainly not the time for love. They all were preparing for the looming war.

22

GOOD MEETS EVIL

A S ALL THE land was preparing for battle in the hidden forest of Demble, the evil was growing ever so closer. Seitor and his army were moving at a swift pace, and at this point, they were already close to the end of the land of Castillo and at the edge of the border with Demble. The Dark Lord's entire army surrounded the entire land.

The army was in the land of Castillo to the west and in the land of Flora to the east. Nothing would pass them, and they would consume all the people. Seitor was focused, and he knew what he had to do. He had to kill the new family, and get their powers.

King Daniel and King Simon were with each other, talking about the future.

"What lies ahead?" asked King Simon.

"I don't know, brother, but there is one thing I do know. Yesu is with us," said King Daniel.

"I had such a strong faith like you, never bending, never straying away. I know Yesu is there. I have seen the so many wondrous things, meeting your family, the angel Michael, but I don't know if he will come to save us this time. The Dark Lord is so powerful, and his army is like no other ever formed. I hope you are right," shared King Simon.

King Daniel looked at King Simon as they reached the top of a high mountain, and said, "Remember one thing and never let this go, if God put you in it, He will see you through it. All you have to do is believe. Believe in our Savior, and with everything in your heart, trust in the Lord and in His mighty power."

After saying this, King Daniel smiled, and he and King Simon clasped hands and embraced each other's shoulders. "I will very much enjoy fighting beside you," said King Simon. "By the way, where did you learn your fighting skills? Young Ladam and the others tell me you fought so bravely and craftily."

King Daniel, really not knowing what to say, replied, "Well, I have had no training at all. I have never even used a sword before."

"Never used a sword before! This can't be. I have trained since I was a child, and I am still learning. How then can you have fought like this?"

King Daniel stood there a bit silent and said, "I don't know, but what I do know is that when I take hold of the Sword of Yesu, something comes to me, and I feel light as a feather but quick, like the strike of a lightning bolt. It is as though all my senses are heightened. My strength is increased, my heart is bolder, and I can see everything before it happens."

King Simon took out his sword and swung it toward King Daniel, and King Daniel quickly called out the Sword of Yesu and blocked the strike.

"Very good, Your Majesty! Now let's put it to the test."

The two went into a fierce sword battle, and they each tested their own strengths. King Simon was really, putting his full effort toward defeating King Daniel. Strike after strike, King Simon was moving quickly, but King Daniel was keeping up.

"Focus, Your Highness! Focus! But be sure to stay calm. Stay in control," he yelled out as they fought. King Daniel called for the Fariets' shield and fought with both, and he then let King Simon have it. King Daniel swung the shield, twisted, and struck King Simon's sword with the Sword of Yesu, shattering King Simon's sword to pieces. King Simon swung and punched King Daniel on the face. King Daniel flew back and fell to the ground.

"You have to expect everything that can happen, Your Highness, but never let a strike against you shake you. Never be shaken! You are the king. You have the Sword of Yesu!"

King Simon took out his second sword and went toward King Daniel, swinging profusely. King Daniel swung around, and King Simon blocked, but then King Daniel lifted his foot and kicked King Simon in the stomach, knocking him to the ground. King Daniel then lifted the Sword of Yesu and motioned as though to kill King Simon, but he stopped.

The two magnificent kings looked at each other and gave a big laugh. King Daniel extended his right hand and helped King Simon up.

"You are a great king, King Daniel. You fought well."

"They're here, they're here! They have come!" yelled Young James.

"Calm down, Young James. Where have you seen this?" asked King Daniel. Young James, without saying a word, looked between both kings. He pointed into the distance as they stood on the mountaintop. Both King Daniel and King Simon turned around and looked into the distance, and there they were. There was a red glowing light, the light of the spell of Seitor, and beyond that, they could see the massive army approaching the back side of the mountain.

All Seitor and his army had to do was march a few hours around the mountainside, and there they would reach Wizard's Pass, a canal that leads directly to King Aniser's castle, which leads right to the secret forest. King Daniel looked at the massive army he would be facing and said, "It has begun. Emmanuel."

King Simon looked at King Daniel and asked, "Emmanuel?"

King Daniel looked over at King Simon and replied, "He is with us. Let us go and prepare for battle."

King Daniel and King Simon rushed back to the secret forest to gather the others. When they arrived, King Daniel ordered, "Sound the horns of battle! I want everyone to gather to make certain everyone knows the plan."

Immediately, one of the Youngs blew the horn, and all throughout the city, everyone knew it was time. When this was done, everyone began to gather their weapons. Fathers and sons began to leave their homes. Women without children joined in to take part in the battle. All the Youngs gathered their wands, swords, and bows to prepare for the war, and the elders came forward to provide their skills and powers.

As they gathered near the city hall, King Daniel looked around at the many people. There must have been over ten thousand people, including the many creatures, Teimur, and the Fariets. Queen Elena stood by her husband, and on his other side stood Princess Katalina and Princess Violet.

"Just a few days ago, my family and I were ordinary people from the world of Earth. We were living our lives to the fullest, and we lived to serve our God and our Lord. We believe we were serving our primary purpose in that world, and we did all we could to serve others. But instead, our world was changed from one day to the next when we were called by the one you call Yesu." King Daniel paused for a moment, and then he continued, "We are ordinary people, being called by a living God, the Living King. We do not know him, and we have never met him, but we believe he is the one and only God and Savior of both our worlds.

He called us—a man, a wife, and two small children—to hold, what is apparently the most powerful tools given by the Living King for your world to believe in something we have not seen, to believe in something we do not know, to believe in you.

"Just a few days ago, we did not know you even existed, but here we are today, the new king and queens of Heirthia, and let me share with you, we believe! We believe that there is a purpose for all of this! We believe you are more valuable than you think! We believe you are more important to Yesu than you can ever imagine. If we believe, people from another world, then you must believe. You must believe that Yesu is with you. You must believe that no matter what happens today, you are doing what is right because you have believed in something you have not yet seen. Because of this, you are a blessed people.

"Today, you will meet the enemy, the evil one, Seitor. I will not call him the Dark Lord because he is no lord to me! But what I will tell you is that today, he can take your homes, he can take your clothing, your food, your family, and he can take your very lives! But there is one thing he cannot take, and that is your faith in your Lord. Your faith, your spirit, your relationship with Yesu is yours and yours to keep. So go, you people of Yesu, and fight for your freedom, fight for Yesu, and fight for Heirthia!"

All the people began to cheer, and they were encouraged. King Daniel yelled as he held the Sword of Yesu up, "Be brave, be courageous, and be faithful to your Lord Yesu. Let us fight!"

Everyone was ready.

King Elena then prepared the people again, "Okay, everyone, we must move quickly to our places, and remember, move gracefully and very quietly. We don't want to give away our positions. King Aniser and King Jonis have already met with everyone about where you are supposed to be. Remember, be quick to listen, slow to speak, and slow to anger."

The brave souls, creatures, and all the Fariets were ready.

"Wizard Bazar, are you ready?"

"I am," he responded.

"Fariet Bert, are you and the Fariet ready?"

"We are," he responded.

"Remember, you will have three seconds, so grab and go."

"Jities Holmes, are you ready?"

"I, I…" Jities Holmes muttered.

"What's the matter, Mr. Holmes?" asked Queen Elena.

"Well, I, I'm…" he responded in a confused voice. He then looked down.

Princess Violet came to him and said, "Mr. Holmes, don't be afraid. You taught me not to be afraid and to believe in myself, and I did. That's why I'm here. No matter what happens, I will be here for you."

Jities Holmes teared up, and a tear came down his cheek.

Queen Elena asked again, "Wizard Holmes, are you ready? We need you more than ever as your part in this is the most crucial. Can you do this?"

"I will do this, and I will do it well, but only if you hear what I have to say."

They listened carefully.

The Dark Lord and his army had already entered the canal. At the entrance of the canal, there was a fork in the road. To the north was King Aniser's castle. To the northeast was the Backbone Desert, which led directly to King Simon's castle.

At this point, the Dark Lord and his massive army reached the midpoint of the canal. It was a very wide canal and mostly of reddish dirt and few trees. There were many rocks and boulders. Seitor stopped.

He gave an evil smile and said, "We have arrived."

In the distance, Seitor saw King Daniel, Queen Elena, and both their children waiting near the end of the canal. Seitor looked around and saw no one with them. "Kanel, search the top of the canal and make certain there is no ambush. Cauffa, take your pack and sniff out everywhere. I want to know where the people are. Before moving forward, I want it clear."

Kanel and his eagles took to flight and began searching the area. Cauffa turned into a wolf along with his pack, and they too began to search.

"Dawson, spread your Teak creatures outward. I want a spread of our army everywhere." Behind Seitor were the giants, ogres, Blakers, Egwaks, Prosecs, Turks, King Mattei, King Julas, Young Adims, creatures of all kinds, and the six kings and their people. The six kings and all the people were under Seitor's spell.

As the eagles flew, the wolves sniffed out. The Teaks spread out. They searched the land, and found nothing and nobody.

Seitor felt uneasy, "Dawson, Cauffa, did you find anything?"

Both Dawson and Cauffa reported that they found nothing.

"They have left, Your Majesty. They are cowards," voiced Cauffa.

Seitor, still very uncomfortable, whispered, "Ruka, where are you?"

But this time there was no response. "Ruka, I call upon you. Where's the army?"

Again, no response.

Kanel, the Great White Eagle, came and reported that they too did not see anyone for miles. "We see nothing, Your Majesty. Only the four are there."

"They have all left, and you will never find them," yelled out King Daniel as his voice echoed.

"What? The people? Oh, I will find them," replied Seitor. Seitor got off his dark horse, and began walking slowly toward King Daniel, with Cauffa, Dawson, and Kanel beside him. Seitor had on an all-black gown and a red hoodie, and clearly visible was the Ruby Stone Ring.

"What do you want?" asked King Daniel.

Seitor, his face expressionless, whispered, "I only want the powers."

"And then what happens once you have them?" asked King Daniel.

Cauffa growled at the Geminis. King Daniel moved into a battle stance.

"Hold on, Cauffa, hold on. Let the man ask his questions," said Seitor. "I take the powers, and they give me security knowing that nothing will happen to me or my army and that we can have a peaceful life."

"What about the people?"

"They will get their land back, and they will live as they always have. Nothing changes."

"That's it, just like that. I hand you the powers, and you all leave."

"I don't know why you insist on a fight. We never intended to fight. This matter can be very peaceful. I already told you. All I want are all the powers as all they cause is trouble. I believe we have been mistreated our entire lives, and so we just want our place in Heirthia. Besides, you and your family have no use for the powers. You can't even use them."

"How do I know you will keep your promise?" inquired King Daniel.

"I have nothing for you and nothing to show you other than my word. As you can see, you almost have no choice. My army can destroy you within seconds. I know all your powers are not developed yet." Seitor, with his beautiful blue eyes, approached King Daniel and whispered, "It's in your best interests to surrender, and if you do, I will send you back to your home on Earth safe. This I promise."

King Daniel stood there for a moment and said, "My spirit tells me you are deceitful, untrustworthy, disloyal, and devious."

Seitor was taken aback and was becoming visibly angry. King Daniel put his hands outward to move his family behind him.

"Now, now, do we have to get into name-calling, my friend?"

"I'm not your friend. I am a friend of Yesu's," replied King Daniel.

Seitor cringed as though he was electrocuted when he heard King Daniel say this. "Don't say that name for it is only a myth."

"What? The Living King, Yesu?"

Again, Seitor cringed and was not pleased. "Don't be a fool! My friend, the wolf can kill you if I order him, and my valiant eagle can rip your children's bodies apart within seconds with his claws," he exclaimed, beginning to get frustrated.

Cauffa growled profusely.

"So what will it be? Will you freely give me the powers, or will I take them from you and spill your blood?" questioned Seitor.

"Give me a few minutes to talk with my family."

"Take all the time you need," Seitor responded. Seitor and his crew walked back to where the army was waiting. King Daniel stood there with his family for several minutes. Seitor stood by his horse and was growing impatient.

"Master, why are they taking so long? Perhaps they are planning something," questioned Cauffa.

"Be patient," he responded.

Twenty minutes went by, and still they were talking.

"Master, forgive my persistence, but something is wrong. This is too much time. The people are not here, and they are buying time," again questioned Cauffa.

Seitor, now more concerned, began walking toward the Geminis. "What will it be?" exclaimed Seitor.

"I need a few more minutes, and we will be done," replied King Daniel.

"No!" Seitor yelled as his voiced echoed through the canal.

"You may have a grand army, and you may have the ultimate power right now, but there is something you do not have, and that is the love for your army as I do for mine. Today, I have set the people free."

Then a few rocks fell from above and down into the canal. Seitor quickly turned to where the rocks had fallen and looked up, but again, he saw nothing.

"Kanel, go!" Seitor ordered.

Kanel reached the top of the canal. "Nothing, Lord Seitor," Kanel responded as he reached the top.

"I am going to give you one last chance. Give me the powers now, or I will take them from you, and I will kill all the people."

King Daniel looked behind Scitor, and he looked on for a few seconds. Seitor turned around, becoming suspicious.

"Where will you go if I give you the powers?" asked King Daniel, and again, he looked behind Seitor. Seitor, becoming suspicious, looked back, but he only saw his army. Then in the distance behind Seitor, a boulder fell into the canal. All looked up, but there was nothing there.

"Cauffa, Kanel, kill them!" yelled Seitor.

King Daniel took out the Sword of Yesu. "Stand back, or I will kill you, I swear!"

Again, King Daniel looked toward the army. "Where are the people?" exclaimed Seitor.

"They are gone, and you will never find them!" yelled Queen Elena.

"Kill them!" Seitor exclaimed. King Daniel swung his sword, trying to stall the attack.

"I will give you the powers!" yelled King Daniel.

"Give them to me now!" demanded Seitor. King Daniel looked back again, but this time smiled. Seitor looked back but could not see anything other than his army.

Cauffa leaped into the air with his massive jaws open, and Kanel opened his wings, lifting his claws toward Princess Katalina and Princess Violet. The king and queens just stood there without flinching, and Cauffa reached King Daniel's neck and bit into the side. Kanel flew a few feet into the air, and at the same time as Cauffa, he raised his claws, went toward the princesses, and opened his claws to grab the children by the stomach, cutting them open. Cauffa and Kanel crashed into each other.

Cauffa fell to the ground, and Kanel lost his balance and fell to the ground as well. King Daniel and his family stood there, unharmed and untouched.

"Impossible!" yelled Seitor.

He called for his wand through the Ruby Stone Ring and yelled, "Fortis Ignis!" and a red curse came out and went toward the Geminis, but again, the spell missed them, going through their bodies, and still they stood there without moving.

King Daniel then said, "You will never find them."

Seitor, with his right hand, extended his wand, and his left hand, which held the Ruby Stone Ring next to his face, was open.

King Daniel yelled, "Fariet Bert!"

Fariet Bert appeared right next to Seitor out of thin air. He appeared and said, "I'll take that." He then swiftly took the ring out of Seitor's hand and smiled. "Bye, bye!" Fariet Bert said, and then again, he disappeared.

Once the Ruby Stone Ring was taken, Seitor's wand became powerless. "What is happening?" yelled Seitor. The entire army became wary at what was happening.

"Ruka, why are you not responding?" yelled Seitor. "Wizard Leadriz and Young Adims!" called Seitor. These two wizards came quickly. "Give me the sight of invisibility!" commanded Seitor.

"You're too late, Seitor," said King Daniel. Seitor looked back at King Daniel, and the new king and queens disappeared.

"Now, now!" Wizard Leadriz yelled. "Oculos aperi, videre quod non potest erit constare!" His wand cast the spell, and Seitor's eyes were hit. Immediately, he was seeing what was happening.

What none of the dark side could see, what the wolves could not sniff, what the eagles could not spot was that the entire army of King Daniel were everywhere, surrounding Seitor and those who were around that area the entire time. On the cliffs stood the army of King Daniel walking toward the other end of the canal, but again, no one and nothing could see them, hear them, or smell them. Slowly but surely, the entire city walked right past Seitor's army. Many of them could sense something, but because they could not see, they did not know.

Seitor saw that Wizard Bazar had his wand up, and he was casting a spell over the entire region, making all of King Daniel's army invisible the entire time. They were shielded.

"Deus est scriptor protectione! Deus est scriptor protectione! Deus est scriptor protectione!" he voiced. Seitor looked toward the other side of the canal, and to his disbelief, he saw Jities Holmes, also known as Ruka, the witch.

"Ruka!" yelled Seitor.

Jities Holmes was casting a spell over the Geminis that made them appear to be in front of Seitor in the canal when they were actually on top of the canal. All the time they had been talking and all that time the Geminis wasted, the people and creatures had been getting past the Dark Army.

Seitor looked in amazement. The entire hidden city was nearly at the end of the canal. They had truly walked right past his entire army, right in his presence, and he'd never known it. "Give me your wand, Young Adims!" commanded Seitor. The entire army did not know what to do or how to attack as they still could not see.

"I do not serve you. You are evil, and I will not bow to you!" exclaimed Jities Holmes.

"Fulgur!" Seitor cast his spell toward Jities Holmes.

The spell hit him right in the chest, and the spell Jities Holmes had been casting was broken. Jities Holmes was thrown to the ground, bleeding. King Daniel and his family indeed had been behind the army the whole time, but because Jities Holmes was no longer casting his spell, the army could see the Geminis.

"Fulgur!" Seitor cast his spell again but toward Wizard Bazar. Wizard Bazar was also hit in the chest, and his spell was interrupted. He too was thrown onto the floor, bleeding from the spell. When this happened, all the people were no longer invisible.

"Run!" yelled King Daniel and Queen Elena.

"Jities Holmes!" yelled Princess Violet.

"We will get both wizards, my dear!" yelled Fariet Julip. Immediately, all the Fariets gathered and carried both wizards to the end of the canal.

In a panic, all the people began to run toward the near ending of the canal.

"Kill them!" commanded Seitor. Immediately, the army began their attack and ran toward the people. The entire city was running, and although they were now a fair distance away from Seitor's army, they had small children and elders, and so their speed was not quite as fast as that of the enemy.

The wolf pack was so large and fast that the wolves led the way, and they were catching up to the people very quickly.

"Take the girls and go toward Backbone Desert!" exclaimed King Daniel to Queen Elena.

"I won't leave you!" she replied.

"The girls are in danger. You must go!" exclaimed King Daniel. He then reached toward his bride, and he kissed her. He gathered several of the Youngs and instructed them to take his family to King Simon's castle. "Fariets, take the wizards with you and protect my family!"

As they reached the end of the canal, all the people were running into Backbone Desert toward King Simon's castle. King Daniel and King Simon looked back, and there were still people in the canal.

"We cannot destroy the canal yet. There are people there!" yelled King Jonis.

"Come, we need to help!" ordered King Daniel. All the kings—King Daniel, King Simon, King Aniser, King Jonis, and King Jemis—went to help.

"Wizard Wrinkles, old man, wait for my signal to destroy the canal to close it in. Can you cast a spell to destroy it?"

"In a heartbeat, Your Majesty," replied Wizard Wrinkles.

King Daniel went with the others to help them cross the canal to go toward King Simon's castle. King Aniser looked back and yelled, "Wolves!"

King Daniel looked back, and sure enough, about twenty giant wolves were at full speed. King Daniel, knowing the people would surely die, closed his eyes and began to pray. "Lord, come and save us. We need you."

He opened his eyes and lifted his arms, and slowly, many of the rocks and boulders began to rise. Then a great wind came, and a storm began to brew. As the wolves grew closer, King Daniel yelled, "In nominee Yesu!" and he motioned his hand and arms forward. All the rocks and boulders went with such a great speed toward the wolves, and it hit them with great force.

The wolves fell and stumbled to the ground as the rocks and boulders hit. Cauffa was toward the back, and so he was not hit. He leaped into the air and leaped onto King Daniel, who made a loud scream of pain. All the kings stood there, not knowing whether King Daniel was alive or dead. The wolf then moved to the side, and King Daniel could be seen. He was full of blood, but the giant wolf was finally dead. When Cauffa leaped into the air, King Daniel had called out the Sword of Yesu, and Cauffa had leaped onto the sharp deadly sword on his own.

The other wolves were there watching what was unfolding. King Daniel got up and yelled toward the other wolves, "Come, this is what awaits you!" He stood there with his sword drawn. He looked back, and all the people had finally gone through. At this point, the army was growing closer, and the Teaks were ready to battle.

"Wrinkles! Now!"

King Daniel and the other kings began to run toward the end of the canal. Wrinkles closed his eyes and positioned himself. He began to call upon a spell and said, "Exitium, exitium, exitium, exitium!" His spell came out like a wildfire and hit the walls of the canal. Immediately, the walls began to shake. King Daniel and the others were still inside but very near the end. The walls began to shatter, then they began to fall. King Daniel and the others barely made it out. As they leaped out, one of the wolves leaped as well and bit into King Daniel's leg, but then the massive walls came down and killed the wolf.

King Daniel and the other kings rejoiced just outside the canal. Queen Elena's plan had worked. All the people, including the queen, the princesses, and the Fariets were on their way to King Simon's castle, the indestructible castle.

"Your Majesty, Your Majesty! I have it! I have the ring!" exclaimed Fariet Bert in a very excited voice.

"You have done well, Fariet Bert." King Daniel reached over to grab the ring, and *swoosh*, Kanel came and grabbed Fariet Bert along with the ring.

"No!" yelled King Simon.

"Bert!" yelled King Daniel, but it was too late.

There was nothing they could do as Kanel was far too high for any spell. King Jonis lifted his wand and yelled, "Crepitus!" His spell went out into the sky, but they were too high and far the distance.

"They got the ring back!" yelled King Simon.

"The more reason why we need to get moving quickly. They will be out very soon," said King Daniel with a fear in his voice.

Seitor, in a rage, was angry at the entire army. "You all failed. You all are nothing. Take the wall down!" Seitor took out his sword and swung it several times, killing several of his own. Then he heard the yell of Kanel, the magnificent eagle, and he came down.

"Master, lord, I have retrieved the ring for you." Kanel then bowed down and extended his claw toward Seitor.

"My good and faithful eagle. What is this? You have indeed done as you have said." Seitor looked down at Kanel's claw, and there was Fariet Bert, barely alive but still holding on to the ring.

"You will die, Seitor." He then coughed up blood. "Yesu has found favor in the New King, and Yesu will destroy you."

Seitor then took the ring from the frail Fariet and put it on. "Oh, that is not true, but what is true is this: you will surely die. It was a good plan, and it almost worked. If only you had all the powers and knew how to use them, but because of that plan, you will die." Seitor then took the ring, called for the Sword of Yesu, and killed the Fariet where he lay. Fariet Bert was indeed dead.

Seitor then went to the wall and observed how massive it was. They were trapped. He called out, "Wizard Leadriz and Young Adims, come. Let us destroy this wall and kill the enemy!"

The three wizards got together and yelled, "Exitium!" Little by little, the wall was being destroyed, and they were making a path, but it would take time, and it would time enough for the people of Heirthia to reach King Simon's castle.

In a rush, King Daniel and the other kings were trailing behind the people. They entered the land of Exsul. They entered Backbone Desert. It was not very large but still a fair size to cross, and it was hot. In a distance, they could see King Simon's castle in the beautiful land of grasslands, open lands, and small hills. They knew they had to run and get to the castle before Seitor and his army broke out. They were running east, but before them was the scorching desert.

23

BACKBONE DESERT

A S TIME PASSED, they grew very tired as they had been in the desert for over two hours now with no sight of the enemy. By this time, all the people were walking.

"I'm tired, Mommy," voiced little Princess Violet.

"It's so hot," voiced Princess Katalina.

"Don't give up. We're almost there," whispered Young Ladam.
All who were there were growing very tired.

"How much longer?" asked little Jesila to Queen Elena.

"Well, I'm not exactly sure, but I can see the castle in a distance.

"Do we have anything to drink?" asked Miala. Queen Elena stopped in her tracks and pulled out a canteen of water.

"Here. All of you take a drink, but be sure to leave some for the other children." All the children who were there quickly went to get a drink of water.

"We need to keep moving," voiced one of the elders.

"Come on then, children. Move along," he continued.

"They are tired and thirsty. We will give them a few minutes to rest," voiced the queen.

"Well then, suit yourselves, we will keep on moving then," he responded. "Go on, children. Each of you, take your drink."

"Princess!" exclaimed Fariet Elliot.

Queen Elena turned and looked at her daughter, who had been drinking water.

"Violet!" she yelled.

Princess Katalina went to her sister's side. "Violet! Mommy!"

Immediately Queen Elena went to her daughter's aid. "Did she drink water?"

"Yes, plenty. I was watching her, and she just fainted."

Queen Elena quickly lifted the little child's head and gave her some more water. "Daniel!" she yelled for her husband.

"Elena, Violet!" yelled King Daniel. He could see his young one on the ground. He quickly ran to where they were. "What happened?" he asked.

"I don't know. She must be dehydrated!" Then another child fell to the ground and then another. Backbone Desert indeed was beginning to claim its victims.

"It's the heat, Your Majesty. Their bodies are too small and frail for the scorching desert. We need to keep them out of the sun!" yelled Jities Holmes. All the people who were there began trying to help by providing shade, but there was not much they could do. As they went to aid the other two children, three more passed out.

King Daniel was on his knees, crying as he yelled, "Violet!" He continued, "Please, sweetie, wake up. Drink water!" he yelled as he attempted to wake his daughter.

Queen Elena continued to pour water over her head, but the sun was still so hot on everyone. Princess Katalina began to cry out of fear that she had lost her sister.

"Violet, please wake up!" she yelled. "We need shade! Get them out of the sun!" yelled Wizard Bazar.

"Procella!" yelled Princess Katalina. As she did this, she pulled back on the Falcon Bow, and an arrow of fire appeared before her bow. She pointed it up into the sky and released. All that were near her looked up into the sky as the arrow went up into the distance, and then it was gone.

"What was that for?" asked Fariet Ut.

Boom! A loud blast sounded into the sky. Everyone looked up, and behold, a storm was brewing, and it was large. Quickly, the wind picked up, the clouds covered the sun, and there was shade.

The temperature quickly dropped to a safe number, and it began to rain. Princess Violet then opened her eyes, and she quickly drank more water.

"Violet!" yelled Princess Katalina. Princess Katalina went to her sister and gave her a hug. "Don't do that again!"

"I love you, Katalina," whispered little Princess Violet.

"Violet, you're all right," whispered her father. All the other children were feeling better, but they were still very weak.

Then there was a loud battle horn in the distance. All the people turned around.

"The Dark Lord!" yelled Young Jason.

The battle horn was blown by the Dark Army, signaling their army to attack, and indeed, the army began to charge and attack. They were still at a distance, but because the children were still so tired, they would catch up in no time.

"We need to move quickly. Pace yourselves. Run if you can, but move quickly," ordered Queen Elena. All the people, seeing the Dark Army approaching, began to panic, and they all began to run. King Daniel carried Princess Violet, and the Youngs came and helped with the other children who were still weak.

"Run!" yelled King Daniel. The temperature was now much cooler, and the storm was still brewing. The wind was increasing in speed, and thus it made it very difficult to run. The rain was very heavy.

"Mr. Holmes! Can you change the direction of the storm to the west toward the Dark Army?" yelled Queen Elena.

"I'm on it, Your Highness."

"Eurum! Eurum! Eurum," he yelled with all his might, and his wand sent out a beam into the massive storm. Lightning from the storm met with the spell, and quickly the storm began to move westward toward the Dark Army. The storm blew, punching winds. The rain was a downpour. The rain packed the desert ground and created a flash flood, which began to swallow many of Seitor's army. The wind stopped the army in their tracks.

Seitor saw that he was losing much of his army in the flood. He called for the Dragon's Claw Wand and cast a spell to dissipate the massive storm.

"Dilacerare!" His red spell went into the sky, and lightning met with it. The storm immediately died out. The rain stopped, and the wind died down. Quickly, the sun reappeared, and the evil army had their chance, though many had drowned and died.

"Kill them!" Seitor yelled, and once again, they were on the prowl.

King Daniel and the people continued to run with all their strength. Then there was a loud scream, and the ground shook. "What was that?" asked King Daniel. All the people stopped.

"Don't move!" yelled King Simon.

Screech! Again the ground shook.

"What was that?" yelled King Daniel again.

"Don't make a sound," whispered King Simon as he turned and looked at King Daniel and his family with his finger on his lips, gesturing for everyone to be quiet.

"Daddy, I'm scared," said Princess Violet.

Then there was a growl, but it was underneath the ground. "Tonkana," whispered King Simon.

"What's a Tonkana?" replied King Daniel in a most confused voice. King Simon slowly turned around and looked at King Daniel and said, "The desert dragon."

Princess Violet let out a scream, but her lips were quickly covered by her mother. Immediately there was another scream by the beast, and the ground shook underneath them again.

"Not a sound as the dragon can only hear by vibration. Very quiet," whispered King Simon.

"Can we walk slowly?" asked Queen Elena.

King Simon motioned his head back and forth and mouthed the word *no*. King Simon took one step, and the beast growled again. Everyone was still, but all were looking behind at the approaching evil army. The children were visibly upset, and many wanted to cry but were holding it in.

"What do we do?" asked King Daniel. All the kings stood there, not knowing how to handle the situation. Queen Elena looked down and had an idea. She squatted down and grabbed a rock on the floor.

Growl! The ground shook.

"What are you doing?" whispered King Aniser.

Queen Elena lowered her arm with the rock.

"No, don't move at all," whispered King Aniser.

Queen Elena gathered all her strength, and as hard as she could, she threw the rock westward toward the evil army. Everyone stood there in fear that the dragon would hear them and blast out of the dry ground.

The rock hit the ground about thirty yards away. Quickly, the ground shook, but the people could feel the ground dragon moving toward where the rock hit the ground. The enemy was getting very close.

"There they are, Lord Seitor!" yelled King Julas.

"Why have they stopped?" yelled King Mattei.

Though confused and suspicious, Seitor paid no attention. He was after one thing and one thing alone: the powers of Yesu.

Queen Elena turned and looked at everyone. Everyone quickly reached down and grabbed a rock from the ground. Queen Elena then whispered, "One, two, three!" and everyone threw their rocks at the same time. There were thousands in the air all at once.

Seitor looked into the distance and saw what they had done.

"Stop! Stop!" he ordered. The entire army stopped in their trail.

"Don't make a sound!" he yelled. They all stood there waiting quietly as to what might happen.

Then all the rocks fell at once to the ground, and a loud noise it surely made, but it was silent after that. The ground did not shake. Nor did the beast growl or scream. From fifty yards away, Seitor gave an evil smile, and his army chuckled at the failed attempt to summon the beast out of the ground.

Blast! Scream! The massive beast blasted out of the desert floor and onto the ground, facing the evil army.

Immediately the dragon with the shape of a serpent showed its face. Bright green eyes it had. It had two horns on top of its head and three smaller horns on each the side of its face. The beast must have stood fifty feet into the air, and its wingspan must have extended another twenty to thirty feet. Its wings had sharp horns all along its wings, and its claws were massive.

The enemy was still and did not know what to do.

"Don't move. It will not attack if it does not sense you," whispered Seitor.

The dragon stood there moving its head from side to side waiting for any movement. King Daniel looked over at Young Ladam and nodded his head down toward Young Ladam's bow.

King Daniel whispered, "One arrow."

Young Ladam lifted his bow and reached for an arrow in his back. Seitor glanced over and saw what they were doing. Seitor slowly raised his hand with his wand, but the dragon glanced over at him and was staring. Seitor slowly put his hand down and could not cast a spell. Smoke was coming out of the dragon's nose as it waited patiently.

Young Ladam pulled back on his bow and took aim. Young Adims looked at Young Ladam, and Young Ladam looked at Young Adims. Young Adims moved his eyes toward Seitor, and Seitor shook his head back and forth so that Young Adims would not move. Young Ladam took aim. Young Ladam released the arrow, and it flew gracefully toward Young Adims.

Young Adims yelled and jumped off his horse. The arrow missed the horse and hit the Teak standing behind the horse. The Teak fell back in pain and, with its ax, hit another horse behind him, and the horse became spooked and went out of control. The horse went off with the Teak that was riding the horse, and *snap!* Tonkana grabbed the Teak with its massive jaws, crunched the Teak, and swallowed the creature whole. Many of the horses began to become afraid, and there was movement. Tonkana saw another move and grabbed that Turk and ate him the same way. The army was too afraid. They began to move.

Tonkana felt all this and breathed in a very deep breath and then breathed out a huge blast of fire throughout the army. Tonkana was on the attack and was killing all the creatures with its jaws, its claws, and its fire.

"Run!" yelled King Daniel.

Now that Tonkana was fighting the enemy, the people could move again. The entire people ran as fast as they could.

"There, the castle! Go toward the castle!" yelled King Simon.

Finally, they were toward the end of the desert. King Daniel looked back, and the Dark Army was still stuck in their tracks, battling Tonkana. Many of the Dark Army tried to get past Tonkana, but it was too quick and would kill all that tried to pass. As they reached the end, they could see the castle in a distance, and it was not far away.

"Move, everyone, we need to keep moving," yelled King Jonis.

Tonkana was killing the creatures one by one. Seitor then came to a clearing and called for his Falcon Bow. The bow appeared, and he reached out and pulled back, and as he did this, a flame arrow appeared. He released and voiced, "Mors Mortis!" meaning "death."

The arrow flew toward Tonkana, and it hit Tonkana on its left wing. The arrow exploded, causing Tonkana's left arm and wing to be disabled. It cried profusely but continued to fight the army. Then an Egwak jumped onto the back of Tonkana, and another jumped onto Tonkana's right side. The two creatures began to bite into Tonkana's back, wounding it. Tonkana shook like a raging bull, and one of the Egwaks fell to the ground. Tonkana went and killed it with its massive jaws. They just couldn't stop it.

However, when Tonkana did this, two large Blakers jumped onto Tonkana's neck and began to bite into the massive dragon's neck.

Then Wizard Leadriz cast his spell. "Crepitus!" The spell came out aggressively and hit the giant dragon on its right leg, and it blasted it off. Tonkana was doomed.

He fell to the ground, but he had killed thousands and thousands. Even on the ground, the massive beast breathed in a deep breath and breathed out one last line of fire toward the army, burning hundreds of them.

King Daniel stopped and looked back and saw what was happening. Although he was joyful they had escaped the death the dragon would have brought the people, he was saddened for the ultimate death the beast endured. It had saved their lives and given them a lot of extra time to get away. King Mattei opened his wings and flew on top of the dragon. He lifted his sword and stabbed Tonkana in the heart. Tonkana took its last breath and died. He had truly given the people of Heirthia a chance to escape. By the time Tonkana died, he had killed over five thousand enemy soldiers.

Seitor turned around in anger. He had lost over five thousand soldiers to the dragon and over five thousand to the storm's flood. He grew angry. He turned and saw that the people had already gone a great distance, and out of the desert, but he could still see them.

"Kill them all!" he yelled and ordered. The army ran and marched with such anger. The people could hear the cries of the creatures and beasts.

"Mommy, they're coming!" voiced Princess Violet.

"Come now, sweetie, keep moving!"

They continued moving forward, and they had finally reached the grasslands, which is at the edge of Mount Gleamour. Once they got to the top of the hill, they stood there in disbelief. To the far east and opposite side of the castle, they saw something they did not expect. The other half of Seitor's army was closing in. All the kings could not believe that such an army existed. They thought they had escaped the wrath of Seitor's army, but now the people of Heirthia, who'd run from Seitor's army from the west, were now facing Seitor's army from the east. The kings looked on at the massive array of warriors, beasts, and giants. At this point in time, the people knew they had to fight.

King Daniel yelled, "Okay, everyone. It is imminent. The battle is upon us. Now is the time that your faith must be at its highest! If you cannot fight, I will not hold it against you. Continue to the castle as the kings and I fight and hold them off."

"Why don't we all run to the castle?" asked Young Joseph.

"If we all head to the castle, no one will make it," replied King Aniser.

"Look there," King Jonis added.

There in a distance, all the people saw Seitor approaching with his army, and they were moving fast. The army to the east was also moving quickly.

King Simon exclaimed, "The women with children and the elders, go and continue to the castle!" The women with children and many of the elders who could not fight continued toward the castle.

"Elena, my love, continue to the castle with Katalina and Violet. The others will need you to protect them there once you are in."

"I love you, Daniel. Just know that I love you and that you are everything to me," said Elena as she cried so passionately for her husband. They embraced, and Katalina and Violet came to their father and hugged him.

"Daddy, I can fight," exclaimed Katalina.

"I know, sweetie, but I cannot risk losing you. Those people need you and your mother. Your little sister also needs you. Let me and the kings fight this fight, and no matter what happens, Yesu is with you."

Queen Elena took her daughters' hands and began moving with the people. Both Princess Katalina and Princess Violet would look back at their father because they did not know whether this would be the last time they would see him alive.

"Fariet Ut, take the Fariets and escort the people to the castle. Please guard them.

"At your service, sire. In the name of Yesu!" All the Fariets flew and escorted the people to King Simon's castle.

"We need to get closer to the castle and its center point to protect its gates! It's our only hope," exclaimed King Daniel. All the warriors went with him to prepare for battle and to hold off the army so that the people could reach the massive castle of King Simon.

24

THE BATTLE

As THE KINGS arrived halfway between King Simon's castle and the Mountains of Eriol, which divides the land of Exsul and Yesu's castle, King Daniel and his army were ready to battle. They could see Seitor and his army in the distance. The army from the west met the army from the east and created an even larger army.

King Daniel looked at his warriors, and he could see fear in them and doubt in their eyes. With King Daniel were King Simon, King Jemis, King Aniser, King Jonis, Young Ladam, the five Young Brothers, about five hundred of the elder wizards, and about a thousand other Youngs, including Young Caster and Young Lielgab. King Daniel turned and saw his other three wizards—Wizard Bazar, Wizard Holmes, and Wizard Wrinkles.

"Jities, Bazar, are you two hurt?" said King Daniel.

"We will be fine. We have been through worse, and we will survive," replied Jities Holmes.

The two wizards stood there like best friends supporting each other. Wizard Bazar showed them his wound, and although it was still bleeding, it was wrapped, and Jities Holmes did the same thing.

As they rode toward the castle, King Daniel called, "Jities or Ruka—what should I call you?"

"Your Majesty, thank you for forgiving me. I did not mean to give away where you and your army were. I was under the control of Seitor. Please call me Jities Holmes. This is my real name."

"What made you change?" asked King Simon.

"The little princess," he answered.

"Violet?" answered King Daniel.

"Yes. She showed me love. She showed me that she cared. She showed me that people can be family, and that is what I have always wanted. I was never part of any family. I was only controlled by Seitor. When I ended up spending so much time with your family, well, I fell in love with it. There was something there that I just cannot explain which drew me to you."

King Daniel came and embraced Jities Holmes.

"I now serve Yesu, the Living King. He alone is my Savior," exclaimed Jities Holmes.

"I do have a question," asked King Jemis. "Your were called Ruka, the Dark Witch, but you're a man."

"Ruka was my disguise. After the past and history of my dark family, which was filled with evil and sinful ways, I no longer wanted to be known as Jities Holmes, and the only way to change my appearance was to become something completely different. I wanted to get away. So I cast a spell on myself to become a witch that lived in the forest. However, that is not who I am. I am Jities Holmes."

"But why a witch?" asked King Aniser.

"Oh, I tried many forms. Creatures, animals, even a dragon, but for some reason it seemed like everything wanted to kill me. I even turned into a different man, but that was no use. Everywhere I turned, there was a fight, and I was done fighting. However, when I turned myself into a witch, everything and everyone was afraid of me, and so I stayed like that, alone in the forest. The only thing that took over me and threatened my life was the Dark Lord. That is the only reason I served him. He knew my secret, and I didn't want anyone to know."

King Daniel smiled and said, "Well, now you're here with us, and you're family with us."

Jities Holmes smiled and was very grateful for being a part of Yesu's family.

King Jemis said, "Friends come and go, but family will always be there for you."

"King Daniel," called King Simon, "they're drawing closer."

King Daniel turned around toward King Simon's castle, but the people still had not made it inside the castle.

"They're not going to make it, sire," voiced Young Ladam. As they looked at the army drawing closer, they could see into the distance that the wolves were moving much faster than the army, raging for revenge for the loss of their leader, Cauffa.

"Today we fight, and we fight for Yesu. We fight for freedom, and we fight for the glory of God!" yelled King Daniel. His small army cheered on.

With only over a thousand beside him, King Daniel and his army stood their ground, watching the hundreds of thousands of warriors, and as they looked on, they waited for the wolves and the creatures to get within distance.

"Your Highness, I'm at your service," voiced Teimur. The great cat approached King Daniel and King Simon.

"Thank you, my friend. We will indeed need your fierce claws and your massive jaws."

Teimur gave a big smile and a deep growl.

"Archers! Get ready! Wizards, prepare your wands!" Yelled King Simon.

"On my command, archers, go first!" King Daniel yelled. As they waited, they looked on.

The Dark Army grew closer and closer, and they could hear the growls of the wolves and the snarls of the Teaks and the Prosecs. There were just so many of them.

"Archers, fire!" yelled King Daniel. It looked like a haze in the sky with so many arrows being shot above King Daniel and the line of kings.

Then Kanel and his eagles came flying swiftly into the sky, and they destroyed most of the arrows. One by one, the eagles grabbed the arrows. They were stopped.

"Archers, again, fire!" Again the Youngs fired the arrows into the sky, but again, the eagles came and destroyed the arrows. The wolves and creatures were still too far for the wizards to take aim. King Daniel could see Seitor smiling in the distance, and for the first time, King Daniel did not know what to do.

Then there was the sound of one single arrow. All who were in the line looked above, and it was an arrow in flames. They turned around, and behold, it was Queen Elena and Princess Katalina. Princess Katalina had launched an arrow of fire. They looked at the arrow, and not even Kanel himself could get near the arrow as it was covered with flames. The creatures looked up but thought nothing of the single arrow.

"What did you feel when you sent it, Princess?" asked King Jemis. All turned around to her, and she had this look in her face of pure confidence. She whispered one word, "Dragon."

The arrow then become larger and larger, and all the creatures looked up again, and behold, the arrow became a fire dragon. It was a massive beast completely enflamed with fire. It flew to the creatures and enflamed all that were in the front. The wolves retreated backward as they could not pass. The dragon flew upward and again came down and enflamed the land, burning many of the creatures and warriors.

Princess Katalina closed her eyes, and again she pulled the Falcon Bow and exclaimed, "Crepitus Multiplicati!" An arrow appeared before them all, and she released. The arrow went into the air where the fire dragon was stopping the army, keeping them from passing. The arrow went beyond the flames and separated into seven arrows along the line of the enemy, and *blast*! A large explosion came upon them. It was as though missiles had hit. *Blast, blast, blast, blast, blast, blast, blast!* King Daniel knew they had Yesu's favor.

King Daniel looked back, and he was relieved because the people were about fifty yards from the castle's gates. Because Princess Katalina was able to hold off the line of creatures, warriors, and wolves with the Falcon Bow, the people were going to make it.

"Again, Princess, again!" yelled King Jemis.

Princess Katalina pulled back, but nothing appeared. "I can't. I don't feel it anymore," she responded. Still, the dragon was flying between the allies and the enemy. The fire dragon would fly swiftly through the air and breathe fire to the evil army, and they drew back.

Seitor saw this, and so he called for the Dragon's Wand claw and yelled, "Sagittae Glacies!" His spell flew toward the dragon, and it hit the fire dragon, causing it to turn into ice. The dragon froze and fell to the ground, shattering into pieces. When this happened, the army slowly moved its way beyond the fire, which was beginning to die down.

"Hold your ground!" yelled King Simon.

Seitor then cast his spell, "Ignem Vipera!" His spell flew into the air, and a red fire breathing dragon burst out of the spell. It was massive, with red eyes. He cast the spell three more times.

"There are four dragons!" yelled Young Joseph. All four dragons flew swiftly through the air, and they flew downward toward the allies. Blasts of fire were shot toward them.

"Shields!" yelled King Simon. All the allies lifted their shields to protect themselves. It was a wall of shields.

Blast! The flames of fire went over them, and it was hot. About a fifty of the Youngs and elders could not hold on to their shields. As the flames came upon them, they were burned into ashes.

The dragons went up behind them and were circling around to come back for more. Meanwhile, the wolves, creatures, and warriors were within fighting distance. King Daniel could hear their yells and growls.

King Daniel looked into the sky and saw that the fire dragons were coming back. "Wizards!" he yelled as he turned and looked at Bazar, Jities, and Wrinkles.

"Draco Glacies!" yelled Wizard Bazar.

Wizard Holmes and Wizard Wrinkles followed suit.

Their spells went into the sky, and three blue ice-breathing dragons burst out of the explosion. They too were large beasts, with blue eyes.

The blue dragons screamed as they headed for the red dragons. Everyone was watching. The red dragons saw the approaching enemy dragons, and they too went full speed toward the blue dragons. All four of the fire dragons breathed in a heavy breath and they blew fire out. Large flames of fire burst out and went toward the blue dragons. Seitor gave an evil smile.

The blue dragons saw the fire, and so they breathed in deep heavy breaths, and they breathed out a blue haze from their mouths. The blue haze met the fire, and the fires were extinguished.

"Misty ice it is!" yelled Jities Holmes. Indeed, the blue haze was particle ice that froze the fire. As the misty ice met the fire, the fire melted the ice and turned into water that fell to the ground in a rain.

Crash! All the dragons met in an aerial battle of the wand dragons. Claws met claws, and fangs met fangs.

Meanwhile, the ground battle was about to begin. King Daniel looked as the wall of warriors, wolves, and creatures approached them. There were now about one hundred massive wolves in the front line. King Daniel could hear his heart beating as they prepared to fight.

"Wait for them to be in range!" continued King Simon.

The wolves were running and were closing the distance. As they drew closer and closer, the New Faith army became more and more afraid at what was to happen. But right before the wolves were in distance to strike, there was a massive roar.

It was so loud and soul-piercing that even King Daniel and the others were hurled downward to where they had to cover their ears. The wolves fell to the ground as they lost their balance, and they became afraid, crying in fear. Queen Elena had transformed into a lioness.

As she stood there with her head high, she closed her eyes, and the Lion Heart Medallion began to glow. It was a bright light that was illuminating other bright lights, and each time it did this, the light grew larger and larger. The Youngs by her side began to change, and as she walked toward her husband, all who were there began to change and transform. To the king's amazement, there were seventy-seven lions ready for battle.

King Daniel looked at his Queen with such motivation and confidence. He then yelled, "In Nomine Yesu, in Nomine Yesu!"

Queen Elena let out another loud roar, and so, the battle had begun. The queen and all the lions leaped into the air over King Daniel, and they led the battle, and they charged. The wolves and creatures went forward, and thus there were two massive walls of creatures coming at each other—the wolves, Teaks, and Prosecs coming from the south and the wall of lions coming from the north—and both their speeds were incredible.

They ran toward each other, but before they met, the land became silent. The winds died down, and the noise seemed to slowly fade away. There was this melody in the air, as though a choir of angels were humming in the distance. It was truly peaceful, and Seitor saw this, but denied accepting that Yesu was indeed within distance and watching closely. Seitor looked at his massive army, creatures, giants, wizards, and all types of warriors. He became hard and prideful.

As peaceful as it was and as quiet as it seemed, the war was afoot. All that were there could hear their own hearts beating, but then, *crash! Blast! clash!* The wolves and creatures and the lions met in a horrific battle of claws and fangs.

Queen Elena and the other lions took out the wolves one by one, and the creatures were no match. No matter how many creatures came into the battle and no matter how fierce they were, the lions overtook them with their massive size and incredible strength. Queen Elena leaped into the air and, with her massive claws, cut and sliced the creatures.

Three wolves attacked her from different angles, but she bit into the one before her and tackled the one next to her. One of the wolves leaped onto her back, but she quickly turned and killed that one too.

Then the main wolf challenged Queen Elena, and it growled at her. Queen Elena looked at the wolf with her massive teeth and growled back, and she hunched down so as to get ready to attack. The wolf leaped toward her to bite her neck, but she quickly lifted her massive claws upward and then downward, hitting the wolf on the head, and she opened her massive jaws and bit into the wolf's neck. As she did this, she let out a loud roar into the distance, and all the enemies heard this. The Teaks were many, but the lions were overcoming them.

An Egwak came and swung its muscular arms toward the lions in a rage, and it hit several of them, fatally injuring them. Quickly, four lions prowled around the Egwak. One of the lions leaped onto the back of the Egwak, and then two more leaped onto its shoulders. They were biting onto the Egwak. Finally, the last lion leaped onto the chest of the Egwak, and it gave the killing blow. It bit into the Egwak's neck, it died instantly. The massive beast fell onto the ground.

"Rebellis!" called out the dark wizards, and their spells hit the lions one by one. Queen Elena was thrown onto the ground. Although the wolves had been defeated, and hundreds of Teaks and Prosecs killed, the creatures continued to come, and the lions were now faced with the wizards attacking them with spells. The remaining wolves and creatures took advantage of the fact that many of the lions were down. As Queen Elena, still as a lioness, was on the ground hurt, several of the wolves ran toward her, and they leaped to kill her. She was in serious trouble. One of the wolves went and bit into her leg with its sharp teeth. She yelled in pain. Another grabbed her shoulder, and again she yelled in pain. Then she turned and saw that another wolf had leaped toward her head. She knew it was going for her neck.

Crash! Teimur, the great tiger, came to her rescue.

Teimur had leaped and tackled the wolf, and with his massive jaws with rows of sharp teeth, it killed the wolf instantly. Many of the wolves went and attacked Teirmur. Big mistake! The Tiger killed the wolves one by one. They were no match as they fought. Several of the Teaks attacked Teimur, but they too were taken down by the massive cat.

Teimur roared at the enemy. "Retreat, my queen, you and the other lions head back to the castle!" Teimur yelled.

By this time, Teimur was surrounded by the enemy. Queen Elena and the other lions began a second assault, and they attacked the enemy that was surrounding Teimur. It was an awesome battle between the creatures.

"Rebellis! Rebellis! Rebellis!" called the many evil wizards, and each time, the spell hit a lion. Even Teimur was hit several times, causing him to fall to the ground.

"Wizards, cast your spells!" yelled King Daniel to save the lions, Teimur, and his queen. And so it began, the battle of the wizards. Spells of all sorts came about from both sides, many of which hit wizards from both sides.

The lions, including the queen, and Teimur, retreated, as they knew their time for battle had ended for now. It became a battle between the wizards, but then the massive evil giants came and began to swing their massive arms. Slowly, but surely, King Daniel and his small army began to move back.

Queen Elena went to her husband, and she transformed back into her human form. She was hurt, with cuts and bite marks from her battle, but she was okay. They embraced.

"Are you okay?" asked King Daniel.

"I'm fine, sweetheart. I never felt so alive."

"Please, mi amor, you need to take the other seriously wounded Youngs and elders to the castle to get treated."

"I will," she responded. She again hugged her husband, and the two shared a kiss.

"Teimur! Can you take the princess back to the castle and escort the others?"

"Right away, sire!" Princess Katalina jumped onto the back of Teimur, and they immediately went to King Simon's castle.

Meanwhile, up in the air, the battle of the dragons continued. Again, a red dragon breathed fire toward one of the blue dragons. The blue dragon quickly breathed out the blue mist, and at the same time, one of the other blue dragons did the same thing. The first blue mist hit the fire, extinguishing it, but the second blue mist, went past the extinguished flame and directly hit the red dragon, freezing it instantly.

The frozen red dragon fell to the ground, dead. Then out of nowhere, one of the red dragons went behind one of the blue dragons and clawed its back. Blood was drawn. The two dragons fell to the ground. As they landed, the red dragon sank its massive sharp teeth into the blue dragon's neck, killing it.

The red dragon that was victorious let out a loud scream, but then it suddenly screamed again, but this time, it was in pain.

It was Jities Holmes. He had raised a sword and stabbed the red dragon in the heart. "That's for killing my dragon!" he exclaimed with anger as the blue dragon laid its head down and died.

"There, there, my friend. Go in peace," voiced Jities Holmes as he cried for his dragon.

Therefore, there were now two red dragons and two blue dragons, and the four were badly wounded from their battle. The red dragons flew into the distance to seek refuge, and the blue dragons went after them. As the blue dragons approached them, Seitor yelled, "Crepitus," and released a flaming arrow toward one of the blue dragons. It was a direct hit. The arrow pierced the blue dragon, and the arrow exploded, killing the blue dragon. The remaining blue dragon, as fierce as it was, continued chasing the red dragon. The red dragons landed. One of them was more wounded than the other. The blue dragon swiftly went in and grabbed the wounded red dragon with its massive claws and flew into the air.

Seitor again called, "Crepitus," but the arrow missed. The Dark Lord was becoming angry.

As the blue dragon flew high in the sky, its massive claws cut into the red dragon's back, causing it to bleed profusely. The blue dragon then swung the red dragon into the air and let out a heavy breath of blue mist, freezing the red dragon. The red dragon fell to the ground with such force and speed. It hit the ground, killing the red dragon, but at the same time, it crashed onto the enemy, killing several of the giants. The blue dragon, knowing it needed to rest, flew into the distance toward King Simon's castle. Only one red dragon and one blue dragon remained.

Wizards Bazar, Jities Holmes, Wrinkles, and many of the Youngs continued casting their spells.

Wizard Bazar yelled, "Expellere!"

Wizard Leadriz from the dark side responded with "Rebellis!" and the two spells clashed. The battle of the wizards was indeed a fierce one. Spells were everywhere.

Seitor yelled, "Caementa!" The spell hit Young John, the Young wizard. Young John was immediately turned into stone.

"No!" yelled Young Joseph. Young Joseph, a wizard himself, cast forth a spell toward Seitor to cast a large stone. "Lapideas!"

Seitor quickly yelled, "Angustos!"

Young Joseph's spell was destroyed. Seitor gave an evil laugh. Seitor then quickly approached where Young Joseph was standing.

Young Joseph, clearly angry and unstable because of the death of his brother Young John, ran toward Seitor. Jities Holmes saw this and knew Young Joseph would surely die.

Jities Holmes called, "Contortor!"

The wind began to pick up. A storm was brewing. His spell created a tornado in the midst of Seitor's army, and they began to be consumed by the massive tornado. More importantly, the tornado went between Seitor himself and Young Joseph. Jities Holmes went to Young Joseph and hugged him tightly so that Young Joseph would not seek to avenge his brother at that moment.

"He's gone, my friend. He's gone. Don't let your anger control you. Let him go."

Young Joseph was on his knees crying with such sentiment for the loss of his brother. King Daniel saw this and knew they needed to act fast. He and the other kings took advantage of the distraction of the tornado, and it began—the final battle.

25

Full of Faith

THE KINGS BEGAN their assault, and with many of the enemy warriors and creatures killed, they felt unstoppable. King Daniel led the way, and he took out the Sword of Yesu and the Fariets' Shield of Honor, and he and the other kings went into the battle with such confidence and motivation.

King Daniel yelled, "In Nomine Yesu!" and swung his sword, killing a Teak. He spun around killing another Teak. He leaped forward, swinging his sword and shield, and killed two more Teaks. He turned and twisted and continued the battle.

King Simon and the other kings went into battle, and all the kings were fighting off the thousands of Teaks, Prosecs, and creatures of all kinds.

Wizard Leadriz called, "Expellere!" toward King Aniser, and it hit him in the back. King Aniser was badly hurt. King Daniel went to King Aniser, and Wizard Leadriz called again toward King Daniel, "Expellere!" but King Daniel lifted the Sword of Yesu, and the spell bounced off the sword. King Daniel directed the bounced spell toward a giant battling King Simon next to him. The giant was hit on the head and was killed instantly falling to the ground.

Then the Turks were released into battle.

The loyal beasts were ruthless and had no boundaries and no fears, killing anything in their path. The creatures went into battle, and the kings and Youngs went and faced them. King Daniel went to them, and one by one, they were sliced and cut with the magnificent Sword of Yesu. However, the kings and their friends were growing tired, and their minor wounds were beginning to catch up to them. Many of them were losing blood.

Although the kings fought and were successful, they were growing very tired, and the enemy would not stop coming. There were so many.

"It seems that for every one I kill, three more attack!" yelled King Daniel as he stood next to King Simon.

Jities Holmes called, "Fulgur!" toward Wizard Leadriz, sending a lightning bolt, but Wizard Leadriz called, "Contego Scuto!" which provided a protective shield, and the two spells met in the middle.

Both wizards held on with all their strength, but neither would give up. King Simon called, "Daniel, the Egwak!"

King Daniel looked up, and there he saw three Egwaks swinging their arms toward him. King Daniel and King Simon came together and attacked the Egwaks. King Simon knelt down and ducked below the swing of one of the Egwaks and lifted his sword.

The Egwak's arm was badly cut, and it yelled in pain. King Jemis came and helped them from behind. King Jemis, the sharpshooter he was, shot four arrows in a row toward the Egwak, each hitting the Egwak in the chest. King Daniel ran between the two Egwaks and extended both the Sword of Yesu and his sharp shield, cutting the Egwaks' stomachs.

One of the Egwaks swung its arm, hitting King Daniel in the head, knocking him to the ground. King Jonis called with his wand, "Fulgur!" and the spell hit the Egwak that King Jemis had hit, and it was electrocuted.

It fell to the ground dead. "Fulgur!" yelled King Jonis again, pointing his wand, and it hit the other Egwak, killing it instantly.

Then a Turk warrior went and grabbed King Jonis's back and bit into the back of his neck. He yelled in pain. Another Turk went and grabbed onto King Jonis's shoulder, and then another grabbed onto the other shoulder. King Jemis saw this.

Swoosh! Swoosh! Swoosh! King Jemis quickly shot three arrows. Each arrow hit each Turk right in the forehead.

King Jonis then said, "Thanks, brother, but you could have killed me! I'm glad you're a good shot."

King Jemis smiled and said, "I love you too much, brother, but unfortunately, I shot with my eyes closed."

King Jemis smiled, and King Jonis made a confused face, but the two embraced in brotherly fellowship that they were still alive.

King Simon ran toward two Blakers and ran his sword upward, right into one of the Blaker's heart, killing it instantly. The Blaker fell to the ground. A Teak came from behind and grabbed hold of King Simon, causing him to fall to the ground. King Aniser went from behind and stabbed the Teak in the back, killing it.

King Daniel regained consciousness from the fall and got up on his feet, dizzy and hurt. He felt as though he had suffered a concussion and was very unstable. Only one Blaker remained. It let out a loud roar, and so all the kings came together and rushed in, stabbing the giant beast. It finally fell to the ground.

Meanwhile, all the Youngs were battling the Teaks. Young Ladam fought bravely along with his brothers. Young Caster showed his true talent and shot arrow after arrow into the Teaks. It was done with the speed of light, but he was running out of arrows.

The Wizard Youngs also showed promise as they cast spells upon the beasts and creatures. King Daniel looked upon the entire battle and whispered, "Thank you, Father God for the army you have blessed us with." He knew right there and then that this was where God had wanted his family. Although unimaginably outnumbered, the small army was brave and courageous.

Another wave of Teaks and Prosecs came toward the Youngs. Then out of nowhere, Princess Katalina returned to the battlefield.

She yelled out, "Ladam, get down!" and so the Youngs before her ducked down, and she closed her eyes and called. Her arrow of fire came out, and she released it. As it flew, the arrow split into twelve arrows of fire, hitting each of the Teaks and Prosecs that were charging.

Princess Katalina saw what she had done, but then from behind, a Teak came and grabbed her, trying to cutting her arm. Young Ladam ran to her rescue, and he grabbed the Teak, pulling him off the princess.

The Teak was Dawson.

Dawson pulled his sword out, and Young Ladam pulled his out. Dawson struck with such force, causing Young Ladam to fall to the ground. Dawson then made several strikes to the ground, but Young Ladam moved to the side, avoiding each one. Young Ladam lifted his sword as a shield, blocking each strike. Then on one of those strikes, Dawson hit Young Ladam's sword and pushed against it. Young Ladam held on, but Dawson then stabbed Young Ladam in the chest with a dagger he had in his other hand.

Princess Katalina screamed in shock. Young Ladam lay unmoving on the ground. Dawson got up from where he was while Young Ladam lay there with the dagger still in his chest and blood spilling onto the ground. Dawson attacked Princess Katalina, who had no defense, and he grabbed her neck and began to choke her. He looked at her and growled at her, showing his fangs. He then lifted his sword and swung it back and was going to kill her.

King Daniel turned toward her and yelled, "Katalina!"

Stab!

Princess Katalina fell to the ground, and King Daniel mourned and yelled, "No!" as he stared at his daughter on the ground. But then he looked up, and Dawson stood there, blood starting to flow from his mouth. Dawson fell to the ground, and Young Ladam was behind him. Young Ladam had been stabbed in the chest and was hurt, but thankfully none of his ribs were broken. Young Ladam had slain the leader of the Teaks.

King Daniel went to his daughter. She was okay. He held her head to his chest, and he began to cry as he thought he had lost her. King Daniel looked up at Young Ladam with a facial expression of fear and sadness.

He said in a very quiet voice with a knot in his throat, "Thank you."

After embracing her, he asked Young Ladam, "Take her to the castle." Immediately, Young Ladam carried Princess Katalina, and he and some of the other Youngs went to the castle.

King Simon went with King Daniel, and they went toward the others in battle, and that is where they met with King Julas and King Mattei. King Julas went straight for King Daniel, and the two began their sword battle.

King Mattei ran toward King Simon, and King Simon yelled, "I will avenge King Phelo, you treacherous snake! He loved you! You were his friend! His brother!" he cried out as he swung his sword toward King Mattei. King Mattei opened his beautiful white wings and took to flight over King Simon, but King Simon lifted his sword, cutting one of King Mattei's wings. He fell to the ground but immediately got back up, and they began their sword fight.

"Give us the powers! You will be defeated!" exclaimed King Julas, advancing toward King Daniel.

"I am a servant of Yesu, and you have forever betrayed the Living King!" replied King Daniel. He continued, "What happened to you? You've changed. Your eyes are turning a blazing red, and you are not the servant you once were! It doesn't have to be this way!"

King Julas, paying no attention, went toward King Daniel, and the two went into a fierce battle. It was one on one. King Julas, having the Silver Sword, was very quick. King Daniel went toward King Julas and swung his sword, but King Julas moved away and knelt down. He countered with his sword, cutting King Daniel on his leg. King Daniel was hurt. King Julas saw this, and so he went toward King Daniel and swung his sword once again, but this time, King Daniel moved away and knelt down. He then countered with his sword and cut King Julas on the leg.

"What goes around comes around!" King Daniel exclaimed.

King Julas and King Daniel exchanged blows, and although King Julas was much faster, his sword was becoming weaker and weaker from the strikes from King Daniel.

King Julas swung his sword, and King Daniel stepped back. King Julas then kicked King Daniel on the chest and then kicked him again on his right leg, which was cut, sending King Daniel to the ground. Seeing the opportunity, King Julas went to King Daniel and swung his sword repeatedly toward King Daniel on the ground. Strike after strike, he continued.

He then kicked King Daniel on the face, cutting King Daniel over and above his left eye. Again he struck at King Daniel, but King Daniel would not stop deflecting the strikes with his sword and shield.

King Julas yelled, "Why won't you just die!" as he swung and missed.

King Daniel reached up and grabbed hold of King Julas's arm and pulled him to the ground. As he fell to the ground, King

Daniel grabbed a rock next to him and knocked it over King Julas's head, knocking him cold.

King Daniel went over to King Julas, who was on the ground facing up, and whispered, "I am here for you, brother, and I will be praying for you. Although you have turned on Yesu, he still loves you. Your family is still here," he concluded as he cried because of all the fighting that was taking place. King Daniel looked up at all who were fighting. He then looked down at King Julas as King Julas slowly came to, and King Daniel said to him, "Faith, hope, and love. This is what you need in your life."

King Julas whispered to King Daniel and said, "Why do you do this for them? You don't belong here."

King Daniel looked at him and said, "We do it because the greatest of these is love." King Daniel walked away.

Meanwhile, King Simon was battling King Mattie. Although King Mattie's left wing was cut, he attacked King Simon with his sword. King Simon ducked down, but King Mattie twisted and extended his right wing, which smashed King Simon on the chest, sending him flying through the air and falling hard on the ground.

"My ribs! My ribs are broken!" yelled King Simon as he grasped for air. King Mattei went to him quickly to take advantage that King Simon was on the ground. King Mattei quickly swung his sword to the ground. King Simon moved to avoid a direct heart kill but was stabbed in the shoulder. He yelled in pain. Several Teaks came to aid King Mattei.

"The great King Simon down on his back, defeated!" said King Mattei.

"I prefer to be defeated on my back serving the Living King than to live and spend eternity in hell!"

King Mattei raised his sword in anger and was about to kill King Simon when *blast!* King Mattei and the Teaks that were there were blasted and thrown into the air and onto the ground. King Mattei was badly burned, and the Teaks were killed. King Mattei screamed in pain.

"Fariets!" yelled King Mattei. Hundreds of Fariets had come to assist in the battle at the order of Queen Elena.

"Fariet Ut!" yelled King Simon with such relief. The now few several hundred kings, Youngs, elders, and now Fariets stood their ground. Seitor could see that the resistance was strong, and that although they were not many, they were clearly stronger and more effective. Many more creatures and warriors began another attack. Fariet Ut looked at King Daniel and yelled, "Fariets, form the line! Everyone!"

All the kings stood behind the Fariets as they went forward. The creatures and warriors continued to run and attack with swords drawn. All the Fariets were in a line, hovering a few feet from the ground.

"Hold it strong. Hold it strong and give it everything you have in you!" said Fariet Ut as all the Fariets watched this wall of the enemy coming toward them.

As the enemies were within a few feet, Fariet Ut yelled, "Release!" At the same time, all the Fariets released their closed hands, and a most powerful blast came from them, sending all the enemies charging into the air. They fell to the ground and were badly burned from the blast.

"In the name of Yesu, attack!" yelled King Daniel. They went into another attack, and the entire New Faith army was encouraged with the power they had.

Blast! came a frightening sound between all who were fighting. It was Seitor. He had cast a Falcon Bow arrow that blasted the battlefield. The Dark Lord had had enough. He grew angry at all that he was witnessing. The allies were not giving up.

King Daniel and all who were there were thrown onto the ground from Seitor's blast. King Daniel could not hear as the sound from the blast had hit the side of his face. King Daniel then stood in exhaustion and saw that his army had done well and certainly had dented the enemy's size, but he looked into the distance, and the enemy army continued to come in the thousands.

King Daniel's army was hurt. They regrouped, although most of them were exhausted, cut, bleeding, and badly hurt.

"We stand with you," voiced King Simon.

"We will all stand with you," said Fariet Ut.

King Daniel and his army stood there ready to fight, but they were clearly the underdogs. Then King Daniel and the others were surprised. The enemy had stopped charging.

"What are they doing?" asked King Aniser.

"They have stopped fighting," replied King Daniel.

"Do you think they have given up?" asked King Jemis.

"No. Something's not right," voiced King Daniel. Then there was a red glow in the distance. "What is that?" he asked.

King Simon looked closely into the distance. "Dear God, no!" whispered King Simon.

"What is it?" asked King Daniel.

"It's our six fellow kings. They are charging to fight us."

"What is this? Why are they doing this?" asked King Daniel.

"They are under a spell. Seitor is controlling them, and he has sent for them to fight and kill us."

King Daniel and the others stood there in shock.

"Sire, we cannot fight them. Either they will kill us, or we will kill them!" yelled King Aniser.

"If they kill us, it's not their intention, but if we kill them, we know what we are doing!" he added. All who were there looked at King Daniel, needing to know what to do. King Simon crouched down in disbelief. All the kings who were there were deeply saddened at this.

"He is using them because Seitor knows we will not kill them, but they will kill us."

King Daniel looked at the six fellow kings, and they were surrounded with the enemy warriors and creatures. King Daniel knew they would surely not win.

With all the strength in him, he yelled out, "To the castle!"

His entire army, now fewer than a couple thousand, retreated back to the castle. King Daniel waited for all of his army to retreat. He went to the end of where his army was and continued to fight off the Teaks and Prosecs that were now charging.

He did this to stall for enough time for all his army to get back to the castle. King Simon and the other kings continued to fight with him, but then the six fellow kings were fast approaching.

Queen Elena and the rest of the army were waiting back at the castle, and King Daniel and the other kings retreated as well. Jities Holmes cast a spell and yelled, "Crepitus!" and a blast came between Seitor's army, with the six fellow kings, and King Daniel and the others.

"Run, Your Majesty!" he yelled, and all who were there ran to the castle.

Once the dust had settled, Seitor had a clear view that they were retreating back to the castle. "Attack! Kill them! Don't let them into the castle!" he exclaimed.

All had finally entered the castle with the exception of King Simon and King Daniel, and they were ready to close the massive indestructible steel gates. The massive castle within a city was surrounded by water.

"Drop the oil!" yelled King Aniser.

The Youngs spilled the barrels of oil into the water. "Light it!" yelled King Aniser. Young Ladam and his brother let out fiery arrows, which lit up the water.

"Run, Daddy, run!" yelled Princess Violet.

Seitor called, "Mors Mortis!" and a death spell came out and hit near King Daniel, causing him to fall to the ground.

King Simon went into the castle and yelled, "Close the gates!" but then he turned around and saw King Daniel about thirty yards outside the castle on the ground.

Seitor saw this and yelled, "Venenum ut in arce!" and his spell came out with a roar onto the castle. It was too late for King Simon, the gate closed on its own, and the entire castle was poisoned, so anyone or anything that would touch its walls long enough would be immediately shocked and die with its poison.

King Daniel got up, visibly shaken, and ran toward the castle, but the castle was cursed. King Daniel touched the bars on the gate, and he was immediately shot back in pain.

Queen Elena yelled and cried, "Daniel, Daniel! Get him in! Lift the gate!"

They tried to lift the gate, but they were all shot back with the deep poison on the gate. It would not move as it was being controlled by the curse of Seitor. Queen Elena, in a rage, turned herself into a lioness and roared with such passion, and she ran into the gates, but she too was thrown back. Princess Katalina was crying uncontrollably as her father was trapped outside.

"Throw a rope over the wall!" yelled King Simon.

They threw the rope over, but when the rope rubbed against the wall, it burned off. They tried throwing a chain over the wall, but as quick as it touched the wall, it was quick to melt. Jities Holmes and Wizard Bazar called, "Eliminare Venenum!" and their spell hit the gate, but it had no effect. Seitor's spell was too strong.

King Daniel stood there at the gate and looked at his army, then his family. He looked at them with this peace in his heart. "We did it! We saved the people," he said as he stood there, exhausted.

Princess Violet began to cry. "Daddy, Daddy, I love you!" she said. She was consoled by Fariet Elliot.

"Daniel, please, please, come to us, don't leave us!" voiced his wife.

"Daddy, please!" exclaimed Princess Katalina. She was crying.

"I'm so proud of you all. Katalina, I knew you had it in you, and I'm so pleased with the young lady you have become. You have been an amazing daughter to me, and I thank you for being my little girl all these years. He reached his arm through the bars and touched her face.

"And you, Princess Violet, well, that sounds nice. I'm so proud of you too, my dear, and remember, never give up, as I will always be watching you. You are such a blessing to me Violet, and thank you for being a blessing in my life. You both are my shining stars. I love you both very much, and I will always be in your heart."

King Daniel then looked at his bride and said, "My love, mi amor," as they held hands through the bars. "Yo te amo con todo, mi corazon. You are the most important thing in my life and the reason I live. I will always be by your side, my love. I want for you and my girls to rule this land, and I want for you to know that I am so proud to be your husband and to be their father."

"I love you, Daniel, and my heart belongs to you."

He reached and kissed her hands. As he let go of her hands, he looked at his bride and said, "Today, tomorrow, and forever—"

And she finished, "I love you."

Queen Elena fell to her knees and wept. Both Princess Katalina and Princess Violet went with their mother on the ground. King Daniel looked at them and knew they were hurting. He went to his knees and looked at his family. He was tired, sweaty, bleeding, dirty, and exhausted. He reached both his hands through the bars and held them out for his family to hold.

Queen Elena looked up at her husband, and tears came down her face as he began to whisper a song to her and their daughters.

> He is greater than I am
> He is stronger than any power that I face
> He is perfect in all His ways
> Yet He loves me

Then Queen Elena grabbed her daughters' hands. Queen Elena was between the two girls. Her left hand grabbed Princess Violet's right hand, and Queen Elena's right hand grabbed Princess Katalina's left hand. Queen Elena reached with her daughters' hands and held on to her husband's hands, which were reaching inside the bars of the gate, as King Daniel continued to sing.

> His love will always be with us
> His love will always be with me

Although I live a sinful life
He cares so much that he lives in me.
I will believe, I will believe, I will believe

And as King Daniel sang the next chorus, he let go of his family's hands. Queen Elena closed her eyes and began to cry, grasping her hands as she did not want to let go. Both princesses were weeping for their father as they knew what was about to come. King Daniel stood up, turned around in courage, walked, and then slowly began to run toward the oncoming enemy, singing,

And I will believe that He will stand with me
He will fight for me
And He will lead me
I believe!
He will comfort me
He will walk with me
And now I sing
I believe! I believe!

His wife and children looked on, crying at the sight of their father charging to his death, but he had absolutely no fear in him, as he knew he would soon be going home to his Father, the one and only true God and King.

King Daniel lifted his hands, and all the rocks, boulders, and arrows on the ground were lifted into the air, and as all in the castle watched on, King Daniel was going to make his last stand in battle with the Dark Lord. He lifted his hands high, closed his eyes, and motioned his arms forward. All the rocks, boulders, and arrows that he had lifted were forced forward, and they hit the enemy line as he sang with all his heart.

I believe His love will always be with us
His love will always be with me
Although I live a sinful life

He cares so much that he lives in me
I will believe, I will believe, I will believe

Many of the Teaks and creatures were hit, and they were killed. As King Daniel brought his arms back from throwing the things he had lifted, he reached from behind and took out the Sword of Yesu and his Fariets' Shield of Honor. He struck with such force, killing everything that came to him. He turned and swung his shield and swung again with the Sword of Yesu.

One giant came to him and reached down to smack him, but he lunged upward and fiercely struck the giant in the heart with the Sword of Yesu. The giant fell to the ground. The Teaks and creatures continued to come at him, and he continued to fight. He lifted his left hand toward the dead giant and lifted him up with his force and threw him toward the warriors coming at him. He ran toward those coming to him, and again he swung his sword smoothly and valiantly, hitting them all as he sang,

Today, I may die, but I will fight for the One True King
My sins are forgiven
My debt is paid
And there is nothing that can separate His love from me
Because I believe!

All the enemies stopped and were watching King Daniel as he stood there in a battle stance and whispered,

And I will believe that He will stand with me
He will fight for me
And He will lead me
I believe!
He will comfort me
He will walk with me
And now I sing
I believe! I believe!

Seitor then came and swung his Sword of Yesu, which cut King Daniel's arm, making him yell in pain.

"Daddy!" yelled Princess Violet.

Although King Daniel was badly cut, he did not stop fighting. Princess Violet, in a state of panic, looked at the bars of the castle gates, and since she was so tiny, she went in between the bars and made it through.

"Princess!" yelled King Simon as he tried to reach for her. He was immediately electrocuted as he touched the bars and was shot back. All who were there were calling for her to come back.

"Violet!" yelled her mother in a panic.

Princess Violet looked back at them but then looked at her father. "Daddy, Daddy!" she yelled and ran toward her father. King Daniel, fighting, swinging, and using all his strength, continued the battle.

"Let us begin our final battle," said Seitor in a deep evil voice.

King Daniel began his battle against Seitor. Seitor immediately turned himself into a fierce raging lion. He continuously swung his massive claws toward King Daniel, but King Daniel fought valiantly. He swung his sword toward the big cat and cut the cat's shoulder. Seitor leaped into the air and swung his massive claw, cutting King Daniel's chest. King Daniel twisted and swung his sword toward Seitor, and so Seitor turned himself back to his human self and used his sword to defend.

The two pushed away, and Seitor cast a spell using his wand. "Expellere!"

King Daniel blocked it with his shield, shooting the spell back to Seitor and hitting him in the chest, knocking him to the ground. Seitor, badly hurt, got up, and raged toward King Daniel, and the two had a battle of the swords.

King Daniel swung his sword, and Seitor ducked, and so King Daniel twisted and swung it back again and cut Seitor in the stomach, causing him to fall to the ground in pain.

As Seitor fell, he rolled, called for the Falcon Bow, and quickly shot an arrow at King Daniel, hitting him on the shoulder. King

Daniel stumbled a bit as Seitor quickly came to his feet and once again charged. Seitor leaped into the air and transformed into a lion, opening his massive jaw. King Daniel lifted his Fariets' Shield of Honor and swung it with such force toward the lion, cutting it across the face.

Seitor went into a black mist while in the air and fell to the ground as a human. King Daniel stumbled but was ready to battle again, but there was no need to. He had won. All the enemies were in shock that Seitor had indeed been beaten. Seitor looked at King Daniel as he lay on the floor defeated, bleeding, dirty, and badly hurt, knowing he would not win.

Then as he did this, King Daniel heard, "Daddy, Daddy, Daddy!" in the distance.

King Daniel turned around and, in a panic, yelled, "Violet, no!"

While father and daughter stared at each other, Seitor, using his last bit of strength, drove his Sword of Yesu through King Daniel's chest.

All went silent, and all was still. Princess Violet saw that as her father stood there looking at her, calling her name, a sword had gone through his chest.

Slowly, King Daniel fell to his knees and fell to the side. King Daniel was dead.

"Daddy!" Little ten-year-old Princess Violet cried for her father. She stood there, frozen, not knowing what to do but cry. Everyone in the castle was in shock. Queen Elena just stood there with her hands to her mouth as she could not believe what she was seeing. Young Ladam was holding on to Princess Katalina as she mourned for her father. All the people just looked on as they had lost hope.

"No, no, no!" yelled King Simon with such frustration and anguish. They were all in tears.

Seitor, badly hurt and weak, reached down and grabbed the true Sword of Yesu from King Daniel's motionless body. "All hail, King Daniel!" he shouted tauntingly.

Seitor looked at the young princess. She'd dropped the Dragon's Claw Wand on the ground as she cried out loud for her father. Tears poured down her cheek, and she cried so loud and with such agony.

"Daddy!" But her father was gone.

"Get the wand! Kill the girl!" commanded Seitor. The entire army rushed toward the young princess. She was hopeless, and no one could help her. Queen Elena changed into a lioness and let out a roar that shook all of Heirthia, but the armies were determined to kill the girl and get the Dragon Claw Wand. They ran toward her, and she became afraid.

"Fariets, go, protect the princess!" yelled King Aniser.

The Fariets quickly went toward the gate to go through the bars.

"Ignem in murum!" yelled Seitor with his wand. The spell hit the gates, and all between the bars were cursed. The Fariets attempted to go through the bars but were poisoned as they tried. One by one, they fell to the ground.

"Violet, my baby! Violet!" yelled Queen Elena.

Then there was a whisper in Princess Violet's ear. "Don't be afraid, little one, for if God is with you, who can be against you? Trust in the Lord and in His mighty power."

Princess Violet remembered her father and all that he had taught her about love, courage, strength, honor, and, most of all, faith. She continued to cry. She did not know what to do as the raging Teaks, creatures, warriors, beasts, giants, and wizards charged toward her.

As she stood there with tears coming down her cheek, she reached down and grabbed her wand. She continued to sob piteously, but then she closed her eyes and whispered, "In Nomine Yesu," just as she had heard her father.

As the enemy drew closer, with Seitor leading in the front, she again whispered, but this time with more confidence, "In Nomine Yesu." Although it was a whisper, everyone heard it the second time as it traveled throughout the land.

It was silent, but then she yelled at the top of her voice, "In Nomine Yesu Ego Increpa!" as she raised her wand with such confidence and motioned the Dragon's Claw Wand forward, rebuking the enemy.

An enormous, bold, powerful, and massive blue beam came out of her wand, and it was magnificent. It was a blast heard everywhere. The ground shook, the trees folded, the mountains avalanched, and even the wind broke. The light shone brightly throughout the entire land. Although it had become dark, the rebuke she called lit up the entire world of Heirthia. The sky opened like a bright blue day, and there was the sound of a horn of victory, and all could hear the angels singing praises to the Lord, our God, and the angels worshipping Him for His glory.

The rebuke from her wand went directly toward Seitor, and Seitor instantly took his wand and yelled, "Expellere!" His wand shot out its red cursed spell, and the two spells met, but Seitor's was immediately burned and overtaken. The rebuke slammed Seitor right in the heart, and it overtook him. His blue eyes were opened wide as the power of God struck him.

As he was being burned and shocked, Seitor looked toward the young child, and behind her, in the midst of the light, he saw the One and Only Living King guarding her. Seitor looked directly into the eyes of Yesu. Yesu stood there bold and confident, and Seitor was afraid.

Then from the sky, an enormous fist came out and slammed down on the land to the left side of the army, and they were blasted. Then a second fist came from the sky and slammed on the right side of the enemy. They too were blasted. Then one final fist came from the sky, but this one was much larger than the other two, and it came slamming right in front of the young child, and the land was shaken.

Every knee was bowing.

Many of the enemies at the front were killed, thousands were thrown back, and *all* that were in the land could not resist the power of God. The enemies that were not killed and not thrown bowed down before the One True God.

Even those in the castle could not resist. They *all* bowed down before the Lord, their God, for His wonders and His grace had saved them.

You could hear the angels singing praises to God, and all that were in the land were kneeling. Seitor was being consumed by the fire and could not move.

Then the child let down her arm, and the light was gone and the sky closed. The sky was gloomy again, and it was all silent. The flame no longer consumed Seitor. He twisted his cape, and he turned into a black smoke and completely disappeared. He vanished into thin air and was gone.

The evil army quickly retreated into the distance, afraid. They left the land of Exsul and were gone. The battle was indeed over.

26

THE RISE

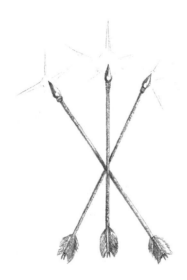

THE SPELL ON the castle was destroyed as Seitor left. Little by little, the spell burned away. The gate reopened, and the army came out cheering the brave young child. Queen Elena went to her daughter and embraced her. King Simon came with the body of King Daniel in his arms. The king was indeed dead. It was a victory, and although some cheered, it was quickly silenced by the presentation of their fallen king.

"Daddy," whispered Princess Violet. She and her mother began to cry at the sight of her father. All were saddened at this great loss.

"The Seven Pearl Arrows!" yelled King Jemis.

"Princess Katalina, you have the Seven Pearl Arrows to use! You must strike your father in the heart, for if you do, he will come back to life!" he exclaimed.

Princess Katalina, overwhelmed, began to cry, very afraid of what they were asking. "I can't shoot my dad!" she cried.

King Simon laid King Daniel on the ground and went to the young child. "Princess, there comes a time when we need to be brave and courageous. I have been the king of Heirthia for a good many years, and I have never seen such courage and bravery like that of your father's. He needs you now more than ever, or you will never see him again."

Princess Katalina stopped crying, and he asked, "Can you do this? Can you do this for the love of your father?"

Princess Katalina voiced in a cracking voice, "I can."

King Simon and King Aniser then went and held up King Daniel, and Princess Katalina called for her bow.

She closed her eyes, breathed in, and whispered, "In Nomine Yesu Ego habent fide." She slowly pulled back on the Falcon Bow, but this time, a white Pearl Arrow appeared. She took aim, closed her eyes, and the arrow went to her father and entered his flesh. The arrow pierced his heart. Upon impact, her father was awakened, and he grasped for air and came to his feet but was still very tired and fatigued.

His family went to him in tears as they thought they had lost him. They embraced with such passion and would not let go. It was a moment of true love for them. They came, they believed, they obeyed, and they were blessed. The Geminis embraced with so much love and ever so tightly.

King Simon went to King Daniel and told him that they had defeated Seitor through the courage of his young Princess Violet, and he told him about the power of Yesu used through the young child's faithful heart. He went on to tell King Daniel that his bold Princess Katalina had brought him back to life through the love of her Pearl Arrows.

All the people were joyful, happy, and very emotional with everything that had happened. In the end, the people gave praise to Yesu for giving them their land back and, more importantly, their free lives. Once again, Heirthia was a free land.

"King Daniel, shall we go after the enemy? We can have the young child cast the spell again," asked Young Caster.

King Jonis the responded, "As former owner of the Dragon's Claw Wand, that spell is the most difficult to come by. I was never successful myself. The amazing child found it in her heart for her father's sake. Chances are, it will never come again. However, don't be fooled, it has many secrets and powers within it."

King Daniel then said, "No, my dear Young. The creatures and beasts knew not what they were doing. They only did as they were told. Remember this: evil or no evil, they are still living things that God created. As king of Heirthia, I will offer the entire land as refuge for those enemies, creatures, beasts, giants to join our army, our family, and to become one of us. For those who do not wish, be assured that they will come back to fight another day, but today, there shall be no more fighting."

King Simon then said, "We also need to save our fellow kings from the seven southern lands. They are still under the spell of Seitor." King Daniel voiced to all the people, "Yes, that is our next adventure my friends—the seven lost."

"What about Seitor, sire?" asked Young Ladam.

King Daniel, standing next to his wife and children, with all the kings, Youngs, wizards, Fariets, and elders listening, said, "I really don't know about him. I know the power of God was upon him, and I know he was consumed by God's fire, but wherever he is, no matter what he is doing, he is still preparing to come back, and he will come back more powerful and more prepared. It is because of this that we must always be ready with the full armor of God."

In a dark room with little light in it, there were several of Scitor's closest allies. In the middle of this room, there was a person lying on a bed with his eyes closed. He was partially covered in a black robe. It was Seitor, but his entire body had changed. It had been burned from the power of God. It was dark, and he looked like of his creatures.

His face has also changed. He looked like a creature—burned, wrinkled, and rough, but then, he opened his eyes, and they were still a beautiful sky blue.

The illustrator who created the above map is Victoria Jimenez (twelve), my daughter. As a young and passionate artist, she certainly deserved a spot in this book to begin her career. Great job, Victoria. I'm so proud of you.

ABOUT THE AUTHOR

Well done good and faithful servant, you were faithful
over a few things. I will make you ruler over many things.

—Matthew 25:21

DAVID JIMENEZ HAS a bachelor's degree in business admin-
istration from Texas A&M International University and
a Juris Doctor from Florida A&M University, College
of Law.

Currently, Mr. Jimenez is the owner, CEO, and president of
the Law Offices of David Jimenez, PL. Mr. Jimenez, his beautiful
bride Erika, and their two children Krystal and Victoria are originally from South Texas until they moved to Orlando, Florida,
in 2006 so that Mr. Jimenez could attend law school and to start
their new adventure.

Mr. Jimenez and his family love traveling and adventure and
anything that has to do with the great outdoors, which inspired
The Living King story. They have three dogs, a Bengal cat, a chin-
chilla, a rabbit, a duck, a giant tortoise, five chickens, a bearded
dragon, and a school of fish.

ABOUT THE ILLUSTRATOR

———◼———◼———

Do not conform to the patterns of this world, but be
transformed by the renewing of your mind. Then you will
be able to test and approve what God's will is, His good,
pleasing and perfect will.

—Romans 12:2

KYLE COTTON CURRENTLY attends Mississippi College
and is pursuing a senior graphic design major. He is in
his fourth year.

Kyle is originally from Orlando, Florida. He has been drawing
and sketching since he was very young. He has worked as a sketch
artist for Walt Disney World for the past two years. This included
sketching and theme park design concept art. Additionally, he
worked on two movie film productions in the art department and
served as production assistant.

He spends a lot of his time watching films, illustrating, paint-
ing, and pursuing photography. He also enjoys exploring and
camping in the great outdoors.

CPSIA information can be obtained
at www.ICGtesting.com
Printed in the USA
LVOW04s2057120816
500060LV00016B/279/P